To my parents, all of them

I have given a name to my pain and call it 'dog': it is just as faithful, just as obtrusive and shameless, just as entertaining, just as clever as any other dog – and I can scold it and vent my bad moods on it, as others do with their dogs, servants and wives.

Friedrich Nietzsche, *The Gay Science*

1

A Season in Paradise

I find him in Empangeni. My father lies on his back at the edge of the sugar-cane valley, one arm under his head, the other flung out, fingers plaiting scrub and yellow weed flowers. The camera next to him is shuttered and blind. He squints at the wavering sky, which moves with heat if not with wind. Empangeni rises behind us: tin shanties glint through the sugar-mill smoke and dusty tracks cross the red hills to mark mission churches, now crumbling. In front of us, the green swarm of cane stretches to the horizon.

'When did you get here?' I ask.

'Just now.'

I stand over him, waiting. We're quiet, at right angles to each other. I close my eyes and lift my face to the sky as though hoping to feel rain. But the early-morning sun burns through my eyelids, red light suddenly inside my head.

'How did you know I was here?' I ask. The heat touches my shoulders and chest, a blessing.

'I read your stuff online. *By Jo Hartslief in Johannesburg, South Africa.*' He speaks in a British accent, mispronouncing my surname the way they all do. His would be no easier for them, the rolling *r* of Roussouw something only the Welsh would be able to attempt. 'The articles were good,' he says.

His compliment surprises me. 'Thanks.' I look down at him, the sunspots fading from his skin and clothes as my eyes adjust to the light.

'Well, not too bad anyway. A bit "human interest" for my liking.' He doesn't move to put air quotes around the term, and he doesn't need to. 'Too many interviews with crying refugees.'

Lying down, my father's belly slopes up from his ribcage. I wonder if it will hang over his waistband when he stands up. He's grown a beard, which is red and grey in patches, and his nose has been broken since I last saw him. It's hooked now, but at fifty-three, he's too old for it to be handsome.

Before I can decide whether or not to get irritated, he asks: 'Were you staying near Alexandra?'

'No. I've been going into the townships with Tumelo, the photographer I've been working with. He knows where to go.'

'He's good,' he says, nodding his approval. 'He's taken one or two nice shots.'

Tumelo's a war correspondent and has been taking photos much longer than my father has. I sometimes search stock-photo libraries for the pictures my father takes – of steaming bowls of pasta and sauce, moist slabs of cake. I want to ask how his slathering shoe polish onto raw meat and frosting grapes with hairspray qualifies him to judge, but I know better, even after so many years.

'Most of the other journalists out here from overseas, it's obvious they're staying in nice hotels in Jo'burg,' he says.

I too have been staying in a nice hotel in Jo'burg, spending the money my grandmother left me on swimming pool access and a queen-sized bed. But I haven't been able to sleep in it.

'And using copy from the news wires anyway, getting the local photographers to do all the difficult work for them,' he scoffs. This is something he's always banged on about, that photographers never get enough recognition. I don't let on that I agree with him. 'But your stuff is different.'

'Thanks.' I wonder how long he'll let me have this.

'Of course you'd be stupid enough to go there. They warned the press that it's too dangerous, especially for a woman, and of fucking course you went anyway.' He looks at me for the first time, his eyes triumphant slivers in the glare. 'I hope those *kaffirs* roughed you up a bit, put their pink hands all over your pasty skin. That'd teach you.'

I gather fistfuls of my skirt at my sides to steady myself against what I know is coming. 'Teach me what?'

'That you can't just come back here after so long and still know how it is – how bad it's gotten – or how to stay safe.' He turns his frown back on the sun. 'You can't come back after ten years and have it be your home any more.'

'I never said it was.'

'I bet they only picked you to come out here because of your surname. That and the nostalgia for swimming pools and Mandela that you whip out when you're trying to be exotic and interesting.'

I force myself to breathe in for four counts and hold it just as long. But my voice wavers with the heat that has come to my face nonetheless. 'You don't know why I came out here, or what happened when I was in Alex.' The words are wet. And he can hear it, has always been able to tell when he's scored a point, even over the phone. In spite of myself, I want to tell him about the fires, the bloody blankets on the side of the road. That before I left London two weeks ago on assignment for a magazine, I'd called a few of my other contacts to see if they'd be interested in a series of articles about corruption and cronyism in South Africa. When the riots broke out, I was a cheap source of copy; 'already in-country' was how they put it. But I know that my father doesn't care about how I ended up in Alex, and if I try

3

to explain myself to him he will have won. Right now, I want to hurt him with something trite and true. 'You have no idea who I am.'

He looks at me and smiles, his forehead moving upwards with the force of it. 'If you're anything like me – and I know you are – you probably need a cigarette right about now. Why don't you sit down?'

Before I can stop myself, I straighten my shoulders and neck to stand taller. My father laughs.

'When did you dye your hair?' he asks.

My hand wants to make a hiding place for my fringe, but I will my fingers to be still. 'I dunno – two years ago?'

'Don't ask me – I dunno the answer.' He watches a hadeda hang in the air above us. It drops lower, lazy with early morning. Its feet rake the cane leaves before it lands near the old Mercedes I rented in Durban. 'Red doesn't suit you. And you've gotten thin. Too thin.' He waves his hand at me as though wiping a mirror. 'Did you do all this for that boy?'

I think he means Dan, the only boyfriend I've ever told him about. 'No.' I broke up with Dan long before I changed my hair.

'For a girl, then.' I wonder if he'll flick his tongue through the V of his fingers. He's done it before. 'Did you let your underarm hair grow out so you could dye that as well?'

'Yeah. I stopped wearing make-up too – oh, and I burned all my bras.' He doesn't react and I keep going, even though I know better. 'And of course I hate all men and only listen to Ani DiFranco.'

'Who's that?'

I shrug. 'It doesn't matter.'

'Every time I see you, I wonder if you'll look like your mom,' he says, his eyes on me again. 'But luckily, my genes were stronger than Karen's.' He laughs again.

'Look, Nico, what do you want from me?' I hope the name hurts him. 'I have to get back and, you know, do my job.'

He turns his head away from me and spits into the grass. 'I'm honoured you'd, you know, come out to the *bundu* just to see me.'

'Don't be. You begged me to come.' Without looking, I find the right key in my handbag and hold it ready for the ignition. 'And it's the first time you've ever needed anything from me my whole life, so that's why I'm here: to satisfy my curiosity, and then bugger off back to the arrangement we had before.'

'*Kak*, man. We haven't seen each other in three years—'

'Three and a half.' I sound proud, like a child bragging about how long she's held her breath underwater. There are so many ways for him to win.

'OK, three and a half years. Not since that shit-hole pub in London.' He smiles, baring teeth too far back in his mouth. 'So you came here today after three and a half years just out of curiosity?'

I shake my head, not wanting to admit that after his phone call I was actually worried about him, but I can see now that he's fine, the same as always. I shouldn't have come.

'Good,' he says. 'I needed to get you here, and what I need from you now…well, curiosity isn't enough to make you give it to me.' He pauses. 'Why don't you sit down?' He stares at me, not really asking.

I sit this time, legs crossed. Sweat is already pooling under my thighs. I bought the skirt at the airport in Johannesburg, an orange, sequinned cocoon; there'll be two damp ovals on the back of it when I get up.

The hadeda hunches closer.

'How's your grandmother?'

He doesn't know she died a month ago. I should tell him. But he turns his head. A check on his to-do list. 'She's fine.'

'Your accent's changed,' he says. 'You sound like a proper Pommy now.' His fingers are motionless as he watches the bird. I stop pulling at grass and watch it too.

In Benoni, where I grew up, hadedas were dull and grey as closed oysters. Mornings I would see them preening in the garden and let the dog out to sprint circles into the frosted grass, driving the squat birds onto aerials and streetlights. There, they complained in mournful kazoos about the Maltese terrier and the pale brunette child too slow to run after them herself. But here, in the sun, the bird is suddenly beautiful, its wings skating the spectrum from green to purple, like the inside of a shell, as it moves towards us.

'In case you haven't been paying attention, the bird's name is Frank,' my father says. 'We've been watching each other since I got here. It seems he's finally decided to come down for a smoke.' From the pocket of his shorts, my father edges a pack of Peter Stuyvesant and a box of matches. His fingers, quick with habit, extract three cigarettes. Frank moves towards us. My father puts two cigarettes on his stomach, motioning for me to take one.

'I'm going to light a match using just one hand,' he brags from around the cigarette between his teeth. The tip bobs as he talks, punctuating his sentence.

The match catches and Frank cocks his head, wary of the flame. But my father and I both breathe it in. He turns his head towards the creature. It stares, curious and suspicious.

'Come on, dickhead.' My father waits for Frank to fetch the cigarette off his stomach. But the bird is still, almost judgemental. 'Well, fuck off then, Frank,' he says, blowing smoke at the bird.

Frank, made grey again, objects: '*How-how-he. How-how-he.*' It's almost as though he's lamenting: *I thought we were friends – how could he speak to me like that?*

I laugh.

'I said, fuck off, Frank!' This time my father sits up, and Frank's cigarette rolls into the scrub, bent. Frank glares, first with his left eye and then with his right, the red on his beak suddenly angry. My father glares back, the ember on his cigarette bright as he takes a long drag.

I sit quietly, a good audience.

Calmly now: 'Frank, let me make myself clear. You are not welcome here. I need to talk to Jo and I won't have you butting in. Your points are trite, your vocabulary *kak* and you always try to make every conversation about you. Now, if you know what's good for you, you'll go.'

Frank huddles lower, his neck folded away like a beach chair in winter.

'And don't even think about making your displeasure known by shitting on my car on your way out.' My father turns, his back now to the bird. Frank pauses and begins to preen himself. In my sunglasses, my father sees Frank's disobedience. He whirls, shouting, '*Hamba!*' Go.

The bird spreads out, grey and suddenly other, in a running start, and I'm strangely afraid of it as it takes off. I duck, but its feet skim cane not skin. It circles the field once, slowly, before straightening out and heading towards the mountains.

My father's shout has stirred the wind; sugar cane clack their objection to Afrikaner words so deep in Zululand.

'When you put your cigarette out, do it properly,' he says. Serious now. 'It hasn't rained here in months.'

I wonder how long he's been in Natal, if he's moved here. Last I knew, he was living in Cape Town. But I don't ask and we sit silently. Beyond the road into town, soil turns into sand and later into red rock. Sparse outcroppings of weeds and abandoned mud huts dot the hillside.

On the way up from Durban this morning I crossed the Tugela River, where the water slows after its long trip and aloes bloom succulent spikes. There, the redcoats had crossed, bringing guns and white man to Zululand. Neither had left yet.

And there I was, a turncoat, making the same trip.

'What're we doing here?' I ask, straightening Frank's cigarette. The paper is wrinkled and dusty.

'I wanted to show you this because I think you'll appreciate it.' My father is being deliberately obtuse, trying to pique my interest.

I won't ask again, so I wait. A bumblebee undresses the daisy weeds.

'I've been here once before.' He straightens his legs out in front of him and points his toes. Both of the shoelaces on his leather walking boots are double-knotted. 'Walked through the furrows in between cane fields. Sat in their shade.'

I think he's quoting, but I don't know where from.

'I've been here before but I must describe it to myself, shape it new each time, to remember it. This whole field is an instrument and every stalk is drink for a thirsty traveller.'

I lean back, my hands in the scrub behind me. Waiting out his preambles has always made me tired.

'I'm wanted for murder.'

I'm awake and upright again. 'What?'

'There's a warrant out for my arrest on suspicion of murder.' He pulls at his beard, twisting the hair between his fingers.

'Wait – *what?*' I can't yet tell if this is part of the performance.

'A week and a half ago, I saw a police car pull up outside my flat, and I knew. So I threw some stuff in a bag and got the hell out of there.' He waves his flat away from his face as though it were a fly. 'Thank fuck blacks are so lazy – they had a smoke first.' He gives a tight half-smile.

'Are you having me on?'

'Fuck you,' he says loudly and spits into the grass right next to me. 'Why would I lie about this? Are you really such a self-obsessed cow that you think I would make this up just to get you to speak to me again?'

I don't know what to say. I want to drive away and leave him here but I've never seen him like this, so agitated. So scared. The few times we've met up since I moved to the UK, and in our occasional emails, he's been expansive, showy. Even when we fought, as we always did – at some comment of his too offensive for me to leave alone, about women or affirmative action or how he would've raised me differently – he's never been this raw. 'No—'

'Look,' he says, bending forward, his hands stopping short in the grass just in front of me. 'I'm sorry.' He stares into the black pools of my sunglasses; something makes me fold them into my lap. 'Please. Running has made me look guilty – I know that. I can't get out of this alone. I need your help, Jo.'

I force my hands to be still in my lap. 'Tell me what happened.'

He sits back, scrub between his fingers. 'Back in April, two cops turned up at my flat and started asking questions about a black man who disappeared back in eighty-three – abducted, probably dead.' He shrugs with only one shoulder; it's not unusual enough for two. 'They showed me this shitty photo of him but I'd never seen him before. I mean, all blacks look alike to me anyway.'

He's always liked to provoke me but I won't react this time. Otherwise, it'll be hours before he tells me his real reason for calling. 'So what happened then?'

He looks away. 'I could tell they thought I was lying.'

'But why?'

He stubs out his cigarette until there's dust under his fingernails. 'Apparently, it happened two years before I met your mom. Things were difficult for me then. Not the kind of life that would give me a good alibi. I was just about to tell them to fuck off, but then they said there was a witness that saw me with the man.'

'Who saw you?'

He picks at the cuticle on his thumb.

I push myself forward over my knees and put a hand on his shoulder, the way I would anyone else. But it feels wrong, touching him. 'Look at me,' I say.

When he does, I can see his eyes are rimmed in red. 'I dunno. They wouldn't say.' He rounds his back. My hand isn't welcome. 'And now they're investigating me.'

'But why would they think you had anything to do with it?'

He looks at the Drakensberg, purple and hazy on the horizon. The skin on his nose is peeling and his hair is short to stave off the grey where it's coming in in a thick band. Bony knees now pulled against his chest, he seems old and vulnerable.

'Because I'm Afrikaans, a white man living in a black man's country.' He scratches at a scab on his calf. 'Because they don't want any truth or reconciliation any more, just someone to blame.' Another speech.

'Can't you just tell them where you were the night he was taken?' I ask.

'You think I wouldn't just have done that if I could have?'

I shake me head, but he doesn't look up to see.

'Eighty-three was when I'd just gotten back from travelling – after the army?' he prompts me.

'Right.' He told my mom that after finishing his minimum compulsory military service in 1979, he'd travelled up through Africa and then across Europe without a passport, crossing rivers and borders under cover of darkness. He'd grown a beard and pretended to be Dutch to fool the Europeans, who'd already begun their sanctions and travelling bans. She thought it glamorous, admirable even, avoiding the required annual conscription duties. Those three years were filled with imagined snapshots of a young man pulling the peace sign in front of the Eiffel Tower, patting a stray dog next to Gaudí's Sagrada Família in Barcelona, teaching himself Latin in Rome. My mom believed him when she was twenty. I wouldn't make that mistake.

He shakes off the fly that has landed on his forearm. 'This hole in my story is all they need. Never mind that the only reason it's there is because I was objecting to the whole war thing.'

Even though I don't really believe his passport-less European tour, I won't let him have this. 'Didn't you go AWOL because they were increasing the number of compulsory years of service and you would've had to do more time?'

'*Ja*, that too.' He shunts the cigarettes towards me with the back of his hand.

This doesn't make sense. Every white man my father's age will have spent time in the army. Surely he wouldn't have been the only one to react to it by falling off the map, as he likes to call it. 'What else?'

He hesitates. 'I have a record.'

'What for? The shoplifting stuff?'

He laughs. 'I didn't know you knew about that. Your grandmother tell you?'

I nod.

'Of course. No, this was something else. Assault.'

'Jesus.' I hold a cigarette between very straight fingers. 'What the fuck did you do?'

'A couple of years ago, in Cape Town, I got into a fight with a *bergie*.'

'What's a *bergie*?' I hate having to ask.

'A hobo. Your Afrikaans clearly needs some work, hey.'

'Why'd you fight him?'

'It was getting dark and I was running along the sea there by Clifton. The man was going through the bins at the top of the stairs down to the beach and just throwing shit everywhere. So I stopped and told him to pick up all the rubbish and that I knew he was looking for food but littering was bad for the environment. He swore at me – coloureds have the best swearwords – so I was just standing there taunting him because what he was calling me was really funny. *Jou ma se slapgenaaide bees-poes.*' Your mother's fucked-loose cow cunt. He laughs again. 'And then, out of nowhere, one of his friends came over and broke my nose.' He pinches the crooked bridge. 'I was halfway to killing him before I was pulled off.'

'Fuck.' I don't know what else to say. The man that did this, the man laughing about it now, is my father, the only family I have left. Dry-mouthed, I put my half-smoked cigarette out against the sole of my sandal.

'Afterwards, they tried to say it was racially motivated, but that's a load of horseshit.' He rolls his eyes. 'I saw a guy who punched me, first; a black guy, second.'

'I'm sure all your nice talk about *kaffirs* really helped the situation.' This is the first time I've ever used that term and I can't help but say it more quietly than the other words, as though someone might hear me, or I might hear myself. I sound too much like other white South Africans with it in my mouth.

'No,' he says, pulling out handfuls of grass. 'Probably not.'

'Why'd you run? Why didn't you just answer their questions?'

'I panicked. But I swear to you, Jo, the day before I left, I came back from work and my whole flat was different. Everything was about a centimetre to the left.' Clumps of red soil dangle from the roots he's pulling up.

'What do you mean?' Instead of putting my hand over his, I watch his grass-stained fingertips.

'The police'd been there, going through my stuff when I was at work.' He rubs his eyes. There's dust in his eyebrows. 'I knew they were going to come for me, and that when they did it would be serious.'

I throw the pack of cigarettes into his lap. I've smoked more on this trip than I have since university and already I feel sick. 'Why do you think I can help you?'

'I need someone who can think like them.'

I can't help myself. 'Do you mean rationally?'

'Fine. Whatever.' He looks away.

I wonder if I should apologise.

'Actually, I've run out of money,' he admits.

'Of course you have.' I knew there'd be another reason for calling me. Maybe this is the real reason, the only one.

'Everyone's taking their own sepia pictures of food now, so work's been slow.' He reaches for the sunglasses in my lap and puts them on.

'Can't you go back to taking photos of lions and Table Mountain?' He used to work for a tourism agency, rich white people in every shot.

'That's not the point. I can't use my cards, obviously, so I've been sleeping in my car the last week.'

I look away from the reflection I can now see in the lenses on his face. The eyes too big and the cheeks too hollow, as though the last two weeks have left me permanently shocked, never hungry.

'I was in Port Elizabeth last week, sleeping in my car, and some fucker tried to break in and I woke up with the glass exploding over me like some Jo'burg firework.' He runs out of breath by the end of the sentence.

I look back at him. 'You don't look cut up.'

'Don't believe me?' He lifts one side of his t-shirt. A bruise stretches from his armpit to his waist, textured and granite-blue. The right side of the bruise is almost perfectly straight. He smiles, but I can't see whether it reaches his eyes. 'It looks like a tidemark, doesn't it?' He lets go of the shirt and sits upright. 'At least it's not on my face, hey.'

'Jesus.' His t-shirt is bunched just above the waistband of his shorts. I can still see a slice of skin, creased and yellowing like an old sheet. 'I'm sorry.'

He catches me looking and tugs at his shirt. 'It's not too bad; nothing's broken, or if it was, it's healed now. But I realised that I couldn't just keep driving around, without a plan or a good cup of coffee, until they caught up with me.'

'When did you last eat?'

'Probably the day before yesterday, but it's not a big deal.' He pinches the fat on his belly. 'I've gone longer.'

I want to ask just when that was, but now isn't the time. 'OK, well, that's the first order of business then,' I say, hoping that the executive-speak will make me feel more in control of the situation. Hoping that after a trip to the nearest Nandos, and, later, an ATM, he'll drop the wanted-man act.

'No.' He takes a cigarette from the pack in his lap and rolls it between his fingers. 'We have to go to Durban airport so I can get rid of my car and you can get a new one.'

'Why do I need a new one?'

'In case anyone sees our two cars together before I dump mine.' He pulls off the sunglasses and rests them on the grass in front of me. Looking down, he says: 'Will you help me, Jo?'

'I dunno, Nico. I can lend you some money.'

He shakes his head. 'No. Please, Jo. I don't have anyone else to ask.' He looks at me. 'I don't want to be alone with this. And it would be good to spend some time with you.'

When I was younger, he'd call and say he was coming to visit that weekend. I'd wait on the steps outside the house, in my only dress, until it got dark and my mom dragged me inside. He never came.

'Nice try,' I say.

He stiffens and I wonder what comeback will follow. But instead he repeats: 'Please, Jo. I know I have no right to ask.'

However obliquely, it's the first time he's ever acknowledged his absence from my life. I close my eyes. Even here, hundreds of miles from the Alexandra, I can still smell burning rubber. I open my eyes and watch him scratching at the scab on his calf. If I go with him, out of the two people in the car, I won't be the worst one. Maybe I'll be able to sleep again.

I sigh. 'OK. I'll help you.'

He grips my shoulder. 'Thank you,' he says, smiling.

He curves his back against the wind to light his cigarette, and I busy my hands gathering butts from the grass around us, his still wet at the tip, older ones fuzzy and innocuous. It's a habit formed at school, when any stray butts would land the entire boarding house in deten- tion, but I realise that if he is telling the truth, it's probably a good idea to cover our tracks.

He takes a deep drag and looks the ember in the eye. 'Fuck, man, the wind's so bad it smokes half of your cigarette for you.' He lies back again, one arm behind his head to give him a view of the horizon.

I wait. 'I'll cancel my flight back to Jo'burg, then,' I say when he closes his eyes.

'Yes.' He scratches his crotch. 'I hate Jo'burg. It's really becoming one of those typical black African cities, you know?'

I shake my head – he doesn't see it – and lie down next to my father. I watch the one cloud in the sky change shape in the wind.

'Like the kind of place that uses mosquito coils,' he says.

I look at the mountains in the distance. 'What's wrong with mosquito coils?'

'Instead of sprays or those plug-ins? Modern-day technology?' He turns, scowling at me. 'You're so fucking irritating. It was a metaphor.

For how Jo'burg's becoming like somewhere in Ghana or something.'

I drop my arms to my sides; the noise of keys in my handbag seems out of place.

'Christ.' He sits up, the sweat on his back an hourglass on its side. 'You know, sometimes you remind me so much of your mom. So literal and so fucking blasé,' he says, standing up and glaring at me. He's always taller than I expect, and rather than softening him, his belly has made him seem stronger, more solid. 'You've ruined it now. Let's go.' He slips a folded baseball cap from his pocket and pulls it low over his face.

I close my eyes against the words, familiar as they are. 'OK,' I say, getting up and beating red dust from my clothes. The sun is suddenly closer, before it sifts out of the sky.

I drive back to Durban airport to return my rental car, with my father following in his own, always three cars behind me. He won't tell me where we're going after that.

On the way to the airport, I call the news desk in London and tell them I won't be filing copy for a few days. Euphemisms like *family emergency* are just imprecise enough to be unquestionable. I don't have a phone number for the editor of the online magazine that commissioned my original piece on South Africa; he lives in New York. I'll have to find an Internet café, I think. Finally, I leave a message for Tumelo, telling him that I've decided to see my father after all. He'll approve; it's less dangerous than following the riots and I know he thinks spending time with family is what I need after what happened in Alex.

Yesterday, when my father called, I was standing over the pulp and teeth of a man. The riots had reached Durban the day before I had. A Malawian had been forced to jump out of a six-storey building to escape the crowd and their machetes. He was dark and half-intact, like fallen fruit. I'd been covering the riots for just over a week, had been into four townships and five refugee centres, and I could no longer count the number of dead I'd seen. Even though I didn't recognise the phone number, my ringing mobile was a reason to step away.

'Happy birthday,' my father started.

'It isn't my birthday.'

'Today is the day you start dying. Everything begins to decline from twenty-five onwards.'

'It isn't my birthday. And I'm not twenty-five.'

'Bet the difference between our ages doesn't seem so bad now, does it? You could go out with a fifty-three-year-old man who works in IT and drink his expensive wine and stroke his back hair and it'd be fine, hey.' He waited.

Men in puffy blue jackets had covered the body on the pavement with a tan blanket, but the blood wouldn't pool in a neat rectangle.

'You there?' my father asked.

'Yes,' I said, walking back to my car.

'I need to see you.'

He asked me not to tell anyone where I was going, but while I was driving along the motorway to the sugar-cane fields where he was waiting for me, the dust making angry scars of the cracks in the windscreen, I called Naledi. She was the closest thing to real family that I had left. And now that my grandmother was dead, she was the only other person in my life – apart from my father – who'd known my mom.

'What's wrong with him?' she wanted to know.

'I don't know that there's anything wrong, apart from the usual stuff obviously. He said he had a story for me.' I wasn't sure if I'd tell her, when I knew, or how much.

'He's lying.' Naledi had never met my father, but she'd heard about him all through primary school and then in emails after I'd moved to England.

'I think maybe he feels guilty about everything, the way we left it.' The tar on the road was starting to crumble into sand at the edges.

'No.' She seemed sure of herself. 'Your father doesn't feel guilt – or if he did, you'd know about it, because he'd be taking it out on you.'

'I know.' I passed a sign warning of potholes in the road and laughed.

'Trust me,' Naledi said, clearly thinking I was laughing at her, finding her paranoid or melodramatic.

'I do. I know you're right.'

'So why are you going to see him then?'

'I don't know.' A row of thin trees separated the road from the cane fields, leaves in clumps and long stretches of bare trunk.

'I think it's a good thing, actually,' she went on. That surprised me. But conversations with her were often like walking out into your garden and finding a baboon in the birdbath. 'It's been too long, and it takes up a lot of your energy to be angry at him. Just so long as you know what he's like.'

'Trust me, I know,' I said. And I did. I was ten when he first began to take an interest in me. Before he moved to Cape Town, he'd take me two weekends a year, on trips up to Kruger Park or the Limpopo River. I'd swim and he'd sit on the river bank, reading. On one of those trips, it was only after I was dry and dressed that he told me there was a crocodile in the water with me.

'It's not your job to look after him.' There was an echo on the line.

'I know.' I turned onto the dirt track my father'd described.

'I know you know all this. I'm sorry I'm getting so *Women Who Love Too Much*. I just don't want you to be let down again.' Her voice was thick. 'But he'll be the one missing out if he fucks it up again.'

'Thanks, but I doubt he'll see it that way.' Ahead, a car quivered in the heat.

'You're one of my favourite people in the world, you know. And if I had the power to make everyone in the world who isn't someone's absolute favourite person disappear, I doubt your dad would be left over.'

I laughed as I swung the car off the road, sending smoke rings of dust into the air.

'Like cauliflower. No one wakes up at 3 a.m. and says: "I feel like cauliflower. I have to have some right now!"' She was laughing too as she said this. 'Do you get the subtext here?' Serious then.

'It's more like text, but yes, I do. Thank you.' Parking, I watched my father against his hill, surveying the cane fields like a colonial lord.

'And this better not get in the way of your actual job, as easy as it is.'

'Ha ha.' When I'd told Naledi, who by then had almost finished her law degree, that I wanted to go into journalism, she'd joked that all it would mean was learning how to add my own byline to press releases. But when I started blogging she was my first commenter. She sent me links to news sites to help me *qualify my opinions*; she even offered to be quoted anonymously: *So people can see you've got some contacts in SA and aren't just pulling this out of your ass*, she'd said. And later she'd asked me to send her print copies of every one of my *Guardian* features. 'It won't, don't worry.'

'Good,' she said. 'Just be careful.'

'I will.'

'Call me if there's anything I can do.'

The red streaks on my windscreen rained blood on my father as he lay in the grass, camera pointed at the sky.

—

After I've swapped the Mercedes for a battered white BMW and my father's moved his rucksack, a coolbox, his golf clubs and three plastic bags into the new boot, we go to a Spur Steak Ranch in the airport. My father orders a rack of ribs, sucking the bones until sauce stretches to the meat of his cheeks in a big brown clown-smile.

'Did I ever tell you about the time I caught you trying to shoplift a pack of chips from the SPAR? You were two and you just sat in your pram, trying to hide them under your jersey.' He mimes the action. 'I love telling people the stories about when you were a baby. They never believe me, because their own children are so fucking boring and stupid.'

I know these stories by heart. I'm not sure any of them are true. 'Yes, you've told me that one,' I say, opening a Crème Soda. Since I landed, I've been going through my old favourites, ticking off brand names, inspecting the packaging to see how it differs to that in the UK. Here, salt and vinegar crisps come in a blue bag, not green. Comparisons have seeped into everything I think and see.

I take a sip, but the Crème Soda is too green and sweet and I can feel it fizzing inside of me. I push it away.

He puts his greasy napkin on his plate. 'I wish that maid would hurry up and clear the table,' he says, gesturing towards the waitress.

'Do you call all black women maids now?' I take out a one-hundred-rand note, blue with buffalo, and put it on the table.

'No.' He smiles. 'Just the stupid or lazy ones.'

'Jesus, Nico.'

'You're not religious now, are you? Did your grandmother finally wear you down?'

My grandmother had blamed my lack of faith on my parents: on my mom's death, on my father's very existence. According to her, I didn't believe in God because he'd taken my mom away from me.

It was pat, like a therapist trying to argue that you dated older men because of your daddy issues. But I never corrected her. It was easier that way and made the weekends I spent with her in St Albans pass more quietly than they otherwise would have.

'I need to go outside to get some fresh air,' I say, standing up.

'The word is pronounced *to*. Spelled *t-o*.'

'Sorry?'

'You say *te* – I have *te* go outside *te* get some air. That's what the English say. South Africans say the word like it's supposed to be said.'

I grab my handbag. 'I'm going outside. Don't come with me.' I walk towards the glass doors, concentrating on not looking back.

Outside, four palm trees line the path from the car park into the building. I lean against the glass. I don't want to be here, and I don't know whether I'll be able to help my father, whether there's anything he actually needs help with. Whether I'm just indulging his bullshit.

I close my eyes; the bandage chafes on my thigh and I'm grateful for the reminder. The horrible things that happened in Alexandra – that are happening across the country – are real, and right now, that's what's important. I almost laugh at myself. *Horrible*: what an English way to describe what happened. There, hurricanes look 'rather windy' and amputated legs 'sting a bit'.

'I'm sorry for what I said.' My father's standing in front of me when I open my eyes. He puts out his cigarette and feels for a bottle of cologne in his jacket pocket. As he sprays his neck, I realise that this is the smell, bitter orange and cloves I think, that I've always associated with him.

'I'm so addicted to this stuff,' he says. 'I had to start smoking just to have a reason to use so much of it.'

I take a step to the left so that my back is no longer against the glass. 'I can't help you unless you stop spinning your usual shit and tell me the truth.' In our reflection in the doors, his face is asymmetrical, the right side lower than the left. My face is how I always see it. 'Are you really in trouble? Or is this just one of your stories?'

He swallows. 'I'm really in trouble. And it's more than that.' He pauses. 'I know that man is dead, because I saw him die. And I want to take you to where it happened.'

A plane comes in low, from Madagascar or Mauritius perhaps, and the palm trees are paintbrushes in the tailwind, streaking white across the sky.

2

Some Afrikaners Photographed

Before leaving Durban, my father wants to stop to eat ice lollies on Battery Beach.

'Last wish of a doomed man,' he jokes as I pay for two fruit ices.

There's no wind and the waves are flat, white fringes. Surfers in wetsuits stand with their feet in the water looking out, their boards waiting for them higher on the beach.

'I don't want to go wherever it is we're going,' I say. My tongue is gobstopper-red, I'm sure.

'Me neither,' my father says. 'But I need you to help me work out how someone saw me with the guy. Who the witness could be and what they would've seen.' He shakes his head. 'What I can and can't deny.'

'Why haven't you told the police you saw where it happened?' I ask.

'They already suspect me, so if I told them and they found something there, that'd be it for me.' He throws the ice-lolly stick at a rubbish bin but misses. 'The man hasn't even been born who'll wipe my arse when I'm ninety and shitting all over myself in prison.'

I smile, though I think he hoped for more. On the beach, with ice creams and bare feet, we're a holiday postcard. Never mind that it's winter and we're both too old for it to be obvious that we're father and daughter. And that one of us is wanted for murder.

'I'd hoped to be able to show you the sardine run,' my father says, raking at sand with his toes. 'The water turns silver with them, sometimes for about ten kilometres. But we're a week or so too early, I think.'

'I've seen it. I mean, I saw it on TV. On the BBC.'

'Oh.'

'The way they move together to avoid predators – in huge funnels of fish – it makes them look more liquid than the sea.' I'm not explaining myself well. 'Almost like mercury. You know, like the baddie in *Terminator 2*.'

'I guess.' He stands up, looking unconvinced, beating his boots against each other so that the air sings. 'I didn't fancy Linda Hamilton in that film; she was too butch. I preferred her in the first one, when she was softer. Pink almost.'

I've forgotten how my father catalogues what he likes and doesn't like in women, and how stridently, almost proudly. Yet another thing I haven't prepared myself for.

'Mariska was quite butch,' I say. She's the last girlfriend whose name I'm sure of.

'I don't even remember what she looks like.' He waits a moment, looking down at me, and turns towards the stairs up to the street. 'Come on. We need to get going.'

As he unlocks the car, he says: 'Take a good look at the sea.'

The ocean is a dirty blue, warm and foamy like someone else's bathwater. There's a reason, I think, that there isn't an Indian Ocean Blue crayon.

'This is the last time you'll see this one for a long time. Years, probably.' He sits down, the car bouncing with his weight, and I join him, squeezing my skirt between my thighs so it doesn't get caught in the door. 'Cape Town's sea is the same sea you have in England. So, if you think about it, we're never really that far apart.' He winks at me:

the action is something he's read in a book or seen somewhere, but it's too self-conscious to work in real life.

I fasten my seat belt.

'I've missed you, hey,' he says, starting the car. 'I almost joined Facebook just to see how you were.'

I can't help laughing.

'What?' He checks the mirrors. 'Wouldn't you accept my friend request?'

'Probably not,' I say, as we pull out of the car park into traffic.

'That's my girl.' Before I can react to his choice of words, he hurries to add: 'Being discerning is good, I mean.'

He's trying.

'Actually, lots of people from primary school have started adding me,' I say. Facebook has only recently caught on here and no matter how many times I ask it not to, it keeps suggesting friends for me based on Naledi's network. 'So many of the girls have their wedding photos as their profile pictures. Or, even worse, ultrasound scans of their babies. Most of us are only twenty-three at the oldest.' I shake my head. 'It's weird. Depressing.'

'If you're not married by then, you've failed at life.'

'I'm glad to be a failure then,' I say. The driver of the car next to us is on his mobile. Cellphone, I tell myself. It's cellphone here, not mobile.

My father smiles. 'And I'm proud to be the father of such a gigantic failure.' He rubs his thigh with one hand. '*Jissus*, I'm not old enough to be a grandfather.'

I'm relieved we've managed to avoid any discussion of him walking me down the aisle or doing a father-of-the-bride speech. I would try to ignore it, but as he imagined an entire cast of characters – my new husband, the best man with the lazy eye, the slutty bridesmaid who put her hand on his leg after his speech – it would become impossible and we'd argue for the next hundred miles. Or however far it is to where he says the man was killed.

We stop at a traffic light and he points. 'Look.'

I follow the direction of his finger. There's nothing remarkable as far as I can tell, just rows of cars and men trying to sell bags of oranges and beaded key rings before the lights change.

I look back at him. 'What?'

'In that car. A black woman driving. You don't see it very often.'

This is one of the reasons we never spoke regularly, even when we were on speaking terms: what's between us changes so quickly and it's too difficult to keep up. To be continually disappointed.

We turn onto the N3, which a military-green sign promises will take us all the way to Pietermaritzburg, and lose the woman in traffic. He goes on: 'It's like when I go running on the beach and I see a black person walking their dog. In my head, black people don't walk dogs. They don't even fucking own dogs. We own the dogs, and the dogs bark at blacks. Not at our maids or our gardeners, but at the rest of them. Whenever I see a black walking a dog, for some reason it makes me think of that Bugs Bunny cartoon where he's in a big cauldron that's just heating up, giving Elmer Fudd advice on what vegetables will go nicely with rabbit.' He glances at the rear-view mirror and changes lanes. 'Or was it Daffy Duck?'

'I don't know.' I find the lever under my seat and move it as far back as it will go, so that I'm behind him and can see only the back of his head, his ear and the slope of his cheek.

'Well, it doesn't really matter. You get what I mean.'

'No, I don't.' I turn away from him and watch the buildings of the city give way to a shanty town as we begin the climb up the escarpment. Shacks made out of corrugated-iron sheets speed by, the washing lines strung between them crowded with checked blankets.

'If there was a switch right here' – he jabs at the dashboard – 'that would make everyone below the poverty line disappear, I'd flick it. Right now. Every day.' He opens his window halfway and spits his gum into the wind that comes wailing around the wing mirrors. 'The stupid and poor procreate and fill the world, while the smart, creative people like you and me feel bad about how poor they are. We think about over-population and don't breed.' The road roars, but his soliloquy is loud enough. 'And yes, clearly I did breed, but remember that I'm making a wider point here, just in case you were gonna get all Karen on me.'

He still knows exactly what to say to provoke me. I rest my head against the window, glad for the sunglasses.

'Morality has developed too far, to the point that one day we'll have given away so much to these bastards that we'll be equal to them. And then what?' He closes the window, trapping the question in the car.

I lean forward and unlock the glovebox, looking for a map I can throw open between us. But all the maps are in books.

'What's wrong with you?' he asks. 'You're like a bullfrog, sitting over there with your *dik bek*.' He turns to look at me. 'You can't block me out forever.'

This is the argument we have every time we speak and I'm ready for it, all the more so because I can't believe I've put myself in the position to have to do it again. I should've hung up on him when he called, or just not picked up at all, I think again. I slam the glovebox shut and sit up straight. 'You know what's wrong.'

He smiles: it worked. 'Not this crap again.' He sighs dramatically and lights a cigarette. His first drag is too deep and he coughs, drop-ping the lighter in the cracked leather folds of the gearbox.

'Yes, this crap again.' I lean forward and find the lighter, its metal top still warm. 'You talk like a fucking fascist. Actually, more like a parody of a fascist.' The last accusation will wound him more than the first, I know. The ashtray is clean and empty, so I throw the lighter into it. 'I feel like such a mug for letting myself get dragged back into your shit again, for thinking – again – that maybe it'd be different this time.' I fumble for something to hurt him with. 'I'm so ashamed of you.' This is a familiar fight, one we had the last time we saw each other. I'm surprised, though, that we've got to it so quickly.

'*Kak*, man.' He speaks quietly, controlled as a leash. 'You're ashamed of yourself. That you come from someone like me.' He offers me a cigarette, lit from his own. I take it; the filter is damp from where he breathed life into it.

'Fuck you,' I say, looking away, but we both know he's right. I'm ashamed of the part of me – biology, genealogy, curiosity, whatever – that has made it impossible to stop loving my father. No matter how foreign and disgusting I find his ideas, the way he makes gardeners and maids eat from enamel cups and plates that he keeps under the sink. How he bragged about bleaching everything a telephone repairman had touched while in the house. Just like in those TV ads where germs spread from raw-chicken cutting boards, my father could see in the imagined red handprints on his light switches and door handles a direct link from a shack to his flat. I'd hoped that he might change – that he'd be the exception and would become more liberal as he got older – or at least not bring it up in front of me.

'You're ashamed that you have white, Afrikaner blood,' he goes on, clearly relishing it now. 'But you'll never get away from that, no matter how many blacks or Arabs you fuck.' The way he says it, all the words in that sentence are as dirty as the last one.

I open my window as far as it will go and let the wind take my cigarette. The car fills with the smell of hot tar and a coming storm. I unfasten my seat belt and push it out from my body so that it whips back into a neat spool behind me.

'What're you doing?' He almost has to shout.

I turn so that my back is against the dashboard. Grabbing my head-rest, I pull myself up onto my knees. Rows of cars stream behind us like ticker tape. 'Getting away from you,' I say, bringing my left leg up over the console between our seats to get into the back of the car.

He grabs my skirt. 'Sit down, you fucking idiot,' he says. 'If people are following us, do you really think it's a good idea to draw attention like this?' He checks the mirrors.

'I don't care,' I say, trying to pull away. He doesn't let go, and the orange cotton rips. The sound seems to shock him, and he takes his hand back. I look over my shoulder and lift my skirt to see the hole. It's long and oval and falls at the tops of my thighs, exposing a pale jellyfish of skin.

I turn to face him. 'Maybe I should get my tits out and press them against the window at passing cars. Just to be even more inconspicuous.'

'I'm sorry.' He looks at me. 'Will you sit down, please? You're mooning every car in the slow lane.' He smiles, but I won't let him have his joke, and he turns his eyes back to the road.

'We're stopping at the next petrol station so I can change.' I slide down into my seat.

He chews his lip. 'OK.'

I turn on the radio and skip through the pre-set channels, listening for news.

'*...bringing the death toll to thirty-two, with at least one hundred injured. Anti-immigrant incidents have now been reported in the North West province and in the Free State.*'

What started in Alex is spreading. I remember running, crouching in the alleyways between shacks. The smell of singed hair and burning rubber.

My father jabs at the radio. The car is quiet again. 'What the hell happened then?' He rubs his left hand up and down his thigh, making his shorts ride up as high as they can go. 'Will you put your seat forward, please? I'm gonna drive into a tree if I keep having to do a fucking *Exorcist* head twist just to see you.'

I can only think in clichés. 'I wanted to be as far away from you as possible,' I say. But even the distance of the last three years hasn't done it. I lift the lever under my seat and row it forward so that he and I are in line again.

'Did you want to hit me?'

'No, I didn't want to hit you.' I pull at the hem of my skirt with both hands so that there are two perfect orange lines running from my waist to the edge of my seat. A cotton trapezium. I try to remember how to calculate angles in an irregular shape.

'OK. Because I'd understand if you did. You looked like you did.' He smiles, and I know something is coming. 'Actually, you've looked helluva like you want to hit me all morning. Which in my experience can mean one of two things.' He looks at me, trying to time his delivery. 'Either you're pregnant or you haven't had a nice fat dick between your legs in a while.' He waits for my reaction. But I'm already tired of being angry.

'I wish it was the latter,' I say, without looking at him. I take the lighter out of the ashtray, pretend to study it, copying all those worried young women I've seen avoiding their fathers' gazes in afternoon films on Channel 5.

He looks at me. 'Do you mean that you're pregnant?'

I round my shoulders, letting my hair hang in my face so that he has to sit forward a little to see me.

'I'm not saying you look pregnant or anything,' he hurries. 'But if you *are* pregnant, we need to do something about it as soon as possible.'

I can't cry on cue but I make myself shudder as I breathe in.

'It'll be OK – it's not like in the old days when girls had to fly to London to get an abortion.' His eyes dart from me to the road and back. 'Let me help you, Jo.'

I can't remember the last time he spoke to me like this – worried rather than mocking or insulting. If he ever has.

The joke isn't funny any more. I lean back in my seat. 'I'm not pregnant,' I say, lighting a cigarette.

'Are you sure?' He looks at me, perhaps expecting to be able to read my face.

'Yes, I'm fucking sure.' I close my window. 'I'm not some idiot who goes for a wee and suddenly pops out a sprog.' The air inside the car is beginning to turn smoke-blue. 'The reason I've looked like I want to hit you since this morning is because you're a fucking arsehole most of the time.' I watch him for a reaction, but he looks straight ahead. 'Not because I'm hormonal or because – God forbid – I've not had sex in a while.'

'Oh.' He pauses. 'So when you said it wasn't the latter, did you mean you're back on men now?'

This again. 'I was never off them.'

He opens the sunroof and the smoke plumes out.

I don't want to have our version of the argument about what parents want for their children – to work until I'm thirty and then marry a nice South African man, or, at a push, an Australian or American, as long as he's not British; but above all, to pick a team and stick to it. We've had this argument so often that it seems scripted, like everything else we row about. The difference is, we're burning through them this time. Normally, they're more evenly spaced, fitted in around his questions about what books I'm reading, his speeches about how disappointing the UK is. I wonder what we'll have to say to one another when the

31

usual arguments are over with. If bigger, more serious ones will follow. 'Can I put the radio back on?'

'No. I never listen to the radio, so I brought some CDs with me from my car.' He points at the cracked cases in the compartment next to the air-con.

'Why don't you listen to the radio?' For some reason, I remember doing this to my mom when I was a child, asking *why?* until she answered me with four-syllable words I had to look up in the dictionary.

'Because I don't like not being able to control what comes on next. And all modern music is shit.'

'I thought you used to be into Van Halen?'

He laughs. 'Yes, but I was young and stupid. It was before I'd listened to Wagner's *Der fliegende Holländer*. That changed my life.' He picks his ear with his forefinger. 'Did Karen tell you about Van Halen?'

I don't want him to say her name. 'Yes.' A Shell sign flashes in the distance, bright as plastic fruit.

'Your mom always had terrible taste in music, hey.' He changes down into first gear.

I won't let him have that easy insult. 'Did you have the poodle hair Van Halen had? Were you hot for teacher?'

'No.'

'That's a pity,' I say as we pull into the petrol station. 'I would've loved to see photos of that.'

'Nope, sorry.' He slows to a stop and turns off the ignition. I only realise how loud the air-conditioning is when it's off. 'Give me your phone,' he says.

'What for?' I look at my handbag, which is lying between my feet. My mobile is visible in the side pocket. I wish I'd zipped it away.

'So that you don't do anything stupid like call someone and let them know where we are.' He unbuckles his seat belt and turns towards me.

'I'm not going to call anyone.' I grip the bag between my feet. 'Now get out so I can change.' I unbuckle my seat belt too, but my legs stick to the leather seat through the hole in my skirt.

He shakes his head. 'Not until you give me your phone.'

'Fine,' I say, picking up my bag and putting it over my left shoulder. 'I'll get out.' I pull at the door handle but nothing happens. I try again. Still nothing. The window won't open either.

'Give me your phone.' He sighs, as though I'm a small child refusing to eat my vegetables, and puts his sunglasses on the dashboard.

'Unlock the door.' Even though I know it's useless, I keep pushing the button to open the window.

'No.' He speaks sharply. 'Give it to me.' He leans over until I can smell the gum on his breath. My back is against the door. 'Give me your fucking phone.' His lips are thin and chapped and there's grey in his eyebrows. The colour in his eyes seems more watery than it used to be, the intention more veiled. Unable to hold his stare, I look down.

'Jo.' He curls his fingers around my wrist and squeezes. I can feel his bones against mine. 'Give it to me or I'll take it from you.'

Suddenly there's a knock on the window behind him. He turns, putting his hands in 10-and-2 position on the wheel. A petrol jockey crouches by the window, miming to my father to roll it down. Nico hits the steering wheel with the flat of his hand, presses a button near the ignition. The car unlocks with a popping sound.

I throw my door open and take a few steps away from the car. Then I remember the hole in my skirt and hold my bag over it, behind me.

'Fill it up, *baas*?' the man asks my father.

'*Ja.*' My father leans across to close the door I left open. He doesn't look at me. The petrol jockey waves him closer to the pumps with the exaggerated gestures of a traffic cop. I should give him a big tip, I think.

While the numbers roll over on the pump, I open the boot, unzip my suitcase with one hand and pull out a black dress from near the top so that I don't have to bend over too far. I slam the boot shut so hard that the car bounces, but my father doesn't look back.

A sign in the window of the station shop says that the bathrooms are around the back. I walk quickly. Tied to a tap against the side wall of the building, a German shepherd waits for its owner. It growls at me as I pass.

The bathrooms don't have doors. Instead, the letters *M* and *F* are painted in black on the building's back wall. Arrows point from the horizontal lines of the *F* down a short corridor of turquoise bricks. The bathroom, empty and smelling of bleach and rotting toilet brushes, opens up perpendicularly at the end of the corridor, hidden from dog walkers by the turquoise wall.

Only one cubicle has a lock. In spite of the lock, and even though I'd be able to hear someone coming, I keep my right foot jammed against the door as I change. It wouldn't slow them down that much but it might give me time to dial the number for the police. I check the bandage on my thigh. It's yellow in places. I know I should change it but I've been going through two a day since the night in Alex and don't have many left. I carefully pull both my t-shirt and my skirt over my head so that nothing touches the floor, shifting the bundle of clothes from one hand to the other as I slip on the dress. It's too short to wear during the day, I realise now, but it'll have to do. The ripped skirt spread over the toilet seat cover, I sit down. The clock numbers on my phone pass two minutes as I wonder who to call. Naledi might say *I told you so*, ask too many questions, care too much. Claire and Hannah, my friends from my first job in London, writing features about local regeneration, would be at their desks, and although they'd probably answer their phones, I hadn't told them any of the backstory.

All they knew about my life in South Africa was a quip I repeated any time it came up in conversation: It's like the American Midwest but with less buying power.

I dial a South African mobile number, relieved when it goes straight to voicemail. Even though I speak quietly, my voice echoes in the empty bathroom. 'Hi, Paul. It's Jo.' Doubled over on the toilet seat, I try to keep the panic out of my voice. 'I'm sorry I didn't call you back. I should've. And we should've done something sooner and maybe.' I close my eyes. I don't know what else to say. 'Look, can you call me when you get this message? I need to talk to you.' Then, lamely: 'Thanks.'

When I walk back around the building, with my phone on silent and wrapped in my shirt at the bottom of my bag, the dog is gone. And so is my father.

The car is locked. His camera is on the driving seat. I don't think he's done a runner. He's not in the shop either. I go into the shop to wait, looking at biscuits, remembering pool parties and home economics class. The way my mom and I used to lick the white animals from the Iced Zoo biscuits. The man behind the counter sells me a packet of paracetamol, water and some chewing gum. Outside, I wait on the kerb by the BMW, my bag tucked under my arm and the shopping bag around my wrist. Four cars pull into the station, fill their tanks and go again.

'*Missies*,' the petrol jockey calls from across the concourse.

I stand up awkwardly, conscious of the short dress. Pushing my sunglasses up into my hair, I walk towards the pumps.

'*Baas* went that way, *missies*.' He points a finger that hasn't been straight in years towards the side of the building.

'Thanks,' I say, and pull a fifty-rand note from my purse.

'God bless,' he says, watching the maroon lion on the note. His palm is rough.

I walk back around the side of the building. There are no trails into the bush, and no broken twigs signalling a newly made one. I'll have to try the bathroom.

The arrow coming out of the *M* points to the floor. 'Nico?' I call down the corridor. 'Hello?' The bricks are stained where men couldn't wait for the urinal; I breathe through my mouth. The bathroom floor is wet in the flickering fluorescent light. 'Nico?'

'Jo?' I hear a sniff. 'Just one second.'

I walk towards the stall his voice is coming from. The door isn't locked, so I push it open slowly.

He stops it halfway with his foot. 'Don't. Don't come in.'

I step into the stall as far as I can. He's sitting on the toilet, bent forward, his head in his hands, his t-shirt pulled up so that it covers his whole face.

'What's wrong?' The shirt is grey where it's wet, a shroud. His belly is hairy and puckered.

'I just—' He breathes in twice without exhaling, as though he needs the air. 'I can't believe.' His voice is higher than usual, pinched. 'What I just did to you.'

'No,' I say, looking down. There's a carnation on the floor. 'Me neither.'

'*Ag*, shit.' His chest judders and he moves a hand over the t-shirt to wipe his nose. 'I'm—' But the words are drowned in sobs and he can't finish the sentence.

I wait, watching him. I've never seen or heard him cry before, not even when I moved to England. Perhaps now is a good time to try to convince him that the best thing to do would be to stop running and go to the police.

But his breathing has already grown more regular. I've missed my chance.

'I'm so sorry,' he manages, still under his t-shirt. 'This thing. It's making me crazy.' He rubs both hands over his t-shirt and lowers it. His face is red and wet, his mouth actually turning down at the corners like a cartoon dog's. He grabs my wrist, the same one he grabbed earlier. 'I would never,' he says. 'I'd never hurt you.' He swallows. 'I love you.' I've never heard him say this before either. He keeps staring at me after he's said it, and I have to look away.

I put the plastic bag down in the cubicle. 'There's some water, and some paracetamol if you need it.'

'Thanks.' He lets go of my wrist.

I step back out of the stall. 'I'll wait for you by the car.'

'OK.' His voice skids on the wet floor and crashes into my ankles.

I have to get out of here. 'See you there,' I say, turning. My face is blurred in the mirror above the sink.

He unlocks the car with the remote as he comes around the corner. His face looks normal again and he's swinging the plastic bag. I get in. He stops behind the car and opens the boot. There's a beer in his hand when he sits down in the driver's seat.

'What the fuck are you doing?' I ask, pointing at the Castle Lager.

He holds the can between his thighs as he starts the car. 'Relax, man. It'll take more than one beer for me to drive even half as badly as all the blacks and women on the road.'

I grip the handle above the window and turn away from him.

When we've pulled out of the service station and into traffic, I ask: 'How long will the drive take to wherever it is we're going?'

'Why does it matter?' He overtakes a pick-up. 'You've become so English, hey. If you listen to Americans having a conversation, the word "dollar" always comes up. With the English, it's transport. Every time I go to the UK, it hits me: public transport over there may be really good, but it also stuffs up your ability to talk about anything else.

37

It's one of the biggest disappointments about England.' He pushes a button and the car is filled with a burst of Bach. He skips between tracks and violins begin their slow build. 'Do you know this concerto? Just listen to how complicated it is.' His fingers follow the movement on the steering wheel.

I watch our progress through the sunroof. Above us, bloated clouds have settled. When my grandmother and her husband drove me to my first term at boarding school one winter's day more than ten years ago, the rich blues and greens of the waterlogged countryside had reminded me of Natal. Then, I'd still thought that in England, the only magic was in the flocking starlings. I'd cried, missing my mom, missing South Africa. But now, in the car with my father, watching the clouds swallow mountains whole, I'm reminded of England in winter.

'They came during the off-season—'

'Who's "they"?'

'I'm getting there,' my father says. 'Jesus.'

We've stopped at a picnic area just outside of Dundee, a small town of low buildings and wide, empty pavements, so he can make sure no one's following us.

The old stone table, missing its benches, is covered in birdshit. He's sitting on the bonnet of the car, leaning back against the windscreen and smoking. I stand against the car, kicking my right heel against the hubcap. The blue gum trees are leaking, spitting at us. Bark comes off their trunks in ribbons.

'Shouldn't the police see this before I do? I mean, there might be evidence there.' I feel ridiculous saying it, like someone out of a TV procedural where everyone is beautiful and the white balance is off, just for effect. 'DNA or something,' I finish lamely.

'These guys would've gotten rid of any evidence. Plus I wanted you to see it first, before the police came raking over the place like vultures.' His choice of words seems wrong. The police wouldn't be looking for bones to pick clean.

After four hours in the car, I need to walk. I push myself off it and head for the picnic table, dragging my feet to stir leaves and bark. 'What were you doing here?'

The little I know about my father's life both before and after he met my mom, I know mostly from her. His life has always been a conversational asymptote. When I was younger I'd tried to find out more, wanting to be able to picture him as a boy or what he was doing on Christmas Day, but he'd told me to concentrate on making my own story exciting and to stop trying to steal his. When I was ten, he said it'd become obvious to him that the only way I'd have an exciting story to tell was if he starred in it. He took me wine tasting and to climb Table Mountain. Remember the things we do together, he'd told me. Remember how nice I was to let you borrow some of my stories. He said he'd worked as a train driver for a travelling circus, and the tall English clown had taught him how to pick pockets; he'd tracked poachers in the Kruger National Park; he'd painted children's faces in Vienna, bringing Africa to Europe in sticky manes and stripes. A different story every time.

'When I got back from Europe,' he says now, 'there was registered mail from the army waiting there for me. I didn't open any of it.' He blows smoke at a circling bee as I bend to brush the dirt from my feet. 'I mean, I knew what it would say: *Refusal to return to base and complete your service will result in six years in jail.*' He puts on a thick Afrikaans accent, with flat vowels and rolling *r*'s.

I straighten, surprised. Once he caught me laughing at some badly edited photographs – celebrities missing their feet – in an Afrikaans magazine and accused me of thinking that all Afrikaners were stupid. You'd do well, he said, to remember where you come from.

'So I packed my stuff that night and left Jo'burg. I didn't realise until after I'd left the Transvaal for the last time how difficult it was to breathe there.'

I nod, remembering running away from the police station in Alex. How thin the air was.

'All I'd been thinking about for months was what I'd seen up there on the border when I was in the army. I didn't know whether I could come back here. But Europe is so boring. So full of churches and shit. In the end, I had to come back.' He pulls a rind of rubber from the windscreen wiper. 'Crossing the Vaal was the first time my brain had worked properly in months. But, *sjoe*, it took a while to get going again.' He laughs at the idea, as though it seems preposterous now. 'And I made a stupid mistake because of that.'

I wait, unsure of which role – enraptured audience member or sympathetic talk-show host – would get the most out of him.

'In my fucked-up state, I thought it would be enough just to get out of Pretoria. So I went to live in one of the houses that your grandparents left me when they died.'

'Couldn't the army track you?' This wasn't something we'd learnt about in primary-school history. Just the Great Trek, over and over again, and apartheid with a capital A.

'Shush, man, I'm getting there.'

'Can we go see the house?' I ask casually, as though I don't care one way or the other. 'I'd like to know more about them.'

'No way.' He rolls his eyes. 'Not making the same mistake twice. Don't you get it? The police will have someone watching the house.'

I don't want to start an argument by pointing out how paranoid he sounds and nod instead.

'Anyway, I thought I was being so fucking clever by hiding down here. No one knew me and I even used a different name.' He pulls the rubber strip tight between his fingers and balls it in one hand. 'I was,' he says, waving his empty hand in front of his fist, 'Erik Klavier.' He presents both hands to me, palms up, with a flourish. The rubber is gone.

I laugh obediently. Eric Piano. 'That's so obviously fake.'

'I know, but the people at the lodge didn't care. They were here from Holland. I was sitting in the Milky Lane in town, and they came in and bought me a caramel sundae with the sauce that goes hard when it touches the ice cream. We got talking about waffles and Amsterdam and they said that they needed someone to watch the place in the off-season, when they went back to Holland. They were quite old and needed help with keeping the place up, so I started working for them in the summer too. At first just things like painting and gardening, but soon I was running the bar, doing all the cooking and taking care of the entertainment for tourists.' He slides down the bonnet and stubs the cigarette out against the tyre.

'What sort of entertainment?' I have visions of smalltown girls dressed in the way eighties movies had defined as sexy, with side pony-tails and baby-blue eyeshadow.

'I started out telling some of Herman Charles Bosman's stories. Do you know them?'

I shake my head.

'Jesus. It doesn't matter. You probably won't like them anyway – not a good representation of the racially diverse population of South Africa. Too many women in bonnets serving men peach brandy.' To imitate my voice, he lifts his chin and looks down his nose at me. 'But the tourists loved them. And soon I just made up my own stories. Stupid, nice things like baboons stealing a car in the Kruger Park.' He throws the butt into the grass.

41

'What were the owners doing while you were taking over?' Some
thing about the story of the lazy owners and the progression of the
lowly handyman sounds familiar. Just like all his other stories.

'They were happy for someone else to do the work.'

'Where are they now? I'm sure they could help.' I realise suddenl
that I expect to be told that they're dead.

'They're dead.' He shakes his head, a TV doctor. 'Killed in a fir
in Amsterdam a few years after I left. I only found out when I drov
through Natal once and stopped in to see them.'

There's smoke coming from the butt in the grass. 'Shit.' I wonde
whether I can get my grandmother's lawyer to check on the Dutc
couple without having to answer any questions about why I need th
information. 'What were their names?' I grind the tip of the butt int
the ground, pick it up and drop it into my pocket.

'I can't remember now. They were really typical Dutch names. I'v
got it somewhere at home.'

He's not being very convincing. You'd remember the names o
people who'd employed you for two years. I wonder how long he plan
to string me along with this on-the-run-from-the-police story. Hov
long he'll double down on the act – to justify tearing my skirt an
trying to take my phone – before he tells me what's really going on

'Was there anyone else around at all that could confirm any of this?'

He looks at me. 'You don't believe me?' He stalks to the picni
bench, leaving the car bouncing slightly. 'Fuck, man, Jo. I ask you fo
help – which is very hard for me to do – and you treat me like an idic
and a liar?' He kicks at the heavy metal drum that no rubbish crev
ever comes to empty. Rusty cans of Coke fall to the floor, spilling dea
bees. 'You weren't exactly my first choice, you know. I've spent week
trying to think of someone else who could help.' He kicks the drun
again. This time, it wobbles.

'Calm down,' I say. Then, quickly, in case that pisses him off further, the way it would me: 'Look, I'm sorry I doubted you.' He is animal, making me animal tamer. But I'm angry at his rehearsed stories, smooth as pebbles, his ready defensiveness. 'This isn't something you can talk your way out of. And your attempts to do so make you seem dodgy. Even to me.' I pause, but there's more to say. 'And now is not the time to play the I'm-your-father card.'

'There's never a time for that, is there?' he asks, suddenly still.

'No, it's too late. I can't just accept everything you say because I'm your daughter. Can you see that?'

'Of course I can see that. I'm not a fucking moron.' He starts pacing.

'Well then, stop behaving like one.' It's a risk, I know, after what happened at the service station. I'm grateful that he's wearing his sunglasses and I can't see his eyes. I don't want to think about what I might have found there. 'And stop kicking that fucking drum. Or I'll kick you in the shins.' The schoolgirl threat makes us both laugh.

'OK, OK, sorry.' He pulls at his beard, frowning again. 'I'm just really worried that being innocent isn't enough.'

It isn't, I think. It never has been in this country. And in the past, that's been good enough for him. But out loud I say: 'It is, and we'll prove it to them.' I force myself to smile. 'So, tell me what happened.'

'Since we're so close, let's just go to the lodge and I'll talk you through it there.' He unlocks the car and gets in. 'We can pretend we're travel agents thinking about bringing large tour groups here. Then we can be as rude as we like. I'll be Andre, a gay from Jo'burg. Sandton, actually. You be Hermione, the snooty British one.'

Inside the car, the leather is cold against my legs and the wind, so quiet in the trees, now wheedles noisily against the cracked windows.

'Can't we just say you used to work there?' I ask as we pull out of the lay-by. 'Something simple?' But I know before he answers what he'll say: my father likes to lie to people, make them believe a complicated and completely false backstory that he's made up on the spot. It's another way for him to measure people.

'No, that's no fun. This way, we'll have stories to tell when this is all over.' He leans forward and pulls another can of beer from under his seat.

'Fine,' I say, knowing it wouldn't matter to him if it wasn't.

'There used to be an elephant's head on the wall behind the bar. And a big swimming pool with water pouring out of the lions' and buffalos' mouths.' We turn left at a sign: *White Elephant Game Lodge.*

'So, no African clichés then.' I hate places like this. It's what people expect my flat to look like.

'But the best thing about this place is how many birds there are. The black crake and the bee-eater. The cut-throat finch with the red on its chin.' We park in the dust in front of a whitewashed one-storey building. Another sign welcomes us in all eleven national languages plus French and German.

I sit with my feet on the pool cover, his camera in my lap. Hermione's prop. Andre the travel agent from Sandton has the lodge owners, two middle-aged Afrikaners who've never left the country, promising package deals, shuttles to the Blood River memorials ('These English, they just love to shake their heads where so many brown people died,' Andre said) and shooting lessons. He's flamboyantly camp and calls them *darling*. I wonder if his entire concept of being gay comes from bad movies.

At first, it's a relief to be alone again. I try to concentrate on the story my father told me about working here, checking it against the few concrete details I have about his life: his date of birth, the semester he moved into the commune where he met my mom, the month he left us. But I can't help thinking about my mom instead. The last spring I had with her, we'd peel back the pool cover every afternoon to test the water. Our feet numb with cold, we'd force ourselves to stand on the first step for at least five minutes. As the weeks passed we went down a step and stayed for longer, building up to the day we pulled the cover off completely and jumped into the deep end holding hands. She always hit the water first.

'I'll see you later, lovelies,' I hear my father announce. 'I'm just going to show Hermione around. Poor thing can't cope with the heat.' As he comes into the courtyard, he turns into himself again, taking longer strides and swinging his arms. 'Did you see me mincing?' he whispers when he's close. 'I felt like Kevin Spacey at the end of *The Usual Suspects.*'

I stand up. 'Have you ever actually met a gay person before?'

'Some of my best friends are gays,' he says, smiling, but when I roll my eyes, he crosses his arms. 'Seriously, though, it's working great – they're so uncomfortable that we get to do whatever we want.' He doesn't usually explain himself. Maybe this is for me. 'And they're making up two rooms for us in the main house as we speak.'

'I don't want to stay.' There's blood in the groundwater here.

'Tough. I'm bored of driving and, frankly, I could do with people to speak to other than you.' He looks around for somewhere to stick his chewing gum and settles for the leg of a rusty pool lounger. 'Dinner is in half an hour. I've told them not to worry about rude ol' Hermione.' He flaps a hand, Andre again. 'So of course they're really worried, since you know the Queen and all that.'

'What?'

'You live in England, so you must be best friends with the Queen.' He bows, one hand behind his back, the other twirling in front of him, but he gives up halfway through. 'So they're doing a *braai* to impress you. Don't fuck it up. We both need to stay in character.' He reaches into his pocket and draws out key rings with cartoon animal charms, dangles them in front of me. 'For the guest rondavels.' He points at the nearest one; a sign just below its neatly trimmed thatched roof identifies it as Rhino. 'Are you gonna put my camera around your neck or should I just take it away now?' He waits while I slide the strap over my head. 'Good girl.'

'Bugger off.'

He ignores me. 'The rondavels have been plastered over now, but when I was here, you could see that the walls were made out of these big red rocks. They looked better that way. Not so beige.' Unlocking the door of Rhino, he says: 'This is where they put me.'

The hut is musty and there are dead flies on the window sills. A bed and a chair touch the wall with only their corners; a cupboard stoops near the window.

'These two army guys came during the off-season, their buzz cuts just beginning to grow out. I told them we were closed but they offered to pay in cash so the owners wouldn't have to know.'

'Nice.' The flies are all on their backs, their legs stiff as aloes.

'I needed the money,' he says. 'Child support isn't cheap.'

I want to say, *You never paid child support*, but instead ask: 'What happened then?'

'The next morning, one of them called me to his rondavel – this one – saying there was a problem with the sockets. I walked in and a third guy – one that hadn't been there when they'd checked in – was pointing a gun at me. That's when I knew I was fucked.'

'Why?' I open the cupboard door; hangers covered in pink foam rattle.

'It's a long story.' He stands in the doorway, leaning against the jamb.

'What about the black man? Where was he when this happened?'

'I don't know where he was.' He straightens, his face half in the light filtering in through the dust outside.

'It's important. It's *the* most important thing,' I insist. 'What's happening now might be about you in some secondary way—'

'Prison isn't secondary.'

'It is compared with someone being kidnapped and killed. And that part of the story is not about you.' I slam the cupboard door shut for emphasis.

'I know that. What do you think I am: a complete dickhead? Anyway, we've only got about twenty minutes before dinner, and I want to show you where I last saw the man.' He nods over his shoulder.

'Fine, but after dinner you'll tell me everything. From start to finish. And again if I need you to.'

'No. Tonight I'm Andre, and I'm going to talk to these people about glory holes and anal fissures so much and so well that they'll tell their grandchildren stories about me. But tomorrow, in the car. We can talk then.'

I walk past him into the courtyard. The list of things that don't add up is too long. Why did they pick this place and how much did my father see? Why didn't they kill him too, when they were done? Why has he never reported them?

He locks Rhino behind us. '*Jissus*, Jo. Why do you always think the worst of me, hey?' Another rhetorical question, I suppose. '*Wa-ngi-buka nge-loku-hlola insimu.*'

His pronunciation is good; he plays marbles with his consonants. I didn't know he could speak Zulu. 'What does that mean?'

'That you look at me trying to find a fault.' He steps over an old hosepipe, faded as shed snakeskin. 'Literally, though, it's *he looked at me as if inspecting a field.*'

My shadow takes a swim in the pool as we cross the courtyard. Underwater, it palms the sun.

'Bullshit is built into the Zulu language, man.' He spits into the grass and unlocks Cheetah, motions for me to step into the rondavel. It's just like the other one, but furnished in louder prints. 'This is where they kept him most of the time. Just him and a chair in the middle of the room on an old shower curtain. They had to keep spraying the piss and blood and shit off of it.' He fills the doorway, and I stand in the centre of the room. What my father says happened here seems incompatible with the cheesy décor, but I can't look at the chair against the wall.

Outside again, he points at a large rectangle of grass halved by a badminton net. 'That's where they submarined him.' I look at him blankly. 'They pissed and shat in a bucket, added some of the dog's crap, and put it all in a plastic bag. Then they forced his head into it and held him there until he stopped breathing.' He bends to drink from a tap on the courtyard wall. Wipes his chin on his shoulder. 'Revived him, just to do it all over again.'

I want to leave this place, this country.

'Then they took him up that hill.' He looks at me, can see I'm pale and unwilling, I'm sure of it.

I back away. 'I have to take photos of the huts, work out how someone saw you—'

'That can wait. Come on.' He grabs my wrist. 'You have to see this.'

From the hill outside Dundee, the horizon is a dried orange peel. We stand together and watch it warp and curl in the late sun.

'This is his last place,' my father says. 'He was dying already. His ears and his nose were long gone. After two days, they let him free here and watched him trying to run.' He kicks at a tuft of grass. 'He fell, dancing like a golliwog puppet.'

'Don't.'

He turns towards me, and I can smell him – cologne and sweat and cigarettes – on the wind. 'Did you ever hear that story about the white man who died and they transplanted his heart into a black man, up in Jo'burg I think?' He doesn't wait for me to shake my head. 'When his family found out, they wanted the heart back.' He laughs at the punchline.

I wipe my nose on the back of my hand.

'For fuck's sake.' He looks up at the sky, as though for confirmation: *Yes, Nico, I see what you have to put up with, and, truly, your patience is astounding.* 'You're such a baby.'

I turn away from him. The hill's slopes have been stripped of grass by the wind and sun.

Behind me, my father says: 'Are you OK?'

'Yes.' With closed eyes, I take two steps away from him in case he tries to move closer or put a hand on my shoulder.

'You look pale.' Quietly now: 'I should've gotten you something to eat.'

I face him, my shoes driving stones deeper into the hard earth. 'I can feed myself.' As an afterthought: 'I've been doing that for twenty-three years without you.'

'I know.' He looks down, rolling a pebble under his foot. 'Do you want to hear more about what happened up here?'

'No,' I say. 'But tell me anyway.'

'He fell. They'd made me carry a generator up here, and they brought it over to where he lay.' He points to a patch of dust, bald as a nectarine. 'Then they taped electrodes to him, one to his right nipple and the other to his penis. I remember, the tape was such a bright blue.' He turns around. 'And then they played radio.'

'What the fuck does that mean?' I don't know what these euphemisms are supposed to do. Maybe they make what's happening less real so that it can keep happening.

'They shocked him and watched him jump, over and over again, until he couldn't even piss himself any more. Then he didn't even jump. He just shuddered in the dust. He was still alive, but only barely.'

I'm crying now, covering my face. My father steps forward, maybe to try to hug me, but I shake my head and put one hand up in front of me. He steps back, hands in his pockets.

'What next?' I ask when I can speak again.

'I don't know. Two of them took me back to the hut.'

'Why?'

'I don't know,' he repeats, squinting up into the sun. 'They knocked me out.'

'Did you see the man again?' I wipe my face with the backs of my hands.

'No. That was it.'

'I thought you saw him die?'

'Don't be so literal,' he says. 'He died soon after that. His screams didn't sound human, which was funny because that's what they'd been saying all along, that blacks aren't human. But as you can see, there's not much around here now, and there was even less then. So there was no one to hear him and go look for the dying animal on the hill.'

'How do you know all this?' I ask, watching him. 'I thought you were down in the hut, out cold?'

He smiles. 'Because, when I woke up, Gideon van Vuuren told me all about it.'

'Who's he?'

'Man, but he was someone I knew from the army. Kind of my *bru* for a while.' He looks straight ahead, away from me, but speaks loudly enough so that I can hear, as though he'd read somewhere that actors don't always have to face the audience. 'And the killer.'

I ball my hands at my sides digging my nails into my palms. 'I thought you said you didn't know them?'

He turns and begins to walk back towards the main house. 'I lied. But wasn't it more dramatic to tell you here?' he calls.

There's no point in running after him, I know. He expects me to be agape at his revelation, at his careful delivery of this important detail, so I turn away from him instead. He's probably halfway to the rondavels by now, looking back, watching me for my reaction. So I close my eyes, tilt my head back just a fraction to feel the last of the afternoon sun on my face and swear quietly, trying to stop myself from crying. I should've known that going to see my father, agreeing to go along for the ride, would be no better than staying on the riots story. Different, but no better.

I lift the camera and shoot a few photos of the lodge from the hill. At least he isn't here to tell me how to frame them. I'll have to wait till we're in the car and he can't stage his revelations.

Of course, after twenty-five years, there are no bones to stumble over among the rocks. No initials written in blood. The rondavels are too sheltered, and this hill too exposed, for someone to have seen what was happening without being spotted themselves. There's nothing here to help my father, just as he'd known there wouldn't be. He's played the entire trip here for effect, composing an image for me to see. The image he wants me to see. But I don't know why, not yet.

Behind me, my father whistles. I lift the camera again to take a photo of the road that heads west, towards the Free State and its frosted yellow grass. Past its dried-up reservoirs and still wind pumps.

The smell of cooking meat is on the wind.

———

I open my bedroom window as far as it will go. The burglar bars have begun to sweat with the frost that's been hanging in the air since Andre said goodnight to me two hours ago. Hermione skipped dinner, feigning the flu, so my father had the stage all to himself.

Branches move in the wind. Being around my father makes me tired – having to be on guard constantly, to question everything he says – but I can't sleep for picturing what happened here, the wires and the bloody shower curtain.

A light comes on in one of the rondavels. I wonder if my father is asleep next door – I didn't hear him leave his room – or if he's down there, remembering. The rondavel curtains move and then are still.

3

This Is How It Happened

I roll an orange between my hands, the smell of the peel filling the car. I hope it sticks to my fingers and stains them. I bite into the top of the orange, pulling out the pith core with my teeth. Keeping it in my lap for later, like the top of a plastic bottle, I lift the orange to my mouth to drink.

Hermione didn't come down for breakfast, but there was fruit in the bowl by the door. Andre left with a promise to call and a kiss on the cheek for the wife of the Boer in short pants.

'I suppose you want to know about Gideon,' my father says, lighting a cigarette. His hair is still wet from the shower.

I hope that my last two weeks in South Africa will go by as fast as the aloes rushing past the windows, that I'll wake up later not to Bach being smokily whistled but to London sweating in the summer, my hair longer and all this behind me. But for now, I have to stay with my father, to convince him that going to the police is the only thing that makes sense. This thought makes me tired.

'We're going to the Swartberg Pass just north of Oudtshoorn,' he says.

I've offered to pay for a lawyer for him, someone who can find out exactly what evidence there is against him, but he won't have it. He wants to figure it out himself. A man doesn't trust his fate to someone else, he said. Obviously, I don't really count as someone else, he'd added, because I was an extension of him.

His idea is to head west, keeping off the big roads, while we work out how to find out who could've shopped him in. The lodge was too isolated for anyone to have seen what happened, and everyone in Dundee knew him as Erik Klavier anyway, so all we can do is work through the list of people involved and figure out who they might have told. We have no destination in mind; we just have to keep moving. And the further away from the lodge we get, the better. But the plan makes me nervous: the further we go into the desert, the fewer options I have but to stay with him and hope he changes his story.

I put the orange in my lap, lean forward and open the glovebox. The road atlas is sticky in my hands.

'There's a waterfall there that very few people know about,' he says. 'You climb a little way off the pass to get to it. We should be there by tonight.'

I look up Oudtshoorn in the index and find the page. The town is surrounded by rivers, thin as thread veins and all with Afrikaans names that promise elephants and monkeys. I remember I have something to ask: 'Won't it be dark when we get there? I won't be able to see anything.'

'Just being able to hear it is enough. It's one of the most beautiful places on earth, better than anything in Europe.'

I close the road atlas and slide it onto the dashboard. He's treating this trip as though it's his chance to be a tour guide.

'Especially England,' he continues. 'The countryside there is pretty at first, but it's garish.' He looks at me, smiling. 'It's like a whore, all lipstick and cheap lingerie. And it's the same all over: there's no way to tell Bath and Edinburgh apart. But this waterfall—'

'Shut up,' I say, fumbling for my handbag. 'I'm not interested in seeing your highlights of SA. Driving around aimlessly forever.' I pull out a pack of cigarettes, my dictaphone and a notepad. 'Just tell me about Gideon, so we can get this over with. And this time I'm going to tape you, so you can't backtrack and deny anything.' I decided last night that I'd tape every conversation we had from here on out as insurance – against what, I don't know exactly. The dictaphone has a battery life of seventy-two hours and I don't plan on still being with my father when it runs out.

He stubs out his cigarette in the clean ashtray. 'I hope we can make it to the Karoo before dusk so you can see the bitter aloes,' he says, keeping his tone light. 'They're red this time of year, and if you get the timing and the composition just right, they look like they're bursting into flame.'

'I don't want to hear about fucking photography now.' I roll down my window and let the orange spin from my fingers onto the road. 'Now you need to tell me about Gideon.' I speak loudly enough so that he can hear me over the road, but when the window is closed again, it's too much.

He sighs. 'OK. Then can we talk like normal people? You know, talk about rugby, chew biltong. Normal father-daughter stuff?'

I flip the pages in my notebook to a blank one, half tearing them from the spiral binder. 'We're not normal people. This is not a normal situation to be in.'

'*Ja*, sure, but—'

'We haven't spoken in three years. That's not normal.' I scratch the date into the top of the page. 'And this sure as hell isn't a normal reunion.' I want to fight.

'I know.' He looks at me. 'And I'm sorry for that. I just don't have anyone else I can go to.'

'No shit.' I look at the clock on the dashboard and note the time in a scrawl. 'That's the way you've chosen to live your life.'

He looks straight ahead again, clearly refusing to bite, and scratches his side. Every time he rakes his fingers upwards, I can see the fading bruise. I open my packet of cigarettes, but it's empty, and I drop it into the footwell and put my feet up on the dash.

'Which is none of my business,' I continue. 'But you've put this massive shitstorm in front of me and asked me to help. And finding out about Gideon is the only way I know how to start.'

He nods at the dictaphone balanced on my stomach. 'OK. Turn that thing on, then.'

I put it in the slot for CDs under the radio, aim the microphone at him and press the red button to record. I bet he thought that his acquiescence would be enough for me to put the recorder away. Notepad against my knees, I draw a margin down the left side of the page in case any of the shorthand needs explaining. I wait.

We overtake a truck with a back light that's flaking off like a scab.

'Gideon was just a nickname,' he says, 'but that's what everyone called him. Gideon van Vuuren. I don't think anyone actually knew his real name.'

I write the name anyway. I'll have to ask Naledi to check for any records.

'Gideon had started his army service a couple of years before I did. I met him up on the border – this big, fat redhead oke.' He looks at me. 'Why are you writing this down too?'

'Shorthand's admissible in court,' I say, wondering if media law is the same in South Africa as in the UK.

'And the recordings?'

Only the conversations that I have his permission to tape would be admissible. I nod anyway.

'So why're you doing both?'

'Shorthand relaxes me, OK?' I say, looking at the outlines in front of me. Gideon van Vuuren is a series of straight lines that taper into curves. 'Just let me do it.'

'OK.' He looks uncomfortable, moving around in his seat and pulling at his shorts before speaking again. 'He was religious – from one of those very white towns in West Transvaal. You know, where they still think horses are intimidating.'

'How old was he?'

'Two years older than me, I think.' He reaches for the nicotine gum in the compartment next to the radio. 'Anyway, I only met him when I got up to the border.' He pops out a piece of gum. It's white and serious as a pill. 'I wasn't very good—'

'You look like you could've dragged logs through the veld or whatever they wanted you to do.'

'Well sure, but just because I could didn't mean I wanted to. Just because I could've killed all the blacks and communists they wanted me to, doesn't mean that I did, you know.' He licks his lips. 'Anyway, I got into a lot of shit for all my backchat – extra push-ups and stuff like that. But they paid a lot more if you went up there and they needed as many soldiers as they could get, so up I went.

'Gideon was really into the whole thing. Yes, sir. No, sir. How many *kaffirs* should I kill for you, sir?' He looks at me and shakes his head. 'He seemed like a nerd, like the kind of kid I used to kick the shit out of in high school.'

'I was a nerd in high school,' I say. He looks away, and I take my feet down from the dashboard and sit up straight. 'Go on.'

'When we started doing actual tours of the Kavango in Namibia, turns out he was a fucking psycho. All that geeky shit was just to hide the fact that he really liked to kill blacks.' His accent is flatter than usual, the word coming out as *blecks*.

Empty fields whip by, but I can only watch my father. 'What did you have to do?'

'Have you heard of Koevoet?'

I shake my head.

'Typical.' He passes me his cigarettes. 'Light one for me, will you? It's Afrikaans for *crowbar*. It was also the name of the counter-insurgency unit that worked on the border with Namibia, tracking and killing communists.'

He drops his balled-up gum into the ashtray and I pass him a cigarette, deciding to light one for myself as a distraction.

'Namibia was still a South African colony then,' he says, exhaling. 'And the government wanted to keep it that way.'

'Is that what you did up there? Work for Koevoet?' I stare at my notepad, not really wanting to know the answer.

'No.'

I didn't realise I was holding my breath.

'I know what I sound like sometimes but I couldn't actually do that. Kill someone. You know that, right?'

I've been hoping he'd say something like this, tell me outright so that I don't have to wonder. I nod.

'Good,' he says, smiling. Then he whistles. 'You should've seen Koevoet work, man. Fucking Gideon was their *bladdy* star player. They even gave him a Southern Cross medal for all his hard work. Everyone else was starting to wonder what sucking dick would feel like because we'd been up there so long, but the boss – Brigadier van der Westhuizen – got Gideon some white Namibian women to *pomp*. He was that good.'

I cough with laughter. 'What the fuck? I can't believe you said *pomp*.'

'What's wrong with *pomp*? It's what you do.' An oncoming car, the first we've seen in half an hour, flashes its lights at us. 'I realised at the time that I actually think gay sex between men is more natural than lesbian sex, because it mimics the normal sex act.' He reaches under his seat for his cap and slips it on. 'And when the camera's really up close, it could be any hole…a woman's even.'

'Oh, for fuck's sake.' I wish I had a cartoon jaw that could drop to the floor and then be rolled up like a blind. 'Please don't start,' I say, taking a deep drag.

'I'm not trying to start.' He looks over his shoulder and lowers his speed to just within the limit. 'I'm just telling you what I think. I don't like butch dykes or faggy men, or even macho men. Anything extreme like that.'

Smoke turns in the air like drops of colour in a cup of water for washing paintbrushes. 'What about me, then?' I regret the question immediately and open my window for it, and the smoke, to drain out.

'You're not a dyke. Not yet anyway, or not that I know of.'

'Can you just tell me what the fuck happened with Gideon, please?'

He checks the rear-view mirror again and speaks quickly. 'Just shut up for a second. And put your seat belt on.'

The car that flashed its lights at us must have put him on edge. 'OK.'

'Just be quiet,' he snaps.

I realise that I'm hoping for a police roadblock, for a ring of sirens to surround us so that he can't take us off-road and into the desert.

He slows down further as we climb a small hill; when we reach the top, there's a dead ostrich stretched out across the lanes. 'That must've been why they were signalling,' he says, relaxing.

I keep my seat belt fastened. The ostrich's feathers moving in the wind fool me into thinking that it might still be alive, but as we pass I can see its neck is limp and twisted as kelp.

'So, anyway, just before I was sent back from the border, Gideon and his unit – these two younger guys who did everything he said – came back to camp. They'd tracked and killed a Namibian guerrilla and Gideon had the guy's ears on a piece of wire around his neck.'

'Fuck,' I say. The shorthand for his last sentence is a scrawl. I cross it out and try again, concentrating on the curves and lines and not on what they mean.

He carries on, 'That night they got fucked up on Mandrax. We were supposed to use it to knock prisoners out, but lots of the guys smoked it themselves. It's called doing buttons. You crush a Mandrax tablet, mix it with *dagga* and then smoke it from a broken-off bottle neck.' He gestures at me with his cigarette. 'You fall over straight away, the shit's that strong, hey.'

On the next page I start a list of things to check, still in shorthand in case he goes through my stuff. 'Did you do it?'

'I wanted to, but I heard it makes your dick shrink.'

I get back to my list. *Call Naledi. Confirm investigation. Check army records.*

'Anyway, they were just outside my tent, laughing about how they'd shot this man in the face. I went out for a piss. Gideon was giving one of the guys shit about not having a crowbar tattoo yet. He had some glass and a pen and was threatening to do it himself.' My father clears his throat. 'I was just standing there, watching this poor guy half-naked and shivering, and then I noticed that Gideon had a hard-on. Everyone else was too fucked up to see it, but it was so obvious. So I got my camera, took a photo and shouted that his meat compass had found north.' He laughs, pleased with his turn of phrase. 'After that, everyone made fun of him for being gay.'

'So being an arsehole is something you've always excelled at.'

He ignores me. 'It was funny. And the whole camp heard me. But he was really embarrassed and at lunch the next day, in front of everyone, he came over and knocked me out with a tray. I woke up in the hospital back in South Africa with three broken ribs. Turns out, he'd really gone to town on me while I was unconscious. Once I'd recovered, I was stationed at the farms near the border, but far away from Gideon, to protect them from the *terrs*.' Terrorists. 'And that was that.'

'Bullshit,' I say, closing my notebook. 'Bullshit.'

'What?' He turns his cap so that it's on backwards.

'So all this happened because you teased him about being gay? He held onto it for years, tracked you down in Dundee and then, what? Made you take part in the torture and murder of a man so he could turn you in to the police twenty-five years later? No one is that crazy.'

'No, you're right.' He checks his reflection in the side mirror. 'How does this look, by the way?' He points at the cap.

'You look like Fred fucking Durst.' I give him my most withering stare.

'Who's that? Someone cool, I hope.'

I shake my head.

'Oh.' He throws the hat into my lap. The underside of the brim is damp.

'Stop bullshitting me.' I push the cap into the footwell and open my notebook again.

'OK, so how about this? By the time I got up to the border, people in SA were starting to think the whole fighting against Namibia thing was a bad idea.'

'How progressive of them.'

He ignores me. 'So they got some journalists to come up and write about what a just war it was. To help with the PR,' he adds, in case I haven't understood. 'Anyway, they saw I always had a camera with me so they asked me to take some photos to go with the articles. Professional development, they called it – when the journos were around, at least.'

I realise now that my father's entire life, or his entire photography career, has been spent distorting reality rather than documenting it.

All of his work has been more about what was left out of the photos than what was included.

'I didn't want to tell you before, but I actually went out on a couple of the missions to take some photos,' he says.

'No shit.' He's always holding something back. I'm just surprised he didn't stage this revelation the way he has everything else.

'One time I went out with Gideon's unit – about six guys and him – and they caught the family of one of the *terrs*. They were trying to get them to rat out the guy, tell them where he was hiding. There was a soldier there from one of the other units – an English guy, I think – who was so obviously a poof.' He flaps his wrist. 'Gideon pointed his gun at him and told him that he had to rape the woman.'

I remember the laughter of the men, the woman's cries.

'So I tackled him. Gideon, I mean.' He sits up straight, his chest pushed forward. 'The rest – the tray stuff – all happened after this. So as you can see, he was really fucked in the head.'

I'm not sure either story is true. Not sure which one makes more sense as an explanation for why Gideon came to the lodge. 'In either case, I'm surprised he didn't kill you.'

He laughs. 'White guys don't kill other white guys. Or they didn't.'

'What about the other guys – the ones who were with him at the lodge?' I turn to a new page. 'Were they up on the border with you?'

'*Ja*, they were in his unit,' he says, sounding bored.

'And?' I prompt him.

He shakes his head. It's not fun any more, it seems, now that he's not part of the story. 'They were just his lackeys. Danie Strydom was really young, easy to control.' He watches me write down the name. 'Jaco Eloff was just dumb. We called him Hammerhead because his brow stuck out so much.' He tries to copy the shorthand outline for Jaco on the steering wheel. 'He came from the wrong side of the mountain in Pretoria. He had this big black mole on his cheek and his skin was that dark brown poor whites get when they spend too much time in the sun. I think he'd left school at sixteen and gone straight into the army.'

I remember his description of what happened in Dundee, the two army guys offering to pay for a room in cash. 'So you already knew who they were when they turned up at the lodge?' He knew too much detail about Jaco to have forgotten, surely.

'I'm not very good with faces. Men's faces, anyway.'

'But when you saw Gideon the next day, you recognised him?'

'*Ja*, of course. You wouldn't forget him.'

'Is that it? Is that the whole story?'

'What do you mean?'

'You keep "remembering" new details. Is there something else you haven't told me?'

'Jesus, Jo. Do you think I'm enjoying this?'

I look away to stop myself from answering him.

'What happened at the lodge, what I saw, has haunted me every day since.'

Before I can stop myself, I say: 'Really? You don't act like it.'

'Fuck you.' His knuckles are white as he grips the steering wheel.

'I'm sorry, OK? I'm just saying that you need to tell me everything, or else I can't help.'

'Yes, *baas*. Do you want me to keep track of my bowel movements for you, too?'

I close my notebook, turn off the dictaphone and slide them both into my bag. 'No, but thanks for the offer.' I'm too tired to fight, so I undo my seat belt and turn to climb into the back seat.

'Whatever you need,' he says sarcastically, leaning to the side to let me through.

In the rear-view mirror, he watches me push empty water bottles and beer cans off the seat. 'I told the guys back in Pretoria about Gideon and said he'd tried to come onto me.'

'Well done,' I say, turning away from him.

'He tied the bodies of the people he killed to the front of the Casspir, the armoured personnel carrier, so that everyone could see how good he was.' My father closes the back window. 'By the time they got back to camp, their skin would be shredded and coming off.'

When I wake up, it's dark. Up ahead, a town flickers, its dark halo empty of stars. I sit up, a headache heavy on my brow.

'It's time for a fill-up, and I need to stretch my legs,' my father says, pulling into a petrol station.

The key for the women's toilet is attached to a two-litre Coke bottle full of sand. I need my father's help to unlock the bathroom door; he holds the bottle and watches my shaking hands fumble with the key. I need food, he says, and he'll get me some. The fluorescent light in the bathroom drones, good camouflage for the flies circling the stall in the mirror. As I count out the paracetamol, wondering if four is too many, I can almost see through the skin on my palm.

Back outside, I sit on the bonnet while my father pays for the petrol and returns the key. I swing my legs and wait for Naledi to answer her phone. My father told me to stay in the car and lock the doors, and I can see him watching me from the back of the queue at the till. I hide my phone under my hair.

He pulls faces at me from inside the shop, tugging on his earlobes to make a monkey face, the basket he's holding in the crook of his arm tilting his head to the left.

'Hello?' Naledi answers, chewing.

'Hi.' I look down at my swinging feet. 'Sorry if I've caught you during dinner. I can't talk long.' There's dust under my toenails. I wonder if it's from the hill at Dundee.

'No problem,' she says. 'Is everything all right?'

'Yeah, it's fine.' I don't know what else to say. I think I'd probably cry if I started trying to explain the not-all-rightness of things.

'I don't believe you.' She's always been able to tell when something is wrong.

'I'll tell you about it later,' I say, looking up and trying to put a smile into my voice. My father sees me and waves, thinking I'm smiling at him; when he sees the phone pressed against my ear, he puts his hand down and turns back to the cashier.

'You'd better.'

'Listen, can you check something for me? It's about my dad.' My flip-flop slides from between my toes and lands just under the car.

'What is it?' I hear the beads on her braids against the phone.

'Is there someone at work you can talk to to find out if there's…' I pause. 'If there's anything going on with him?' I don't want to say the actual words out loud: *Is my father wanted for murder?* 'I don't mean something like loads of women after him for child support for all of his hundreds of illegitimate kids.'

She laughs. 'Sure.'

'Just anything more unusual than that. But can you do it quietly, please?'

She clicks her tongue against her palate. 'What's going on, Jo?'

'Just please check for me.' My father, a carrier bag in his hand, pushes open the shop door and steps down onto the concourse. 'I've got three other names for you to run: Danie Strydom, Jaco Eloff and Gideon van Vuuren. That last one could be an alias.' It's surreal to be using that word. 'And can you do it by tomorrow morning? I'll call you at work if you give me the number?' I slip my hand into my bag to find a pen.

She doesn't hesitate. '*Ja*, sure.'

I hold the phone to my ear with my shoulder and write the number on my palm. 'Thanks.'

My father puts the carrier bag down next to me on the bonnet.

'I have to go.' I hang up and slip my phone into my bag.

'Who was that?' he asks, plastic rustling.

'Just an editor. Wanting to know when I'll get back to Jo'burg.' It's a lie he won't easily catch me in, unless he redials the number. He's only recently taken an interest in my work, but not enough to know who I write for or all the places my copy is used. I don't think he even knows what a blog is.

My father raises his eyebrows.

'And no, I didn't say where I was or anything about my father the fugitive,' I tell him.

'That sounds like the name of a really shit film,' he says, pulling a banana Yogi-Sip out of the bag, balancing it on one palm and waving his other around behind the carton. 'Ta-da! I saw it and remembered that you used to beg me for one of these whenever I took you out for the day.' He pierces the carton with a straw fat as a caterpillar and hands the yoghurt drink to me. 'I hope it's still your favourite.'

I smile at him. 'Thanks.'

'And I got some Ghost Pops and some tinned pineapple rings.' A few of my ten-year-old self's favourite things. He opens the passenger door behind the driver's seat and puts the bag on the floor. 'Let's go.'

I slide off the bonnet and bend to pick up my left flip-flop, putting the Yogi-Sip down next to the petrol pump. I've always liked the strawberry flavour better.

'Jump,' he says. 'Jump in.' He drops an empty beer can – his fourth of the evening – onto the rocks.

I'm in my bra and pants, shivering in the dark. The torch beam wavers on the surface of the water, a drowned moon. I can't work out how I've ended up agreeing to swim in the waterfall pool at 11 p.m.

'Why aren't you coming in too?' The sound of falling water rises up from the surface like steam.

'Someone has to hold the torch. I'll go in after you.'

'I don't want to.' The water is black, mouth-dark.

'Jump in,' he shouts. 'For once in your life, do something spontaneous!'

His voice echoes, hitting me from more than one direction. To prove him wrong – as he knew I'd want to – I jump into the water.

It's cold, colder than the sea at Brighton. And sharp as the rock it has come through. The water is clean enough to drink, but I imagine fallen climbers, their twisted, sun-bleached skeletons and flapping, faded windbreakers, how only this river will find their bodies, and I keep my mouth shut. I keep my eyes shut too, my own darkness far more comforting than staring into the black of the water. But when I resurface and open my eyes, it's dark there too. The torch beam has gone.

'Nico?' It's quiet, just my voice and the water. 'Nico, where are you?' There's no answer, not even a snigger. The stars, so silent by day, now seem to buzz. 'Hello?' I feel for the rock, trying to find crevices for fingers and toes. There's a chip in the rock just below the surface, big enough for one foot. 'This isn't fucking funny,' I call out. My fingertips brush only smooth rock and I fall, a backwards belly flop. Water rushes into my nose. I push myself up and cough into the night air.

I'm too close to the waterfall; even though it's thin with winter it churns up the pool around me. I let my legs buoy to the surface and swim away from the sound, doing breaststroke kicks but paddling with my hands as I don't know how close I am to the rock. On a downstroke, my right hand becomes webbed for a second, catching something big, soft and heavy. I scream, pull my hand up out of the water. The thing takes flight, following my salute, and I hear it hit the rock before it falls back into the pool. A dead bird, maybe. I kick harder, trying to keep my breathing even. 'Nico?' I look up, hoping to see the whites of his eyes or his teeth, but there's nothing. Just rock and a narrow channel of stars.

I wait, shivering. 'Please.' I don't want to cry or scream but I can hear the fear in my voice. 'Dad?' My fingertips find the wall and I bring my body against it, a castaway washed up on a beach, hugging the sand and smashed shells. 'Daddy?' The moon is the eye of a dark bird.

I begin to move along the rock away from the falling water, hoping to find where the deep pool spills over into a smaller one. My fingers are numb on the rough rock. 'This isn't funny,' I shout again. I find a toehold, and a small ledge for my fingers, but there's nowhere for me to go and I slip back into the water again.

This is punishment for all my questions.

His voice comes from above me, moving in an arc as he jumps out from whatever rock it is he's been hiding behind. 'Yes it is!' I've forgotten what he's affirming. He switches on the torch, shines the beam in my eyes, but I look down so he can't see my face. I'm crying and I'm sure that my lips are blue.

'Help me out.' I put up my hands, wedging my toes against the rock, and he pulls me out of the pool, the torch gripped between his thighs. I move away from the edge and feel something warm on my foot. Blood. I must've cut myself on a sharp edge my feet are too cold to feel. The night wind lashes at my wet skin. My father bends and hands me my clothes; as soon as he's close enough, I hit him, hoping to land it on his cheek but catching his nose instead.

'Ow, fuck, man! What was that for?' The torch falls and rolls into the dark water, where it glows like the lure on a deep-sea fish. He sniffs.

'Fuck you.' I try to pull on my dress but it sticks to my wet hair and I can't tell the armholes from the neck.

He sniffs again and spits. 'Can't you take a fucking joke, man? I'm bleeding.' I can't see him tilting his head back or pinching his nose, but his voice reverberates through the ravine above me, the *m*'s and *n*'s heavy and airless.

'Not that kind of joke, you arsehole,' I shout, pulling my dress back over my head and inside out. I'll have to put it on in the car. 'I thought you'd left.'

He spits again. I think he's looking at me. 'How could you think that?'

'Easily.' I hope I can keep my voice steady and my teeth from clattering. 'You're a fucking nutcase sometimes, you know that?' I want to go further. 'You think it's normal to be the way you are?'

He exhales hard. There are small splatters against the rock wall. 'What do you mean?'

'You know what I mean. Everyone knows – they just have to spend an hour with you to know.' Standing there in my bra and pants, my stomach moon-pale, I start to regret trying to hurt him by pointing out what he must already know. He must know. But I don't want to get into that here, in the dark. 'Fathers aren't supposed to do that to their kids.'

He sighs. Although I can't see his face, I can picture the disappointment that will have crept onto it and settled, like a bad smell you can't find the source of. 'I thought we were done with this shit.'

In London three years ago, we hadn't been. But I've given up my right to have this conversation by answering his call two days ago. 'Let's just get out of here.' Spray from the waterfall stings the side of my face. 'Unless you want to swim? Get the torch?'

'Fuck no,' he says. 'Last time I was here, with a woman from Oudtshoorn, she said this pool's really dangerous. Nine people have disappeared in it – sucked into the underground water system.'

In the dark, I take a deep breath.

'She was quite sexy, actually. For a coloured woman. We swam together in the smaller pool and I saw part of her nipple. It was pointy with dark ridges. Like a pecan-nut shell.'

'Give me the car keys.' I hold my damp dress against my chest and put out my hand.

'Sure,' he says. He unclips the keys from his belt, muffling the metal with his hand. 'Actually, you'd better come here and get them in case they go the way of the torch.'

Strategy, again. I'm an isolated pawn, but I just want to be off the board. 'Fine.' I inch forward over the uneven rocks, hand outstretched. I'm closest to the water. The torch beam has sputtered and disappeared, swallowed by a creature waiting in the depths. It's so dark I could close my eyes and it wouldn't make a difference, but I won't believe that I can feel the wind and the rocks against me and the blood between my toes and yet be unable to see anything.

'She wanted to fuck me,' he says. 'I could smell it on her.'

He's so close that I can hear his breath over the water. I don't want to touch him.

'She brushed up against my dick in the pool.'

My fingertips graze his t-shirt. The thin cotton reminds me of how little I'm wearing. He puts his hand over mine. It's warm, and I wonder if it's bloody.

'She was quite light – almost white – but she had lips like a black, thick and fat.' He turns my palm to the sky and folds my fingers over the keys. Holding my fist tightly, as though he's trapped a spider, he says: 'I knew those lips would've felt good on me, but they were too black for me to want to *pomp* her.'

My heartbeat is louder than the churning water. He brushes the inside of my wrist. I pull my arm towards my body, but he only lets go when his fingertips touch the skin just above my belly button.

'Anyway,' he says, cracking his knuckles. 'Before all this, she told me that nine people had disappeared swimming in the pool you were just in – sucked into the underground caves, apparently.'

I push a key between my fingers like a weapon, the way I do on dark streets in South London. 'You're a fucking psycho,' I say. I don't want him to hear me cry, so I turn and start to feel my way along the rock wall, hand over hand. The ravine opens up above me like a mouth, shouting the sky.

'You're so easy to fuck with,' he calls behind me.

My feet slide in their own bloody trail – I've forgotten my flip-flops, but I don't want to ask him to bring them. I keep my eyes on the edge of the rock above. Empty branches lean out over the edges, like hikers drawn to the cliffs, looking down.

4

Bad Conscience

In the grey pre-dawn light, the trees are darker than the sky, cut out from the horizon by a hurried hand, branches curved and jagged as nail clippings. My father sleeps in the back seat. I've been driving barefoot for five hours, disobeying his instructions and keeping to bigger roads. I need to see other cars, remember it's not just him and me.

When we pulled away from the waterfall outside Oudtshoorn, I switched on the radio to spite him, but he fell asleep anyway, and all I found was Afrikaans I couldn't understand and concertina music, so I turned it off. In the silence, I played games with myself, trying to remember Afrikaans children's songs about how to kill mambas. I listed the words I still knew – those for *elf*, *spell*, *magic* – and gave up listing the ones I didn't know or thought I should learn – *torture*, *accomplice*, *complicit*.

I haven't made good time. There are rabbits everywhere and they like the light; I've been driving slowly so I can swerve when they jump out in front of the car, shadow puppets bouncing across the light-white tar. They're long and fast, with the exaggerated ears of children's drawings. There's nowhere we have to be – I don't know where we're going – so I decided to stop and wait awhile.

Now, parked in a lay-by in Langkloof Valley, I open all the windows and listen to the cicadas glittering in the fields around us. The valley smells of apples. Even with the headlights still on, I've never seen this many stars. In the back seat, my father grunts and turns, the towel he's sleeping under half falling into the footwell behind the passenger seat, his arms bare and goose-pimpled. I light a cigarette and leave the towel where it is.

I've decided to call Naledi first thing in the morning, to check whether my father is telling the truth about the police investigation. If he isn't, I won't be there when he wakes up.

One of the rabbits wasn't fast enough, or I wasn't, and I don't want to get out of the car to see fur and blood on the bumper. I wonder if it would be better to die like that. Blinded. Quickly.

'You're still here, then.' My father stands up out of the car into a stretch. 'I take it that means you'll stop acting like you're bleeding between your legs and actually be useful now?'

I don't answer. Instead, I point the hose at his face, moving my thumb over the mouth of the hose so that it shouts water in jagged streams. He laughs as it hits his face, and opens his mouth to drink from the spray.

'Thanks. I'm awake now,' he says, shaking his head.

He takes my reactions and makes a game for himself out of them, like a child licking a whole bar of chocolate so that his friend won't ask for a piece. I turn the water back on the car.

'Now I understand why we went to war against the red danger.' He dries his cheeks on his shoulders and looks at me, smiling. 'Women are dangerous, crazy bitches when they've fallen to the Communists.' He takes a few steps towards the petrol pumps and drops into a push-up. He breathes in a way he was taught to, somewhere along the line, and I'm surprised by how effortlessly he finishes a set.

'I dreamt that you were older,' he says, standing up and brushing the gravel from his palms. 'I was still the same but you were folded

73

over on yourself, you were so old.' He bends forward to touch his toes, his voice muffled by his knees. 'We talked, and when you laughed you came open a little bit, like an oyster or something.' He stands upright, lifts his arms above his head and leans backwards, a brown wedge of stomach showing below his t-shirt. 'So I told lots of jokes – I can't remember them now – and they prised you open more and more. But when you were finally flat on your back, your whole middle was crawling with maggots and falling away.' He takes his sunglasses from his pocket and puts them on. 'What do you think that means?'

'Fuck knows,' I say. Since the night in Alex, there's been no subtext to my dreams, just women crying and fires that I can't put out.

When I pulled up just after 9 a.m., Gert – of Gert's Petrol Station – offered to clean the bumper for me. It happens all the time, he said. Then he saw my bloody feet and hands and asked where my husband was. I only shook my head, unsure of how to answer and allowing him to choose my backstory – *he's the one who did this to me*; *I don't have a husband but now I wish I did*; *this is punishment for betraying him with another man.* He pointed me in the direction of the hose. Later, while I was drying my feet, he brought me an enamel mug of sweet coffee and a homemade rusk full of raisins and cinnamon. It was too hard, so I let it soak in the coffee while I called Naledi.

My father was the prime suspect in an open murder investigation, she told me. Her clearance at the Justice Department wasn't high enough to find out any actual details. 'What's going on? Have you seen him?' she asked. 'I'm worried about you.'

I had to stay with him, I realised, for now at least. I couldn't be sure what he might do if I left, and I knew I'd feel responsible if he hurt himself. Or anyone else. I wanted to tell Naledi that if she hadn't heard from me in a week's time, that she should call the police. The British embassy. But instead I said: 'And Gideon van Vuuren?'

'No record of him, not even as an alias.'

'Shit.' Had my father lied about knowing Gideon's real name?

'Jo, what's going on?'

'I'm OK, I promise. But what about the other two guys, Jaco and Danie?' Maybe one of them knew more about Gideon, enough to help us – or the police – find him.

She sighed and told me what she had found out. I thanked her, and hung up on her mid-question, turning off my phone.

My father walks around to the front of the car, holding an unlit cigarette above the fine mist coming off the bonnet. 'How many'd you hit?'

I turn off the nozzle, the last of the rabbit running red into a drain. 'Just one.'

He turns and walks to the wall, as though to wind up the hose, but unzips his trousers instead. 'I fucking hate Joubertina.' Dark yellow pee joins the puddle under the licence plate.

I take a step back and walk around to the driver's seat. All four doors are open to air out the car.

'All it has is a Dutch Reformed Church, a dam and this *bladdy* petrol station. You can't buy booze here, you know.' He zips himself up and turns back towards me, his finger deep in his nose. 'One of the founding principles of the town. Luckily, I've got my beers in the back.'

'I'd have thought you'd like it here,' I say, bending to pick up a butt that's fallen from the car. 'Mountains on either side; everything yellow and red. You could commune with nature.' I put the cigarette butt into my dress pocket with all the others. 'Talk about the sun and farming.' I shield my eyes with my hand and put the other on my hip, surveying the car park as though it's my own cotton field. 'Deign to greet some non-whites. And all while you chew grass.'

'Fuck you.' He puts a foot on the bonnet, bouncing the car, and lights the cigarette. 'Whenever I'm anywhere like Joubertina, I suddenly want to overdose on technology and everything that's modern. Like get a friend with benefits and pour soya milk all over her.' He takes a drag, holding court. 'And I want to join Facebook right now, goddammit, just because I don't even think they have dial-up Internet here yet.'

'Well, that's good,' I say. 'Because it means maybe people won't recognise your face from all the "wanted" posters.'

'I'm on "wanted" posters?' His hairline moves back as he smiles.

'Yes. Online. With a number to text if you're spotted.' I take out the mat from beneath the driver's seat and beat it against the door. Cakes of mud flake off. 'A lifelong ambition?'

'No,' he says. 'It's just like a western, that's all.' He turns to face me, pushing his sunglasses up onto his head. 'How'd you find out?' he asks.

'It doesn't matter.' I walk around to the back of the car. 'You were right and I'm still here.' I find socks and trainers for my cold feet, and when I close the boot, he's leaning against the open driver's door, gripping the aerial, his fist white. I can see from his face that it does matter. 'I called someone I know at the Department of Justice.'

'Who?'

'You don't know her.' My friends: another aspect of my life that my father has never had any interest in.

'Did you say where we were?'

I shake my head.

His hand slides to the base of the aerial and opens only briefly before it forms a fist again, hitting the plastic sunroof so hard that it cracks. 'You stupid little cunt.'

Without realising it, I've brought my shoes up against my chest and moved to the other side of the car. Faded leather and two layers of metal separate us now. 'It was a good friend, and I didn't tell her anything.' The bell on the shop door chimes.

'What did you say? Exactly?'

'I didn't tell her that I'd seen you.' It's the truth but it feels like a lie the way he's looking at me.

Gert steps onto the concourse, holding a *knobkierie*, a walking stick with a heavy, rounded top that can split skulls open like watermelons.

'I just said I couldn't get hold of you,' I go on.

'And what did she say?'

Gert is approaching, but my father doesn't hear him.

'That the police are looking for you. There's a reward for information, something like ten thousand rand.'

'Did you tip her off, take the money?' He flicks the half-smoked cigarette at me. I try to dodge it, but the wind carries it back into me, and my hair singes before I can shake the butt onto the floor.

'Hey!' Gert, in a green floppy-brimmed hat, stands just behind my father. 'Are everything aw'right?'

I want to laugh at his English, its way of sounding earnest and stupid all at once. Instead, I say: 'Thanks, Gert,' rolling the *r*'s in his name so that he knows I'm not a Pommy, or not only a Pommy. 'Everything's fine.'

'*Draai om, laaitjie,*' he says to my father, prodding him in the back with the stick. But my father doesn't turn around. He closes his eyes and tilts his face to the sky. The message is clear: handle this.

I look at Gert. His eyes are deep-set and hooded, his moustache grey; his terracotta cheeks shine as though they've been polished. I want to put on my shoes and take the walking stick and smash every window and every glass bottle full of purple Fanta or Crème Soda and walk away, further down into the valley to the orchards or the dam. I hate my father for putting me in a position to need rescuing by another man. And I hate Gert for rescuing me.

'Gert,' I say, making two syllables out of his name with a singsong voice I learnt watching women on TV asking for jewellery. 'Thank you so much for the coffee. It really helped me come back to my senses a little bit.' I move around to the other side of the car. My father stiffens as I pass him, but doesn't open his eyes. 'I left the cup on the petrol pump for you,' I say, pointing over Gert's shoulder.

Gert looks back at me, unconvinced.

'I was a bit *babalas* this morning,' I say. I'd rather claim a hangover than something hysterical and typically 'female', but it'll be more difficult for him to accept. 'I feel better now, though, so we'll be leaving you in peace soon.' He stares at me, rolling the cane between his fingers. 'But before we go, I want to buy some of those delicious rusks. And some cigarettes.' When compliments fail, offer money.

'*Ja*, OK,' he says, lowering the walking stick.

'I'll be in just now,' I say, with a bright smile. He nods and turns away, the cane over his shoulder like a rifle. Faith in God and the Mauser.

'Nicely done.' My father sits down in the driver's seat, knee against the steering wheel, one foot still on the gravel. We watch Gert disappear into the shop.

I sit down on the back seat and toss my shoes on the floor in front of me. I brush the dirt off my feet with my socks before swinging my legs into the car.

'Does your friend…?' He leaves it open, the inflection in his voice a lure, feathers and hook.

'I'm not going to tell you what her name is.' I put my left ankle on my right thigh and pull a sock over my toes. The cut is beginning to bleed again. 'Just like I didn't tell her that I've seen you or that I know where you are. Anyway, she tracked down Danie. He's taken his mom's maiden name. He's Danie Gerber now and he lives in Potchefstroom.' Now the right foot. I'll feel safer when both shoes are on. 'My friend couldn't find Jaco – nothing on him since ninety-seven – but she

78

found an old girlfriend, Wilna. They had a son together in the early nineties. The address is in my bag.'

'Excellent,' my father says. I decide now isn't the right time to push him about Gideon's real name. He takes the keys out of the ignition and slips them into his pocket. 'Did you call her from the shop?'

'No, from my mobile.' I finish doing the laces on my trainers. With shoes on, I feel on surer territory, less as though what's in the ground is seeping into me. When I look up, my father is staring at me, cigarette dangling from his bottom lip. 'This isn't some spy movie where she would've traced my call, you know,' I say.

He looks away. 'I know. But I wanna get out of this fucking place as soon as possible.' He grabs my bag from the footwell, puts his sunglasses on and stands up into the light. 'I'll go get some smokes.' He turns and walks quickly across the concourse, gripping my bag tightly.

I lie down on the back seat. There are dark berries ground into the carpet behind the passenger seat, flat and dry as pennies. I don't know how they got there. Nowhere in South Africa is safe from the wilderness. And everything is so much closer to the body here, more dangerous, unmediated by yellow lines and tinny voices repeating *Mind the gap.* My bare legs are already beginning to stick to the seat. I close my eyes and turn onto my side, pulling my feet into the car. I want tea, even though I never drink it, and to salute the magpies that peck over the bins outside my flat in London. My life there seems so far away, less real than the two weeks I've spent here. For the first time since the funeral, I miss my grandmother.

'*Jissus,* Jo, what did you say to that man?'

I open my eyes, back in my sticky, dirty body. My father drops a plastic bag full of colourful cartons onto the seat in front of me.

'He kept the *knobkierie* on the counter the whole time I was in the shop.' He slams both passenger-side doors shut and walks around to

79

the driver's side. 'I had to buy two packets of rusks and a milk tart just to keep him from beating me up.'

I turn onto my back and look down to see him standing at my feet.

'Nice double chin,' he says.

'Bugger off.' I tilt my head back and watch the light coming through the crack in the sunroof. The light is sharper, as though it's broken, like a straw emerging from the water at a different angle.

'I put the change in your purse,' he says, throwing my bag into the footwell behind the driver's seat. 'There's some water in there for you.' He slams the door and sits down behind the wheel.

'Where are we going?'

He puts the keys in the ignition. 'I think we're gonna drive with the sun.'

'Cape Town?' I smile – somewhere I've been before, somewhere I know people – and sit up on my elbow to pull my bag onto the seat.

'No, to see Jaco's girlfriend.' He starts the car. 'It's not a holiday, you know.'

'I know.' I unzip my bag and find my sunglasses. I'm too tired to argue, tired enough to sleep in spite of the light, but I don't want my father to be able to see me doing it. The seal on the water bottle is broken, but I drink until it's empty anyway.

'Oh, and I got a newspaper too. *The Bugger*.'

I think he means *Die Burger*.

'Nothing in it about me.' He drops the paper into the footwell behind the passenger seat as we pull out of the car park.

I slide the empty bottle back into my bag and look for my phone. It isn't there. Neither is my South African passport. I'm stuck with him, in this country. I feel flushed, my skin suddenly itchy. Should I have expected this from him?

'But the fucker who's started this whole investigation is mentioned in there.'

'What do you mean? Gideon?' I decide to wait out the rant before I ask about my phone. The picture on the front page is of a dead man doubled over on a dirt road in Cape Town. His clothes and the soles of his shoes are still burning, and the earth is scorched where he lies, melting into the track.

'No, he's a politician, so he's always all over the papers talking shit and quoting Shakespeare.' He coughs into his hand.

'Who's a fucking politician?' I sit up and throw my arms around the headrest in front of me. We drive past handwritten signs for home-made jam and honeybush tea.

'Like "his people" even know who Shakespeare is.' He opens his fist, the phlegm unfurling in his palm like a sick anemone.

'Shut up, Nico. Who's a fucking politician?'

'See, I knew you'd flip the fuck out about it.' He leans forward and wipes his hand on the leather under his seat. 'He's the one after me.'

'Of course I'm gonna flip the fuck out about it,' I say, sitting back and opening the paper. 'Why's he after you?'

'It's his dad, the man I'm supposed to have killed.'

'What?'

'That's why I had to go on the run. There's too much power behind this.' He catches my eye in the rear-view mirror. 'It's good politics to get a white man for it.'

'No, we have to stop. Stop right here and go to the police.' We speed past dead rabbits in dark heaps.

'I can't.' He pushes down the lock on his door with his elbow; the other three locks follow suit. 'I can't go back until I have proof that I'm not guilty.'

I was wrong to think I could handle him, that I had a say in what we did. 'And how do you suggest we find it?' I wonder if he got to my British passport too, folded into a pair of pants in my suitcase.

'Go talk to the other guys who were there.' He keeps his eyes on the road. 'Figure out who saw us and who's started talking now.' The speedometer reaches a hundred and twenty. 'I think he's on page five.'

I turn the pages quickly, tearing past articles about bank robberies and the World Cup.

'It's Paul something.'

There on page five is an article about changing Afrikaans town names in Gauteng back to the original Sotho and Zulu. Next to it is a photo of a man. He's standing in front of a hall, its name spelled out in a lighter shade of stone than the rest of the building. He's laughing, holding a ribbon between the blades of a big pair of scissors.

I close the paper, throw it into the footwell. I move into the middle of the seat and lie down so that my head is behind my father and he can't see my face.

Paul something is Paul Silongo. I know him.

5

Too Long

16 days ago

From the plane, the Highveld was one big motorway and Johannesburg an oil stain, the city's colours swirling into one another in the smog, as though it had just rained. But here it wouldn't rain again for months. As we circled the airport, the city was iridescent in the morning light; flying into the headwind it was plate-glass blue; and as we turned, parks and mine dumps coloured the smog. I remembered again winter in South Africa, when the sky is washed out and the fields are either yellow with drought or scorched by fires. Winter here looks better through sunglasses.

I came back on my South African passport, which was stiff and empty of stamps. I'd read somewhere that the South African government had a problem with dual citizenship. Better to keep my UK passport in my handbag, ready to be waved easily back into England with no threat of chest X-rays. Two women were scanning barcodes and checking photos, talking loudly to one another from their booths. I recognised the word for *tourist* from primary-school Sotho – *bahahlaudi* – although I knew I would no longer be able to say it without stumbling over the *hl* sound. The women laughed, and even though I was in the queue for citizens I was suddenly worried that they were talking about me. My passport photo was taken seven years ago, just before I turned sixteen and my child passport expired, in a pharmacy near my boarding school, before I'd discovered side partings and make-up. But Prudence – according to her name badge – scanned it, stamped it and waved me on. As far as Immigration was concerned, I was the same person.

Everywhere, the airport was under a crust of construction. Signs promised that it would be all new and improved for the 2010 World Cup. The billboard at the baggage carousel promised the same thing, except this time for the electricity grid. My suitcase was one of the first out, and I wheeled it behind me through customs and into the arrivals terminal. I'd forgotten how warm it could be, even in winter. But it was a better heat than in London: drier, lighter against my skin. Everything was bigger than the last time I'd been here. The airport had a different name and new information points; shops and restaurants lined the concourse to the car-rental desks. Almost ten years ago, Naledi and I had gone to the Wimpy and eaten as many plates of vinegary chips as we could before my flight was announced. At the gate, she'd given me a present: a stick with brown paper wrapped around the top. I'd opened it on the plane to find a South African flag, and I cried as lightning made pink the sky over Zambia. The two British women next to me had given me tissues that smelled of lavender.

I waited in line at the Hertz desk, resting my handbag and a shopping bag containing sunglasses and a too-bright orange skirt next to me on my suitcase. This would be the first time I'd rented a car; I was just old enough to do it, another reason I'd decided to come out. My grandmother's death certificate was in my bag, along with her will and bank details. My ticket, the return date chosen at random four weeks from now, was the first and only thing I'd touched the money she'd left me to buy. She'd intended the money as a dowry, I knew. As a single woman, my owning property would be off-putting to men, she'd said. I'd thought briefly about ignoring her, putting the money towards a deposit on my small rented flat in East London, but hadn't wanted to be tied to the damp basement rooms with their dehumidifiers and dull energy-efficient light bulbs.

I would need to come up with more exciting observations about England before seeing Naledi that night, I thought. I was now foreign – or half-foreign – and therefore exotic. My stories had to live up to that expectation.

'You'd better watch it,' a man's voice said behind me. I turned. A tall black man in a suit picked up my handbag and slung it over his shoulder. 'You're not in Kansas any more.'

'Hey—' I stepped quickly towards him, reaching for the strap across his shoulder, and bumped into my suitcase. It fell over, and the shopping bag slid across the tiles into the ankles of the woman queuing ahead of me, who had turned to stare.

'Relax,' the man said, putting the bag down, this time at my feet.

I picked it up immediately and slung it over my shoulder. My mom's death certificate was also in the secret pocket just in case I needed it, and I could almost feel it against my back.

'I'm not gonna steal your bag, but someone else might've,' he said as he pulled the suitcase upright. The woman queuing ahead of me smiled as she gave him the shopping bag, their hands touching briefly over the thick plastic. 'Thanks.' He bent to tie the bag to the suitcase handle with a fat double-knot and stood, smoothing his hands over his suit jacket. 'That's better.' He lifted his sunglasses. 'You can't be so unaware of your stuff here. Just a friendly warning.'

'Thanks.' I felt as though I'd just said all the consonants in the word *croissant* in front of a native French speaker. I was blushing.

'You're welcome,' he said, smiling.

I turned away from the man, keeping my suitcase pulled into my hip. The line had shortened and only the woman stood, tapping her foot, between me and a way out of there. I stared at her shoes, willing the colour to fade from my cheeks, not wanting to look around in case the man was loitering. Over the tannoy, in five languages and twice in English, a man reminded customers to pay for their parking at the machines by the lifts before going to their cars.

Key ring around my forefinger and a map with the route to the car park pressed between my lips, I turned away from the desk and looked around. The man with the sunglasses was sitting at the end of the row of seats parallel to the hire-car desks. He leant back, one arm along the seats next to him, legs crossed. He was reading a paper, which he held low against his thigh. I folded the map in half and pulled at the knot on the shopping bag until it was loose enough that I could get to the sunglasses. As I began to pick at the sticker on one of the lenses, I saw the man stand and do up the buttons on his charcoal suit jacket. He left the paper on the seat and came towards me, his shoes clipping against the tiles. I put the sunglasses on, grateful that they covered so much of my face.

'Hi there,' he said, stopping in front of me. He smiled a very white smile. 'I thought I should apologise for earlier.'

'No apology necessary. I should be more aware of things like that.' He had an angular jaw, a stud in one ear. There was a half-inch-long scar above his left eyebrow, near the hairline. I waited for him to speak or move out of my way, but he just smiled expectantly. 'Well,' I said, pulling up the handle on my suitcase, 'thanks again.'

'Wow,' he said as I stepped past him. 'The English really are unfriendly.'

I kept walking, hoping a child's hope that if I just didn't look at him he would go away. He followed, clipping all the way. I wanted to be the man running on all the exit signs.

'And awkward, too.' He moved up in front of me, walking backwards so as to face me. 'That's what you always hear about them. They're drunks – unfriendly drunks at that – and when they're not pissed, they're awkward bastards.' He smiled again.

I stopped. 'Can I help you with something?'

'You could help me by recognising me so we can get this uncomfortable stuff out of the way.' He straightened the cuffs on his jacket. 'Frankly, it makes me think you're not too hot as journalists go.'

I pushed my sunglasses up into my hair. 'Why'm I supposed to recognise you?'

He stepped closer. 'Because I'm one of the guys you came out here to interview.' He held out his hand. 'You are Johanna Hartslief, right?'

In the UK, when I introduced myself, it was always with the post-script *like heartsleaf*, but he'd said my name right first time.

'I'm Bangizwe Silongo, Deputy Premier of Gauteng. But you can call me Paul. We spoke on the phone, remember?'

'It's Jo.' I shook his hand. It was soft, the cuticles perfect. I'd been surprised by his call. I'd emailed the ANC's press office only a week earlier, including the name of the magazine in bold, its Nobel Prize-winning contributors too, and asked if they could suggest an appropriate spokesperson for me to interview. I was in my flat, still wearing pyjamas, when he rang. We'd spoken for almost an hour, about the article at first – income inequality, public resources and tax subsidies – and then, somehow, his career, our favourite pubs in London. There'd been a delay over the phone, so that our voices sometimes overlapped.

'Nice to meet you, Paul.' On the phone, he'd introduced himself as Paul and I'd accepted it without thinking, but now that I was back in South Africa, I felt foreign and other calling him that, being told I could call him that.

'I was sure you'd recognise me,' he said, the light behind him, his outline dissolving. 'Google image search my name at least.'

'I should have.' I'd have to find a way back to equal footing. I smiled. 'I thought we were meeting next week. Are you stalking me, Paul?' How had he known which flight I was on? I wondered, unsure whether to feel flattered or worried.

'I just thought I'd come to meet the prodigal daughter returned to interview this humble civil servant,' he said. 'It's the least I can do.'

I looked beyond him to the shops flanking the door. I recognised crisp packets and sweet wrappers that I hadn't realised I remembered. I wanted to buy one of everything – not to eat, just for the familiar branding. 'Don't you have a province to run?'

'Nah, I'm just the face. The brains can get on without me for a few hours.' This was a joke he used a lot, I could tell. I imagined he was used to people making a comment about what a nice face it was.

'I'll be sure to quote you on that.' I looked at my watch, grateful that I wore it on my right wrist so I could keep one hand on my suitcase. But this action, universal shorthand for *Will you look at the time? I have to run*, didn't seem to register.

'Let me help you with your luggage.' It wasn't a question. He put his hand over mine on the handle of my suitcase.

'OK. Thanks.' I pulled my hand out from under his and we walked through the automatic doors, into the sunlight sharpened on winter's whetstone.

'It's been a while since you've been back here, hey?' He was too tall for the suitcase and kept pulling it into his heels. 'Ten years?'

How did he know that? Had I been that specific over the phone? I couldn't remember now. 'Yeah,' I said, wishing I was alone for this. The light was different here. Outside smelled like burning grass and I wanted my mom, more than I had in years. My eyes were full under my sunglasses.

'You've lost your accent.'

A sign above the zebra crossing welcomed me to South Africa, the Rainbow Nation. I cleared my throat. 'Would you be happier if I was speaking Afrikaans?'

'Yes, because *Afrikaners is plesierig*.' Afrikaners like to have fun.

I couldn't help laughing to hear him quote the cheesy folk song.

'It's this way.' He pointed. We crossed the drop-off lane and went into covered parking. 'Where are you staying while you're here?'

'I'm at the Mercure in Bedfordview for a few nights, but after that I'm all over the shop, depending on how the stories go.' I looked down at the licence-plate number stamped on the key ring, and up at a row of Toyotas.

'Impressive.'

'I'm not trying to impress you. Just do my job.' I pressed the button on the immobiliser and the lights on a silver Toyota flashed. 'Here we go.' I pulled off my handbag and unlocked the boot.

'How well do you know Jo'burg?' He stood the suitcase against the car and half sat on it.

I put the bag in the boot, unzipped it and pulled out a bottle of water. 'I used to know Benoni quite well, but that's not the same thing, is it?' Our flat there was the best place we'd ever lived, small and almost too expensive, but worth it. Benoni was suburban, full of trees; there was an art deco City Hall, a bunny park. Even back then, Jo'burg was a very different place.

'So, how's this for a deal? We lock your stuff in your car and you let me take you to Lookout Point, so you can see all of Jo'burg and get your bearings. Plus it'll be useful background for our interview.'

'Won't the brains miss the face soon?' The water was warm. London water.

'Nope. There's time for this booked in my diary.'

I laughed. 'That's presumptuous of you. I have work to do, you know. I'm not just here for you to insult.'

'I promise to stop taking the piss.' The last part his best attempt to emulate the Queen's English. 'Let me take you on a tour and then I'll stop bugging you. You have my word.'

I paused. We were both being caricatures of ourselves, exaggerating sarcasm or self-deprecation and expanding to fill the space. It was fun, but I wanted it over with or it would be all I remembered about my first few hours back in South Africa. And this ride could be useful. 'OK, I'll come with you, but only if you drop the bullshit act.'

He raised his eyebrows. 'What act?'

'Come on, Paul.' I balanced the water bottle on top of my bag. 'We don't know each other, but I think you can drop the charm offensive.'

'OK.'

'Good. Now, I need to change before this tour begins.' I waited.

'Sure.' He put his feet out in front of him and stared at his shoes.

I waved my hand in front of his face. 'Get off my suitcase then.'

He stood up, brushing at the pleats on his trousers. 'Shall I turn around?' He lifted the suitcase into the boot.

'No, you can go fetch your car and I'll meet you by the drop-off point in ten minutes.' I unzipped it and pulled out a green top, ballet pumps, deodorant and a hairbrush.

'OK.' He bowed. 'But you'd better not just drive away. I could have you arrested for resisting my charms.'

I rolled my eyes. 'You're not helping your case, Paul. Now bugger off and I'll see you in a bit.'

'Yes, ma'am.' He turned, whistling as he walked away.

I got into the driver's seat and put the keys in the ignition so I could turn on the radio. I wanted to hear a song I recognised. I scrolled through the stations but got only fuzz, so I switched the radio off and climbed into the back seat. I took off the jeans and jersey I'd travelled in and stuffed them under the front seat. Wishing for a shower, I sprayed deodorant until I coughed. It was warm enough for bare legs, and I ripped the tags off the new skirt with my teeth. I brushed my hair in the rear-view mirror, sprayed deodorant over my feet and slipped them into the pumps. I went around to the boot to grab my purse and some gum. My reflection in the surfaces of the car was stout and mushroom-like; from head to toe, red, green and orange: a traffic light, but in the wrong order. Everything locked and alarmed, I walked back into the sunlight, wishing I could whistle.

I couldn't see him at the drop-off point, just taxis and people stopping to say goodbye quickly and cry in their cars on the way home. I stood under a white sign that shouted parking time limits in yellow capital letters. I should have called someone or read all the hire-care crap in the glovebox, I thought. Waiting made me look keen.

'Jo!' I looked around. A hand waved from the tinted window of a dark Mercedes. The back door opened and Paul stepped out, without his suit jacket and sunglasses.

Look straight ahead and don't fall or walk into anything, I thought as I headed towards him.

'Ready for your tour?' he asked. Up close, his shirt was covered in thin, pink stripes. To make him look softer, probably.

'Can you even see out of these windows?'

'Of course. I have to be able to see the province I'm trying to fix up, don't I?' He lifted his arm, gesturing theatrically to the taxi ranks and the passengers coming through the glass doors.

I laughed, surprised. 'Of course.'

'After you,' he said, stepping aside. It wasn't far enough, though: he smelled of mint and the pleats in his trousers were starchy against my legs as I edged past him and got into the car. He closed the door softly, leaving two handprints on the window, and I could hear him whistling again as he walked around the back of the car.

Inside was cool and tinted blue. I pulled the skirt over my vein-pale knees and put on my seat belt. 'Hi,' I said to the driver, watching him not watch me in the rear-view mirror. He was in a suit and dark glasses. At least he isn't wearing a cap, I thought.

Paul was leaning against the passenger door, talking on the phone. 'OK,' he was saying. 'I understand. Let me know what you find out.' He slipped his phone into his pocket, opened the door and slid in beside me. 'Sorry about that.'

'Problems with your underlings?'

He slammed the door and fastened his seat belt, frowning. 'I'd prefer it if you didn't refer to them like that.'

I put my sunglasses on and looked away. I'd dropped my guard too quickly, I thought. I'd have to wait for him to offer me a way out. The driver pulled out of the lay-by, and the airport rushed past through two layers of blue, like the bottom of the rock pools my mom and I used to go snorkelling in during summer holidays. It was quiet in the car except for the motorway humming beneath us.

He took a deep breath and puffed up his cheeks. 'Sorry,' he said, exhaling loudly. 'You didn't deserve that. I was dealing with some family stuff.'

I let him wait for a moment. 'That's OK,' I said finally, looking at him. 'Is everything all right?'

'No.' He looked down. 'But I can handle it. Usually, anyway.' He paused. 'So, what is it you want to talk about?' he asked.

'We could talk about the World Cup.' I tried to rub the goose pimples from my knees. 'Or how you're being touted as a prime example of the changing face of the ANC.'

'What do you mean?' He unbuttoned the cuff on his right shirt-sleeve and folded it over a few times.

'That's your party line. Surely you know.' The veins in his forearm were slightly raised, like new scars.

He started on the left cuff. 'How the rest of the world sees us is not something I have time to think about.'

'Why was it so important for you to come meet me then?' Back on familiar territory.

'Because I wanted to meet you face to face.' He turned in his seat, leaning against the window, one leg bent against the leather. 'I don't like getting to know someone over the phone. You can't see their reactions.' He watched me then, for mine.

'I know.' I'd forgotten that the traffic-light poles were yellow here. That people called them robots.

He smirked and I knew what was coming. 'I also wanted to meet one of the most unpatriotic journalists ever to flee our shores.'

'Unpatriotic?' I'd expected it, just not so soon. He must've read my blog.

'Criticising the government like you have – it's bad for the country. It makes us look bad to the rest of the world, which ultimately has a negative impact on everyone still loyal enough to stick it out here.' He rubbed at a scuffmark on his shoe, keeping his eyes on me.

'I thought you were smarter than that.' I pulled off my sunglasses and folded them over my fingers like a knuckleduster.

'Why? Because I speak good English and drive a European car?'

'You don't drive it.'

He sighed. 'I'm not saying that this is the case in every country. But South Africa is a post-conflict society and nation-building is an integral role of journalists here.'

'Well, if nothing else, thanks for thinking of me as a South African journalist.' I couldn't keep the sarcasm out of my voice.

'The role of the journalist is to serve the public interest, right? And public interest is in the preservation and proper functioning of society.' He tapped his knee, keeping time with his speech. 'How can you criticising the electricity-supply issues and calling into question the integrity and competence of government officials be serving the public interest? It just works people up, makes them stop trusting us.' He could've just said blackouts. Everyone else did.

I turned further towards him. 'You're confusing public interest with national interest. It's a journalist's duty to tell the truth – it's about empowering ordinary people, not governments.'

He laughed.

'But that's OK: party men older and more experienced than you do it too.' That little bit of condescension silenced him. I smiled, enjoying myself now. 'And it's dangerous, especially when it comes to the party line about HIV not causing AIDS.'

He frowned. 'What, you think HIV really causes AIDS?' He waited. 'Sorry, that was a bad joke. I totally agree with you on this one.'

'Good. Otherwise I would've asked to get out right here, wherever we are.' I hoped he realised I didn't mean it. 'This isn't much of a tour, you know.'

'I only promised Lookout Point,' he said. 'Or did you want to see more?'

I looked down, trying to remember what we'd been talking about. 'You have an example of so-called patriotic journalism on your door-step. Any critic of Mugabe is automatically a traitor to Zimbabwe, and that's the problem. It's Zimbabwe or death.'

'But the South African government isn't going around killing its critics,' he said. 'This is all off the record, by the way. The party line on Zimbabwe isn't one I agree with, but I shouldn't let it get out that I've called Mugabe a killer. And an idiot.'

'Don't worry. I don't have a tape recorder on me,' I said, putting my hands up. Then I realised what I'd implied – *You can search me if you like* – and put my hands in my lap. I'd always been comfortable with banter as a way of flirting, but trading political insults was new to me. 'It's good to know that you don't think Mugabe is…' I tried to find the right way to finish my sentence, 'a stand-up guy.'

He laughed. 'No, I don't.' The car drew to a stop and he looked around. 'We're here.' He opened his door and white afternoon light slashed at the leather. 'Come on.'

I stepped into dusty scrub and straightened up, squinting.

'Here we are. Lookout Point,' he said as I circled the car. We'd stopped midway up a very steep hill. Beneath us, rows of bare trees measured visibility in the smog and the tarps covering swimming pools cut blue oblongs out of the land. The screen at an old drive-in cinema nearby was white and tattered.

Thirty feet away, a small group of black people were kneeling in the scrub, praying in French. None of them was wearing shoes. One of them, a man in a denim jacket, turned to look at us, rubbing his hands together, and smiled. Paul nodded at him.

'These are the Northern Suburbs,' he said. 'The rich ones, in case you can't tell from the number of pools. All the trees here make Jo'burg the world's biggest man-made forest.'

'Sometimes you speak in capital letters. Johannesburg: The World's Biggest Man-Made Forest.'

'I'm proud of my country. Our country.' It was a warning. 'That's Hillbrow Tower. The tourist board wants to push it as Jo'burg's answer to Table Mountain, but to me it just looks like a big syringe. You can't really see any of the castles because of the smog, but in that direction – pretend you see it—'

'I see it,' I said obediently.

'—is Soccer City, which we're expanding for 2010. When it's done, it will compare proudly with the world's greatest wonders, such as the Statue of Liberty, the Eiffel Tower and the Sydney Opera House.'

I looked up at him. 'Please tell me you're quoting.'

He smiled. 'Do you think we'll finish everything in time for the Cup?' He leant closer and stage-whispered: 'I'll give you a hint: that was a test.'

'Yes, of course you'll finish everything in time for the Cup,' I said, bobbing my head as I spoke.

'Good. You've been paying attention,' he said. 'Actually, I'm worried we'll miss the deadline. Tomorrow and tomorrow and tomorrow.' He turned towards me. 'Speaking of which, what are you doing tonight? Are you free for dinner?'

'I'm meeting my friend from school tonight.'

He looked back into the yellow smog. 'Naledi?'

'Yeah,' I said, surprised he remembered her name. When we'd spoken over the phone, I'd told him about her as proof that I hadn't become completely unmoored from the past, this country. I'd also told him about my mom, how I hadn't been back to South Africa since she died.

'Dinner before you go? Maybe if you get down to Cape Town to see your dad, we could meet up there. I'm there a lot.' He remembered everything I'd told him.

'Yes,' I said.

He clicked and pointed finger-guns at me. 'Shot.' Good.

'Oh God, I haven't heard that in years.'

'Prepare yourself for tonight then. The kids have all sorts of new slang you won't understand.' He opened the car door. 'I'll take you back.'

I turned in the dust. Nearby, a field was burning: the flavour of winter.

I sat wrapped in a towel, hair still wet, trying not to drip onto my laptop as I listened to Naledi uncork a bottle of wine over the phone. I was already late for dinner.

When Paul had dropped me off at the airport, I'd reread the directions to my hotel, but I'd still taken the wrong exit off the motorway, ending up in rush-hour traffic. There was too much noise and too many lanes. Men tried to wash my windscreen or sell me bin liners and bead necklaces at every traffic light as I wondered if here, this junction, was where my mom had died. Dusk was hanging low over the city by the time I'd made it to my hotel. I'd ordered a glass of wine from the bar downstairs before I showered. And then another one.

'How was your day?' I asked Naledi, feeling as though I was wasting time by asking something so mundane.

'Not too bad. Although seeing Lauren every day is a bitch.'

Naledi had come out of the closet a few years ago and hadn't seen her parents since. Being gay didn't sit well with either God or the ancestors, she'd said. 'You finished with her then?'

'*Ja*. Seeing someone from the office is a stupid thing to do.'

I had no similar experience from which to draw an insightful, empathetic comment and settled for a quip instead. 'I think they call that shitting where you eat.'

She laughed the laugh of someone who doesn't whisper, either because they physically can't or because they're against it on principle. 'Here's to not shitting where you eat.' She drank. 'Toasting would be a lot easier if you were here, you know.'

I clicked to open a game of solitaire, closed it again before all the cards had even been dealt. 'Actually, I don't think I'm gonna be able to make it over tonight. I didn't sleep well on the plane and it's all been a bit much today,' I said lamely. It was nothing to do with jet lag. There'd be too many questions I didn't have answers for, that I hadn't even asked myself yet.

'Hang on,' she said. 'I'll be right back.' She wasn't talking to me. Mpho and Monica were already there, helping her make dinner. They were the only other people from South Africa I kept in touch with any more – these days, just a text on our birthdays.

I'd messaged both of them before I left London to let them know that I'd be around. The idea of seeing them all together had seemed like fun then. Even when Monica had responded: *You're looking so thin, Jo. I'm so jealous! How do you do it? I was looking at pictures from school this afternoon and I was so skinny then. It's good motivation.* Followed by an emoticon and two *x*'s.

I hadn't known how, or whether, to respond. In London, I walked everywhere. It was the only way to get to know the city, and after two years there I was starting to recognise street names and to be able to recommend small old-man pubs on the corners of residential streets. Knowing the city this way, its short cuts and dead ends, might make it feel like home. The route back to my flat from a magazine I sometimes freelanced for took me through some of the oldest parts of East London. On Fashion Street, a half-timbered Elizabethan building was now an office block, pink and blue spotlights directed at the white panels on the exterior. Even after ten years in England, the age of everything still surprised me. To think that London was already a city, with roads and plans, when Jo'burg hadn't been settled yet, made me feel as though I was always behind, trying to catch up. Whether I was homesick for London or for Jo'burg, I didn't know, and I wasn't sure how to explain all of this to Monica in a Facebook message. I didn't think I'd be able to do much better over one dinner.

'Hurry up, Jo,' one of them now called in the background. 'And bring more wine.'

When I'd left South Africa, I'd been jealous of them, getting to go to high school together. I hadn't expected to feel exactly the same, ten years on.

I heard Naledi sliding a door closed. 'Are you sure?' she asked. There were frogs somewhere in her garden. 'It might help to be around people who know you.'

'I just don't think I'll be on good form tonight,' I said. 'But I'll come over tomorrow, I promise.'

'Are you OK, Hartslief?'

'Yeah. I'm sorry. I know I'm being weird.'

The frogs seemed louder now. I'd hoped to hear crickets. My first summer in England, I'd met my grandmother's neighbours. They let me swim in their pool, even though my grandmother had told me not to ask them. The neighbours bred crickets for their leopard geckos. That summer, the crickets had found a way to escape from their aquarium. In bed at night, I'd listened to them shimmer in the garden next door. It had felt like home and I'd cried every night until I started back at boarding school.

'That's OK. It must be weird to be back.' I heard her glass clack against her teeth. 'Have you missed it?'

I reached for my wine. 'Yeah. I didn't realise how much.' Jasmine didn't smell the way it was supposed to in England. All that rain seemed to wash the fragrance from the flowers.

'What're your plans while you're here?' she asked, trying to rally. 'I know you've got to join the global conversation with your international perspective on the abundance of experience in South Africa.'

She was misquoting the magazine's manifesto on purpose. When they'd commissioned my article, she'd spent a few hours reading back issues and sent over an email that contained only a paragraph of exclamation marks. 'Could you live off granny for a while?'

I laughed. 'Only for three or four months, according to my spreadsheet.'

'Sexy.'

'Other than the lawyers and you, obviously, I should probably see Lynda too.' I leant back against the headboard, my eyes closed. Lynda and my mom had met when they were both at Wits University, she studying communications, my mom reading anthropology. When, after another round with my grandmother, my mom had decided to move out, Lynda had offered her a room in a commune near campus. It was through Lynda that she had got into campaigning for women's rights. But it was also through Lynda and her commune that my mom had met my father.

I went on: 'She sent this card after the funeral saying she would pray for me, so I probably owe her a visit.' For as long as I can remember, Lynda had sent me a birthday card. Each birthday, the same message: *May all your endeavours be crowned with blessings this year.*

'Yuck,' Naledi said. 'Or is that something non-horrible people would think is nice?'

'Maybe.' The laptop had suspended and the room was suddenly very dark. 'I wouldn't know though.' I wished then that she hadn't invited the others, that we could just sit together getting drunk and watching our favourite nineties action films. 'Anyway, I'll let you get on with dinner. You guys have fun and I can't wait to see you.'

I needed to hang up before I changed my mind and drove over there.

———

Apart from the vaguely African print on the runner across the foot of the bed, my room could've been anywhere. There was satellite television, room service menus in French and German. I pulled on the jeans and jersey I'd flown in. I needed to get out.

I sat on the kerb in front of the lobby, under a flickering light, and lit a cigarette. Balancing my handbag on the edge of a flowerbox, I dug one-handed for my purse and phone. The business card was there in the front pocket. I dialled. It rang twice.

'Hi, Paul? It's Jo Hartslief.' I kicked at an uneven brick. 'My dinner was cancelled and I was wondering what you're up to tonight?'

When we'd both hung up, I zipped my purse and phone back into my bag and rested my forehead on it. I finished my cigarette, staring at the stitching, the way the teeth of the zip fitted together. At the petals and dark green stems. There were chicken bones among the flowers.

I'd need to change my clothes, I thought. I stood up, picked up my bag and went back into the hotel.

6

The Right to Make Promises

'It's a bad time now.' A woman's voice, an accent I can't place.

Telephone poles measure our speed, the lines rippling across the pumpkin-soup sky. I don't know how but I've slept the day away. I can see a rectangle of late afternoon through the sunroof, perfect as a postcard except for the birdshit and blue-gum sap on the plastic.

She clears her throat. 'Do you mind? It makes me feel sick.'

I raise my head slowly to see the stranger talking to my father. A thin black woman, not much older than I am, sits in the passenger seat, her hair knotted at the nape of her neck and a checked blanket in her lap. She sits stiffly, her shoulders straight and not touching the seat.

'Sorry, I'll put it out,' my father says. The window opens a crack.

'Thank you, *baas*.' She looks down as she speaks.

He laughs. 'Who taught you *baas*?'

'The man I work for now. It's a good job – I look after the baby.'

'What were you doing in Zim before you came down?' my father asks, changing gears.

'I was a primary school teacher, but when they shut the school, I had to come here to find work.'

'Christ,' my father says. The woman flinches. 'Sorry.' I can hear him drumming his fingers against the steering wheel. A nervous noise rather than a rhythm. 'So you're a nanny now.'

'Yes. They want me to teach him too, though.'

'What do you teach him?'

I can hear the woman's bracelets clacking together as she smooths the shawl in her lap. 'I do vocabulary exercises with picture books mostly. But I was teaching him to sing too – he'd never heard singing other than opera. Now he sings along with me. He just makes noises actually.' She leans forward and pulls her handbag up onto her lap. 'I've bought him a *mbira* to play on,' she says, pulling a thumb piano from a plastic bag. Silver keys that look like spoon handles fan out against a small wooden board, each attached to the base by a nail. She runs her fingers across the Coke bottletops hammered onto the base of the instrument. 'They'll probably want me to take these off. They attract the ancestors' spirits.'

'It's beautiful,' my father says. She rests the piano on her lap, out of his reach. 'Was it expensive?'

'No – not when you have rands to buy in Zimbabwe.' She puts the little finger of her right hand through the hole in the bottom corner of the board and plucks a few keys with her thumb.

'Play something,' he says, but she shakes her head.

My father is quiet as she runs her fingers over the scalloped edges of the keys before putting the piano back in her bag. He changes lanes and we speed past a sign for Mangaung. I thought we were heading for Bloemfontein. Maybe this is its new name. Or its old one.

'Where do you live?' he tries again.

She folds her hands over the bag in her lap. 'Thabong, near Welkom.'

'Does your family live with you?' I hear him moving CDs to find the gum in the compartment next to the radio.

'No, they're still in Harare.'

'That must be difficult,' he says.

The woman sighs. 'Yes. I send money to them but there's nowhere in Zimbabwe to buy groceries, so my husband has to get the bus to Jo'burg to buy food. It takes him a whole day to do the shopping.' She watches the road. 'I want to bring the children down to live with me – my sister can look after them in the day while I'm at work – but with the troubles now, I will have to wait.'

I wonder how many times she has given this speech to white people who are frowning and asking how things are. The short history of Zimbabwe, easily retold over a round of golf.

A pause. 'Gosh,' my father says. I have to swallow a laugh. Without the swear words and shock value, he seems insincere. 'Is it bad in Thabong?' he asks.

'No, not yet. But it's coming. Just before I went away, some of the men attacked a Malawian woman living in another township near Bloemfontein. I don't know what they did to her but she had to go to hospital.'

My father breathes out loudly, the air whistling over his teeth. 'What are you going to do?'

She sits back in her seat for the first time. 'Nothing, for now. Just wait and see. I have to keep working to send money back, so I'll stay as long as I can.' She looks at the watch on her right wrist. 'How much longer do you think it will take?'

'A few minutes? The turn-off to the shopping centre is coming up,' he says, pointing.

She ducks forward to check the road sign passing above us, then nods. 'OK.'

'Will you go back to Zimbabwe if the riots start here?' my father asks.

The woman looks at her hands. 'I've been in South Africa for two years. If I go back, they might think I'm a spy or that I'm working against the government. There's nothing to go back for – no food, no clean water. Disease. Did you know that an egg costs almost fifty billion Zim dollars?'

'Fuck.' That's more like him. The woman looks at my father. 'Sorry.'

She smiles for the first time. '*Baas* says much worse than that.'

The sound of the road changes as we turn off the motorway.

'Do you miss Zimbabwe?' my father asks.

She lays her head against the headrest, her chin in the air. I wonder if my father is staring at her neck. 'The light,' she says. 'My people.' She opens her eyes and looks at my father. 'You can never really forget your own land.'

We turn left and slow over a speed hump. 'Here we go,' my father says. 'Anywhere in particular?'

'No,' she says, pulling the shawl over her shoulders. 'Anywhere is fine.'

'OK, I'll get as close to the shops as possible,' he says as we turn right.

The woman nods.

'Are you sure you want to stop here?' my father asks. 'I can drop you at home if you want? Or at work?'

She clasps her hands together and bows her head slightly. 'Thank you, but their house is not far from there and I need to change before I go to work.'

'Why?' he asks as the car comes to a stop.

'I have a uniform that I have to wear. A maid's uniform.' She opens the passenger door. 'A light blue one with a white apron and collar.' She steps out into the car park, straightening her skirt, and slings her handbag over her shoulder.

'I'll get your bags,' my father says, leaning across the console between the seats so that she can hear him.

I close my eyes again, pretending to be asleep. The car shudders slightly as he gets out. I can feel the light change as he opens the boot. Propping myself up on my elbow, I turn to watch them through the rear window.

'Well, I hope that everything goes well for you, Maria,' I hear him say as he lifts a duffel bag onto the gravel. I wonder if she can see the empty Castle cans or if he covered them up before he put her stuff in the boot.

'Thank you – me too.'

My father slams the boot shut, camera in hand. 'Is here OK for a few photos?' he asks. 'It was part of the deal.'

I wish he hadn't said that. The lift, the conversation – all of it part of a transaction made on the side of the road.

'Yes, OK. Yes.'

I wonder if he'll try to photograph her again when she's changed into her uniform.

'Thank you,' he says, putting the camera down on the boot a few moments later. 'Maria, I want to give you something,' he says, reaching into his back pocket and pulling out his wallet.

'No, no, *baas*,' Maria says, taking a small step backwards.

'Please. Take it.' He offers her what's left of the folded wad of notes, purple and shiny, that I gave him at Durban airport. 'Please.'

She hesitates, looking around to make sure no one is watching, and steps forward. 'Thank you,' she says, stuffing the money into her handbag without taking it off her shoulder. 'Thank you very much.' She redoes the clasp.

'Keep safe,' he says. 'And don't stay longer than you have to.'

She nods. 'Go well.'

He pulls a cigarette out of the packet in the breast pocket of his shirt. 'You too.'

Maria lifts her duffel bag, turns and walks towards the shopping centre, her upper body slightly tilted to the right. I wonder what's in her bag to make it so heavy, if she's bringing home back with her, bit by bit, every time she visits.

I lie back. Birds scissor across the sky. The sun should be setting soon. I don't even know where we are.

'Get up!' my father shouts at me, banging his fist on the boot. 'Or I'll lock you in there with your farts.' I sit up and my father comes around to the open front door. 'Morning, sunshine,' he says, blowing smoke into the car.

'What?' I look at my watch. It's eight o'clock.

'You've been asleep for about twenty hours, lazy cow.'

I wipe the sleep from my eyes. 'Fuck off.'

He holds his watch up to the window. Like mine, it says eight o'clock. But where the three should be is a small white circle around the number twenty-six. I've lost a whole day. How could I have slept so long? Maybe all the sleepless nights have finally caught up with me. Or maybe I'm getting sick. The burn on my thigh is throbbing and I wonder if it's infected.

'While you were snoring, I've already been up to check out Wilna's flat.' He opens the back door. 'Now get up and get some air onto that body before you stink me out of the car,' he says, dropping his cigarette onto the gravel. 'And tidy yourself up a bit. You're not going to find a husband with a face like that.'

Before he can ask, I give him all the money I have left in my purse. He smiles. 'See, I can be nice to some black people,' he says.

I wonder then if he knew I was awake and watching when he gave her the money.

'Stay here,' he says. Key ring helicoptering around his finger, he heads towards the shopping centre.

I change my underwear and wash my face with water from one of the half-empty bottles on the back seat. I check the front of the car for my phone but there's no sign of it. When I look in my suitcase, my UK passport is missing too. He must've taken it while I was sleeping.

He comes back to the car with two fishing rods under his arm, a tackle box in one hand. 'We *have* to go fishing,' he says, putting the box on top of the car. 'There's a dam near here.'

'I hate fishing.'

'Have you ever even been fishing?' he asks, opening the boot.

'Yes. Enough to know I hate it.'

'When, then?' He stops trying to manoeuvre the rods into the boot and looks at me.

'Once when I went to France on a school trip,' I say. 'It was really boring.' I look at my nails to emphasise my point.

'You've been to France?' He opens a beer. 'I am not happy about that. No one called me to ask if you were allowed to go. I would've said no.' He takes a long drink and wipes his mouth on the back of his hand.

In the past, talk of permission would have made me angry. I would've listed the other places I'd been, and some places I hadn't. Describe how New York smelled of flowers near Central Park and food everywhere else. But it's a small thing now, after everything else he's done.

'Anyway, fishing isn't boring. And we're doing it.' He bends, one of his knees cracking loudly, and puts his beer down in the shade of the car. 'It'll be father–daughter bonding time.'

I scratch at the edge of the burn on my thigh where the glue on the bandages is causing a rash. 'How much did the rods cost?'

'I dunno. They were the cheapest ones the shop had. Two thousand bucks each?'

'Don't ask me how much they cost. You made me wait by the car,' I say. 'For fuck's sake, Nico, I gave you that money for food and petrol.'

'Don't have a cow, man.'

'Go return them. They're too big for the boot, anyway.'

'We're not returning them.' Giving up on fitting the rods in the boot he leans them against the car.

'Yes, we are,' I say, grabbing my handbag from the back seat. 'Where's the receipt?'

'We're not returning them. They're damaged.' My father stands very still.

'They're not damaged.' I slam the door and take a step towards him. 'Don't be such a baby.'

He grabs both rods in his hands and lifts them above his head. Men gathered around the *boerewors* stand turn to look at us. 'I'll break them rather than give them back,' my father says. 'Don't make me do it.' The rods quiver against the morning sky as though there's water nearby.

'If you do it, it won't be because I'm making you,' I say and turn to walk towards the shopping centre, forcing myself not to look back.

I spend a few minutes looking for a working payphone; when I don't find one I sit in the bathroom, contemplating stopping someone in the centre and asking them to call the police for me. I wouldn't be able to wait in the mall until they arrived – he'd know something was wrong. I'd have to be out there with him, see him realise I've betrayed him. I can't do it, I decide. Not yet. But since he's spent all the money I gave him and not yet taken away my cards, I buy dried fruit and meat, Diet Coke for the caffeine, and a newspaper. I find an ATM and withdraw as much money as the bank will let me. Then I pace in front of two CCTV cameras, looking straight up at their blinking lenses. If Paul knew who I was when he met me at the airport, maybe he'll have a trace on my bankcards.

When I get back to the car, the rods are angled through the sunroof into the back seat. My father is sitting sideways in the passenger seat, his socks balled into his walking boots next to the car and his legs in the sun.

'I'll pay you back,' he says. 'I promise.'

'Will you pay for all the therapy I'm going to need after this road trip?'

He laughs, crushing the empty beer can in his hand. 'You're on your own on that front, man.' He stands up. 'Let's eat. It's been far too long since I last had a *braai*, hey.'

'It's been like two days.'

'Doesn't matter,' he says. 'I'm owed some meat and beer.'

He buys us *boerewors* rolls and a bottle of peach-flavoured fizzy water, which is already open by the time he reaches the car.

'Are you tasting all my food and drink for poison now?' I ask as he hands me a fresh white roll that drips fried onions and sauce.

'Shut up and be grateful, hey,' he says. 'In Zimbabwe, they have no food or clean water – people are dying of cholera over there, you know.'

'I know.' I take a bite and memories of *braais* with my mom under the mulberry tree surface suddenly. 'Thank you,' I say, turning away from him.

Almost instantly, my hair smells of fried onions.

'How did you find Wilna?' I lick mustard from the corner of my mouth. Jaco's ex-girlfriend lives twenty minutes from here, just outside of Bloemfontein.

'Phonebook,' my father says, his mouth full. 'Not bad, right? Call me Magnum PI.' He opens another beer.

We watch the men sell meat to early-morning shoppers. A white man in a khaki utility vest sits in a camping chair under a beach umbrella, while black men in hair nets and plastic gloves turn the sausages on the barbecue. When the shoppers pay, they pay the white man.

We sit in the car outside a block of flats just north of Bloemfontein. Most of the narrow windows are bare, thrown open against the heat, and a satellite dish leans out from one of the top-floor flats. The lawn around the side of the building is patchy, with more bald spots the colour of old bone than grass. This is where Wilna Dell lives.

Of the row of shops underneath the flats, only the off-licence is still operating, the other lots boarded up. A sign dangles by one nail from the façade on the corner where an Italian restaurant has long since closed.

My father pulls a baseball cap I've never seen before out of the cubbyhole in the door next to him. The peak is bent in the middle, almost like the roof of a house in a child's drawing. 'What a fall it was,' he says.

'Huh?'

'It's a pun.' He rolls his neck from side to side and turns to look at me. 'She fell pregnant?'

'Oh.' I pull my hair into a low ponytail, checking it in the wing mirror.

'I'm not surprised she ended up in a shithole like this. That's what you get for being a loser like Jaco's baby mama.'

'What a contemporary reference,' I say, wishing for a snappier comeback. 'Nice.'

'*Jissus*, man,' my father says, leaning over and slapping my shoulder. 'Wake up already.'

'I'm trying,' I say as I pull my handbag onto my lap, but I don't know what I'm looking for and zip it shut. 'I feel like shit.'

'It's probably the *boerewors*,' he says, slipping on his sunglasses. 'You can't handle that much meat.'

'Right, I get it.' I try the door handle but the car is locked. 'I'm surprised you didn't grab your crotch when you said that.'

'Christ, Jo.' He shakes his head and pulls his cap as low as it will go. 'You're really nice and everything, but I'm just not that into you.'

I lean back against the headrest, eyes closed. 'Wow, have you been watching MTV or something? You're so full of the latest idioms. Really down with the kids.'

He laughs. 'No, I was just stalling.'

'What for?' I hear the central locking pop and feel for the door handle, hoping that fresh air will help me wake up. I don't know why I'm this tired.

'For some way to work beef flaps into the conversation.'

'Gross!' I punch his upper arm as hard as I can.

'Or man-meat.' He smiles. This, at least, is familiar, in between the glasses, cap and thickening beard.

'You're disgusting,' I say, shaking my head.

'What? It's your fault.' He rubs his arm. 'Fuck, man – you gave me a dead arm.'

'Good.' I sling my bag over my shoulder. 'What do you mean it's my fault?'

'You gave me that dictionary of swear words. What did you expect?' He pushes his door open and pockets the car keys. 'It's been my toilet reading ever since London.'

I turn on my dictaphone before I step out into the sun and slam the door shut behind me.

'Plus,' he says, doing a drum roll on the car roof, 'if you're gonna swing both ways, that means I can be twice as rude to you.'

'There it is.' I should never have told him that I'd had a crush on a girl during my first year of uni.

'Too obvious?' The car beeps once as it locks.

My bag feels very heavy. 'What do you think?' I slide it off my shoulder and onto the bonnet.

'OK, OK, no more easy targets, ma'am.' He stands, both of his knees clicking, and salutes, his flat hand whipping away from his face much faster than seems possible.

I don't know what else to do and give him two thumbs-up. I want this to be over so I can crawl into the back of the car and sleep another three hundred kilometres away. 'You ready?' I ask.

'Almost. Just one more thing,' he says, pulling my bag towards him. 'Our story.'

'What? Are we from a travelling circus, looking to recruit one more clown?'

He picks at the knot in the chiffon scarf tied at the base of the handles of my bag. 'Nope.'

'Jehovah's Witnesses telling her off for celebrating birthdays?'

He shakes his head.

'Reformed characters selling sponges and felt-tip pens door to door?' I hope there's a lift in the building; the way I'm feeling, four flights of stairs will be more than I can manage.

'No.' He pulls one end through the knot and the scarf is free, wrinkled and fraying at the ends. 'Good one though.'

'I give up then,' I say, leaning against the bonnet.

He loops the scarf around my neck, tying a bow under my chin. I can see sweat stains on his cap just above the peak. A once-yellow springbok is caught in mid-flight on the front of the cap.

'There.' He twists the bow so that it lies over my left shoulder.

'What am I s'posed to be?' I ask as he turns back to my bag. The dictaphone is in the side pocket. I hold my breath. If he finds it, there'll be another argument.

'You'll see,' he says, pulling my glasses case out of the bag. 'Put those on.'

A blurry picture: my father, looking ready for a rugby match, smiling in front of boarded-up shopfronts, all framed in dark-green rims.

'*Parfait*,' he says, pronouncing the *t*, and turns towards the building.

I sigh. 'Tonight, Matthew, I'm going to be…a French person.'

'Huh?' He looks over his shoulder.

I pick up my bag; it bumps against my leg as I walk past him towards the flats. 'Never mind,' I say. 'It doesn't matter.'

The door of 4D is open despite the stink of overcooked stew coming from the neighbouring flat. My father shakes the security gate by way of a knock. I wait behind him, leaning against the railings, out of breath from the climb.

'Hello?' He grabs the gate with both hands this time and rattles it again.

'Don't,' I whisper, pushing myself up off the railings and stepping closer. 'The neighbours.' I can't see him do it, but I'm sure he rolls his eyes at me over his shoulder. 'Well, their flat reeks and I don't want them to open the door,' I say.

He turns and lowers his sunglasses. 'Pull in your stomach. The French are supposed to be thin.'

'She's never gonna believe this.'

'Yes, she will. She's probably never even left the country,' he says, as though that settles it.

In a back room, a child screams and starts to cry. 'Stop fighting or I'll get the wooden spoon,' says a woman's voice inside. The threat sounds more severe for being in Afrikaans.

'Hello, Miss Dell?' My father steps back from the door. Through the white diamonds of the security gate, I can see the beginning of a green and white marbled knitted scarf on the dining table. A ball of wool trails over the edge, around a chair leg and under the couch.

A naked child with a bowl haircut and a red face lurches around the corner. There's eczema on its arms and legs and a yellow dummy in its mouth. In its fat fist is a Barbie with no hair. The toddler glares at us the way teenagers are supposed to, and then forms a screech around the dummy.

'Sht, sht, it's OK,' my father says, holding up both hands.

A bigger child, same haircut but wearing a pink tracksuit, appears behind the naked toddler, as if it has been summoned in some secret language. It's on a black plastic motorbike, the wheels of which are flayed. 'Hello,' it says, rowing itself closer. 'Who are you?' The easy rider smiles at my father. It's missing a front tooth. Based on the pink tracksuit, I'm guessing it's a girl.

'Hi, can I help you?' It's a woman – Wilna. Her hair is scraped back from her face into a high, looped ponytail, secured with a purple scrunchie. She grabs up the naked child on her way to the door. There isn't much of a waist for the child to sit into.

'Hi, Miss Dell? My name is Erik Klavier.' My father holds his hand out through the gate, but she doesn't take it. He waves towards me. 'And this is my associate, Jolie Bourdeaux.'

I expected his French pronunciation to be better, given that he's supposed to have spent time there. I know we can't tell Wilna the truth about why we're here, but I won't take part in my father's charade. I look down. There's a dark red stain on the carpet.

'Jolie doesn't speak much English.' He shrugs. '*Bladdy* French.' He smiles and ducks his head before looking back up at Wilna. It's an old move, one I've seen him use with women before, mostly the younger ones. On one of the two visits I'd made to Cape Town as a child, he'd taken me to a pizza restaurant; there he'd used the same duck-and-look move – combined with a monologue about how hard but rewarding it was to be a single dad – to get the waitress's number. I want to tell him that he's too old for it to work any more, even though I may be wrong. Women have always seemed to like him.

'What do you want?' Wilna asks, looking between us. The child on her hip glares at us and drops the Barbie through the gate.

'I'm looking for Jaco Eloff.' My father crouches to pick up the doll.

Wilna frowns. 'I'm sorry but I don't know where he is.'

The child on the plastic bike rolls closer to the gate.

'Has the tooth mouse come to fetch your tooth and leave you a present?' my father asks. The child grins and holds out a sticky fifty-cent coin. What looks like peanut butter and syrup is matted on its cuffs. That was the only sandwich I liked at aftercare. I wonder if this is how my mom and I looked to outsiders.

'Sorry, what was it you wanted?' Wilna shifts the child higher on her hip.

He stands up. 'Can I come in for a minute? It's about Jaco.'

Wilna shakes her head. 'I'm sorry, no: the girls caught lice from some of the other kids in the flats. I was just about to bath them.' Maybe that's why the doll doesn't have any hair.

'The thing is, Miss Dell, a distant relative of Jaco's – a great-uncle who lived in France his whole life – died recently and has left Jaco quite a lot of money. So I'm helping his lawyer find Jaco to give him the money.'

'Oh.' The naked child leans out from Wilna's body and grabs at the Barbie through the gate. 'How much money?'

'I'm not at liberty to say, but it's quite substantial and really in his interest to get in touch with us.'

I can tell he's smiling; he's enjoying himself, quoting clichés from legal shows.

'Well, I haven't heard from him in more than ten years,' Wilna says. The child wriggles against her and keens to get down. Once on the ground, she hankers at the motorbike, trying to lift her baloney-pink leg over the seat behind her sister. 'Not since ninety-six, I think.' Wilna bends to lift the child onto the toy.

'What about your son? Doesn't Jaco come to see him?' My father slides his hands into his pockets, code for a casual question.

'No.' She wipes her hands on her jeans.

'Oh.'

'Look, I haven't heard from Jaco since the police came looking into the drug-dealing stuff. Which wasn't a surprise, by then.' She hugs her shoulders and I wonder if she's remembering that first night, when it was still a surprise. 'He was an asshole.' The older girl laughs, as though she understands that her mom just swore. 'And he owed us too much child support to ever risk asking for my help.'

'Are you at least getting some from their dad?' my father asks, gesturing at the girls.

Wilna looks at him sharply. He's pushed it too far and I wait for the door to slam. But she sighs instead. 'Not enough,' she says, resting a hand on the older girl's head. 'I think they miss him, but who can tell what they're thinking most of the time?' It isn't really a question. Guilt settles in a frown between her eyes at the admission that her children are foreign to her, alien.

'Maybe they're better off without him,' my father says. Then, in case this is the door-slamming limit, he hurries to add: 'They're going to be such pretty girls.'

Wilna smiles. 'The one in front is Elani and the grumpy one is Ellen.' With their matching bowl cuts and pose on the motorbike, they look like a portrait gone wrong.

'Hi, Elani. Hi, Ellen.' My father waves at the children, but they stare at him blankly. 'Listen, Wilna, if we can't find Jaco, that money belongs to you and your son.'

'Really?' A smile reaches her eyes for the first time today.

'Yes, really.' He steps closer, one hand on the gate. 'But you can help us move this along if you know anything that can assist us to prove that he's not coming back.'

I realise he's asking if Jaco is dead.

'Last I heard, he was in Cape Town for his unit's reunion,' Wilna says. 'But that's all I know.'

My father takes his hand back.

'But,' she says, stepping forward, 'he was back on his drugs by then and out of it all the time. I wouldn't be surprised if something bad happened to him.'

'I see,' my father says. He turns back to me. '*Vous avez une carte d'affaires pour le madam?*' he asks, before mouthing the words *business card* at me. I don't know what he'll do if I sabotage his story by saying no or walking off, so I unzip my bag, hoping my grandmother's lawyer's card is still in my purse. When I can't find it, I write my UK mobile number on the back of an underground travel card.

'You'll let me know if you find anything?' Wilna asks, her voice as light and hopeful as a helium balloon.

'Sure,' he says. 'You'll be our first call.' He passes the card to Wilna through the gate. 'The French aren't very organised,' he says apologetically. 'But please do call us if you hear anything.'

She smiles, fingering the magnetic strip on the ticket.

Ellen wants the bike to herself. She takes the dummy out of her mouth, storing it safely in her fist, and bites her sister's shoulder. Elani's face reddens as she screams. Ellen begins to cry too, perhaps to seem more sympathetic. With their upturned faces and open mouths, they remind me of cuckoo chicks.

'Look, I'm going to have to go,' Wilna says, shouldering the door. 'It was nice to meet you. I hope I'll hear from you soon.' She smiles again and shuts the door softly. From inside comes the sound of two sharp smacks and then silence, like the quickly hushed applause of someone who's forgotten that it's inappropriate to clap after hymns.

'*Allons-y,*' my father says, turning.

I sit on the pavement, legs stretched out, while my father photographs the flats behind me. A black van is parked in front of the off-licence, the air flickering with heat above it.

Jaco couldn't have been the one who told the police about my father. Wilna hasn't heard from him for over ten years and Naledi didn't find any activity since 1997, not a parking ticket or a speeding fine. No death certificate either, but that didn't mean much. That leaves Danie or Gideon.

My father drops his camera onto the driver's seat and sits down next to me, lighting a cigarette. '*Jissus,* those kids were gross,' he says. 'I'm so glad I wasn't around when you were that age.' He puts a hand on my knee and squeezes. 'Or I might like you even less than I already do.'

I pull my knees up to my chest and wave the smoke away from my face. 'Why'd you get her hopes up?'

'About the money?'

'It was cruel to do that.'

'No, it wasn't,' he says, exhaling. 'Her life is one long fucking disappointment because she makes it like that.'

'So it's her fault her ex was an army creep who disappeared and never paid child support?' I take off the scarf and wind it around my fist, a boxer's hand wrap.

'*Ja.*' He coughs. 'If you always pick losers, that's what you're gonna get.'

'Obviously I have yet to learn that lesson,' I say, nodding at him.

'You didn't pick me.'

'No.' I stand up and lean against the car to let the warmth of the metal seep into me. I can't seem to control my temperature.

'And I didn't pick you either,' he says. 'But you turned out all right.'

'Why, thank you.' The sarcasm doesn't register.

'You give me a bit too much backchat, but otherwise you're OK.' He stubs out his cigarette against the kerbstone. 'That'll do, pig.'

I shake my head. 'Fuck you.'

He stands up, dusting his hands against his shorts. 'No thanks.'

'You're disgusting.'

'But you love it. Why else would you be here?'

I straighten up, squinting. 'Not for you.'

'Why then?'

'Never mind.' I turn away from him, towards the passenger door.

'No.' He grabs my wrist. 'Why are you here, if not for me?'

Because when I'm with him, I don't have to think about what I've done. Or haven't done. He's the baddie in this story for a while, not me. And, if I'm honest with myself, my father is the one person who, if I told him what happened, would see no reason to feel guilty. No shades of grey or moral dilemmas. Black and white. That's what it always comes down to for him.

'Running away from your problems?' He tugs at my arm to get my attention. 'Or does being with me make you feel better about yourself?'

'No, that's what *you* do: run away,' I say.

He smiles and I can see he doesn't believe me. 'Maybe we're more alike than I thought, or than you'd like to admit.' He nods at the car. 'Let's go.'

'Yes, lets,' I say, walking around to the passenger side.

He opens the back door and reaches in, taking out a bottle of water in one hand, a beer in the other.

'If you're gonna drink, let me drive,' I say as he balances the can on the car roof.

'No chance,' he says, pouring water over his hands and rubbing them together. 'If I go to sleep now, I'll have nightmares about those kids.'

'They weren't that bad.'

'Yes they fucking were.' He rubs his hands on his jersey. 'All sticky and pink and stupid and with nothing interesting to say for themselves.'

'That's normal for that age.' I sit down in the car, pushing my bag onto the floor.

'It wasn't for me,' he says, getting in next to me. 'It wasn't for us.'

I don't like being included in this statement. 'Please, just shut up.' I bend forward and find my perfume. 'For once.'

'Why're you so grumpy?'

I spray the fabric at my armpits. 'Having you for a father will do that to a person.' Both wrists.

He waves the perfume away. 'Personally, I think I'm delightful.'

I close my eyes and lean forward so that my forehead touches the dashboard, but it's too hot and I sit up straight. When I was six, I left my first and favourite cassette – the *Dirty Dancing* soundtrack – in the back seat of my mom's car one morning. By that night, it'd warped, the tape crinkling in the sun. I hid it under my bed and pretended I'd gone off it, found something new to like.

'Are you still feeling sick?' my father asks.

I sit up. 'Just tired, although I can't see how.'

'Well, go back to sleep then,' he says.

'OK,' I say, just as tyres squeal somewhere down the road.

My father slots the key into the ignition, but the sound of advancing

121

sirens, the tones lower and faster than those in the UK, fills the car, pouring in faster and colder than the air-conditioning. He twists in his seat. 'What the fuck did you do?' he shouts.

'Nothing.' Blue and yellow lights flash across the windscreen as the car speeds up behind us. 'I swear I didn't do anything.'

'Duck!' He turns and slides lower in his seat so that he's crouching in the footwell, then grabs my cardigan and pulls me down over the gearbox and the fishing poles towards him.

'It's not gonna help,' I whisper, but I can't even hear myself over the sound of rubber wailing against tar. They must've turned back towards us or braked suddenly. He pushes his camera under the driver's seat as far as it will go.

Now there are two sets of sirens, keeping different times: the second one is longer, less urgent, but just as close. They've stopped moving, are right behind us, piercingly loud, and I cover my ears.

There must be a lot of police: I can feel them running towards us, their heavy boots pounding out yet another rhythm. One that I can feel in my chest.

My father grips the back of my neck and pulls me closer to him so that his mouth is in my hair as he speaks. 'I'm sorry,' he says. 'Don't believe what they say about me.'

The car darkens and I hold my breath. They're coming as much for me as for my father. Aiding and abetting is what they call this on TV.

But then it's light again and the policemen have passed us, shouting instructions to one another that I can't make out. Maybe they're waiting at the front of the car. I pull away from my father's grip, but he jerks me back towards him.

'Let me look,' I say, grabbing his wrist with my other hand and twisting the skin.

He shakes me off and I slowly raise my head, fingers sliding on the hot dashboard. I'm sweating now and my mouth is fuzzy. The fishing poles quiver above the car as I sit up.

'Be careful, Jo,' he whispers.

The radio filling half of my view, I can see the block of flats. Someone is leaning out of a window on the top storey, looking down at us. I push myself up higher. All I can see is the parched grass in front of the building, the open door of the off-licence. The policemen have disappeared.

'What is it?' my father asks, pulling at my sleeve.

'I can't see them.' I look around. 'But we can't get out.' A police car is parked behind us, blocking us in.

'Fuck.' He rests his head on the cracked leather. 'Fuck!' Punches the seat back.

'Stop it.' The fishing poles roll under me as I pin his arms into the seat. 'We're gonna be OK.'

Then, behind me, someone raps on the passenger window. I turn. It's a policeman, his gun shining at his side. He motions for me to roll down the window.

I nod. 'What did you do with your beer?' I ask my father through my teeth as I sit up.

'It's under the seat.' He looks only at the man on the other side of the glass.

'Open up,' the policeman says, trying the handle on the door.

I smile up at him. He's white and short, his neck thicker than his head. A rugby player, maybe. 'Sit up,' I tell my father and, before he can argue, I roll down the window. 'Sorry about that, sir,' I say.

'Out,' the policeman says. 'Now.'

I don't know whether to risk pissing him off by arguing. Behind me, I hear my father's door open. 'Sure,' I say, unlocking the passenger door. 'What's this about, officer?'

He backs away from the car as I step out into the dry heat. 'Turn around.'

'If you just tell me what—'

He moves towards me quickly, slamming the door shut with one hand, the other on his gun. 'I said, turn around.'

'OK,' I say, raising my hands and turning towards the car. My father's hands are on the sunroof, his chin tucked into his chest. Another policeman, this one tall and tanned, stands behind him, patting him down, looking for a gun. I haven't seen one, but that means nothing.

The policeman behind me pushes me against the car, kicking my legs apart with his boot. My father won't look at me.

'We haven't done anything wrong,' I say, as the officer's hands run down my back. I wonder if he can tell I'm lying, if my racing pulse will give me away.

'Turn around,' the taller one says to my father.

Hands over my breasts now, onto my stomach.

'What's this?' the tall one asks. I can't see what he's pointing at. Surely he's not that stupid, I think. He can't have a gun on him.

'To keep my money safe,' my father says, his voice and his head low. He's good at making himself seem small, despite his height.

The hands pause over the bandage on my leg before skimming up my thighs.

'He's clean,' the tall one says across the car.

The hands drop from my body. 'Her too,' the policeman says behind me.

'Can I turn around?' I ask over my shoulder.

'*Ja.*'

I look up, wanting to catch my father's eye, to decide on a story to tell them with just a glance, but all I can see is the back of his head. 'Thanks,' I say, pushing myself off the car.

'Jooster, bring him around here.' The policeman on my side keeps a hand on his gun. Jooster leads my father by the arm around the car. 'Do you have any ID?' The short policeman looks at me.

'Do you?' I ask, heart humming. My father leans against the bonnet next to me, his eyes on the ground.

His badge is blue and gold. 'Sergeant van Niekerk, with the Bloem-fontein Police,' he says.

'My driver's licence is in my bag,' I say. 'In the car.'

'Step away from the door, please, ma'am.'

Jooster watches us as Van Niekerk finds my handbag on the floor by the passenger seat and empties it out on the roof of the car. Jooster copies my father's details out of his ID book. 'I've never seen it spelled like that, with two *l*'s,' he says. There are no *l*'s in my father's name. I wonder what this alias is and how long he's been using it.

My father clears his throat. 'It's French, I think.'

Van Niekerk checks my make-up bag before opening my purse and finding my licence. He hands it to Jooster, who writes down my name and address in London.

'What're you doing here?' Van Niekerk stands with his thumbs through the belt loops on his trousers.

I take a chance. 'Visiting family,' I say, my palms sweating.

'Do you have family in this building?'

My father straightens. '*Ja*. Well, a family friend. Wilna Dell in 4D.' He's trying to help, but I think he just made this worse.

'I didn't ask you,' van Niekerk says, squinting at my father.

'He's telling the truth,' I say. Van Niekerk looks back at me. 'Wilna Dell.'

Constable Jooster writes down her name too before handing my licence back to the sergeant.

'How long were you visiting with Ms Dell?' Van Niekerk asks.

Shit. 'What's this about, Sergeant?' I ask, doing my best impression of my grandmother.

'Answer the question, Ms Hartslief.' *Ms* is an insult the way he uses it.

I look at my watch. It's twelve thirty. 'We got here at around eleven fifty, so…' I leave the sentence dangling in case my father has a way out of this I haven't thought of.

Van Niekerk smiles. 'That's not a very long visit with an old family friend, is it?'

'Her children had lice, so we couldn't go into the flat.'

He looks at my father. 'You accompanied Ms Hartslief up to 4D?'

'Yes, sir.' My father pulls his cigarettes out of his pocket. 'Do you mind if I…?'

'Go ahead,' Van Niekerk says, as Constable Jooster walks around to the front of the car to write down the licence number.

'What's your relationship, then?' The sergeant wags his finger at me and my father, but he's asking me.

'He's my driver,' I say. Jooster writes this down too.

'And where were you before today?'

Now they have our licence number, they'll be able to track us in grainy shots taken by roadside cameras. It's better not to tell too many lies.

'Langkloof,' I say.

'And before that?' Van Niekerk prompts. 'I want the full itinerary.'

'Oudsthoorn.' I won't admit to being in Dundee. 'Empangeni, Ladysmith – all around Natal.'

Van Niekerk flexes my driver's licence between his fingers; it bends so far I'm sure it will break. 'That's a lot of family friends, Ms Hartslief.'

I wonder if they'd been told to do this, when they arrested my father, to drag it out like this. 'Look, Sergeant—'

'Jooster,' Van Niekerk calls, 'radio in these two's names and see if anything comes up.' He spits onto the asphalt. 'And get someone to check with Ms Dell.'

'Yes, Sergeant,' Jooster says, turning away from us and walking up the bank of yellowed grass towards the flats.

My father is still, his hand cupped around his cigarette. I don't know what this means. If it means anything.

'Now,' Van Niekerk says. 'I wanna know, if all you're doing is visiting old friends, why you two hid from us.'

'We didn't hide,' I say, stalling. Part of me wants to tell the truth and get it over with. With every lie, the trouble I'm in gets deeper. 'We just ducked.'

The sergeant laughs. 'You ducked.'

'Yeah, in case bullets were gonna fly everywhere. The British Foreign Office has warnings about that kind of thing. It says South Africa is a very violent country.'

'Is that right?' Van Niekerk looks at my father for confirmation.

Nico puts his hands up in front of his chest, as though to defend himself from accusations of treason. 'Look, the lady pays me, so I do what she says. And she said duck, hey.'

The sergeant shakes his head. 'So you're telling me you have no reason to avoid the police?'

'No.' Our voices a chorus, my father and I agree for the first time, on a lie.

'Nothing to do with what was going down on the seventh floor?'

We all look up at the block of flats. 'What's happening on the seventh floor?' I ask.

'None of your business.' Van Niekerk adjusts the volume on the radio at his waist and it begins to buzz.

They're not after us. When I open my mouth to speak, my jaw clicks; I've been grinding my teeth. 'Nope. Nothing to do with that.'

Van Niekerk looks up at me from under his brow, perhaps sensing my relief, or just angry at my tone. 'We'll be confirming that with some checks down at the station,' he says. 'You don't mind, do you?'

My father stiffens, but the sergeant doesn't see it.

'No,' I say. 'Run whatever checks you like.'

He pulls the radio from his belt. 'Wait here,' he says, turning away from us, the radio covering his mouth.

My father drops his cigarette near where the policeman spat. He pushes himself up off the car and stretches. I wonder if he's looking for escape routes, somewhere to run or hide. I shake my head at him.

'Can I have my ID back, please?' I call after the sergeant.

Radio to his ear, he turns and holds the licence out. I'm careful not to take it too eagerly.

'*Ja*, OK,' he says into the static, as I repack my handbag. 'I'll be right there.'

Two policemen, puffy with utility belts, come out of the building, a young black man sagging between them, his arms behind his back.

The sergeant turns. 'Ms Dell has a different version of events.' He smiles. 'But we'll talk about this at the station.' They'll have the 'wanted' poster at the station, the one with my father's photo on it.

The policemen walk their prisoner through the car park to the police car parked behind us.

'I'm gonna go speak to her now,' Van Niekerk says. 'Give me your keys so I can be sure you'll be here when I get back.' He waits.

I nod at my father, who walks around to the driver's side, pulls the keys from the ignition and lobs them at the sergeant.

Van Niekerk catches the keys against his chest. 'I'll see you soon.' He turns towards the building, holstering his radio.

Behind me, the sirens start up again. My father and I turn to watch the police car pull into the road.

'What the fuck now, Jo?' he asks across the roof.

I drop my bag onto the passenger seat through the open window. It could all be over. Catching my father could make smug Van Niekerk's career. 'Open the boot,' I tell my father. I'm not ready for it to be over. Even if prison is the best place for him – and I'm not sure it is, not yet – he's not the only guilty party in this mess. We know where Danie lives and, if we're lucky, maybe we'll be able to track Gideon. They deserve punishment too. And when the time comes, I want to be the one to take him in. To ask Paul not to see him as a man outside of history but as a man who acted in the context of a culture that normalised violence and brutality. But I won't waste this opportunity: it's the first time I've had anything like a bargaining chip.

'Why? What's the plan, Jo?'

I wait for him to look at me. 'I'm not gonna let him take you in,' I say. 'But you will talk to the police about all this, eventually.' He frowns, but I cut him off before he can speak. 'It's that or we go down to the Bloem police station right now. Do you understand me?'

He looks over my shoulder at the block of flats.

'Nico.' I have his attention again. 'Do you understand me?'

He shakes his head. '*Jissus*, you're a drama queen. But *ja* – I get it.'

'Good,' I say, opening the passenger door. 'And one more thing.'

'What?' He watches the stairwell for signs of Van Niekerk.

'I want my stuff back. I could've turned you in so easily, but I didn't. I think I've earned it. Give back my phone and passports.'

He lifts his cap and wipes the sweat from his forehead. 'OK, fine. Whatever.'

'Good. Thank you.' I slide into the passenger seat and he bends down to look at me through the open window on his side of the car. 'Now hurry up – there's a second set of keys in my suitcase.'

He smiles. 'That's my girl.'

7

The Structure of Things Then

I dream of Maria, the hitchhiker my father photographed. I think it's Maria; she's covering her face but the same checked shawl is tattered over her shoulders. She lies on her side in the dust, covering her head with her arms, her knees to her chest to protect her softest parts. Men and women surround her, heavy clubs raised above their heads. Maria is already dead, the carved knots at the ends of the *knobkieries* shining and wet like plums.

I wake up sweating in the back seat, alone. The car is parked in the shade before a whitewashed colonial building, the gables over the front door rounded and ornate. I don't know how long I've been asleep. I woke to use the bathroom at a service station and then again a few hours later, when we were parked outside a shopping centre somewhere, my father asleep in the front, the seat tipped back as far as it would go, his profile just visible above the headrest. The car was stuffy, but I'd sat up anyway to check that the doors were locked and the windows closed. On his lap, his fist gripped around the handle, was a cricket bat. I'd fallen asleep again quickly, and woken only briefly I don't know how long ago when he prodded my leg with the bat. I check my watch. It's 3 p.m. Looking at the shuttered windows of the building, its thatched roof, I wonder for a second if we're back in the Karoo.

The breeze coming in through the sunroof is dry and shimmering. I open the door and step into the light, rolling my head from side to side to stretch my neck. My mouth tastes sour, but my water bottle has rolled under my seat and I'm too stiff to try to reach it. The back door is unlocked, so I pick through the rubbish in the back-seat footwell. Empty cigarette packets, sticky juice boxes. Fingernail-sized pieces of silver foil, stamped with tiny blue trademark signs.

The water is warm but I finish it, wishing for floss and my toothbrush. The parking area in front of the house slopes down into a dry riverbed. Weavers' nests hang like yellow teardrops from the branches of the trees along a stream. I have no idea where I am. I walk around to the back of the car to add my bottle to all the empties; the boot smells of stale beer and there are more empty cans than I remember him drinking. My father's rucksack and my suitcase are gone. I hurry back to the front seat. My handbag is missing. And so are the car keys. Laughter comes from inside the house, as though calling the rest of the pack to a stolen feast.

'Bastard.' I want to push the car into the riverbed and walk away. Instead, I check to make sure no one has come out of the house, then run back around to the boot. Three plastic bags are jammed into the centre of the spare tyre. He'll know I've been looking if I move them, but I don't care any more. I pull out the bags, searching through them for my phone, my purse, anything that I can take back, that I can keep in my pocket and make talisman. But I know he's probably already taken my things into the house. One bag contains a pair of still-damp swimming trunks; another, dirty clothes. The third holds three tennis balls, scuffed and fuzzy, four packs of cards, red rubber bands double-looped around them, and a few dice. Warm lager dribbles onto my hands as I move the cans to get to the coolbox and black golf bag. The ice he bought in Welkom has melted already, and the Castle Lagers in the coolbox are sweating; I rinse my hands in the water. I close the coolbox and push it to the other side of the boot to make room. But the golf bag is wedged into the back and I can't get it loose.

A wind pump turns slowly nearby, or someone opens a gate. Just the driver's seat left. I glance back at the house again before I open the door and sit down. The seat smells of his cologne, and my feet don't reach the pedals. In the utility box under the armrest in the front door I find only a folded Cussler paperback, a bottle of headache tablets and a pocketknife. The centre console is empty. I lean forward and feel under the seat. A cellophane wrapper, a comb. I run my hands over the levers that open the boot or adjust the seat and my fingers brush against something taped to the leather.

Kneeling in the dust, I look under the seat to see what he's hidden in the dark interior, the one secret I've discovered for myself, that he's not been able to reveal dramatically or feed to me like breadcrumbs. Under the seat, in a nest of sticky tape, is a gun.

I rest my forehead on the warm leather of the seat. I wonder if it was already there when the police pulled us out of the car, if this is why he's since caked mud in such thick layers over the licence plates. A dog barks somewhere. I sit back on my heels and look around for my own hiding place for the gun. Next to the house, a light blue horse cart with yellow wheels is mounted on two sleeper beams. Bunches of grapes are painted along the side of the cart. A sign is nailed to the spokes of the wheel: *Jacobsdal Lounging Lizard B & B*. We're still in the Free State, I think, but I'd need to check the road atlas. A shadow passes across the windows of the house. I get up, wiping the dust from my legs, and shut the car door as quietly as I can. I run to the boot and stuff the bags back into the tyre, piling a castle of crushed cans over them.

The front door opens just as I'm closing the boot. Two men come out onto the porch.

'Jo, love,' my father says in Afrikaans. 'Come meet Marius.'

I slide my sunglasses out of my hair and onto my nose. '*Ja*, sure,' I say, looking up at the men. My father waves me over, a whisky glass in his one hand.

I follow the trail the broken wheel on my suitcase has carved into the hard, splitting ground towards the front door of the house. My father steps down from the veranda and takes my hand. He turns back to the bald man on the porch.

'Marius, this is Jo.' He smiles. 'My beautiful wife.'

For dinner, we eat *bobotie* and saffron rice with raisins. The egg on top of the *bobotie* is undercooked. There is a seven-layer salad, and tomato chutney.

'Sometimes I get so sick and tired of "South African" food that all I want for supper is cheese on toast,' Marius says, filling his wine glass and then my father's. 'But the guests love it. So that's what Leonie cooks.'

Six of us are seated at the table: as well as my father and Marius, there are Marius's wife, Leonie, and two men, Rian and Colin. The two guests know the house, where the whisky and the ashtrays are, which chairs they can lean furthest back in. Colin is young – English-speaking, I think – and there is a comb sticking out of his sock. Rian is wearing a green rugby shirt with a white collar and cuffs and the number twelve in white on the back. Our hosts are more formally dressed, Marius in a checked shirt and cords and Leonie a long-sleeved dress with small brown flowers on it. The four men do all the talking, addressing only each other, except when Leonie asks if anyone would like second helpings. They speak in Afrikaans, and I can't follow it all.

Earlier, while Nico and Marius drank whisky on the porch, Leonie showed me to the room my father had rented for the night.

'Twin beds,' she said in English, smiling. 'He said you kick in your sleep.'

'*Dankie*,' I said. Thank you. The room was at the back of the house and looked out onto the pool. The cover was anchored with bricks, but the wind had tugged one corner free and I could see that they'd let the water go green.

'Do you have anything you'd like washed? I thought I'd check before I put Nico's things on.'

I shook my head, hoping he'd at least waited for her to offer to do his laundry.

'Dinner will be ready in an hour,' Leonie said. 'We have some friends coming from town.' She waited.

'Oh, of course.' I smoothed my hair. 'I'll change.'

She nodded, turned and shut the door. My suitcase was open on the nearest bed, my handbag sitting on the bedside table. I locked the door and kicked off my shoes. The peach-stone floor was warm and red beneath my feet. I checked my handbag – no sign of my passports or phone. I should have forced him to hand them over immediately outside Wilna's flat, even if it meant Van Niekerk came back before we could find the spare keys. At least the dictaphone was still there.

While the bath was running, I emptied my father's backpack onto his bed. Three pairs of socks rolled into balls, cargo trousers, one clean t-shirt. Another, bigger pocketknife than the one I'd already seen. His ID book – the real one – the plastic cover tacky and splitting at the corners. Condoms. Two cameras and a spare battery. I switched on both cameras. The most recent photos on the first one were of Maria. She looked embarrassed, unsure of what to do with her hands, the shopping centre in the background out of focus. I scrolled through the rest of the images, which were all of me. There were no pictures on the second camera. I wondered what had happened to the photos

I'd taken at the lodge, and those he took at Wilna's flat. He must have hidden a memory card somewhere. I'd just started unrolling a pair of his socks when there was a knock at the door.

'Jo, honey?' It was my father. He tried the door. 'Is everything OK in there?'

'I'm just getting into the bath,' I called as I repacked his bag and propped it next to the bed where I'd found it.

'OK.' The doorknob turned again, more quietly this time. 'Wear something nice to dinner.' The light under the door changed as he moved away.

'Fuck you,' I said to no one.

I sat in a shallow, hot bath, my left leg dangling over the side to keep the bandage dry. A series of studio photos of black men hung above the bath in gold frames. In the first, a boy posed with a football in front of a yellow curtain. In the second, a greying man in a hat and brown suit stood with his foot on top of an old suitcase, leaning forward onto his knee and smiling. In the third, a teenager in skinny jeans and sunglasses pulled his cap lower, his right foot in the air. He was dancing. The backdrop was a deep red, a stage curtain perhaps. When I sat up to get a better look at the photos, bath foam fizzed on my back.

The gun changes things, I thought. My father must be very scared of Gideon. But would he use it to save himself from prison; would he point it at me? I couldn't answer either of my own questions.

Leonie serves milk tart and coffee for dessert.

'Right, Jo,' Rian says in English. 'Nico here says you're a journalist.'

I nod, sipping at my coffee.

'What do you write about?' He looks around, getting the men ready for a joke. 'Clothes and make-up, I'm sure,' he says before I can answer. They laugh, my father more loudly than the rest of them. 'Just kidding, hey.'

They're my father's kind of people, the type who would call themselves *traditional* rather than what they really were, and he wants to be liked by them. Maybe I can use that against him.

'Of course,' I say, my mouth hidden behind my coffee cup. They think I'm smiling. 'Actually, I don't know if you've told them this, *liefie*,' I say, looking at my father, 'but I actually write about sex.' I put my hand on his arm. 'You know, different positions, reviewing sex toys.' I sit back in my chair, keeping my eyes on him. 'What was that one we tried the other night? That was just – wow. It just blew both our minds, didn't it, sweet cheeks?' I cross my legs, my dress rising on my thigh. I don't look to see who notices.

Colin clears his throat.

'Now Jo—' my father starts.

'I mean, I know we sometimes get a raw deal, us women, but multiple orgasms just about make up for that, wouldn't you say, Leonie?' I turn to look at her, doing my best to toss my hair.

She's staring at the flecks of egg on the neatly gathered knife and fork on her plate, her fingers fraying hair out of the long plait hanging over her left shoulder. I feel terrible for bringing her into it.

'Leonie,' Marius says, putting his hand on her knee. 'Why don't you clear the table?'

'Yes, Marius,' she says, rising.

'I'll help,' I say, putting my napkin on my plate.

She looks at me and I can see her face is flushed. 'No thank you, Mrs Roussouw.' She bends over my father to gather his knife and fork. 'You're the guest. You relax and enjoy yourself.'

I nod, pulling down my skirt and uncrossing my legs. 'OK, thank you.' I wonder if I should compliment the food again, but I settle for tracing Leonie's name across my thumbnail in shorthand. The outline is smooth and curved, with a sharp, straight tail.

Marius coughs and takes a sip of his whisky.

'Right,' Rian says, rolling the *r* and rubbing his hands together. 'Time for some poker.'

An antelope's head is mounted above the fireplace. I wonder if it too is just for the tourists. On the sideboard behind Rian, a stuffed rabbit runs in a glass case. Under the rabbit are rocks, brown ferns turned up at the edges and balls of green cotton wool. The animal's glass eye is angled so that it's looking over its shoulder, perhaps at the thing chasing it. A red bird with a black mask is perched on the ledge above the rabbit, tilted forward slightly to survey the scene below it. The windows are open and the room no longer smells of meat and smoke. It's cold and Marius has plugged in the gas heater. It gurgles in the corner. I stand in front of it, trying to warm my legs.

Leonie went to bed as soon as the washing-up was done. Women weren't allowed in the poker game, Marius said. House rules. But since I was a guest, I'd be allowed to watch. I poured myself some more wine and said I'd be honoured to. Marius glanced at my father before nodding.

'So where are you from, Nico?' Colin asks, halving the pack and shuffling the cards. The men look at my father.

'Pretoria,' he says. I wonder why he's lying. Maybe so he can bluff better later on. 'Anyone else from that part of the land?' he asks, stubbing out his cigarette. He looks at the other players, who shake their heads. 'Well, then, I can say it. It's a shithole.' He smiles, stacking his chips into three towers. 'I haven't been back in twenty years.'

'I was going to say, *bru*.' Colin cuts the cards. 'The Highveld is a shit place to be, and not just in winter.'

'What are you doing in Jacobsdal, then?' Rian slides one chip into the centre of the table for the small blind. Marius throws two into the pot.

'We're on our way to Nature's Valley,' my father says.

I turn to look at him.

'*Ja*, my family used to come down to Plett every Christmas, and I wanted to show Jo the place.'

I've been to Nature's Valley once before, to the beach house my father's parents owned on the Garden Route. It's where I spent my last week in South Africa, just after my mom died. I wonder if this is another bluff.

Staring at my father, Colin deals two cards to each player.

'Nature's is nice,' Rian says, looking at his cards. 'But Knysna is *lekker*. I once had a cherry in Knysna.'

'*Ag*, quit, man, you've had a cherry in every town,' Marius says. He reaches for his lighter.

'This one was special, hey,' Rian says, tracing patterns on the table-cloth with the bottom of his glass. 'The things she would let me do to her in the bioscope. *Sjoe!*'

My father laughs, picks two red chips from the stack in front of him and slides them into the middle of the table.

'Aren't you going to look at your cards, Nico?' Colin asks.

'Not yet,' my father says, interlocking his fingers behind his head. In his armpits, his jersey has felted into navy bobbles.

Colin shakes his head. 'It's your funeral,' he says, throwing two chips into the pot. 'Call.'

Rian slides another chip into the pile in the centre. 'Call,' he says, looking at Marius.

Marius knocks twice on the leg of his chair. 'Check.' The word is smoky.

Colin deals three cards face up into the centre of the table. Three red cards. I move back to the table and stand behind my chair.

Rian looks at his cards again. 'Check,' he says. He sits back, his hands behind his head, copying my father. The green of his rugby shirt is darker under his arms. Colin sees me notice the sweat patches and smiles.

'Rian here has eaten at just about every fish bar in town, if you know what I mean,' Marius says, leaning over to tap my father on the leg.

'What can I say?' Rian says. 'I'm a hungry man.'

They laugh, and Marius sits forward for another look at the flop. 'Raise you sixty,' he says, throwing three chips into the pot.

'Well, you know what they say, my *brus*.' My father rests a hand on his thigh while he checks his cards. The others wait. He scratches his cheek and throws three chips into the pot. 'The key to happiness is to live well, laugh often, *pomp* much.'

The men laugh. My father only smiles, rolling a chip between his thumb and forefinger.

They talk as though I'm not in the room. I'm used to this from my father, but I wonder if the others are doing it to make me feel uncomfortable, as payback for mentioning multiple orgasms.

'Call.' Colin adds three chips to the pile in the middle of the table. 'What about it, Rian?' he asks, reaching for the sugar pot on the sideboard. He sucks on a sugar cube.

Rian takes another look at his hand and shakes his head. 'Fold,' he says, pushing his cards to Colin, the tablecloth creasing under his hand. As he leans forward, a thin gold necklace with a horseshoe charm falls out of his shirt. He catches me looking. 'It's for luck,' he says, fingering the chain. 'Not that I need it.'

I sit down as Colin turns a fourth card face up onto the table. The queen of clubs.

Rian whistles. 'Fuck, man. I'm an idiot.' He's missed out on a good hand.

Marius smiles. 'Not so lucky now, hey, Rian?'

Rian sits back from the table, his arms folded, knees spread. 'That's not what your mom said last night,' he says.

A pause. They laugh.

Marius stands up to pour another round of whisky. '*Ja*, no, she told me you were a very considerate lover,' he says before sitting down. He looks at his cards and knocks once on the table. 'Check.' My father does the same.

'That's not what I've heard,' Colin says, knocking. He deals a fifth card into the centre of the table. The ten of hearts. 'Lena from the post office said you were nothing but a two-push Charlie.'

Rian bangs his fist on the table, his chips jumping slightly. 'It was at least three, hey,' he says, smiling. 'Don't be so full of vinegar, Colin. Just because you can't get a girl to milk you.' He moves the five cards on the table so they're equally spaced.

Marius sips his whisky loudly and coughs. 'Nice one, *bru*,' he says. 'I never want to touch milk again now.' He slides five chips into the centre of the table. 'Raise you a hundred.'

My father counts out ten chips. 'Call, and raise another hundred.' He sits back and lights a cigarette. 'So, Colin, do you have a case of the blue balls then?' he asks. I know now that he's going to win this hand.

I drain my wine glass.

Colin blushes. 'Shit, man, Rian,' he says. 'Look what you've started.' He taps the cards in front of him with two fingers. 'Call,' he says, pushing ten chips into the pot.

'Jeez, OK,' Marius says. 'Call.' He adds another five chips to the pile on the table.

'Before we show our hands,' my father says, raising his tumbler, 'I want to propose a toast to the best men in the Free State.'

The men lift their glasses. '*Tjorts*,' Marius says, nodding.

'And the bluest balls in all the land,' my father adds, looking at Colin.

'For fuck's sake, man,' Colin says, the heavy glass bottom on his tumbler loud on the table. 'I have a piece on the side. My balls are the opposite of blue.'

Rian slaps Colin on the back. 'What's the opposite of blue?' he asks. 'Red?'

'Empty,' my father says, and the men laugh.

I stand up. 'I'm going to bed.'

My father grabs my hand. 'So soon, sweet cheeks?'

'Yeah, the excitement is too much for me.' I shake him off. 'Thank you for dinner, Marius.'

He nods without looking at me.

I pick up my wine glass and go through to the kitchen, where I wash it up and leave it in the drying rack. Leonie has already laid out the mugs for her and Marius's morning coffee. The kettle is full. A cake tin next to the breadbin is covered in jacaranda flowers, gold showing through where the purple paint has begun to flake. I open the tin quietly; inside are rusks, irregular and homemade, jewelled with sultanas. There is a mug tree on the counter, and all the cups have 'Love Is' cartoon designs on the front. A naked little girl aims an arrow at a naked little boy; *Love is your secret weapon*, the mug says.

I run my fingers along the terracotta tile trim that lines the wall. The fruit bowl on the counter is full of light-yellow apples. I pick one and find a butter knife with a serrated edge in one of the drawers. They won't miss it. I hold the knife with the blade against my forearm.

When I return to the dining room, Rian is talking about the new waitress at the Wimpy. 'It was two inches of turf and then I hit the red soil,' he says, gesturing with three fingers. 'All women, even the black ones, are the same on the inside.'

My father shakes his head, laughing. Seeing him drunk and stooped over the table, his neck brown and beginning to sag, I think for the first time since he was asleep in the Langkloof Valley that I might be able to handle him and his mess. How much the knife in my hand has to do with this feeling, I don't want to know.

'So are you going to get your driving licence and marry her?' Marius asks, leaning forward to tap Rian's knee. I can't be sure but I think the slang is a South African spin on having to buy the cow to get the milk.

'It was nice to meet you,' I say from the doorway. Rian looks down. Marius waves over his shoulder as he deals the next hand. I turn and head for the bedroom.

'Are you joking me, *bru*?' I hear Rian say. 'I'm not gonna marry her – I was doing her a favour. I can ride any girl I want at any time I want. That's why they call me Michael Screwmacher.'

They laugh again.

Even though I know we have to be up early to drive to Danie's tomorrow, I can't sleep. The covers are pulled tight over me, tucked in deep under the mattress. The room is very dark, even with the curtains open, and smells of wood polish. I lie awake thinking about Paul, parsing our conversations for evidence that he didn't know Nico was my father.

The sky is sugared with stars. There's no phone here, nor in any of the rooms I'd stopped in on my way to bed, only in the dining room where the men would overhear me. I'm not sure who I would call anyway. I don't know any numbers off by heart, except my own, and my father has probably turned off my phone in case the chime of a text message coming in gave away its whereabouts.

I could leave tomorrow. Get him to stop at a petrol station, go inside and ask someone to call the police for me. Forfeit my passports and report my phone as stolen. A few hours at the British Consulate in Pretoria would be better than who knows how long with my father. But I'll give him one more chance, I decide: if Danie is nice and normal and has never heard of Gideon, I'll turn him in. I have to do it.

'Fuck,' I hear my father say outside the door. I'd thought about locking it, but I wanted to be up and out of here as soon as possible tomorrow, ideally without seeing Leonie. A half-drunk argument wouldn't help.

I switch on the dictaphone, which is hidden inside my handbag on the bedside table.

'*Jissus*, Jo,' he says in the dark. 'Turn on a *bladdy* light, will you?'

I pull an arm free of the cover and grope for the switch on the lamp. In the low light, I can see that he's eating a thick crust of brown bread. He sits down on his bed.

'Drink some water,' I say, sitting up and moving my bag onto my lap. I don't like being pinned under three taut blankets. Not when he's in the room.

'I'm not drunk.' A small piece of half-chewed bread falls out of his mouth as he talks. He laughs. 'You're such a joykill. But I won back your fishing pole money.' He pulls a wad of crumpled notes from his pocket and throws them onto my bed.

'Thanks,' I say, hugging my knees into my chest, trying to force the covers loose. Maybe I can use how drunk he is against him. 'Listen, why didn't you tell the police about Gideon when they questioned you?'

'Christ, really?' He lies back on the bed.

'I know some people who could help. Who would listen.' Quietly then: 'I could go in with you.'

He takes a bite of bread. I wait, straightening out the notes against my thighs.

'Why not?' I ask again.

'Because, Jo,' he says, sitting up, crumbs rolling down his shirtfront, 'I know what Gideon will do.' He looks at me and I can see his left eye is a little lazy when he's drunk. 'There's something I haven't told you.'

What a surprise, I want to say, but it will only distract him.

'When I moved down to Dundee, I was so happy. I could be outside all the time and I didn't have to be afraid of the army finding me and taking me back.' He puts the rest of the crust on the bedside table. It's wet at the edges. 'It was the best time of my life.'

A few days ago, this statement would've made me angry.

'But in late eighty-two, they did find me.' He feels for his cigarettes. 'Actually, Gideon found me.'

I slump back against the headboard. I already know this part.

'He just pitched up at my door one night, all smiley and friendly. Said that he'd tell the army where I was unless I helped him. Said he couldn't have planned it better.'

So the first time my father had seen Gideon again was not at the lodge, like he'd said, Paul's dad already in one of the rondavels.

I don't want to ask, but I know I have to. 'What did you have to do? What couldn't he have planned better?'

'His blue plan.' My father tries to push one boot off with his other foot.

More euphemisms. 'What's that?'

'His front.' He bends forward to untie his laces. 'He said he'd keep my secret if he could use the lodge in the off-season, posing as a landscaper or something.'

The room is too dark for this conversation. I want to see his face, whether he's actually sorry.

'I wish I could say I didn't know what he wanted to use it for. But with a guy like him, it was always going to be something bad. I think he was working for the security forces.' He throws his boots over his shoulders. 'When they pitched up with that black guy in the boot of their car the next April, I knew what his red plan was.'

'How long did this go on for?'

'Two winters. Then I left for the commune where I met your mom.'

I close my eyes. 'How many people?'

A pause. Drunk, it takes him longer to work out whether or not to lie. 'At least ten.'

'Jesus, Nico.'

He swipes at the bread and it falls to the floor. 'I made a choice. It was me or them,' he says, standing up. 'If I'd said no, you wouldn't exist.'

'Don't,' I say through my teeth. He's trying to make me complicit.

'But I want you to know that I never got involved with what they were doing. I stayed in the main house and I hardly ever saw them. They wanted me to help – to take photos to show the next guy they picked up, to scare him.'

'And did you?'

He stoops to pick up the bread, suddenly too close to my bed. 'At first. Just once.'

I wonder if this is why he's spent the rest of his life with his lens turned away from reality.

'Of the man they're accusing me of killing.'

'Do you know why they took him specifically?' I want to know in case I ever have to tell Paul.

'It was random. It could've been anyone.' The worst possible answer. 'As long as everyone in his township knew he'd been taken, that was enough. It was a message for the people there who were plotting against the government.'

Plotting is the wrong word. Maybe if he was sober, he would've chosen something else, I tell myself. 'So did you take photos of him?' I ask.

He shakes his head. 'I told Gideon I couldn't do it. He hit me and then he took my camera and all the film.'

Before he can complain about how much that camera cost him, I say: 'So this is why you can't tell the police about him – because you'd be an accessory to at least ten murders.'

He laughs. 'You think I'm the first oke who wants to turn him in or tell stories about him?' He walks towards the bathroom, one hand on the mattress to steady himself. 'Jaco wanted to go to the TRC about what happened up on the border.'

TRC. The Truth and Reconciliation Commission.

'He was just stupid enough to think that it was a good idea. I think no one's seen him for ten years because Gideon killed him. Probably with the army's blessing.'

'Why didn't you tell me this before?'

'I was worried about what you might think of me. Being scared like that.' He looks around as though trying to get his bearings. 'So weak.'

I rest my chin on my knees. 'I'd rather know you were scared – that you had some actual human emotion.' But, as ever, my father's humanity cost other people more than it ever did himself. I wish I didn't know how weak and selfish he'd been. 'Is this everything? Is there more you haven't told me?'

'This is everything.' He struggles to focus on me. 'Promise.'

'There were no records of a Gideon van Vuuren,' I say. 'Is there anything else you can remember about him?' But he's more interested in the clasp on his watch. 'Could you maybe remember his real name, if you thought about it really hard for a minute with your brain? Or would you get a nosebleed?'

He ignores me, untucks his shirt from his shorts and pulls it over his head. 'Gideon's probably seen the dead guy's photo all over TV by now.' Strapped around his waist is one of those security pouches the

Foreign Office advises you to buy before coming out to South Africa. 'That's why I want to know who told the police about me. Who's talking.' There are rectangular bulges in the shiny material of the front pocket, and the zip doesn't quite close. My phone, I think. My passports. The car keys.

'If I even go near the police,' my father says, 'he'll kill me.' He catches me looking at the pouch. 'Or he'll kill you.' He turns and closes the bathroom door behind him. For a long time, I can hear the water running.

8

The Greatest Weight

There's a one-armed bandit on the veranda. The cherries and watermelon wedges are dark, and the plug lies prongs-up on the bricks, kicked against the base of the machine. On the stool in front of it is an orange lunchbox filled with coins. We drink tea from glass mugs. Bougainvillea is stitched through the wooden trellises above us; faded papery flowers hang low over the table.

'The army was all hurry up and do nothing,' Danie says, pouring tea. 'We were always rushing and then waiting for the idiots to come inspect us.' He pushes the biscuits towards me.

Danie Strydom's house is the first stop we've made since leaving Jacobsdal early this morning. The B & B was sleep-quiet when we got up, but Leonie had left a thermos of coffee and a Tupperware container full of boiled eggs, sandwiches and rusks on the sideboard by the door. My father took out two rusks and put the rest in the coolbox. He was hung-over and didn't want to talk. He'd shaved badly and his beard was longer on one side than the other. He looked rough, as though he was losing feathers. We pulled out of the driveway as the church bells marked 8 a.m. Five blocks later, the bells at another church began to chime.

'This is why you should never let the church tell time for you,' my father said, unscrewing the cap on the thermos.

The Free State had passed me by in partial glimpses. *Welcome to Kimberley. Take the right-hand lane. This section of the N12 is financed by Old*

148

Mutual. Outside Klerksdorp, a brown sign with a white border listed the museums we could stop and visit, but never would. I watched the mountains play shadow puppets – here a crocodile, there a ribcage – with the rising sun.

I knew I'd missed my chance to get my phone and passports, to get away, while my father was snoring off the whisky. But he'd slept on his stomach, the buckle of the security pouch only just visible under his ribs. It'd shifted higher as he slept. Kneeling next to his bed, I could see that the belt was fastened so tightly around his waist that it had stuccoed his skin; there wasn't enough slack to pull the buckle closer. I'd thrown the blanket over him, then checked his clothes on the floor, but there was nothing in his pockets. Finally, I'd got back into my own bed, lying on my side, my back to my father, hands jammed between my thighs to warm them. Dawn was slow and grey, like fog moving in.

Danie was in the pool when I arrived. I rang the bell twice, waiting in front of the heavy green security gate, and switched on my dicta-phone, which was still in the front pocket of my handbag. His house was on the corner of a quiet street in what my father told me was a university town. Back in the fifties, no one was allowed to dance here, he said. Maybe the place had its own version of Kevin Bacon.

Danie came out into the front driveway in his Speedos and waved. I reminded myself to use his new surname, Gerber. Water pooled at his feet as he pointed a small remote at the gate. He was thin, very tanned and not much taller than me. The muscles in his thighs swelled out over his knees.

'Sorry – I thought you were coming later,' he said as we shook hands. He smelled of chlorine and his eyes were dark and deep-set, seemingly lidless. I wondered if, like a fingertip straying into every photo, he could always see his brow bone.

I smiled, pushing my sunglasses into my hair. 'Nope – 3 p.m.' We'd agreed to the time yesterday, when I'd called from the phone in the B & B dining room, my father standing behind me. I wanted to interview him about his company, I'd said. As an example of South African business success. I'd written down the time, drawing over the number until it was thick and the outline went through four pages.

'*Ag*, sorry, man.' He patted his stomach. 'But I gotta keep in shape, you know?' He was blocking the doorway.

My father was waiting for me in the car, parked around the corner. Even from this distance, with all the windows rolled up, I thought I could hear his Beethoven; my own version of the tell-tale heart. I needed to get inside before Danie went looking for the source of the noise.

I lowered my head slightly. 'I'd say you're doing a pretty good job of it,' I said, looking at him through my fringe.

He stepped aside and escorted me through the kitchen to the porch, his hand where I'd expected it to be, in the small of my back. The veranda stretched along the length of the house, a *braai* at one end and a table-tennis table at the other. The garden, green and neat, sloped down to the pool, which was steaming. We sat down and I pulled out my notepad and pen.

The maid, who was wearing a bright pink smock and a green headwrap, brought tea and a folded towel. Danie pulled on a pair of chinos over his Speedos. I complimented him on his house, feeling for the right questions to ask to get him to warm to me. He showed me pictures of the cheetahs his contributions had helped to be released back into the wild. I told him about my imaginary cat back in London. Eventually, I decided to risk it and asked whether he'd learnt his self-discipline in the army.

'We had inspections at 5 a.m.' He leans back, his chinos sitting low on his hips. 'So we had to get up at three thirty to start straightening things up.' He rolls the *r* in 'three', the one word so far that's given away the fact that English is his second language. 'Everything had to be perfect or we'd get punished. Sometimes we'd only been to bed at two, staying up to polish the floors in our socks. We called it the discotheque.' He laughs. 'Your bed was the main thing they could nitpick about. I used to put washing pegs under my mattress to stop it from sagging in the middle. Jesus, but the frames were old. And I'd put toothpaste on the edge of my blanket and iron it straight and stiff. Then I'd sleep on the floor.'

There's a black tattoo of a cross on his upper arm, the horizontal line curving downwards at both ends. To hide the crowbar? I think.

He leans forward. 'Is this the kind of thing you wanted?'

I dip a Marie biscuit in my tea. '*Ja*, it's perfect. Great background.' A half-moon of biscuit crumbles and silts.

He smiles. 'Rags to riches, hey? Self-made man?'

I lick a drop of tea from the rim of my cup and nod. It feels too obvious, to flirt with him to get him to trust me, but it seems to be working.

He clears his throat. 'Well, there's lots to tell, but it might not be quite suitable for a girl's innocent ears.' I raise my eyebrows. He looks down. 'Maybe later.'

'So when were you discharged?' I ask.

He pours soya milk into his cup. 'Early eighty-three. I'd done my two years.' He stirs and sits back. His nipples are stiff and almost white. 'Of course, they'd extended the military service so I had to do thirty days a year for the next eight years after that.' He shakes his head. 'I remember my twenty-first birthday. I had to do twenty-one push-ups on my fists that morning. And then go run ladder drills until I puked.'

'No cake and party hats?'

He laughs. 'That came later, after the vomiting.' He sips at his tea. 'The army was really good for me in some ways. The self-discipline, as you said.' He pulls in his stomach. 'I still do a thousand sit-ups every morning, and five hundred push-ups. But we had to take blue vitriol – copper sulfate? – so that we wouldn't miss, you know, women too much.' A fly lands on the biscuits. 'And ultimately, I think we all knew that on the border we were fighting against the people who were gonna be our government some day.'

I'm surprised he's mentioned the border so easily. I knew he wouldn't deny being in the army if I asked him: a man his age would have been conscripted. But given his change of name, I didn't expect him to be so open.

'How long were you up on the border?' I ask.

'Almost two years,' he says. 'In a way, I was glad for it. My family was back in Pretoria and really poor. Things were bad then. Being up there, I got danger pay, which meant I had more to send back to them.' He folds his arms and squeezes his right upper arm. 'The AWB would deliver a meal for my little brother every day. In the winter, blankets, sometimes shoes. That's how those fuckers tried to win supporters. Please excuse my French,' he says, smiling.

I try to remember what the AWB stood for. White-only states, I think. 'Don't worry about it,' I say, finding that his scorn for the AWB, no matter how calculated or expected in polite conversation, makes me like him more.

A small bird in a green cummerbund lands on the lawn. Its beak is long and slightly curved and its tail feather rustles in the grass.

Danie points at it. '*Jangroentjie*,' he says.

'Sorry?'

'A sunbird,' he explains, then goes on: 'All the mail I got from home was censored, but I could tell how bad it was for them. The army was really, for me, about money to send home to them. And to meet people who could help me get a good job after I left.' The bird freezes, listening or watching for something.

I want to hear more about the job he had, working for Gideon, but I know that will have to wait.

'We'd been preparing for the war all our lives,' he says. 'They got you early. Every Wednesday you came to school in cadet uniform, marching around and learning to shoot.' There are white marks on his arm where his fingers have been. 'All your life, you hear about the *terrs*, the black tide, the *rooi gevaar*.' The red danger. He looks at me, frowning.

I wait, not wanting to interrupt his train of thought. The bird's smooth head flashes in the sun.

'They show you videos of the enemy – communists and black guys – doing the most terrible things. And they tell you that you're fighting for your country, that God's on your side. That us Afrikaners are the chosen people and that the blacks are the Canaanites.' He closes his eyes. 'One of the guys told me that we all died up there in the bush. The lucky ones were those that never made it back.'

He pushes his chair back, standing up, and the bird is gone. 'Do you mind if I smoke?' he asks.

'Go ahead.'

He picks up my mug, the biscuit lining the bottom like the last jam in the jar. 'Actually,' he says, stacking the milk and spoons on the tray, 'is it OK if we go inside? It's getting a bit cold.'

'Sure.' I bend to pick up my bag, dropping my notepad and pen into it and slinging it over my arm. 'You are half-naked, though,' I say, standing up.

He laughs and the cups on the tray clink together. '*Ja, ja*, if I *have* to put a shirt on I suppose I will.' He turns and I follow him across the veranda and up the stairs into the house.

The kitchen is dark. Tiles the colour of chocolate icing line the walls behind the countertops. Stew simmers on the hob, and a flat glass dish full of vegetables waits on the counter under clingfilm. The ceiling is low, the skylight dirty. Bunches of keys hang from the coat hooks behind the door. There are burglar bars across all of the windows.

'I'll just say goodbye to Patience, and then we'll go to my study,' Danie says, carrying the tray past me into the scullery, where I can hear washing-up being done.

The clock on the wall, made out of an old brass pan, has stopped. There's a lettuce spinner in one of the three sinks in the kitchen. I wonder if all this food is for him, or if he's expecting someone later.

'OK,' he says, behind me. 'This way.' He shakes open a folded green shirt as he passes me and turns left into a passageway. 'It's still warm,' he says, pulling it over his shoulders. I can see the outline of his Speedos against his trousers, the fabric darker and still drying.

'I'm sorry if it got a bit heavy before,' he says, pushing the door to his study open with his foot and switching on the light. 'But you should know that every day I ask God for forgiveness for what I did in the army.' He shows me to an armchair in front of a floor-to-ceiling window that looks out onto the driveway. There are burglar bars here too. Even after almost three weeks in South Africa, the levels of security still surprise me. 'I guess I'll have to wait and see what He makes of me.' He puts a heavy glass ashtray down on the coffee table, then turns and opens a shallow drawer in the desk behind him, bending forward and reaching into the back.

Built-in bookshelves in a dark wood stretch along one wall of the room. The books are mostly electronics textbooks and computing titles, but near the window is one shelf of colourful spines. I step closer. Oscar Wilde plays, Beat novels and five Calvin and Hobbes books. Further along the shelves, an Escher print – a reflection of trees in a pond, leaves floating over a large catfish – leans against the books. It's my favourite Escher too, and I smile and sit down on the edge of one of the chairs, my knees together.

'I know they're here somewhere.' He talks into the drawer, moving notepads and boxes of paperclips. 'Smoking's just another thing I have the army to thank for.' He straightens. 'Aha!'

He turns, a packet of Peter Stuyvesant in one hand, matches in the other, and sinks into the armchair opposite me. His shirt is unbuttoned. The flame wavers as he lights a cigarette. I shake my head when he offers me one.

'I've tried to pay my dues,' he says. The words come out grey. 'I give millions of bucks to charity every year. I pay for my guys to finish matric and get their qualifications. That's why I live in Potch – so many schools here. But I know it's not enough. Nothing will ever be enough to make up for what we did.' He chews the inside of his cheek and takes another drag.

On the wall behind him, in square black frames, a younger, bearded Danie gives a cardboard cheque to a black man, smiles as he holds up an award, poses with a policeman in front of a 4x4.

'Do you want to talk about it?' I put my notepad on the coffee table. 'Like, just to talk, I mean. Not for the article.' I want to delay what I know I have to do.

He sits forward. 'Fuck man, this is gross,' he says, looking the ember in the eye. 'I just always think, maybe this time it will be different, hey.' He stubs out the cigarette in the ashtray.

'Can I ask you something?' I finger the studded wood at the end of my armrest.

'*Ja*, shoot,' he says, his elbows resting on his knees.

'What did you do when you came back from the border?'

He coughs. 'The army put me through university.'

'That was nice of them,' I say. His smile is more of a grimace. I doubt he'd laugh when he told stories about the border. 'You weren't tempted to work for the government when you got back?'

He frowns. 'I'm not sure how this is relevant?'

I don't want to ask, but I know I have to. 'What can you tell me about the lodge outside Dundee?'

He blinks. 'What?'

I clear my throat. 'Dundee.'

'I think you've got the wrong end of the stick here.' The butt smokes in the ashtray. 'I don't own any property in Natal.'

'I know that.' In the gloom of the study, I can get away with looking past him rather than at his face. I know I have to do this to help my father, and Paul, but I don't want to do this to him. I believe that he's sorry, that he's changed.

'Listen, I don't know what you're talking about,' he says, his eyes narrow.

'That's not what Hammerhead says.' I use Jaco's nickname to scare him, to show him how much I know.

His wet trousers make balloon noises as he moves forward in his chair. 'You're lying.'

Does he know that Jaco has disappeared? Or did they promise each other they'd never talk? 'Well then, what about Nico Roussouw? Or Van Vuuren?' I ask. 'You were on the border with them.'

He stands up and walks towards the window, snatching at the curtains to pull them closed. 'Did he send you here?'

'No.'

'Don't lie to me,' he says, stepping quickly across the room and grabbing both my shoulders.

Maybe I was wrong to think he wouldn't hurt me.

'I'm not.' I shrink back into the chair, but he jerks me towards him.

He must have seen my father on the news, realised the police were investigating the murder at the lodge. I try again, hoping he might know Gideon's real name. I've got nothing to lose now. 'What about Van Vuuren?'

This time, he lets go of my arms and buttons his shirt quickly, his hands shaking. Flecks of spit gather in the corners of his mouth.

'I'm sorry, I'm just trying to find out what hap—'

'Get out,' he says, stepping closer to me. The hem of his shirt is askew and there's one buttonhole spare.

'I didn't mean—'

'Just go,' he shouts, turning back to the window.

Patience shows me out, the gate at the end of the driveway already half-open. I steady myself against the garage door, trying to even out my breathing. When I look back at the study, the curtains are closed and motionless.

My father folds over the corner of the page he's on and drops the novel back into the cubbyhole. He points to a bottle of water at my feet. 'Just got it out of the coolbox if you want some.'

I shake my head. 'I'm OK, thanks – we had tea.'

'Tea?' He laughs. 'Not what I pictured.'

'That didn't used to be his drink?' I pull the seat belt over my shoulder and buckle it.

'Nah,' he says, pushing his hips up off the seat to search his pockets for the cigarettes.

'Well, a lot about him has changed.'

'Like what?' He opens the packet and offers me one.

I shake my head. 'Like everything. He knows there's no way to ever make up for what he did.'

'I think we're all in that position,' my father says.

I turn to look at him as he lights a cigarette between his thumb and forefinger. He closes his eyes as he inhales. It's the first time he's ever acknowledged that he has something to make up for. Maybe this is the one thing – the best and the worst thing – that we have in common.

'But I feel I should point out that me and Danie are not even in the same league,' he says, opening the sunroof as far as it will go. 'My sins are minor, comparatively.'

I look away. 'Whatever.' The tips of the fishing rods shudder in the wind.

He sighs. 'OK, let's make a deal. The whole I'm-a-bad-dad thing is off the table as of now. I admit it and will always feel guilty about it. But I want a relationship with you now and I don't know if we can do that if we keep having this same fight.' He puts his hand on the back of my headrest. 'Deal?'

'Maybe,' I say. Two weeks ago, this would've been all he needed to say. It probably would've made up for everything. But now, I've lied to Naledi and the police for him, been made to confront Danie alone. I know too much about my father, too much about what he needs from me, for it to be that easy. 'We'll see.'

'Good enough for me,' he says, taking a drag. 'So what else did he say? Anything useful?'

The smoke is making me thirsty. I decide not to tell him I used his name. He doesn't know I taped the conversation. 'I asked him about the lodge—'

'What did you ask? Exactly?'

I open the water bottle. 'I just asked him to tell me about it.' I half expect him to make some crack about my sharp interviewing skills. 'An open question to get him talking,' I say defensively.

'And?' he asks as I drink.

'As soon as I even brought up Jaco's name, he flipped.'

'What do you mean, flipped?'

'He kicked me out of the house,' I say, screwing the cap back on. 'He seemed really scared.'

My father grunts in disbelief.

'I don't think he's said anything to anyone about what happened at the lodge,' I say, finding myself wanting to elaborate. 'He's too scared.'

'But did you get anything out of him about who could've gone to the police?'

I shake my head.

'Great.' He throws his cigarette out of the sunroof and it lands on the bonnet of the car. 'Well done, Jo.' He pounds his fist against the steering wheel.

'What was I supposed to do? Get him to confess to it and promise to go to the police?' I hold my handbag tighter.

'*Ja*, actually. That's exactly what you were supposed to do.' He picks up the cigarette packet in his lap and throws it at me. It hits the window behind me harder than I thought it would. 'You're fucking useless, you know. I should've done it myself.'

Just knowing that the knife I took from the B & B is in my bag makes me calmer. 'Why didn't you?' I ask.

'Because I thought for once I could trust you not to be a moron. That you'd be a little bit more like me,' he says, spitting as he talks. 'And less like your fucking mother.'

'Fuck you,' I say from between my teeth. I should've let the police take him, back in Bloem. I thought I knew what I was doing, but I've been lying to myself.

'Shut up and let me think.'

When I look at him now, all I can see is a man who let at least ten others die so he wouldn't go to prison. A man who lies for fun, who holds his own daughter hostage on an aimless trip through South

Africa, every doubling back like water spinning down the drain. Even if I can help him, the two of us together like this are headed only for disaster. He's asking too much of me, and I of him. He can't be a father to me, not in the way that I want, and I'm beginning to hate him for that. Beginning to hate myself for going along with him, for lying so easily on his behalf. For thinking that I could save him.

'No,' I say, opening the door before he can lock it again. 'I'm finished.'

He grabs my arm below the elbow. 'Jo, don't be an idiot.'

'Give me back my stuff.' I dig my nails into his fingers and push his hand off.

He lets go and sits back. 'Come on, Jo. Calm down.'

I look at him and can see he doesn't believe I'm serious. 'Give it to me now or I'll go back to his house and call the police.' I step out of the car and stand up.

He leans forward and looks up at me. 'Stay right there, you stupid bitch.'

'So much for a relationship.' I slam the door in his face and walk quickly to the back of the car. I hear his door open as I feel for the button that will release the boot.

'Please, Jo, don't do this,' he says, walking towards me.

The boot pops open. 'Take your stuff,' I say, pulling at the handles on the plastic bags and dropping them on the road. 'Take your fucking coolbox and your fishing rods and go.'

He grabs my wrists again. 'I'm sorry, OK? I'm sorry.'

'I don't care.' I pull back, but he holds on, stepping closer so that I can smell the beer on his breath.

'What can I do to make this up to you?' His breath comes in short, phlegmy rasps. 'Anything.'

'Turn yourself in,' I say. He lets go of my wrists. 'Tell them about Gideon and the lodge.'

He shakes his head. 'I can't do that, Jo.'

'Goodbye, then,' I say, pulling his rucksack towards me.

He pushes me away from the car, hard, and my heel catches on the kerb. I drop my bag and stumble backwards onto the pavement, twisting to break my fall with my right hand and hitting my coccyx hard on the concrete. He runs his hand over his beard.

'I'm not scared of you.' I try to control my breathing to stop myself from crying. 'Hit me if you want, lie down and beat your fists on the ground like a fucking five-year-old, I don't care.' I sit up, blowing on the graze on my hand.

'Now is not the time for you to talk, it's the time for you to listen.' He walks towards me, slowly, as though he's worried I'll bolt. 'You think I like traipsing around this godforsaken country with you?' He offers his hand to help me up, but I ignore it and he cracks his knuckles against his hips. 'I don't, but keeping you close is the only way to keep you safe. Gideon will kill us both right here.'

I push myself up off the concrete with my left hand, keeping my other arm close to my chest. 'Where is he, then? Hiding behind a bush waiting to jump out?' I sidestep my father and bend to pick up my bag. 'You keep the car. And my phone.' My hands shake over the zip.

He steps past me to pick up a plastic bag of dirty clothes and hits the licence plate with it. 'Do you think I'm fucking joking?' The bag is splitting at the bottom. 'He killed your mom!'

I blink. 'No,' I say, stepping back. 'It was a car accident.'

'It was a warning to me, not to talk to anyone. I was seeing a shrink at the time and he found out.' He drops the bag into the boot. 'You were supposed to be in the car. That's why I let your grandmother take you out of the country.'

He's lying. He has to be. 'I don't believe you.'

'Gideon fucked with the car – probably the brakes or something

– and then he chased her.' He takes off his cap and I can see his eyes, but I can't read them. 'The day after it happened, there was a letter in my postbox from him, telling me that if I didn't keep my mouth shut, it'd be you next time.'

The blood in my ears makes his voice sound like it's coming from far away.

'I'm so sorry,' he says.

The electric gate in front of Danie's garage starts to open. My father looks over his shoulder. 'I'm gonna go check if he's running. Will you get back in the car, please?'

I hold my bag in front of me.

'Please, you have to be here when I get back,' he says, putting on his cap. 'I don't wanna lose you again.'

Before I can answer, he turns away from me and runs towards the house, keeping low. I wait until he's fifteen yards away and hurry to the driver's seat. The door is still open, but the keys are gone. I kick the cubbyhole in the door and his novel falls to the floor.

'Fuck,' I say, hoping the keys give him away, jangling in his pocket as he crawls through the bushes near the gate. I look back at the house; I can't see him. The knife isn't enough. I lean forward, one hand on his still-warm seat, and reach into the footwell. The gun is still in its honeycomb of Sellotape, pointed towards the back seat. I find the grip and pull downwards until the tape begins to come away from the seat.

I don't know who it's for yet, but when it comes I'll be ready. I slide the gun into my bag.

9

The Transported

The bracelets are on special: two for one. They're stacked over the necks of brown beer bottles with the labels scrubbed off. I lift a giraffe-print bangle and try it over my hand, but it's too small. I try another, in zebra print. I want to take something back with me to the UK, some sign that I'm not English. But the zebra bracelet, an ear and snout etched into the wood, won't fit over my thumb and I leave it on the counter, turning to look at the small shelf of guidebooks and maps above the ice creams. The spine of *102 Things to Do on the Garden Route* is creased.

At the end of the aisle, a hand-painted sign promises homemade fudge and chocolate tiffin. I pick up a packet of fudge. Made in the kitchen of Mrs Nel of Coldstream, the label guarantees, next to a clip-art oven glove. A ribbon gathers the green cellophane, the ends of which have been curled with scissors. The whole thing looks like an anaemic plastic pineapple.

I brushed my teeth in the service-station bathroom. Beer had helped me sleep and I woke at dawn still in the front seat, holding my bag against my chest. My father was pulling at his leg hairs to keep awake as he drove, and I pretended to doze off again, listening to the road and trying to work out what to do. By the time the signs started promising bungee jumps in the Tsitsikamma Forest, I knew.

My father is at the till, paying for water. Over the tannoy, the DJ is asking listeners to call in and say which South African sportswoman they'd most like to see naked.

'Can you turn it down?' Nico asks the man in the green cap behind the counter. 'Jo,' he calls. 'Do you want anything else?'

I look up from the fudge. 'Yes – some Marlboro Lights.' I want a brand I recognise.

He shakes his head, disapproving of my choice, turns and points to the display behind the teller.

I've been at this service station before. Two hundred yards from here is the bridge over Storms River. You can't see the mouth of the river from there, just a blue haze of sea evaporating into the horizon. We'd stopped here, my father and I, the Christmas I'd spent with him just before I moved to the UK. The week in the family house was his one condition for signing the papers that let my grandmother take me out of the country. In a box under my bed in London I still have the photos he took. Me in front of a statue of a seal. Me waving from the rope bridge over the mouth of the river. A snake, its head held high out of the water, swimming alongside the boat. One of the two of us giving the thumbs-up, my father's face only half in frame. I don't remember taking the photos, or anything else about that visit, other than the feeling of surreality that was draped over every day like a mosquito net, compounded by the strangeness of spending that much time with my father. And waking up every morning surprised not to be in my own bed with the sounds of my mom in the bathroom getting ready for work. Even at the time, I'd known I wouldn't want to remember much about the visit. For once, my brain had complied.

'Come on,' my father says in my ear. 'Let's go watch the water under that bridge.'

'Did you know that some tourist was killed here when he was rubber-tubing down the river and a bushpig fell off the cliff onto his head?' my father asks.

I laugh, knowing he wants me to. We're standing halfway across the bridge on the narrow hard shoulder. A truck speeds by behind us, honking.

'How much would you pay me to take a piss from here?' my father asks, leaning out over the guardrail.

The forest on one side of the ravine is blackened. Even the rocks are scorched. I wonder how they kept the fire away from the road.

'Feeling better?' I didn't count the empty, crushed cans of beer in the back seat; only four of them were mine, and I knew he'd carried on long after I'd fallen asleep.

'What?' He straightens. '*Ja*, sorry. I felt like a dead dog's asshole this morning.'

I point at the empty trees. 'For the veld fire project?' I ask. Last I knew, he was planning to put together a book of photos of wildfires as some sort of political comment. He'll like that I've remembered, that I called it a *project*.

'Nah, I've given up on that idea.' He slides his sunglasses from his nose and hooks them onto his shirt.

'Why?' I ask. 'I thought that was the plan.'

'What's the point?' He shrugs. 'What can art show you that you can't see in the shops or on TV?'

'Who are you quoting?'

He reaches out and ruffles my hair. I duck my head, and he takes his hand back to the guardrail, looking at it as though it were a naughty dog that was supposed to wait outside the post office for him but had run off to watch rotisserie chickens instead.

He leans forward on his elbows and looks down. 'Do you remember when we came out here last time?' He looks away, I can't see where. 'That was one of the best weeks of my life.'

A car passes behind us in the middle of the road. My skirt moves in its slipstream. 'It was just after she died.'

'*Ja*, no, of course,' he says, straightening. He spits his gum into his hand and drops it into the ravine. 'It would be so easy for you to push me,' he says, turning to face the road. 'Here – I'll make it easy for you.' He stands against the guardrail, his arms held out at shoulder height. 'All your problems would go away.'

I step back into the road. 'I'm not gonna push you.'

'Come on,' he says, leaning back. 'You won't even have to push very hard. I promise I won't fight it.'

'No.' A jeep speeds by in the far lane. The driver shouts at me but I can't make out the words over the noise of the engine.

'I'm ready.' My father closes his eyes. 'Do it!' he shouts.

I wait. There are cars coming, on this side of the road. They're already honking their horns.

My father opens his eyes, lowering his arms. 'Chicken.' He smiles.

I wait, the cars just fifty yards away. This isn't part of my plan, but it'll work.

'Get out of the road, you moron,' he says, stepping forward to grab my shirt and pull me back onto the hard shoulder as the car speeds past behind me, the driver leaning on the horn. We wait for the caravan to pass, my father still clutching the shirt at my stomach in his fist, his breath coming fast.

'Why are we going to Nature's?' I ask. I can see a fleck of chilli between his teeth.

He sighs, letting go. 'I know there's a lot of stuff you don't under-stand right now.'

'I'm not twelve any more,' I say, smoothing the wrinkles in my shirt. 'You can't just expect me to drive around with you forever, never knowing where we're going or why.' I decide to take a chance. 'You owe me the truth,' I say, watching for a reaction.

Instead of laughing at my overwrought sentences, he looks serious. He feels guilty, I think. It's enough. I turn and begin walking towards the service station.

'Jo, wait,' he calls.

I hesitate but keep walking, hoping he'll interpret it as my attempt to avoid getting reeled back in again.

'I've thought about what you said,' he says, running up behind me. 'You're right. I'll go to the police. Just please wait, hey?'

I turn to face him. 'You're lying.'

'Not this time.' He squints, shielding his eyes from the sun with his left hand. 'Later today, after we've gone to the house in Nature's, we'll go to the station.'

'Do you promise?'

He nods. Something flashes in the ravine below us.

'Why now?'

'I think Gideon's the witness. He dobbed me in to watch me squirm, to make me run. But I'm tired of running now. And I'll probably be safer in prison.'

I wait, hoping for something more.

'Do you think I could go into witness protection?' he asks. 'That'd be fun.'

My father opens the toilet door, his shorts and jersey in one hand. He drops the clothes onto the rocking chair in the corner of the living room. He's changed into olive-green cargo pants and a khaki utility jacket over long sleeves, and evened out his beard. In the middle of the room, five black and red wooden pelicans turn slowly on a mobile, the white feathers of their wings ragged and curling.

'Next time you see me, I'll be in an orange jumpsuit, so take a good look.' He rubs his hands together and crosses the wood-panelled living room, smiling. 'Do you remember any of this?' he asks, stepping out onto the balcony.

I stub out my cigarette against the railing and cup the butt in my hand. 'Some of it.' I point at the neighbour's house, a yellow and grey wedge with triangular windows. 'That.'

He laughs. 'Anything else?'

I shake my head. I don't want to remember.

The balcony wraps around three sides of the house. White paint is peeling off the banister in large islands. The plastic roofing is missing in parts and a barbecue near the front door is rusted. 'Should we be out here? Someone might see.'

'I called ahead and the woman who rents the place out is in George today, so we're OK,' he says, pushing the glass sliding door open as far as it will go. Across the road, a wooden house huddles among trees, its windows boarded up. A potholed tennis court is dark yellow with dew. Beyond that is the dune, which moves every year, my father says. It's unmarked and white as butterfat. An old black pick-up passes the house, the driver flickering his lights at us. As we drove along the lagoon earlier it overtook us on the dirt road, shooting stones up at our windows like children spitting watermelon pips. We watched it rocket through the dust.

'Why do you still have a key?' I ask.

'Because I like to be able to get into my own house whenever I want to.' He turns and leans back into the house. 'Duh,' he says, lifting wooden wind chimes out of a bowl on the table by the door.

'You're like the poster boy for the nineties.'

'Please – duh is forever,' he says, hanging the chimes from a hook above him. 'There.' We watch them, waiting for a sound, but the air is still. Hadedas on the grass play join-the-dots with molehills.

'Come on,' he says. 'I want to show you something.'

There's too much furniture in the living room, all of it cane, the cushions covered in a faded tan and green pattern that looks like mould. 'I like what you've done with the place,' I say, realising as soon as I've said it that it used to be something that only people on TV say, like *This is me*, or *I'd like that*. Beach chairs are folded under a duck mobile. I pull the string hanging from its fat stomach and its wings flap.

'*Ja*, I know.' He looks around. 'Everything in this room is basically crap, so that it doesn't matter when kids wipe their snot on the furniture.' He pushes a hanging basket and it swings on its braided white ropes. 'Anyway.' He opens a door and leans over the threshold into the darkness to feel for a light switch on the wall. 'This is the dining room. Maybe this will be more to your taste, madam.'

The dining table is under a heavy black drape. I kneel and lift the old curtain; the table is made of yellow-wood and covered in a plastic film to save it from jam and vinegar.

'This was Ma's,' he says, smoothing a bubble in the plastic. 'I don't care who the woman rents the house out to, but this is the one thing she knows to stress about.'

'Why's it covered?' An orange conch shell is balanced on the sideboard, its pink lips pointing up at the ceiling. Next to it is a stack of board games. The door to the kitchen is shut, the keys on a purple tag in a bowl on the sideboard.

'There's too much salt in the air.' My father pulls the drape back over the table. 'Too much light. The sun bleaches everything if you're not careful.'

I try to imagine the colour evaporating out of wood and linen but can only picture cartoon glass jars turning white, shivering with fear as though a hammer had just sauntered into the room.

'So when I put the house up for rent, I worked out a system with the agent.' He straightens the Monopoly box. 'Three days before the guests arrive, she's supposed to come scoop spiders out of sinks, turn on the gas, fetch water from Plett.'

'Why water?' I ask, walking back out to the living room.

'The water here is too brown for most people,' he says, turning off the light. 'It comes from a borehole – it's clean, but they're sissies. They don't even want to wash their clothes in it.' He closes the door behind him. 'She emailed me to say that one guest had actually complained that it upset his stomach.' He shakes his head. 'My fist in his stomach would upset it more.'

On the trolley against the wall is a terracotta pot full of shells. I pick up a piece of dried coral, shaped like a wishbone, expecting it to smell of the sea. There's nothing salty to it. 'Can I keep this?'

'Take anything you want,' he says. 'It'll all be yours someday anyway.'

I tuck the coral into my handbag.

'This way,' he says, turning towards the stairs. 'I dunno if you can remember, but this staircase used to be full of photos of the Roussouws, back to the early nineteen hundreds.'

'I'm not sure,' I say, following him down the creaking stairs. 'Maybe.' The wood panelling on the walls of the staircase is lighter where the frames used to hang.

'I used to sit for ages when I was small, looking at the photos,' he says, tracing his fingers along the edges of a rectangle above the bottommost step. 'Trying to get up these *bladdy* stairs without waking Ma and Pa.' He sighs. 'Anyway.' From the top of the stairs I can see his hair is starting to thin at the crown.

'It must've been really nice,' I say. 'Coming here every Christmas.'

'Don't say "nice",' he says and jumps from the third-last step down into the hallway. 'But yes, it was.' He looks up at me. 'I'm sorry you didn't have that.'

I nod, biting the inside of my cheek. 'Me too.' We get on better when I lie to him. I trail my fingers over the wooden panelling and shake my head. 'Get out of my way, old man.' I swing my arms and bend my knees, ready to jump.

'Take off your flip-flops or you'll kill yourself.'

I straighten up as he turns and disappears from my view. 'Right.' I wait a few seconds, then climb down to the last step as quietly as I can. I jump from there, landing noisily. 'Ta-da!' I call. 'From two steps higher than you.'

No answer.

The walls down here are white and made of plaster. It seems like a different house. A series of drawings hangs in the hallway in bronze frames. Black women in traditional dress, their heads swaddled in fabric. One holds a baby to her naked breast; the other, an empty pail. There are no blues or greens in the sketches.

'Jo?' my father calls. 'We're leaving soon so pee now or forever hold your peace.'

'OK.' The bathroom, with its mustard tiles and yellow sink, is at the end of the corridor, past the room my father's voice came from. Through the gap between the door hinges, I can see him listening, waiting for me to pass. He's trying to hide something from me.

I hurry to the bathroom and, without going in, close the door loudly, hoping my good-daughter act has made him less vigilant. Hugging the corridor wall, I edge back to the bedroom, where I can hear my father moving something heavy.

My eye to the half-inch sliver between the door and its frame, I watch my father step backwards out of the wardrobe, lifting a dark brown speaker. He places it on the floor, looks up, listening, and I hold my breath. He pulls a pocketknife out of his utility jacket and moves around the back of the speaker. I lean closer, changing the angle, to follow him. He flicks open a short, thick blade, which he slides into the gap between the speaker and its backing. The wood pops free and he places the board somewhere I can't see, before bending forward and lifting a pencil tin and a plastic Checkers bag from inside the speaker.

I can't risk watching any longer and creep back along the hall. The bathroom doorknob turns silently. I flush the toilet without lifting the seat. I wonder what he could be hiding in the pencil tin. What would fit in it – a key? A ticket somewhere? Would a passport be too wide?

Water sputters into the sink.

A list of names? And in the plastic bag, perhaps, faded passbooks, bundled in date order, once used to restrict the movements of black people in apartheid South Africa – now all that's left of the men who were taken to the lodge.

I open the bathroom door and cough so my father knows I'm coming. 'In here,' he calls.

There are two single beds in the room, pushed against opposite walls. Between them, in front of the window, my father leans against a chest of drawers. The speaker, the pencil tin and the plastic bag are gone.

'This used to be my room,' he says. 'It was very different then, but you get the idea.' He knocks on the chest of drawers. 'I kept my comics in here.' He turns and holds open one curtain. Light trips in over plants – succulents and fynbos – and sprawls into corners slightly coloured. Beyond the greenery, the car shimmers in the heat. 'I used to climb out the window sometimes to meet my friends.'

I stand in the doorway, waiting.

'But what I want to show you is this,' he says, walking across the room to the built-in wardrobes. He opens two of the four doors before he makes a show of finding what he's looking for. 'By George, I think we've got it.'

I step into the room and join my father by the wardrobe. He's put the speaker back inside it. The front of the speaker cabinet is made out of fabric. 'It looks like tweed,' I say, scratching it with a fingernail.

'Be careful,' he says, shouldering me out of the way. 'This is older than you are and way closer to my heart.' He smiles and reaches into the wardrobe, past the speaker. 'Sit down.'

I stand in the middle of the room. Both beds are covered in plastic. I wonder how many children have woken up in puddles here, their parents quickly awake and having to help them wipe down the mattresses and find clean pyjamas.

'This wardrobe is my secret hiding place,' he says.

Another half-truth. I wonder what he'll pretend to discover.

'Man, but it's stuck in there good, hey.'

I want to tell him that he's overdoing it.

'Here we go.' He backs out of the wardrobe and lowers a familiar-looking plastic bag onto the floor. The pencil tin is silver, with a navy lid. Up close, I can see it used to be a maths set. Why send me to the bathroom when he was going to let me see what he was looking for anyway?

'What is it?' I ask.

'My treasures,' he says, sitting down on one of the beds.

I sit down next to him. 'Can I see?'

He opens the lid. Inside are four marbles, two pieces of frosted glass, a small metal ruler and a sea-urchin shell.

'My Superman.' He holds up a cat's-eye marble. Red, yellow and blue veins curve through the centre of the glass. 'I won a lot of games with this one.' He looks at me. 'I even stuck it up my nose a couple of times.'

'Galaxies are my favourite,' I say, pointing at a speckled marble.

He picks up a piece of orange frosted glass and rubs it between his fingers. 'I found this on the beach here. Orange is the rarest colour for sea glass. Only one in every ten thousand pieces is orange.'

'Why do you have the shell?' It's light green and cracked, with white bumps where its spines used to be.

'Just because.' He puts the marble and sea glass back into the tin and closes the lid. 'It used to be alive. And now I have it. But it's yours if you want it. All of it, I mean.' He balances the pencil tin on my knee. The silver plating is coming off at the corners.

'Thank you.' I put both hands over the tin and pull it into my stomach. 'Thanks.' I know he wants this to be a moment I'll remember, but all I can think about is what he told me about my mom on the street outside Danie's.

'No problem.' He stands up. 'And I'll give you your phone back – it's in the car.'

'Really?' I look up at him and he winks at me. I'm grateful to him for a second, before I remember that there's nothing to be grateful for.

'Actually, these are the real treasure,' he says, fetching the plastic bag.

'Let me guess – a domino set?' I say lightly. Matching my tone to his is making me tired.

He shakes his head as he unties the knotted plastic.

'Pebbles?' I squeeze a dent into the pencil tin.

'No.' He lowers the bag for me to see. Inside are at least twenty inch-wide gold coins. He reaches into the bag. 'One-ounce Kruggerrands,' he says, handing me a coin.

'How much are they worth?' On one side is a springbok; on the other, the profile of Paul Kruger, state president of the South African Republic, enemy of the British during the Second Boer War. Here, finally, is something I remember from history class. I think the coins were banned in the West as part of the sanctions against South Africa during apartheid.

'Depends on the price of gold,' he says, knotting the handles of the bag again. 'More than a thousand bucks each, at least.'

At last, I think: the real reason we're here. 'What do you need these for?' I ask, holding the coin up to him.

He shakes his head. 'That one's yours. For all the money you've lent me.'

I don't want it, but I don't want him to know that. I add it to the pencil tin; next to the sea glass, the coin looks gaudy, like a shopping-centre Christmas decoration.

'I need them to pay for my defence.' He loops the bag over his wrist.

'Where did you get them?'

He rolls his eyes.

'Your lawyer will want to know,' I say.

'In that case, I'll tell him. Now, let's get out of here. Will you lock up this room for me?' he asks, lifting the speaker back into the wardrobe. 'I need to go to the bathroom.'

'*Ja*, sure.'

As I turn off the lights in his old room, the toilet flushes. I can hear him humming; Handel maybe. On the doorjamb are short pencil markings, slightly curved, alongside names and dates. *Nico, 1965*. Six inches higher: *Nico, 1969*. The markings grow less frequent after that and stop in 1972, three years before his parents died and he stopped coming here altogether, when he was already over six feet. I run my finger over the smudged pencil and crouch down to see the marks for my father as a small child. There, between Nico at eleven and thirteen, is *Jo, 1997*.

———

'Every Christmas Eve, we'd come down here.' My father has pulled the car onto a grass bank next to the Groot River lagoon on our way out of Nature's Valley. The water is dark, the lagoon empty of wind-surfers and swimmers. The sea shines beyond the dunes. I remember standing at the mouth of the lagoon, my feet in the water, crying, as the water washed the plough snails in and out.

'Everyone would be there, all the kids, sunburnt and with the black-est feet from running around barefoot. And Father Christmas would row across the lagoon and bring us presents. He was always drunk but I never once saw him fall in.' He opens the windows on his side of the car. 'I wonder if they still do that.'

The clouds moving in over the escarpment are heavy and pink with promise. Rain is coming. To leave the earth steaming and clean. The drought is over.

'It's getting late. Maybe we should wait till tomorrow to go to the police.' I lean forward so that I can see the lagoon past the fishing rods. My notebook, the taped conversations and the lodge – it should be enough, when the time comes. But I need to know everything about Gideon, the man who killed my mom, before I let the police at my father.

'No.' He shakes his head. 'I said I'd do it today.' He pulls a plastic bag out from under his seat. The handles are double-knotted. For a second, I wonder if he's giving me all of his Krugerrands, trying to buy me off. 'I promised,' he says, dropping the bag – too light for gold, and too square – into my lap. 'Your stuff. All of it.'

I pull the plastic taut and push my finger through it. My phone, my passports, all there. 'Thank you.'

He starts the car and pulls onto the dirt track next to the lagoon. I turn my phone on and wait for it to find a network.

A sign warns us to keep our windows closed in case of baboons.

My phone beeps; unread messages. I open the first one. It's from Paul, sent three days ago. *We need to talk.*

'You've been getting a lot of messages actually,' my father says, driving across the intersection.

I slip the handset into a zip pocket in my handbag, gripping it between my knees.

He catches me staring at him. 'Don't worry, I didn't read any of them. It's just the vibration was turning me on a bit, so I had to switch the phone off.' Behind us, a car turns into the dirt road, stones skittering out from under its tyres.

'Right. OK, so,' I say, trying to remember what we were talking about.

My father laughs. 'Lots of sexy messages on your phone that you don't want your old man reading?' He coughs. 'Do you want to stop to get something to eat before we go to the police? The nearest station is in Knysna, so it's about an hour's drive, more if it rains.' He glances at the clouds, low on the mountain and getting darker.

'Please,' I say, knowing that wherever we stop, there'll be another reason why we can't go to the police just yet. A bedpan museum I just have to see, a severe iron deficiency requiring immediate attention with steaks, a newly remembered witness we need to talk to. But now I can use my phone to call Naledi from the bathroom. Tell her where we are, to send the police. 'Are you sure we shouldn't wait for the storm to pass?' Ahead of us the dirt road meets the R102, which climbs through the forest up onto the plateau.

My father stops at the intersection with the furthest inland of Nature's Valley's four roads. It's dark, set into the mountain forest. He waits for a blue car coming from Plett to pass us and turns left after it. 'Nah, I know this road really well,' he says, turning on the headlights. 'We can drive through the storm and then above it.' He closes the sunroof as far as it will go around the fishing rods.

A dead baboon lies on the side of the road, its chest flat and dark red, its fingers curled. Tread marks in the road show that a car swerved onto the hard shoulder to hit the animal. My father slows, shaking his head.

We cross the low bridge over the Groot River just as the rain starts. 'The river's as thin as a mamba. Not for long, though.' He starts the windscreen wipers.

I tilt my head back and watch the forest pass above us through the sunroof, feeling the rain on my face. The fishing rods are our masts, water coming in around them. Ragged orange rocks jut out over us where the mountain was cut to build the pass; sometimes they stick out as far as the solid white line in the middle of the road. Dark leaves fan out against the sinking cloud. The rain on the canopy is noisy as traffic.

'Here we go,' he says, changing gears. He slows the car as we near the foot of the pass.

I lean forward to look up at the road. The turns ahead are tight and many, the lanes narrow. I open my window. The car is so close to the rockface I can touch it.

'You can put the radio on if you want,' my father says.

'Really?'

He's smiling. 'Sure. It'll give me something to complain about.'

I push the button marked AM/FM. Static fills the car. 'Thanks.'

He nods, his eyes on the road. I pause for a few seconds on the first channel I find – a song by the Black-Eyed Peas is playing – wondering how long he'll be able to stand it.

'*Fok*,' my father says in Afrikaans.

'What?' I turn towards him, quickly switching the radio off.

He checks the rear-view mirror. 'Behind us.'

'What is it?' I twist in my seat, but I can only see as far back as the last turn and there's only one car behind us. 'What is it?'

'I should've known. I should've fucking known.' He slams the flat of his hand against the steering wheel.

'It's a woman driving,' I say and turn back to him.

'Not right behind us, you fucking idiot.' He checks the mirror again. 'Behind the bitch. In that *bakkie*.'

We're going faster now. Rain lashes in through the open windows. I look again. The yellow bumper of the woman's car is just visible around the rocks as we turn again. She's slowing down. 'I can't see anyone behind her,' I say.

He reaches out his window and wipes the side mirror with his sleeve. 'Of course you can't,' he spits. 'That would require you to actually be useful.'

We've caught up to the blue car in front of us. My father starts to flash his lights.

'You can't overtake here!' I grab the handle above the window as he swerves out into the oncoming lane. 'You can't even see around the next corner.'

He presses down on the horn. The blue car flashes its hazards. I can see the passenger turned in his seat, shouting at us. A fish sticker on the bumper before it turns.

My father checks the rear-view mirror again. It's beaded with rain. 'Fuck, fuck, fuck.' He swerves out and back into our lane again, trying to see if there's a car coming around the next turn.

I twist again to look back. The road behind us is empty now, just a sharp turn dropping off into forest. No pick-up truck, no crew cut behind the wheel with a gun and a tattoo of a crowbar on his arm.

'There's no one behind us,' I shout over another blast of the horn. 'Please slow down.'

The rain comes in brooms. I can barely see the car in front of us. The wipers drag a sickle-shaped leaf, dark green and thick, across the windscreen. Mud washes down the cliff walls over the pass and into the road. A sign at the edge of the road warns of falling rocks. There are so many ways to die here.

I find the seat-belt buckle behind me but pull too hard and it locks. Everything is wet. The blue car has pulled over at a narrow lookout point at the edge of the road. The gravel washes away under its tyres, but the occupants are safer there, just a couple of feet from the cliff edge, than in front of us. The driver presses down on his horn as we flash past. We're driving at twice the speed limit for the pass.

My father ignores the blue car. 'It's him,' he says, checking the rear-view mirror. 'Fuck.' He hits the dashboard. 'Sooner than I thought.'

I look at him. 'Did you know he'd come for us?' The seat belt is twisted across my body. 'Were you trying to lure him out?'

'Just speeding up the inevitable, hey.' He shakes his head, almost smiling. Scree showers down from an overhanging rock ahead, mud streaming towards us. 'But you've slowed me down too much,' he says, leaning forward and reaching under his seat. 'I work better alone.' His face is turned towards me, his ear pressed against the horn. The car drifts into the oncoming lane.

'Stop it,' I shout, grabbing the steering wheel with one hand. The car is heavy, skidding back into our lane through the falling scree. Slates of mud and pebbles drop onto the bonnet and into the car through the sunroof. I can't see the road.

'Where the fuck is it, Jo?' He sits up and grabs my arm, squeezing.

The rain begins to wash the windscreen clean. Cracks vein the glass. The turn ahead is tight, a hairpin. The road seems to fall away into dark canopy. Only the curving solid white centreline promises otherwise and I don't believe it.

'What are you talking about?' I try to pull my hand away and the car swerves towards the cliff wall. CD cases slide out of the cubbyhole next to the radio and onto the floor. 'I didn't do anything.'

'He's gonna kill both of us, you stupid bitch!' he shouts, wrenching my hand from the steering wheel and throwing it back at me. A white handprint on my skin.

The speedometer needle jumps. I look over my shoulder. The road and the rain are the same shade of grey. 'There's no one behind us,' I say, feeling for the gun in my bag. I'll make him slow down.

He takes the turn too fast and the back wheels skid out to the edge of the road. One wheel spins above the forest. I brace myself against the dashboard. Thick mud slides down onto the windscreen from the roof, too heavy for the right wiper. The driver's side of the car is dark.

'Fuck,' he shouts.

Around the corner, a boulder squats in our lane, just touching the centreline, as tall and wide as a door. I wonder if my mom saw it this clearly, the wall that killed her. If she closed her eyes just before she died.

Water whips off the steering wheel as it spins.

10

On Being Sane in Insane Places

13 days ago

'Don't be scared: you're white foreigners – they won't hurt you.' Standing in the aisle of the minibus, the tour guide smiled and shook his head. 'Just each other.' He turned and leant forward to speak to the minibus driver. The couple across the aisle from me took the lens caps off their expensive cameras.

The winter afternoon in Johannesburg was greyer than usual, smoke hanging in the air above the township. A truck had passed us on the way into Alexandra, driving in the opposite direction, two bikes in the back, the frames covered in brown tape. Pot handles poked out of a lidless plastic drum. Two people had been killed overnight. Johannesburg police, toting shotguns, their navy trousers tucked into big black boots, had come in early this morning and people were leaving while they could. All but one of the roads out of the township would soon be barricaded, the tour guide had said, blocked either by burning cars and minibuses or by armoured police vans.

The minibus was almost empty and the tour company had charged us double the usual price for a township tour. In case of damage to the vehicle, they'd said. At a police stop at the Canning Road entrance into the township, we'd waited behind a dark car as officers searched the boot for weapons. They'd waved us straight through. Just beyond the police stop a bedsheet was strung between two shacks. It had been hung up before the spray paint had dried, and the words – *Drive all foreigners away* – were running down the banner.

I was meeting Tumelo Kgotso, a longtime stringer for *The Star*. I'd been woken that morning by a call from the editor of a London daily. I'd never wanted to work in news journalism – even now, it was too full of Oxbridge graduates and men who gave no thought to adjusting their balls mid-conversation – but it was something to add to my portfolio. The editor had told me that the paper would need its own photos and suggested a few photographers that had worked for her before. Tumelo was the first one I'd called.

Tumelo had told me he would be waiting outside the Alex police station on 15th Avenue, where the refugees were sheltering in tents. He'd advised me to come in with the tourists; it would be safer that way, he said. I'd told him I'd be wearing jeans and a black jumper, with a green messenger bag slung across my chest. Our version of a red rose.

There were more trees than I'd expected. According to Wikipedia, this was 'old Alex', originally intended for whites; there were two-storey houses with brick walls and sloped roofs, and streetlights shaped like candy canes lined the paved road on the right. Plants yellowed under an old beach umbrella in the front garden of one house. Its windows were dark. The hotels and office buildings of the suburb of Sandton rose above Alex on the left. We passed a football field, the grass black and still smoking, and headed deeper into the township.

The tour guide turned again to face the passengers. 'Listen up, guys,' he said, lifting his baseball cap and wiping the sweat on his forehead into his hair. 'When we stop, you can get out, but stay close to the bus, hey? We might have to move quickly.' We pulled across an intersection, the houses smaller now, their front doors just a few feet from the road. 'Normally we'd take you to Madiba's old house and to the river, but today we're only gonna go to the police station.' He grabbed the back of the seat next to him as the minibus bounced over a sheet of corrugated iron. 'Also, keep your bags close to you. And be careful who you take pictures of.' We passed a riot van, neon-yellow stripes across the body, joining in a V at the front beneath the windscreen. The tour guide smiled unconvincingly as we crossed Roosevelt Road. 'And remember, not all South Africans are like this.'

The houses gave way to informal settlements, the tin walls white in the sun. I pulled my sunglasses out of my bag and put them on. There was no room for trees here, just as many shacks as could be built on the lots lining the street. The minibus slowed as we passed a burnt-out car, its tyres missing.

'That's the stadium up ahead,' the tour guide said, pointing, his back to us. 'Home to Alexandra United.'

He can't help himself, I thought.

We swerved to avoid a man lying on his side in the road. Four women were standing nearby in a semicircle. He reached up to them. His head was bleeding, the pillowcase wrapped around it dark and wet. Further along the road, a policeman pinned a man down with his knee.

We turned right. On the corner, a shirtless man in black jeans and a studded belt bent and picked up a rock. In his other hand he held a machete, and a doormat was draped over his arm, ready to be used as a shield. His ribs stuck out as he raised the rock over his head, keeping his elbow straight, and threw it at a police van. The doors opened and two policemen in bulletproof vests jumped down from the cab. The shirtless man stood his ground. I twisted in my seat but the back window of the minibus was too dirty to see out. Someone had drawn a smiley face in the dust.

Four policemen, one at each corner of a mattress, carried an injured woman past me to the station entrance. Her breasts were bare and bloody, her face hidden by a towel. Tumelo lowered his camera, whistling through his teeth. He was in his late fifties, his hair greying and his skin slightly too big for him.

'This is bad,' he said, looking around. 'I haven't seen anything like this since before ninety-four.'

A man limped past us, holding his ID book out in front of him. His face was covered in mud, a cut on his cheek jagged as barbed wire. Being South African was no guarantee that the mob would leave you alone.

I was the only one to get out of the minibus; to get to the door I'd had to climb over the tourists, who were taking photos through the open windows. The tour guide, smoking in the front with the driver, told me to stay close to the bus. When I answered him in Afrikaans, he pointed at his watch and held up both hands. I had ten minutes.

Across the road from the station, about a hundred and fifty feet away, men had gathered, watching. It was strangely quiet, apart from an occasional ululation that would ripple through the crowd, a war cry. This was where the taxi rank normally was, Tumelo had told me, but the only taxi on the street had been burned and tipped over. Its tyres were also missing. A broken Heineken bottle lay in the large puddle surrounding the taxi. The road was police territory, for now. Five guarded the gates, ready to lock them at any sign of trouble, and more than fifty were fanned out around the station, shotguns raised.

The south entrance to 15th Avenue was barricaded with burning rubbish, the smoke acrid and thick. Tumelo had taken a series of photos of men throwing the abandoned possessions of foreigners into the fire. A crucifix. A doll. This was a place abandoned by God and the whites.

'Should we get some of the kids?' I asked, pointing at black children kicking apples among the remains of a hawker's stand, then feeling rude for suggesting shots to this experienced photographer.

But Tumelo just nodded, adjusting the strap on his camera. He was only an inch or two taller than me, wearing brown walking boots and dark clothing. Around his neck on a bright blue lanyard was a press pass issued by *The Star*.

'I'll try to get one of the policemen to talk to me. Will you be OK?' I asked, rubbing the back of my neck.

Tumelo looked surprised. '*Ja*, sure,' he said. 'I'll pass the elbow test no problem.'

'What's the elbow test?'

He tutted. 'If you know the Zulu word for elbow, you're not a foreigner. It's like the old pencil test.'

Behind us, a woman began to cry. She was asking for her children. I looked at Tumelo. 'The pencil test?'

'*Eish.* You know? If they put a pencil in your hair and it stuck, you were black. If it fell out, you were white.'

'Fuck,' I said.

He laughed and the bags under his eyes became more pronounced. 'What did they teach you at those English schools?'

'Not that,' I said, shaking my head. 'World War Two mostly.'

He smiled. 'Look, I'll meet you back here in half an hour.'

I hoped so. I liked him already.

'Don't worry about me.' He pointed at his forearm. 'I'm not dark enough that they'd stop me.'

'Jesus.'

He laughed again. 'Stick with me, *tsotsi*, and I'll have you singing "Shosholoza" by the end of the night.' He waved and turned away, his camera already raised.

I pulled a notepad and pen out of my bag. Next to the police station entrance, a man in jeans and a black t-shirt knelt in front of a crying woman. I walked towards them, then thought better of trying to interview her. Behind me, the shouts began again. The man looked over his shoulder at the crowd, and I realised it was Paul.

He turned back to the woman and helped her up. The baby on her back had a bandage wrapped around its head. I hoped that he'd seen me and waited as he took her through the gates of the station grounds.

The crowd was growing. A man in blue workman's overalls, open to show a t-shirt that said *100% Zulu boy*, dragged his finger across his neck, a promise to the foreigners behind the police lines. He tapped his palm with a length of pipe, keeping time. A metronome.

'What are you doing here?' Paul asked behind me. He stood close, watching the crowd, his arm touching mine.

'Hi,' I said. There was blood on the tar. It was an impossibly large stain.

He looked straight ahead. 'This is not a good place for you to be, Jo.' He frowned.

'Is that because if something happens to me, it'll be bad PR?' I knew as soon as I'd said it that this wasn't the time or place for such a flippant comment.

'Yes, frankly.' He looked down, turned to face me. 'But it's good to see you.'

I nodded. 'You look weird in a t-shirt,' I said, smiling. 'Like you're not fully dressed yet.'

'You've seen me in less.'

I cleared my throat and adjusted the messenger bag across my chest.

'Best not to dress like a politician today,' he said. 'The party doesn't even know I'm here. They wouldn't like it.'

Four policemen carried an injured man past us into the station grounds, one at each arm and leg. The man was wearing a red t-shirt that looked as though it was unspooling, blood trailing behind him like thread.

'This is our fault, you know,' Paul said, shaking his head and turning towards the crowd. There was a thin silver chain around his neck. 'We did this.'

'How?' I remembered that my sunglasses were still pushed up into my hair, as though I were at the beach. I pulled them off and hooked them onto my bag strap.

'How long do you have?' He counted his points on the fingers of his left hand: 'We've cleaned up the city for the World Cup and forced people further away from jobs. We talk about "illegal immigrants" like they're responsible for all our problems. We've failed to raise people up out of a hand-to-mouth existence. We should've refused to build any more golf courses until everyone in this country had a house. But wealth is still white and poverty is still black.' He spat into the dust to his right. 'Apart from in the ANC, of course. The oil rises to the top. It's always going to take a tragedy for poor blacks to be seen.'

'I won't ask if I can quote you on that,' I said. He smiled and lifted his face to the sky. I watched him swallow.

'*Amangundwane!*' A man had climbed onto the burnt-out taxi. He was wearing a striped jersey, maroon tracksuit bottoms and trainers. He was ready to run. Or chase. He raised his fist.

'It means rat,' Paul translated for me. 'Scab. That's what foreigners – the *kwerekwere* – are.'

'Kill the foreigners!' the man shouted. The policemen near the taxi lifted their shotguns to their shoulders.

'Those are the community leaders,' a woman said next to me. 'The guys shouting at the front.'

I turned towards her. She was black, tall and very thin, with short hair in a middle parting and a wide, flat forehead. She wore a polka-dot rollneck jumper, black jeans and a band around her right arm. The logo on the armband was a black circle with a red star in the middle and the words *Abahlali baseMjondolo* around the circumference. 'Hi. I'm Lindiwe.' She smiled and there was a dimple in her right cheek. 'His sister.'

'Oh, sorry,' I said, tucking my notepad under my arm. We shook hands. I wondered if she, too, had an English name. What she thought about Paul using his.

'I take it he's told you all about me?' She raised her eyebrows. I shook my head apologetically. 'That's OK. He's the star of the family and likes to keep it that way.' She turned her back on the crowd to check her phone, an old Nokia that was bigger than my dictaphone. I smiled, unsure of what to say.

'Jo,' Paul said, rolling his eyes. 'This is Lindiwe, my little sister. She works for the shack-dwellers' association – the AbM.' I'd never heard of the AbM, but now wasn't the time for a current affairs lesson. 'I'm working for her today.' He pointed to the band around his right upper arm. 'Helping with refugees.'

Lindiwe nodded as she put her phone in her front pocket. 'Yes he is.' She turned back towards the growing crowd.

Five men, carrying spears, now balanced on the blackened metal shell of the taxi, rocking it back and forth. A policeman shouted at them to get down, but they laughed and stamped their feet.

'This is only going to get worse,' Lindiwe said. 'People think that refugees have more rights than they do. That they get houses, water, healthcare, sanitation. It won't stop.' She gestured towards the station. 'I've got to get back, but it was good to meet you, Jo.'

'And you,' I said.

She touched my shoulder. 'Don't stay too long, hey.' Behind me, she punched Paul in the arm. The sibling banter seemed incongruous. Maybe that was the point. 'See you later,' she said, before walking back towards the station. At the gate, she turned again, and I waved, but she didn't see me. Behind her, just inside the doors of the police station, Tumelo was photographing a mother and child, both of them crying.

'*Amandla!*' The men on the taxi shouted together this time. Power.

The man in the *100% Zulu boy* t-shirt stepped forward, pipe raised. Then he brought it down on the road. It was an old sound, one I hadn't heard before, but I knew it meant that something was about to happen. I slipped my notebook into my bag and pushed the pen into my pocket. I looked around; the minibus had left without me. I'd been more than ten minutes, like I'd known I would be, but it wasn't going to be as easy as I'd thought to get a lift out. I stepped closer to Paul.

The leader jumped down from the taxi, water splashing up onto his tracksuit bottoms. 'Give them to us,' he shouted. He turned to the crowd. '*Umshini wami mshini wami,*' he sang.

'*Khawuleth'umshini wami,*' they responded, beating their pipes against the tar. Those without pipes raised their weapons: machetes, rakes, axes and spears harrowed the smoke rising from the burning rubbish nearby. Spades, grey as headstones, shivered in the dusk.

'It's "bring me my machine gun",' Paul said through his teeth. 'Let's go.' He grabbed my arm and took a step backwards. 'Slowly,' he cautioned.

'*Umshini wami mshini wami,*' the leader sang again, turning back to the station.

A policeman fired a warning above the crowd, his shotgun a starting pistol. The men began to dance towards the station, lifting their knees almost to their chests as they advanced. Hammers, clubs, even a golf club throbbed in the air as they *toyi-toyi*ed. Behind us, the police station gates swung shut, locking Lindiwe and Tumelo in, locking us out. A riot van, high off the ground, crossed the burning barricade on 15th Avenue, but the men kept dancing and singing as they moved closer. The policeman fired again; the birdshot swarmed. The man in the *100% Zulu boy* t-shirt fell, heavy and damaged.

We ran. The cement breath of Jo'burg hung over the city. Women and children scattered ahead of us, disappearing into the dark, narrow alleyways between shacks. To the right of the station, men crouched in the road, blocking off Selborne Street. Behind them, tyres burned: No one shall pass here. They laughed at us as we ran past them, one man hacking at the tar with his machete. They were biding their time.

'This way,' Paul shouted over his shoulder. A riot van sped past us towards the station, cutting an arch in the smoke.

'*Wen'uyang'ibambezela*,' the *toyi-toyi*ing crowd sang behind us.

I sped up, drawing level with Paul. 'Where are we going?' The messenger bag banged against my back as I ran, the strap chaffing my shoulder. On the side of the road, a dog lay under a scab of flies, its intestines spilling out.

'We have to find a way out.' Paul pointed at an alleyway on the right. 'Before it gets dark.' A man ran past us, his eyes on the station. He was smiling, hammer raised and ready.

Barbershop was written in chalk on the wall of a shack, but the door was closed and there was no one waiting for a haircut. The street's kerbstones were missing, stolen to build a barricade somewhere else in the township. Paul ducked between two shacks and I followed, out of breath. The alleyway was narrow, the roofs of the shacks almost touching above our heads. It stunk of sewage. We stopped and stood facing each other, our bodies touching. Gunshots sounded in the distance.

'The gates were closed, right?' Sweat shone above his eyebrows. 'Lindiwe was inside?'

I nodded, catching my breath. 'I saw her go in.'

He lifted his t-shirt and wiped his forehead. 'Good.' His back against the tin, he edged towards the entrance of the alleyway.

'What are you doing?' I asked. My bag scraped against the metal.

He leant out of the alleyway and looked in both directions, as though at a zebra crossing. 'Getting my bearings. That way,' he said, pointing at the dark passage behind me. 'We need to get to the river.'

'OK.' I turned, but he caught my arm.

'Get behind me,' he said. 'And if you have a camera on you, take it out. They're less likely to hurt you if you're taking photos.' He looked back at the road as he spoke. 'There's power in your skin, but only so much.'

'We're gonna teach you,' a man said inside the shack. 'After this, you're gonna know the way which is nice.' The woman screamed. No one would come running so they let her. 'You'll become a woman after this.'

I could hear belt buckles being undone. Paul grabbed my hand.

We'd made it over 16th and 17th Avenues, picking our way through rubbish-filled alleyways by the light from our phones. By now it was 6 p.m. and already dark. Progress was slow: we had to be quiet, and some passages turned out to be dead ends. My shoes were covered in sewage. We had been about to cross to 18th Avenue when a car pulled up at the end of the alleyway. Paul had dropped into a crouch, holding his phone against his chest. I'd ducked behind him, holding on to his t-shirt for balance, leaning around him slightly to see why we'd stopped. A group of men in caps and hoodies had got out of the car carrying AK-47s, guns I'd seen on the news in stories about Africa, the taillights glowing red behind them. They'd dragged a woman out of the back seat. She'd kicked out at them, and one man had punched her in the stomach. When she'd sagged, gasping for breath, the man had laughed and poured beer over her head. They'd taken her into the shack, but one of the men stayed leaning against the bonnet, smoking. We waited, crouched in the alleyway, with no choice but to listen to what was happening inside.

'You're supposed to be with a man.' A different voice this time.

'I am,' the woman said, her breathing ragged. 'I have a boyfr—' she started, but they'd filled her mouth.

'This is gonna turn your mind to be normal.' He grunted and she cried out. 'It hurts me when you're being inhuman,' he said, spitting. 'It pains me a lot.' He spoke in English. She was *kwerekwere*, a foreigner.

Something banged against the table, faster and faster. A beer was opened. Someone laughed.

'We must rape you,' another voice sang. 'We must rock you.'

The woman screamed again. This time, it was silenced quickly by a knuckle or an elbow. The woman gagged and the men laughed. I wiped my nose on the back of my hand and tried to stand, wanting to run into the shack and drag the men off her, but Paul tightened his grip on my arm and pulled me closer to him. He shook his head, closed his eyes. His face was wet. I rested my forehead against his shoulder.

'I don't appreciate your lesbian style.' Buttons hit the wall of the shack as fabric ripped.

I swallowed the sound that was gathering in my throat.

He grunted. 'And this is just to let you know that you must live in a straight motion of way.'

The men laughed again. Piss ran out under the tin sheeting.

'Who's next?' Someone crushed a beer can.

'Me,' said the man leaning against the car. His cigarette butt rolled into the alleyway entrance. He opened the door to the shack and slammed it behind him. Inside, there was a slapping sound, but I couldn't tell if they were hitting her or high-fiving each other.

Paul lifted his head. He motioned for me to stay close and straight-ened, edging forward towards the road. My knee clicked as I stood up.

We paused at the entrance to the alleyway, listening. The woman was crying. Table legs scraped against the floor. The men laughed again.

Paul leant forward and checked that the shack door was shut. He nodded. I flipped open my phone to provide light, but there was no need: the next block was burning. We walked quickly, keeping low.

It was quieter here. The shacks looked empty, abandoned earlier in the day. Doors hung open. Pots and plastic chairs were piled outside, ready for looters. Clothes were strewn across the road. The street was empty but for a man lying in the dust on the opposite side of the road, his tracksuit bottoms pulled down and his underpants showing. His eyes were closed, his tongue protruding from his mouth. He was still leaking. He was not long dead.

They were coming. The ground shivered with the force of them all, moving together, hunting for trophies.

Two women pulled tin sheeting behind them, away from the fire. We came out onto a dirt road between 18th Avenue and the river. The shacks were too close together, sagging and spitting out wire mesh, for us to edge through the alleyways any more.

At the end of the block, a barricade burned. Small groups of people warmed their hands around the fire. Branches had been cut down and dragged into the street, whether to slow the police or the mob I didn't know.

We crouched behind a blackened car. Paul was bleeding from a deep cut in his arm. We were dirty and stinking.

Across the street, two teenagers pushed a blind beggar over into the dust. They picked up his cap and cane and ran, singing, to join the mob passing a few blocks behind the barricade.

'We'll cross the Jukskei there,' Paul said, pointing at a dirt path a hundred feet away under a washing line. 'It's shallow this time of year. Then follow the river and cut through the cemetery.'

More dead bodies. The earth was full of skeletons.

'Where to?' I asked.

'The M3.' He readjusted his AbM armband to cover the cut. Blood seeped out below it as though the ink on the red star was running. 'I'll call someone to pick us up from there.'

Suddenly, the small crowd by the barricade scrambled, screaming. A man was running towards them, swinging a burning tyre around his head on a long piece of wire, the fire a rocket exhaust. Smoke rose in a spiral. He let the wire go and the tyre joined the burning rubbish on the street. He laughed and chased a group of women around the corner.

It was just us and the beggar.

'Now,' Paul said. He stood up and walked quickly into the road towards the path between the shacks, marked by washing line. I followed him, keeping close to the shacks.

Someone screamed nearby. I stopped about twenty feet from the path. Under a length of tin sheeting on the ground, I saw a handle. It was a spade. I picked it up.

Paul had stopped and turned back towards me. 'What are you doing?' he called.

The path lit up behind him. A man ran into the road, screaming. He was on fire, a burning tyre around his neck. He fell onto his hands and knees, the fire underneath him, fanning out like an Elizabethan collar. Another man came up from the river bank, a machete raised above his head. He paused, his outline wavering in the heat coming from the fire. There was a *knobkierie* in his other hand. He smiled at

Paul, seeming eerily calm, and lowered the machete. I shrank back into the darkness of the shacks, spade raised and ready to swing. But the man just laughed and jogged past Paul towards the township.

The burning man had stopped screaming. His arms gave way and he slumped face down in the dust.

I dropped the spade and sprinted towards him. I pulled a sheet from the washing line, knelt and threw it over his back and head, trying to put out the flames. He smelled of petrol and rubber. The top corners were burning and I was sure I was patting the sheet too hard. Something hurt on my thigh. It felt good, necessary; it was paying dues.

Someone came running up the path behind me. 'Get away from him!' a woman screamed. Her face was wet and wild. 'Leave my husband alone!'

I could hear the traffic on the nearby highway, soft and regular as water. I realised then that she was shouting at me.

'Jo!' Paul shouted behind me, grabbing me under my arms and dragging me away from the man. 'He's dead.' He pulled me onto my feet.

The woman had ripped back the top of the sheet. I turned and ran down the path to the banks. I could hear Paul behind me.

The smoke over the township had swallowed the stars. The river was wide but shallow. People were crossing here, carrying all they could on their backs, balanced on their heads. Behind us, the township burned.

11

Intersections

Clothes are folded on the chair next to the bed. They look like mine. I close my eyes, count to five and open them again. The room is bright. The bed is angled beneath me; I'm lying uphill. Above the chair, green and white checked curtains are half drawn. The window is closed. Terracotta roof tiles and white stucco shine through the window.

I feel sick. Something is wrong.

My right hand lies on the pale blue blanket, veins fat as worms. It seems far away. The fingers curl. I exhale and realise I've been holding my breath. A suitcase lies flat next to the chair. The floor is light brown. I feel too high off the ground. A big TV hovers against the wall opposite the bed – Oprah is on. There's no sound when she speaks, just a low drone I can't identify the source of. My throat is raw, my chest heavy as I try to calm my breathing. To the left of the bed is a blue plastic wall. There's no door I can see. I can't move my left arm.

I blink, trying to remember what happened. A tear clings to the lobe of one ear.

'Jo.' A man touches my right arm, his hand cool and smooth. He's blurred, the light behind him too bright. I blink again.

He squeezes my hand. 'You're in George Hospital. You're OK. Just go back to sleep.'

Water runs down onto my face and there are leaves in my hair.

I wake suddenly. It's raining. The curtains are drawn but I can hear it. I'm out of breath.

I close my eyes, waiting. The buzzing is gone. There's just rain.

The TV is off. The long neon light hanging above me flickers.

I have a headache.

The light-blue plastic curtain hanging to the left of the bed moves as the door behind it opens. A woman clears her throat, closing the door behind her softly. The top edge of the curtain becomes scalloped as she pulls it open, the folds moving down towards me like icing.

'Nice to see you awake, Ms Hartslief.' She clicks her pen as she moves to the end of the bed and picks up my chart. She looks down at the clipboard as she talks. 'Apart from cuts and bruises, you dislocated your left shoulder in the crash. We've reduced it and it'll hurt for a few days.' She looks up at me. 'Keep it in the sling, hey?' Her face is oval and pale, her hair pulled back into a ponytail. She has purple eyeshadow on.

I try to nod. She looks down and signs the chart. Her name is one long stripe. She moves closer but I can't read the name printed on the ID badge around her neck.

'The burn on your thigh is healing well.' She watches me for a reaction. 'I gave it a good clean and some fresh bandages, though.'

I nod again – *Thanks*. The headache gets worse.

'You had a pretty serious concussion as well, when they brought you in. But we've been monitoring it over the past thirty-six hours and things look good.' She holds the clipboard against her chest and pockets her pen. 'I would've preferred to keep you here a day or so longer, but your friend assures me he'll keep an eye on you in Cape Town.' She shakes her head. 'He's very insistent.'

I swallow. 'Where is he?' I ask. It doesn't sound like my voice.

She nods at the door beyond the curtain. 'Just outside.'

I move my right hand level with my hip and push down, shifting straighter in the bed. 'Is he OK?'

She smiles. '*Ja*. He's worried, sure, but he's a big boy.' She pats the blanket over my foot. 'He can handle it.'

I lie back slowly, vertebra by vertebra, and close my eyes.

'I wanted to talk to you before I called him in, though.'

I hope she doesn't sit down next to me. I don't think I can move to make room for her on the bed.

'We ran some blood tests.' She steps closer. 'There was a lot of temazepam in your system.'

Temazepam. Is that a sleeping pill?

'Did your doctor prescribe it for you?'

I don't remember taking anything other than paracetamol. How else would it get into my system? Then I realise: all those already-open bottles of water. The bastard.

'No.'

She's wearing the same perfume my mom used to. I want to ask her what it's called so that I can fill my suitcase with bottles of it.

'Ms Hartslief,' she says sharply. 'Were you having trouble sleeping?'

'Yes. But I won't take them any more, I promise.' I want her to call him into the room now so he can see what he's done. I bet he'll have a cut on his forehead, which will make him wince every time he puts on a baseball cap, but no other injuries. I lift my hand to my face to wipe the corners of my eyes.

'It's possible they caused the accident, you know,' she says, rubbing her forehead.

I shake my head. *I wasn't driving*, I want to say, but my mouth is too dry. And I don't yet know who was behind the wheel in the story my father will have been telling about the accident.

She sighs, rolling her head from side to side. I want her to stay, to sit at the end of the bed, but talking to me seems to be making her long for the end of her shift. 'OK, well, I'll go get him,' she says.

'Thanks,' I say as she turns away from the bed. I wonder what he needed to do that I had to be asleep for, apart from going through my stuff. Or was it just to make me more compliant? I'll ask him as soon as we're alone again.

I hear her open the door behind the plastic curtain. 'Mr Silongo?' she calls. 'She's awake.'

In the mirror I watch the nurse retie the sling.

She shook her head as she pulled off my hospital gown; as she knelt in front of me, holding open the waistband of the skirt I'd picked out, I saw the marks on my body. A purple beauty-queen sash was coming up where the seat belt had been. My right forearm was covered in red welts; it looked like I'd been stung by a jellyfish. A weal stretched across my right hip. Each bruise was payment towards the debt I owed.

'Thank you,' I say.

She nods and turns; I'm alone in the bathroom. Paul is waiting outside. I can hear him flick between channels.

I comb a side parting into my hair with my fingers. Open with my teeth the thin plastic packet that holds the toothbrush. The nurse has already unscrewed the cap on the toothpaste for me. I let the water run, counting to sixty and back down again as I brush. I close the tap. Paul's turned off the TV.

I walk back out into the room, past the curtain. From this angle, I can see the mountains rising over the hospital car park. The sun is still low in the east and the ridge shadows are deep. They look like knuckles.

'You ready?' Paul's sitting on the bed. He's wearing a navy suit and has lost weight since I last saw him that night after Alex, sitting in the back of a car outside my hotel in Jo'burg, bleeding through his AbM armband.

'No.' My suitcase, dented and stinking of beer, is packed, standing on its wheels next to the bed. My handbag, still wet, is balanced on top of it. 'Did you know who my father was when you met me at the airport? Is that why you called me in London?'

He pinches a pleat in his trousers.

'The night at your house?' My shoulder felt better out of the sling. I'll have to wait until we're in the car to take it off.

He nods, looking down.

'Wow.' I shake my head.

He looks up, not quite at my face. The top button on his shirt is undone.

I have no right to be hurt. 'It's fine. Really,' I say, sitting down next to him on the bed. He is heavier than I am and the mattress slopes down to him. I grip onto the metal bar at the foot of the bed.

He turns towards me, bringing his right knee up onto the bed between us. His trouser leg bunches at the calf. His socks have a cartoon-animal pattern on them; he catches me looking and smiles. 'Lindi gave them to me,' he says, tracing the outline of a giraffe with his finger.

'Is she OK?'

He nods, staring at the knot on my sling. '*Ja*. She's in Du Noon now, setting up a refugee camp.'

I wish for a newspaper and a map, something to help me know what day it is, what's been happening. Where I am.

'You ready to go?' He pulls his phone from his pocket, holding it so I can't see the screen. 'I have to be on a call at seven.'

I put my hand on his leg, surprised when he doesn't flinch. I have to ask. 'Is he dead?'

'I don't think so,' he says. 'Most of the blood in the car was on the passenger side, and only your luggage was in the boot.'

The phrase *he's in the wind* comes to mind, another useless pop culture reference point.

'Are you relieved?' he asks, still looking at his phone. But his fingers are still.

'I dunno.' I try to measure my reaction, but everything is slow and dulled. 'Not really – part of me wants it to be over.' I think this could be true, and I can tell it's what he wants to hear.

He slips his phone into the breast pocket of his jacket. 'I wanna keep talking to that part.'

I nod. The headache is going, but I can't stop thinking about the temazepam. I look at him. 'Why're we going to Cape Town?'

'We're going to find Gideon,' he says, standing up.

I turn quickly, too quickly, to look at my handbag. Inside, the notes and tapes I made. The gun. I could explain why I had it, but I'm not sure he'd believe me. I wait, bent forward, forehead on the bed, for the spasm in my back to pass.

'Are you OK?' He puts his hand on my shoulder.

'Uh-huh,' I say into the mattress. I take four slow breaths. 'Do you have any leads?' I ask, the words equally spaced, but not mine.

His hand is heavy. 'The old government destroyed most of their records before we came in. So that they couldn't be prosecuted for it.' He remembers where his hand is and steps back. 'Your dad's whole story sounds like a big, fat crock of shit. There's no record of a Gideon van Vuuren anywhere. Not even with the army.'

'I know. My father – Nico...' I don't know what to call him in front of Paul. 'He said he never knew Gideon's real name.'

'Convenient.' Paul turns his wrist so that he can see the time. 'But obviously your references to Gideon, your father and the lodge touched a nerve with Danie Strydom.' His watch, like mine, tells only time. I wonder what day it is. 'And the brigadier your dad mentioned, Van der Westhuizen, actually exists. He lives just outside Cape Town. We're gonna go talk to him.'

I breathe in for five seconds and try to hold it as long.

'Actually, *you're* gonna go talk to him. Just to see if there's anything to what your psycho dad said.' There's a smile in his voice. 'He'll take to you a lot better than he would to me. I mean, look at me.'

His shoes are new and polished, two white circles shining on the toes. At school inspections, they'd called it the black mirror effect. It was that or detention. I close my eyes. 'OK.' I talk through my teeth. 'Will you be giving me a list of questions to ask? How about a microphone in a brooch?'

He laughs. 'No, man, nothing like that.'

I breathe out and sit up slowly. 'Have you talked to Danie yet?'

He looks down at me. 'Yes. Not me personally, but he was down at the station for a couple of hours yesterday.'

I wonder if Danie had seen it coming, after my visit. 'And?'

'He was much better prepared this time. Couldn't get anything out of him. So when we're done in Cape Town, we'll go speak to him together – he seemed to respond to you.'

I remember laughing at Danie's jokes and have to look away.

'And you should know that I'm sending some people to the lodge in Dundee. I'll join them as soon as you're settled in CT.'

'OK.'

'Your dad is a fucking crazy person, by the way,' he says, scratching his thigh. 'Flipping moods all the time.'

Like an unfunny, one-person sketch show, I've always thought. But I don't say it.

'I listened to the tapes. The one from the crash.' He shakes his head.

'I don't know how you managed to stick it out with him so long.'

'Me neither.'

He holds out his hand. 'Let me help you up.'

I sigh. 'Thank you for looking at the lodge,' I say, pushing myself up off the bed with my right hand.

He frowns and I realise it was the wrong thing to say. He was doing it for his father, not for mine.

'Have you checked his car at Durban airport?' I remembered it while I was brushing my teeth. 'And his flat? In case there's anything there.'

'We've been through his flat, but I think it'll help if you're there to tell us what we should be looking for.' He pauses. 'When you can, I mean,' he says, looking past me. Perhaps at the mountains or at the pattern on the curtains.

'Sure. Maybe tomorrow?' I offer.

'Let's see how you feel.'

'Were you here earlier?' I ask, remembering the man at my bedside when I first woke up.

'Yep,' he says, pulling up the handle on my suitcase. 'You didn't think he'd risk getting caught just to see you were OK, did you?'

'No,' I say, realising as I speak that it's true. 'You got here fast.'

'The phone company notified us when you turned on your cell. Just before you crashed.'

'Wow, OK.' I wonder if he'd been tracking me, drawing pins piercing the map wherever I withdrew money or paid by card.

'We've searched the forest around the pass and we're looking at the car too.'

'What for?' I can't unzip my bag with one hand. I pull it onto the bed and squeeze it, feeling for anything gun-shaped.

'Anything that can help.' He tips the suitcase onto its wheels. 'Ready now?'

I swallow, nodding, and pick up my handbag. The gun, like my father, is gone.

Once again, I'm nothing but a passenger. The road flashes by behind my reflection. *Mossel Bay, 40 km. Cape Town, 436 km. Turn here for San cave paintings.* There's graffiti on the sign, initials I can't make out. I wonder if the paintings have been graffitied over too.

They'd found me in the road next to the car, surrounded by leaves and soggy playing cards. The front door on the driver's side was open. So was the boot. There was a jack of spades in my hair, Paul said. The woman who'd found me and driven me to the hospital had taken photos. But I wouldn't want to see them, he told me.

The road looks familiar. I turn to look at the signs on the opposite side of the road. Kouga. Humtata. I've been here before, avoiding rabbits, my father asleep in the back. It was the last time I was allowed to drive. Behind the Hottentot signs, a building-length banner in teal and orange tells us to bank with FNB.

The land throbs softly in the background.

'Keep your eyes on the road,' Paul says, changing gears. 'It'll help you not to feel sick.' He smiles at me.

'Thanks.' I don't know why we're driving instead of flying to Cape Town. Maybe there were no seats on such short notice. Or maybe it's to punish me.

'Are you OK?' he asks, checking the rear-view mirror. His shirt-sleeves are rolled up to the elbows and there's something written on his hand.

I shake my head. 'It doesn't matter.' I lean back slowly and close my eyes. The car is stuffy and my left arm is heavy against my chest.

'Listening to the tape of you and Danie was really informative,' he says. 'Do you always flirt with guys to get information?' I can tell the question is prepared, the words carefully chosen. 'Tell them what big muscles they have?'

'No,' I say. 'Not back in the UK, but here – I don't know, it felt like the only power I had.' I don't know if the past tense is accurate. 'It wasn't like that with you, though. Really.' I open my eyes, realising that I could ask him the same question. 'Was it like that for you?' I ask before I can stop myself.

He shifts up into fourth gear. Instead of answering me, he asks: 'How long did you know that I was his son?'

I've been expecting this question, and I try to work out how long it's been since the petrol station in Joubertina. 'Six days, I think. I'm not sure – there are a lot of holes.' I look at him, contemplate putting my hand on his arm. 'I wanted to call you, but he had my phone.'

He nods. 'Sure, OK.' He swallows and I remember tracing his Adam's apple with my lips.

I pull the hem of my skirt down over my knees. The headache is back. I'm supposed to fly back to London next week, I realise. I'll need to change my ticket.

He unhooks his sunglasses from his shirt, driving with his elbows as he opens the arms. 'His name was Vusi, you know.'

'No, I didn't know that.' I doubt my father had either.

'I can't remember him ever living with us, but he came back to visit a few times. Then, when I was five, he just stopped.' He slides the glasses over the bridge of his nose. The lenses are gold. 'For a while, my mom said he was coming back, that he was just busy and couldn't get back from the city.' He clears his throat. 'But six months later – thirteen December 1983 – a woman came to visit us from Jo'burg. Thembi something. My mom told me to take Lindi outside to play. But I could hear her scream all the way down the hill. I knew then that he was dead.'

I don't know what to say, so I wait.

'When I was old enough, I got my aunt to tell me everything she knew. Thembi was his girlfriend. I guess it makes sense that he'd have one, because he couldn't come back to see us very often. Anyway, they were in bed when three or four guys in uniforms started banging on the doors and windows. My dad let them in – he knew it would be worse if they had to break down the door – and they took him away. Thembi went to the police station looking for him, but he wasn't there. She told his friends at the shebeen what had happened, but they couldn't really do anything because the cops were always finding reasons to pick them up. For a while I hated Thembi, because she was the last person to be with him and she wasn't my mom, but she risked a lot – her passbook, her right to stay in South Africa – and it cost her almost everything she had to come tell us what happened.' He wets his bottom lip with his tongue. 'I've looked at hundreds of police photos, searching for his face on the dead and beaten bodies.' Behind him, tree trunks blur into each other. 'I know basically nothing about him, apart from that he played Stevie Wonder on the guitar.'

My ears feel blocked and I want to open a window. I know I should keep my eyes on the road ahead to stop from feeling car sick but I can't look away, not now.

'I've never thought of him as a real person,' Paul says. 'Just a victim of something that in some ways has defined my entire life.'

A blue mist hangs a foot above the forest floor. Flowers, I think. Do bluebells grow in South Africa? 'Pull over,' I say, leaning back against the headrest. 'Please.'

He looks at me. 'Christ, Jo.'

We're in the fast lane, three rows of cat's eyes from the hard shoulder. He checks the mirrors. I hold my breath, trying to starve the spasms in my stomach.

'Almost there,' he says. 'Hold on.'

Closing my eyes, I wait for the road to stop roaring as we slow down. I want to be empty. We brake heavily, him cradled by his seat belt, me bracing my right arm against the dashboard. I'm fiddling with the door handle before we've even come to a complete standstill.

'Wait,' Paul warns. 'Let me help you.' But I'm out onto the tarmac and running into the long grass at the roadside before he can unbuckle himself. Kneeling among hairy yellow flowers and stems flushed with pink, I retch. Between heaves, I can hear Paul locking the car, his footsteps in the grass behind me. I cough and spit, trying to get rid of the bitter taste.

'Are you OK?' He puts a hand on my back.

I retch again, although there's nothing left to throw up.

He takes his hand back. 'I'll wait by the car. I've got some water in the front.'

The spasms roll up my body in waves. My breaths are wet as sobs. Doubled over, I wait, watching ants and cloud shadows. My right arm shakes.

Behind me, his phone rings. He answers and talks quickly. I can't follow any of the Zulu.

On my first night back in South Africa, Paul gave me his address over the phone, and the GPS in my rental car brought me to the house from my hotel in less than half an hour. I hadn't planned to call him. But that night I wanted to be a different version of myself, rather than being compared to an out-of-date original, like I was some sort of inventory. It wasn't Naledi's fault and I knew that the next morning I'd feel guilty about not going round to her place.

The swallows had made their nest in the extractor fan. I woke them with the doorbell, and we kept them awake opening and closing cupboards looking for the right kind of glasses. Paul turned on two floor lamps in opposite corners of the open-plan living room because he didn't know which switch would turn on the overhead lights and which would blade matted feathers and pulp onto the walls.

'That's what you get for not having your own house,' he said, measuring out teaspoons of white sugar into two glasses half-full of ice. He was still in his suit trousers, but his shirt was untucked, the top three buttons undone.

'Are you telling me you're a homeless politician?' I quartered an orange. 'If so, you could definitely get your own reality show,' I said, licking the juice from my forefinger.

'All part of my master plan.' He rubbed his hands together and laughed.

'Why don't you have your own place?' I spooned two cherries onto the chopping board.

'I move around a lot for work,' he said, pouring a thumb of water into the glasses.

'So the taxpayer puts you up?' There was a half-smoked cigarette, ash in a perfect cylinder, in a saucer on the counter. Empty beer bottles were stacked next to the rubbish bin.

'I pay rent, thank you very much.' He passed me a glass. 'Stir.'

'Where are your parents?' I regretted asking immediately. After he answered, a question about mine would be inevitable, and I didn't want to talk about them.

He turned away and reached for an almost-full bottle in the cupboard above the microwave. It looked expensive. He dropped a cherry and a wedge of orange into each glass. 'Strike one,' he said, smiling.

'Sorry?' I said, watching him measure out bourbon whisky.

'How about we make a deal?' He stirred both drinks before

throwing the teaspoons into the sink. 'No politics, no religion and no family talk.' He handed me my glass. 'And no pets, either,' he said, unplugging the kettle in the corner to make room for a docking station for his MP3 player.

'But don't you want to see the photos of my cat, Lord Meowberry Fluffington?' I asked, sniffing my drink. 'I keep them in my purse.'

He laughed as a song I recognised started up. Ten seconds in, I knew what it was. Nine Inch Nails' 'With Teeth'. I wasn't sure what I'd expected but it wasn't that.

'Let's sit,' he said, nodding at the couch.

His briefcase was closed at one end of the dining table. At the other end, wicker coasters orbited the wood. Nothing in the house looked like Paul's taste. I realised that while I could confidently say what he wouldn't like, I didn't know what he would. Or whether I fell into the latter category.

'So, if religion and politics are off the table, what's left?' I asked. We were sitting cross-legged at opposite ends of the couch, turned towards each other but careful not to stray outside of our own cushions.

'Sex, drugs and rock 'n' roll?' he suggested from behind his glass.

I laughed. 'OK, drugs first.' I sipped at my drink; all I could taste was whisky. 'What the hell is this?'

'It's an old-fashioned.' He wiped the corner of his mouth. 'I think it was the world's first cocktail.'

'I'm surprised the world tried again after this,' I said, taking another sip. No doubt it would get easier to drink the drunker I got.

He shook his head. 'Obviously you need to be schooled.' He stirred his drink with his finger, holding my gaze.

'Last thing on the topic of drugs,' I said, putting my glass down on the no-man's-land cushion between us. 'Would you be up for sharing a cigarette?'

He smiled. 'Absolutely. Hold this for me?' He passed me his glass.

'Did I interrupt a meeting or something when I called?' I asked his back as he walked to the kitchen. The song finished and I could hear the birds complaining.

'No politics,' he said, returning with the saucer and a pack of Stuyvesants. 'But no, they'd already left.' He dropped the cigarettes onto the couch and sat down. 'This is a good one,' he said as 'Hurt' came through the speakers.

I handed him his drink and pulled a cigarette from the pack. 'Yeah, it's so much better than Johnny Cash's cover.'

'I know.' He passed me a lighter, still warm from his pocket.

'One of my friends saw Nine Inch Nails at Reading Festival.' The lighter caught and I inhaled, careful not to wet the filter. 'She was pretending that she knew them well to impress a boy, but when they played "Hurt", she told everyone that she thought Johnny Cash's original was much better.'

Paul laughed as I passed him the cigarette.

I took another sip of my drink. 'What next?'

'You choose,' he said. He held the cigarette between his thumb and his forefinger. It suited him. It looked like he enjoyed smoking rather than needing to do it.

'OK.' I leant against the armrest. 'Tell me about your first girlfriend.'

He coughed. 'That doesn't count as sex – I was fourteen.' He flicked ash into the saucer.

'I should hope not, then,' I said, taking the cigarette. The filter was slightly damp. 'What base did you get to, though?'

He shook his head, smiling. 'Second, I think?' He was drinking faster than I was, I noticed.

'Wow – you were an early starter.'

'What about you?'

I put my glass down in the valley between my crossed legs, pulling my dress up slightly over my knees. 'It's kind of a cliché – I was eighteen, had just gone to uni and had never really spoken to a boy before.' I took a final drag before offering the cigarette to him. He shook his head and I put it out in the saucer. 'So I fell for a guy on my course who was twelve years older than me and liked to make me feel bad about myself.' In fact, after an argument about how I was too intelligent to waste my talents on journalism, I'd realised that he had a lot in common with my father. It was a cliché too far, and we'd broken up a week later.

'Sexy,' he said, stretching one leg onto the cushion between us.

'I thought so,' I said, sucking an ice cube. I could've told him about Dan, two boyfriends later. How he'd downloaded South African music that he would play when we went to bed. How he'd ask for my definitive, potted take on South Africa whenever there was anything about SA in the news. How we'd fought about it. *Like one person can say everything you need to know about a country*, I'd told him. *Like everyone there is a fucking archetype.* I could've told Paul about how I'd bought Dan a DVD of an Afrikaans film Naledi had recommended. The eBay seller had promised it would come with subtitles, and if not, that I could send it back for a refund. When the DVD had arrived, there'd been a sticker on the back of the package that had the old South African flag on it, and one sentence in Afrikaans: *Ons sal oorwin.* We shall overcome. Even though there weren't any subtitles, I'd refused to send it back, to have anything more to do with the seller and his stickers.

'Hey, the music's stopped,' I said.

He finished his drink. '*Ja*, I don't have the whole album.'

'I do,' I said, standing up. 'It's on my iPod.' I carried it around out of habit, even though I wouldn't be walking or taking public transport here. Halfway to the kitchen, I stopped to rub the back of my calf with the top of my foot. I'd seen that portrayed as a seductive move some-where, but I didn't want to think too hard about where. It could've been a soft-core porn film.

Paul followed me into the kitchen. 'Another one?' he asked, motion-ing at my glass.

'Sure.' I downed the rest of my drink, my eyes closed against the taste. 'Jesus.'

He smiled and dried a teaspoon on a tea towel. 'So we're onto the rock 'n' roll part of the evening.'

'Yes, we are.' I left the headphones in my handbag and unplugged his MP3 player. 'Least favourite kind of music?'

He spooned sugar into the glasses. 'Power ballads.'

I laughed. 'I thought you'd be partial to a bit of Journey or something.'

'Fuck off,' he said, stirring.

'OK, favourite band.' I wiped the iPod's screen with the hem of my dress.

'Too many to pick one,' he said, squeezing the orange wedges before dropping them into the glasses.

'Lame.' I plugged my iPod into the speakers. 'What about guilty pleasure?'

He looked up. 'You first.'

'I get it.' I watched him pour the whisky, more in this batch than the last. 'You don't want to pick the Backstreet Boys or something if my guilty pleasure is something cooler.'

'Yep, you got me.'

'OK.' I scrolled through my music library. 'I'll play you my guilty pleasure,' I said, leaning against the counter. 'It's pretty bad though, so you've been warned.'

He tasted his drink before putting both down on the counter. 'OK, then. Hit me.'

I turned the volume up slightly. 'Here goes,' I said, pressing play.

The first beats of the song kicked in. Paul smiled. 'Is that Jay-Z?' He pushed the drinks closer to me. 'He's good.'

'Wait for it,' I said.

We stood at right angles, nodding to the beat, as Jay-Z flowed from coke to Glocks to K-Y Jelly. Then the guitar riff came in.

I laughed and turned down the volume. 'See?'

I reached for my drink, but Paul pushed me hard against the counter, his mouth over mine, his fingers digging into my back, pulling me closer, the other hand in my hair. He lifted me onto the counter, pushing himself between my legs, as Linkin Park's frontman sang about his scars.

I pull at some grass to wipe my mouth and nose, and sit back onto my heels. Smooth my skirt. Looking around for the first time, I see that the grass blushes into mauve tufts as it climbs up the slope away from the road.

I stand up carefully, left leg first, leaning on my right arm. I turn back to the motorway. Paul is watching me, squinting. His sunglasses flash on his head, bright as headlights. As I near the car, he holds out an open one-litre bottle of water.

'It's a bit warm,' he says.

'Thanks.' I gargle and turn away from him to spit into the grass.

'How's your arm?' he asks, screwing the top back onto the bottle.

'Actually, can you untie the sling for me please?' I turn, gathering my hair over my right shoulder. 'It feels better when it's out in front of me.'

He balances the water bottle on top of the car and steps closer. I can feel his breath on my neck. 'Tell me if it hurts, OK?' he asks, picking at the knot. He has to use his fingernails.

I close my eyes. 'I know I don't have any right to, but can I ask you to do something for me, please?' I don't wait for him to answer. 'Can you get the police report from my mom's accident?'

'Why?' He drops his hands and I turn to face him. His earring is missing.

'Because my father said that Gideon tampered with her car and ran her off the road.' I speak slowly, trying to control my voice.

He rubs his forehead, his fingers digging into his skin. 'Yes, OK.' A truck honks as it passes us. 'Fuck!' he shouts, hitting the roof of the car with the flat of his hand. The water bottle bounces and falls into the grass. I step back, remembering that my father had done the same thing at the service station in Joubertina. Maybe that's what South African men do: abuse their cars when they're angry.

My father has done so much more than that.

I want to pick up the water bottle but I can't bend that far.

'Sorry,' he says, leaning against the car, hands behind his head.

'It's OK,' I lie. 'Do it again if you want, this time for me.'

'Maybe later.' He pushes himself upright and motions for me to turn around. Before he tries the knot again, he brushes my hair out of the way, his fingers stroking my neck. I have to concentrate not to shrink away from his touch.

'Almost there,' he says.

There's one more thing I want to ask. 'Do you think he checked I was OK before he left?'

Paul's fingers stop tugging at the gauze. 'I don't know,' he says. 'I hope so.' He finds the right loop and pulls it through the knot. The gauze falls onto the tar. 'There,' he says, trapping the sling under his foot before the wind runs away with it. 'Are you OK to get going again?'

I knuckle the wet out from under my eyes and turn, nodding.

'Are you sure?' He looks at me closely, as if trying to read my face.

I smile quickly. 'Yes.' I lift my left arm slightly. I take a deep breath.

12

The Tame People

Two days later

The fence is at least ten feet high, topped in snarls of razor wire. The gate is open, but I don't think it's an invitation to visitors. More of a dare, perhaps. I wait on the pavement.

A brindle dog – a boerboel, I think – licks itself in the shadow of a muddy pick-up, one hind leg lifted over its head. The truck is parked in front of a double garage, between the two doors, one of which is open. The mud on the truck is thick and light grey, like a rhino's hide; it's old mud, boasting of the hunter's skill with a gun. It tells of many kills. I'd bet the truck has a name.

It's too dark inside, and too bright out, to see into the garage. But in the back of the truck, balanced against the half-open canopy, is a shotgun. I look down, balling my fists. I can still feel the weight of the Sellotape-wrapped gun in my hands, the way it stuck to my palms, almost as though the glue is still there in the creases, like the residue after a plaster has come off. But here the gun looks so casual, propped up in the back of the truck like a fishing pole.

I have to do this, and not just for myself.

'Brigadier van der Westhuizen?' I call.

The dog tips itself over, falls to its feet, nails scraping against the brick. It points its black muzzle at me and begins to bark, jogging closer. I stand still, holding my handbag in front of my body, as though to cover the scent of my fear.

'Riebeeck, shuddup.'

The dog stops and looks over its shoulder at the silhouette in the dark mouth of the garage. There's a white blaze low on its chest, tapering to rounded points near its shoulders. It lowers its flat head, the loose skin over its forehead wrinkling as it frowns.

'*Kom!*' the man calls, the *k* so hard that the word sounds like swallowing.

The dog turns and lopes up the driveway towards the garage. It's still young, its white-tipped paws too big for its legs, and blocky, as though it's the midway step in a 'how to draw a dog' tutorial.

I step over the tracks of the electric gate. The man has retreated further into the garage, perhaps defending his position. I walk up the driveway towards the sprawling house, hands open at my sides so that he can see they're empty.

'Brigadier Christian van der Westhuizen?' I call again, more loudly.

The dog yelps and scuds out of the garage and under the truck. I stop and bring my hand up to shade my face from the glare. The dog whimpers as I wait, watching for movement in the dark. Then, behind me, I hear a motor whirring, metal engaging. I turn. The gate is closing.

'Hello.'

The first thing I see is a gun at his side, fat fingers curled loosely around the barrel. A rifle, maybe, with a sight. Hundreds of spy movies have taught me what I'd look like through the scope. Sweat traces my spine.

Only the left side of his mouth curves upwards as he smiles. He looks me up and down slowly, and I let him, waiting for him to decide on an opening gambit. I know how to play men like him – two parts scared little girl, one part vixen – or at least I thought I did. My attempts to play my father have left me doubting myself. I thought

217

only I was pretending during the father–daughter bonding in Nature's Valley, but Nico'd had a game plan all along, one that didn't involve talking to the police.

The brigadier's dressed for a hunt, in an olive shirt, blotted with oil, and tan shorts: a mix-and-match safari suit. A camouflage-print baseball cap hides his eyes; a silver beard and black moustache take care of most of the rest of his face. The man is at home in this country – with his gun – in a way I never will be. For a moment, I hate him for that.

'What do you want?' he asks in Afrikaans.

'*Om te praat*.' My tongue isn't loose enough to roll the *r*. 'To talk,' I say, letting my hair fall into my eyes.

He lifts the gun and slides it across his shoulders behind his neck, hooking both arms over it. The stance pushes his chest out, like some dull bird in its mating stance, and his gut juts out even further over the waistband of his shorts. I know it's only because of my skin – and possibly my skirt – that the gun isn't pointed at me.

'Are you the brigadier?'

He nods.

'Do you have a minute to talk?' I concentrate on his beard, trying to block out the gun over his shoulders and the hairy belly showing where one button is missing on his shirt. I can't help but think of Mr Twit, the cornflakes and baked beans hidden in his hair as tasty snacks. Mr Twit was cruel to animals too. Believed the birds that landed in his garden belonged to him.

'Come with me.' He turns back to the garage, not looking to see if I'll follow.

I drop my sunglasses into my bag and resist the urge to wipe my palms on my sides. Against the paved front garden, with its bricked-off islands of aloes, I'm conspicuous in my dress and boots, chosen to cover the bruises: the modern version of the redcoat. I straighten, breathe as deeply as I can, and walk towards the garage.

I woke late this morning, stiff and bruised. Whenever Paul was in Cape Town, he'd told me on the drive from George, he stayed at a government-owned house on Lion's Head, and one of the spare rooms on the second floor was mine for as long as he was in town. We'd arrived two nights earlier at dusk, just after the floodlights at the foot of Table Mountain were turned on. Paul had helped me up the stairs to my room, but had stopped at the threshold and said goodnight. My shoulder was too painful for me to undress myself and I'd slept in my clothes.

From my window, through the trees and scrub, I could see Camps Bay and Clifton Beach. Two cranes perched on the hillside. Construction on the World Cup stadium had started. A toothbrush and a bar of soap, both still in their wrappers, lay on the bedside table where Paul had put them yesterday morning. There'd been a young nurse with him who'd changed my dressings and washed my hair over the sink. I hadn't been hungry, and she sent me back to bed with painkillers, a sleeping pill and a promise to return today. I'd asked her what she was giving me; it wasn't temazepam and I was grateful for that. For being able to see the pills before I swallowed them.

Paul was gone when I woke up this morning, and I was alone in the house. The bed in the room he'd said was his hadn't been slept in. He'd left the brigadier's address and a driver's phone number on the kitchen counter. The nurse would be coming by at one to check me over, the note said. I traced my finger over my name in his handwriting.

The fridge was empty, and the cupboards held only coffee, tea and powdered milk. I'd made myself a cup of rooibos and climbed slowly to my room. One-handed, I dug through the clothes in my suitcase, dusty and smelling of smoke, and found a clean dress. I wondered if I could use the washing machine in the kitchen but thought it might seem presumptuous, too at-home. After that, I tipped my handbag out onto the bed, making piles of cigarette butts and chewing-gum wrappers. My dictaphone still worked, but I decided against taking it with me to see the brigadier. I tried my phone, but it wouldn't turn on. I prised off the back, looking for water damage, and put the battery on the window sill. But something else was wrong. The SIM card was missing.

I sat on the bed, my useless phone face down in front of me, wondering if, like the gun, my father had taken that too.

The garage smells of coriander. I wait for my eyes to adjust.

'Why would a khaki like yourself come behind the *boerewors* curtain?'

'Excuse me?' The switch to English surprises me. His vowels are so 'flet' that he sounds like someone making fun of Afrikaners' English.

Two green and gold lamps, more suited to an office, glow at each end of the workbench that runs across the back of the garage. The brigadier, his back to me, leans to switch off the oscillating fan, pointed upwards, buzzing next to a small fridge.

'A Pommy like you? Out in Brackenfell?' He turns to face me, a meat cleaver in his hand. 'Have you come to annex the place?' He laughs, dropping the blade to his side and tapping it against his thigh.

'No, sir.' I try to smile. 'I came to talk to you about one of your soldiers.'

He half turns and fumbles with something metal on the workbench. I can't see the rifle anywhere. '*Ja?*' he prompts me.

I remember how Danie reacted when I mentioned Nico's name. 'Jaco Eloff.' It's almost a question.

'What's he got to do with you?'

'He's my father.' I stare at the lamp, waiting, surprised at how easily the lie came.

He laughs loudly, leaning back against the workbench. 'You poor cow.'

I sigh and look down, hoping he'll take my relief for offence. 'I know.'

'*Ag*, sorry, hey,' he says, sliding the cleaver onto the surface behind him. 'You'll have to excuse me – I spend all my time with old boys. Not used to talking to little girls like you.'

I wonder if I should reply in Afrikaans, and if so, whether I should use the formal version of 'you' – *U* instead of *jy*.

The workbench rattles as he pushes himself up from it. 'What say you we turn on some lights in here?'

I nod, keeping my eyes lowered. 'Yes, please, sir.' Three parts scared little girl it is.

The brigadier feels for the switch on the left wall. I blink as the strip light flickers and hums. 'That's better,' he says, as he sinks to his haunches, one hand on the wall to steady him, and reaches into a gap under the workbench. 'I'll just find you something to sit on.'

Parked in the second bay is a red two-door Mercedes. The driver's cream leather seat is pulled too close to the steering wheel for it to be the brigadier's car. The rifle shines dully on the bonnet of the car, the shoulder strap hanging down over the tyre. He has a wife, and he doesn't like her enough to worry about scratching the paintjob on her car, I think.

The brigadier drags a wooden crate out from under the counter. He pulls the crate into the middle of the empty parking bay and pushes down on two corners to check it will hold my weight. 'Sit.'

He's used to having his orders followed. 'Thank you,' I say.

He waits behind the crate as I crouch and drop my bag onto the concrete. I sit, my back to him.

'No, man,' he says, gripping my shoulders.

The pain is immediate, and I push my nails into my palms, forcing myself to resist the urge to lower my left shoulder out from under his fingers.

'That way,' he says, turning me towards the workbench.

I move as quickly as I can, keeping my left arm close to my chest, willing his hands off me. He steps past the crate and walks towards his cleaver. I blink away the tears, trying to slow my breathing. At least he didn't turn me towards his belly.

'Something to drink?' he asks, turning over two tumblers on a tray next to the fridge.

I think I'll vomit if it's anything stronger than water, but the tray holds only bottles of spirits. It's a test, just like his hands on my shoulders had been. 'Whisky?' I guess. 'Neat.'

He nods, unscrewing the cap on a bottle with a black label. 'Good girl.'

I slowly straighten my left arm out in front of me until my palm is flat on my knee, wishing for the nurse and her cup of pills.

'*Tjorts*,' he says when he hands me the tumbler, clinking his two-thirds-full glass against mine.

I bring the whisky up to my lips, just wetting them, and smile around the glass. 'Cheers.'

He turns back towards the workbench. 'Now, what can I do for you?'

I wipe my mouth on the back of my hand.

'I'm sorry that I can't sit and have tea,' he says over his shoulder. 'Heading off into the Karoo tomorrow morning for a hunt.'

'No, I'm grateful for any of your time.' I hope he'll switch back to English soon: I know the Afrikaans for animals and food, but not for torture. 'What are you hunting?'

'Lions.' He leans and pulls the cleaver towards him.

I stare at him, hating his back and his baseball cap. 'Wow.'

'*Ja, nee.*' He moves along the workbench towards what looks like an old, industrial pencil sharpener. 'Maybe later I'll show you the heads I've got mounted in the house. The *kaffirs* up there know what they're doing when it comes to taxidermy.' He says the last word in English, looking over his shoulder again to let me know that it's for my benefit.

I smile and pretend to take another sip. 'This is great, thanks.'

'You looked like you needed it,' he says, blowing on the sharpener. 'You English girls always do, or else you'd never drop your panties.'

While he laughs at his own joke, I dip the hem of my dress into the tumbler and let it soak up an inch of whisky.

'So what do you wanna know?' He turns, a long wooden pole in one hand – the kind that you use to open tall sash windows. The other hand is in a blue plastic glove. I watch as he lifts the S-shaped hook towards the ceiling. Above the workbench, thick strips of dark meat hang from a washing line strung across the garage. He's drying biltong.

'I was hoping to find my father.'

He lowers the pole, a piece of dried meat hanging on the hook. With his gloved hand, he lays the meat on a piece of muslin on the workbench.

'My mom didn't know him well,' I improvise. 'They met when she was over here from England in 1984.'

He lifts the pole again, fishing for another piece.

'She died recently and I wanted to get to know my father. I hoped you could help me find him.'

He adds another strip of meat to the pile. 'And how did you get to me?'

Shit. I fake a long sip of whisky, covering the front of the tumbler with my fingers so that he can't see how much I've drunk, and cough. 'Sorry,' I say, looking up at him. 'This is just really difficult.'

He reaches for his glass, watching me as he drinks.

'Other than his name, all my mom really knew about my father was that he went on about you and how you helped him on the border.'

He lowers his glass, his eyes dark underneath his cap. He reminds me of the worst things about my father. I realise he's waiting for me to talk.

'I know he isn't worth much, my dad, but you were kind to him, and that means a lot to me,' I hurry on. 'I don't want to cause any trouble, I swear.'

He drains his glass and slams it down on the counter. I'm surprised the glass doesn't shatter.

'I'm sorry.' I lower my eyes, pushing my knees together so that my legs are in the shape of an A. 'I'll try to find someone else who can help me.'

'There's no one else,' he says in English, leaning the pole against the workbench.

I look up at him as he pushes his cap up and wipes his forehead on his arm. 'What do you mean?'

'Everyone he used to know is dead.' He turns, head bent over the pile of biltong. 'Those that aren't haven't had anything to do with him for a long time. When Eloff left the army, he didn't cope so well.'

'Drugs?' I ask, back on firmer ground.

'*Ja*. Mandrax.'

I find another length of hem to soak up more whisky.

'Eloff wasn't good enough to go on to Special Forces work. Most of the others in his unit did – Barnard, du Plessis, Van Vuuren – and he took it hard.'

Is the Van Vuuren he's referring to Gideon? I don't think now's the right time to ask.

He turns, working a hook out of the end of a strip of dark brown meat. 'For a while, we all tried to help him.'

'How could you help?' I ask, cradling the wet stretch of fabric in my hand so that it doesn't drip.

The brigadier sighs. 'We'd give him Mandrax to sell. He could make a ten-rand profit per pill.' He throws the hook into a bowl on the counter. 'But you can see where that led.' I nod. He picks up another strip and pulls at the hook. 'He almost fucked up a few CCB ops, going around his friends and asking for money for more pills.'

I almost lean forward. 'Sorry – CCB?'

He reaches for the whisky bottle, which is still open on the counter, refills his glass. 'The Civilian Cooperation Bureau. A hit squad.' He puts one finger on his lips. 'But don't tell anyone, hey.'

'No, sir,' I say, shaking my head when he offers a top-up.

'The idiots who hanged a baboon foetus out in front of Tutu's house and hoped it would bewitch him.' He laughs. 'They did some good work against the *terrs*, but that was just stupid.'

I wait, not knowing what to ask.

'After he almost blew the ops, some of the guys made sure Eloff knew not to come around any more.' He pulls the muslin along the worktop towards what I now realise is a biltong slicer.

I put my glass down next to the crate. 'Were they undercover? I mean, is that how he almost ruined things?'

'*Ja.*' He turns, both hands gloved now. 'Especially the ones in Region 6 – that was here, SA.'

Gideon.

He walks past the crate to a door in the side wall of the garage and pushes down on the handle with his elbow. 'Sarie,' he shouts. 'I need the jars.'

The dog comes running, ears perked and tail wagging. I hope it stays out of the brigadier's reach.

'Those were the days, hey,' he says, back at the workbench. 'But

I'm not your history teacher, so go read a fucking book if you want to know more.'

I hold the glass for the dog to drink from, watching the brigadier in case he turns around. 'So did you see my father again?'

He shakes his head. 'Not until our reunion in ninety-seven.' He begins to feed a strip of biltong into the slicer. 'And by then, no one wanted anything to do with him.'

I stroke the dog's ears as it noses my hem. 'How come?'

The brigadier pauses before he answers, weighing up how much damage I could do, how much power I have. 'He was planning on talking to the TRC,' he says, deciding I'm just a girl and no threat to him.

The door behind me opens; the dog starts but doesn't run. I turn and smile at Sarie, a woman in her late fifties wearing coral lipstick and smelling of potpourri. She nods, carrying a heavy-looking tray of sterilised jars past me to the workbench.

'Bean stew for supper,' the brigadier says as she slides the tray onto the counter. Another order. Sarie picks up my now empty glass on her way out and closes the door quietly behind her. The brigadier chooses a jar from the tray. 'I'm sending you off with some of the best kudu biltong you'll ever taste,' he says.

I wonder if that means our time is up. 'Did he talk to the TRC, then?' I try.

He holds the jar at the edge of the worktop and pushes thin slices of meat into it. 'No.' The dog watches as slivers of biltong miss the jar and fall to the floor. But it knows better than to go for them.

'Why not?' I'm pushing my luck, I know.

He finds the lid for the jar and turns towards me. The dog pulls its head out from under my hand and scurries out of the garage. I keep my face blank and try to look as small as possible.

'I think you know the answer to that question,' the brigadier says finally, screwing the lid onto the jar.

I nod. I do know.

'It was the best solution for everyone, your father included. He was useless by then, and he knew it, so I don't think he fought it.'

I decide to risk it. 'Do you know who helped him realise that?' I hate him for forcing his euphemisms on me.

'The okes in his unit. It was only right.'

The gate begins to open. I can't leave without asking. 'One last thing, sir, if that's OK?' I keep going before he can tell me *no*. 'My mom said she met one of his friends from the unit who was really kind to her, and I was hoping to track him down. She thought his name was Van Vuuren and she said he had red hair. It's not much to go on but you wouldn't happen to know where I could find him, would you, sir?'

He holds the jar out to me. Its lid is green; it probably once held the gherkins he no doubt likes cut in a specific way for his lunch. 'Even if I did, I doubt he'd like to be found by the likes of you.'

Is that a warning? I stand up and take the biltong from him. 'Thank you,' I say.

'I didn't put it on too tight,' he says. 'Just in case there's not a man around to open it for you when you want some.' He winks.

I force a smile. 'Thank you for your help, sir.' I turn towards the sunlight. Almost there.

'Wait.'

I stop. He might as well have said *heel*.

'You won't get away that easy,' he says, next to me. He smells of oil and meat. 'Your bag.'

'Oh.' I realise I've forgotten it next to the crate.

'Let me.' He slides the handles up around my left arm, careful not to touch it, as though it were an electrified wire that would buzz if he touched it, like in the children's game Operation. Does he know about the crash? Or could he tell I was hurt when he touched me earlier?

'Thank you,' I say as he gently lowers the handles onto my shoulder. The bag is light enough that I can stand it, just until he turns away.

'You're welcome.'

I look straight ahead and walk out into the late afternoon.

Back on the road, the driver gets out of the car and opens the back door for me. For a second, I'm surprised it's not my father waiting for me.

Before we drive away, when I'm sure the brigadier is no longer watching, I open the jar of biltong and pour it through the gate on the driveway. The dog comes running.

13

Please Do Not Feed the Animals

The olives come in a blueberry dressing.

'Trust me,' Lindiwe says when I raise my eyebrows. 'They're yummy. That's why I bought a bucket of them.'

I laugh. 'Do olives and tequila even go together?'

'As of now, yes.' She lifts olives with a slotted spoon and tips them into a brown bowl. 'I just invented it. You can say you were there. It'll be your claim to fame.' The olives are purple, but the oil in the dressing makes them look milky. 'Now we need something to spit the stones into.' She ducks behind the counter and holds up a brandy glass.

'Nice,' I say. I probably shouldn't be drinking, but even being close to alcohol makes me feel freer, to talk, to cry. I've always thought that's why people in England drink so much. Just another way in which I've been assimilated.

She slides the brandy glass across the bench and reaches back into the cupboard. 'We'll have to drink out of normal glasses.' She stands up, three tumblers between the fingers of her left hand, a plate in the right.

'Where's Paul?' I ask. The wind is picking up outside. The trees in the garden look like washing-up brushes in the heavy cloud.

She leans forward, elbows on the counter. From around an olive, she says: 'In Dundee.'

'Oh.'

She nods. 'But he'll be here soon. He called when he landed and asked if he should bring anything. I told him actual food and a new personality.' She chews and shows me the stone between her teeth.

I hold out the brandy glass. 'How much has he told you?' I have to ask.

She spits the stone into it. 'That he thinks your dad had something to do with the murder of our dad. Or that he knows more than he's said, anyway.'

My reflection in the worktop is speckled. 'Oh.'

She laughs. '*Eish*, Jo, is that your favourite word now?'

'I just dunno what else—'

'I'm just giving you shit,' she says, putting her hand over mine. 'I don't know what to say either.' She turns and opens a drawer.

My shoulder throbs where the brigadier squeezed it but I wouldn't be able to tell if he left a mark.

I got back from his house at sunset. On this side of the mountain, it was still light. Further along the street a big man sat reading next to three open garages, guarding the imported cars on display inside. He'd been there that morning when I'd left for Brackenfell. Lindiwe was waiting in the kitchen, wrapped up like a present in a long yellow and orange scarf. She was in her socks, the soles of which were waxed black with the grime from the tiles.

'Do you know if they found anything at the lodge?' I ask now.

'Paul didn't say. I dunno if he'd tell me anyway. We never really talk about it.' She rinses a knife.

'Why not?'

'Because we'd get into a fight.' She turns and wipes a drop of water from her forehead with her sleeve. 'It's all he can think about these days, finding out exactly what happened to him, but I don't think it matters any more.'

I suck on an olive stone.

'I mean, obviously it matters.' She pulls a tall stool out from under the breakfast bar and sits down, reaching for a lemon. 'But it matters less than right now does. Basically, what I'm saying is that I don't care if Batman has some tortured origin story. Stop crying about it and fight some baddies already. I just think there comes a time when you have to stop blaming the past for everything and actually deal.' She cuts the lemon in half.

My mom and I used to eat lemons straight from the tree that grew in our complex's small garden. We'd each have a half, sprinkle the top with salt and eat it like a grapefruit. 'Maybe that's what he's trying to do.'

'Maybe.' She shrugs, halving a second lemon. 'All I'm saying is focus on what you can do right now, you know? Face forward.'

'Is that your mantra or something?'

'No doubt. I should get it on a bumper sticker.' The stool tilts as she reaches for the salt shaker.

'I'd buy one,' I say. 'Even though I don't have a car.' The last words quieter as I realise how bad the joke is.

She smiles and raises her glass. 'Now, please: drink with me. To…' She pauses; nothing we have in common is worthy of a toast. 'To new friends.'

Tequila reminds me of university drinking games, cheap cocktails, requesting 'Killing in the Name' on cheese nights at the club with a stripper pole in the middle of the dance floor. Even though it will probably make me feel sick, I raise my glass, lick salt from my wrist and throw it back. It's good enough to drink straight.

'Damn, today sucked,' she says.

'No shit,' I say, nodding at the lemon peel she's shredded.

'I was at the shelter at the Killarney race track, taking down the names of the refugees from Du Noon township, and these rich white guys got all nervous about them trying to steal the cars. It was surreal, hey. Women braiding each other's hair, people playing soccer or checkers.' She looks down and pushes the red plastic Alice band further back onto her head. 'And then I talked to one of the women and it turns out they haven't had food or water for four days. They say they love peace, that they've shown SA how much they love us,' she says. 'But we don't love them. We treat our dogs better than we treat them.'

Or our cars, I think.

A roof tile lands on the porch, terracotta flak. I flinch and take a deep breath to slow my pulse. I've heard that living in South Africa means jumping at every noise, a weapon next to your bed, an alarm code punched in every night, but Lindiwe hardly notices.

'And now,' she says, 'they have to choose between going back to the countries they ran from or going back to the townships where they are being beaten and stoned. Where's the choice in that?'

I shake my head. Rain licks at the windows.

'It's just one more thing on the long list of shit.' She picks up the bottle of tequila and wipes the ring of condensation under it with a dishcloth. 'Did you know that it's possible to be too black?'

'What do you mean?'

'If you're too dark, the police stop you in case you're here illegally. Even if you're legal – whatever that is – if you won't bribe them, they tear up your papers and send you to Lindela.' She balls the dishcloth and throws it into the sink.

'What's Lindela?'

'Yo, are English newspapers just full of photos of badgers and Prince William?'

'You're forgetting the boobs and radical Muslims.'

She shakes her head. 'Lindela is a concentration camp for refugees being deported.' She raises her hand. 'Hold up – it's for *black* refugees being deported. There are no white *kwerekweres* in SA.' She smiles. 'Not even you.'

'Jesus.' I slide off the stool and rinse my glass in the sink. 'I'm surprised the tabloids aren't all over this as an example of what the UK should do.' I fill the tumbler and drink. The water is different here, softer.

Lindiwe swivels to face me. Her shoes are under the counter, the outer edge of the soles more worn than the rest. 'The people I saw today lived in Wendy houses that the rich whites and blacks in this neighbourhood wouldn't even let their kids keep their bikes in. So I think we should put our glasses down on any and all wooden surfaces in this house as a protest. That's some resistance right there.'

I smile and lean against the sink. 'Maybe key some of those cars next door?'

'*Ja*, for definite. What kills me is that no one from the government will go out and speak to them. Instead, they'll declare some sort of day of healing or something, as if a public holiday is a big enough plaster for this.'

'How does it work, you and Paul on opposites sides of this?' I ask, sitting down again with my glass of water.

She pours herself an inch of tequila. 'Not well, most of the time. But worse for him than for me. The party doesn't like it.' She twists her glass. It sheds salt in concentric circles, like a firework. Then she looks up at me. 'But what I really want to know is what the hell is going on between the two of you?'

I laugh. 'Smooth segue.'

'I know,' she says, pushing my glass towards me. 'Finish that water so that I can get you drunk.'

I put the empty glass down, panting. 'Just give up already.'

'*Eish*, Jo.' She pours tequila into the glasses. 'I'm gonna keep trying, you know.'

'Well, it's not gonna work.' I swill the tequila around. 'Any of it. I can't come live with him and be his love.' Saying it out loud makes it seem even more laughable. Romanticism is out of place here, dated and naïve.

'*Haw wena*. Think positive.' She raises her glass. 'Face forward.'

I lick the back of my hand and reach for the salt as she bites into a slice of lemon.

'Is it because he's a bad kisser?' she asks, her eyes watering.

I pick out the pips, dropping them onto the plate. 'Why do you think he's a bad kisser?'

'Please, man. I've seen the guy eat soup.'

We shrug with laughter.

'Shit, but it's quiet in this house,' she says.

'I know. I couldn't find a TV or a radio anywhere.'

'Maybe they don't want to be able to hear about all their fuck-ups.' She reaches down and lifts her backpack onto her lap. 'Speaking of which, would you mind helping me with something?'

'Sure.' I push the plates and glasses along the breakfast bar, clearing a space. 'What is it?'

'A mailshot to the Durban council.' She tips a plastic folder out onto the counter and starts separating envelopes and letters into piles. 'A campaign for electricity in the shacks there.'

'OK.' I wipe the worktop in front of me with my sleeves.

'I'll write the addresses on later.' She slides a pile of paper towards me. The red and black logo I'd seen on her and Paul's armbands in Alex is stamped in the top right corner of each letter. 'Thanks.'

I turn the first letter lengthways, lining up the edges. Thunder shakes the windowpanes. 'So what made you join the AbM?' I ask, running my fingernail over the fold.

'Growing up in a shack will do it,' she says, smiling.

I shake my head. 'Sorry, stupid question.'

She puts her hand on my arm. 'No, it's not. I mean, we were lucky. After Mom died, we went to live in Jo'burg with our aunt who was a maid for a nice English family in Brentwood.' She pats the air out of an envelope. 'Getting out of the homeland meant we could go to school. The family helped pay for it,' she says, pulling a sheaf of paper from her pile. 'So I guess it's because we were lucky that I joined.'

'Is that why Paul joined the ANC?'

'He joined so that what happened to Dad wouldn't happen again,' she says in a deep voice. She looks down. 'It was worse for him because he could remember them both, Mom and Dad.'

'You can't?'

'No – I was two when he disappeared and just five when the TB took her.' She smooths the fold in the paper with her thumb. 'In a way, I'm grateful for that.'

I put the envelope on the stool next to me. 'I want to give you something,' I say, reaching into my handbag.

'OK.' She looks up, her hands still.

'If you don't want it, just say.' I find the coin in the inside pocket. 'Here.' I put the Krugerrand down in front of her.

She picks it up and runs her thumbnail over the ridges scoring the rim of the coin. 'Is it real?'

'Yes.' It doesn't look real, though. More like chocolate money, or a doubloon. When I first arrived in England, I'd hoarded the pound coins my grandmother gave me; they made me feel like a pirate. This coin would have been a prize possession back then. 'My father gave it to me.'

Lindiwe looks up, frowning. The Krugerrand shines dully, like a bell, in her palm.

'But I want to put it towards something good, like your work,' I say. 'Is that OK?'

'I dunno.' She closes her hand around the coin. 'Let me think about it.'

'OK.'

She stuffs it into her back pocket. I wish again for music or a TV; the rain isn't loud enough to fill the silence.

She slides a letter into an envelope. 'How old were you when your mom died?' She's working much faster than I am.

'Twelve.' I fold five sheets of paper at a time.

'And when did you move to England?' she asks.

'About three weeks after that. My grandmother moved there in ninety-one to be with her second husband, Uncle Rob. He was Scottish but he'd worked in London so long that I could understand most of what he said when I met him; just as well, or it would've been even more awkward than it was.' I'd cried more at his funeral, five years ago, than at my grandmother's. 'And then I was off to boarding school the week after that.'

She whistles. 'It's like a ye olde book. All it needs is an evil governess and a magic cupboard.' She looks down. 'Where was your dad?'

'Here.' I shrug. 'But he wouldn't take me. My mom didn't want that, anyway.'

'They didn't get on?'

I add four more envelopes to the pile on the stool. 'No. They hadn't seen each other in years, not since they broke up before I was two.'

'Do you remember them together?'

I shake my head. 'But he told so many stories about that time that it's almost like remembering.'

I know these stories off by heart. We lodged with an old woman, a Mrs Pienaar, living in the annexe intended for maids and gardeners. My father gave me bowls of cool, milky coffee so we could stay up till 4 a.m. while my mom slept. He read to me, played Wagner and let me draw on the walls in sticky pastels. When our routine wore him out and he went to bed, I'd climb out of my cot and trek to Mrs Pienaar's side of the house.

My father said I was expert at opening olive jars with my small, fat hands. I ate all the pickles in Mrs Pienaar's fridge. I gnawed on cheese corners, leaving spit and gum marks. I tried to feed every last sausage – pink tubes bright as Barbies – to her goldfish, who sulked below the crust of floating meat. I tore out the price tags she'd stapled into expensive home-knitted tea cosies. I trailed wool and peppercorns.

According to my father, and until I was old enough to know better, this was my story: I was olive thief, sausage socialist, anti-capitalist. My mom swore none of this ever happened.

'Drink?' Lindiwe nods at the tequila bottle.

'Yes, please.'

The front door opens and the windows rattle in their frames, the room colder. 'Jo?' An umbrella drops on the tiles.

'In here, big brother,' Lindiwe shouts.

Paul turns on the light in the corridor and comes into the kitchen. Drizzle shines in beads on his jacket. Lindiwe clicks and points finger-guns at him, and I wonder if he picked up the habit from her or if it was the other way around.

'I didn't really feel a lot,' Paul says behind me. 'And then I felt so bad for not reacting the way I should. I was standing where he died.' He clears his throat. 'Likely died. Allegedly.'

'How're you supposed to react?' Lindiwe asks. In the reflection above the sink, I watch her rub his arm.

'I dunno – cry or something.'

I rinse a plate and slot it into the drying rack.

'I thought trying to find out what happened to him would help.' A pause. 'I just hoped it would help me to stop obsessing over this. That maybe I could think about it once a day rather than twenty times.'

Lindiwe puts her arm around his shoulders. 'Maybe you should try to focus on him rather than on what happened. Learn the guitar maybe.'

'What are you? A motivational speaker?' There's a smile in his voice.

'Yes, actually. Jo thinks so too.'

I duck my head. I can't tell if the brown mark on the plate is food or the pattern.

Paul's phone rings in the entrance hall. A stool scrapes against the tiles as he runs to get it. He's in his socks now, too. I pull the plug and water begins to drain out.

Lindiwe puts the empty wine glasses down on the counter next to me. 'Is this awkward?' she asks, leaning against the worktop. 'I can't tell.'

I smile, grateful for her joke.

She sighs. 'When we were younger, he used to build traps outside the house in case anyone tried to come in and take us the way they did Dad. And he'd hide weapons all over the house – cricket bats with nails sticking out of them and homemade spears.' She looks at me. 'Did you see any when you were at his house?'

I shake my head, squirting dishwashing liquid onto a sponge.

'But maybe you were too naked to pay attention.' She elbows me, and I pull away, holding my shoulder. 'Shit, sorry,' she says, bringing her hands up to her cheeks.

'It's OK.' I try to smile.

She looks down. 'I'm just gonna go check that he's all right,' she says, straightening.

I nod and dry my hands on a damp dishcloth. I tip the uneaten olives back into the bucket, turning it to close the lid. The olives join the milk, cheese and tomatoes Paul bought in the fridge. I leave the tequila on the counter, wiping the surfaces around it and catching salt and pith in my hand.

Outside, the sky is drizzle-pink, the mountain behind the house disappearing into a cloud bank. I sit down and open the envelope of photos Paul had printed from the camera my father left in the car. He'd already looked at them, he told me as he slid them across the counter during dinner. Nothing useful, he said. The memory card containing photos of Wilna's flat, the lodge, maybe even Danie's house, was still missing. I wonder what else was on it that he had to take it with him.

I spread the photos out in front of me in a grid. Many of them are of me, of the back of my head. Me on the balcony at Nature's Valley, looking out at the sea. Me on the hill in Dundee, his other camera raised in my hands. Me smoking outside the airport. One is taken through the sliding door and you can see my father's reflection in the glass; I stand, arms folded, within his outline. The rest were taken in the car, my head turned away from the camera, yellow and grey blurs in the window frame.

I wind a sheaf of hair around my finger. The rest of the photos are of car parks, some I don't even remember stopping in, and the road behind us, framed by the back window of the car. I cover my half-portraits with the roadscapes, searching for a repeated car or a figure in the distance – the only reason my father would have had for taking them. But the question remains: was he looking for Gideon in these pictures, or for the police?

'What the fuck is this, Paul?' Lindiwe throws something down on a table in the next room. He answers in Zulu, his voice low.

In one photo there's a red pick-up three cars behind us, one lane over, and again passing the petrol station near Storms River. Or is the second one orange? Maybe he wasn't lying about the *bakkie* behind us. Maybe he crashed the car and left me there because it was the only way to keep me safe.

'Will a confession from him really solve everything?' Lindiwe asks. 'Has it ever been that easy? How long are you gonna keep doing this to yourself? And to the rest of us?'

'*Hhayi*,' he says. No. He slams his briefcase shut. 'But I don't know what else to do.'

'Here's what you can do.' She's shouting now, the rest in Zulu.

'Lindi—' Paul tries to talk over her.

Lindiwe slides on the tiles as she comes into the kitchen. 'I'm sorry, Jo,' she says, kicking her trainers out from under the counter. 'I've gotta go. Give me a call if you want.' She bends and pulls her shoes on. 'That idiot in there can give you my number.'

'OK. Here,' I say, handing her my pile of envelopes.

She stuffs them into her backpack and slings it over her shoulder. 'Call me if you need anything,' she says and shakes her head. 'Or better yet, call someone that has absolutely fuck-all to do with this family.' She turns, her shoes squeaking. The front door opens.

I wait for it to slam, but she closes it quietly behind her instead.

Paul takes two tumblers out of the drying rack and checks them for foam. He pours an inch of tequila into each glass while I read the letter.

It's dated 1 April, but the contents are clearly no joke:

240

Mr Silongo,
Nico Roussouw of Flat 2, Malabor Court, Newlands, Cape Town,
killed your father.
Good luck.

There's no signature. The letter is typed on plain white paper. Paul's name and office address are printed onto a label on the envelope, which is postmarked Johannesburg.

'Why say good luck? What does that even mean?' Paul asks as he slips onto Lindiwe's stool. 'Did he really want me to get Nico or was he being sarcastic?'

I fold the letter into its envelope. 'How many times have you read this?'

'Fifty.' He inspects the tequila in his glass before he swallows it. 'More.'

'I'm sorry.' I don't know where to look.

'You didn't send it,' he says, pushing the other tumbler towards me.

Paul and I haven't been alone together since the drive from George. We haven't mentioned my visit to the brigadier, what happened in Alex, or that night at his house.

'Who do you think did send it?' he asks, pouring again, more this time.

'I don't know. Gideon, maybe.' I haven't told him about the temaz-epam or the gun.

'Just for fun?' he asks.

'Possibly.' Worst of all, I haven't been able to tell Paul about his father's last moments on the hill near the lodge. I shouldn't have to be the one to do that, I keep thinking, but there's no one else.

He clinks his glass against mine. 'For old time's sake,' he says and we both drink.

14

Particulars

A drowned gecko floats in the drain outside the flat. I stand under the awning by the letterboxes while Paul talks to the policeman inside. At the end of the road, behind an electricity pylon, Devil's Peak climbs into the cloud. Palm trees bend in the wind.

The driver had come to bring me to Newlands at eleven, as Paul had promised last night after his second shot of tequila. Without my phone as an alarm clock I'd overslept, and my hair was still wet as I ran out to the car. Paul was late meeting me here, and I'd waited in the car, thinking about buying cigarettes.

Now the policeman pulls his cap lower as he steps out into the rain. He's not in uniform. I avoid his eyes as he runs past me down the grassy bank to the road, not knowing what Paul's told him about who I am or why he's waiting for my father. Out from under the awning, I close my eyes and lift my face to the sky, as though hoping to feel sun. My hands are sweaty under the latex gloves Paul's told me to wear.

Part of me hopes the walls will be covered with posters of naked women holding guns, White Power manifestos on every surface, the medicine cabinet lined with bottles of anti-psychotics – the not-normalness of my father finally made trite and obvious.

'You can come in now, Jo,' Paul says. 'They'll come back when you're done.'

I nod, my eyes still closed, and turn.

The doormat is soggy. It says: *Please remove your clothes*. I doubt it came with the flat.

I step past Paul into the flat. The front door opens into the living room. 'What'll they come back to do?' I ask.

'Tear it apart,' he says.

I feel as though theme music is about to start up. Something by The Who, maybe.

'Search it properly, I mean.' He buttons his suit jacket. His suit and shirt are two different shades of black, and the jacket is too big at the waist and arms.

A framed embroidered tapestry of a piece of scripture hangs above the TV. 'What do you want me to do?' I don't know where to start, and I don't want to touch anything.

He folds his arms. 'Check for the obvious. See if there's anything that means something to you.'

I turn back to him. 'Like what?' The rain is blowing into the room at an angle and his shoes are getting wet.

'You tell me. You know him.'

I put my handbag on the armrest of the couch. It's covered in brightly coloured scenes from someone's idea of a cave painting. 'No, I don't.' This is not the time or place to try to make that point. 'But I'll try.' Stick figures chase a buck across the armrest.

'Fine,' Paul says. He pulls his phone out of his pocket and looks down at the screen.

There isn't much in the living room, but it's neat. The coffee table and sideboard don't match, one made of cheap pine, the other dark and glossy as hair. There are only two windows in the room, dirty and sulking behind mauve floral curtains. The kitchen is one long counter, running along the right wall of the flat. A fern wilts next to the fridge.

None of this feels like my father. I open both windows and the curtains breathe with wind.

'Where'd you go this morning?' I ask, opening a kitchen cabinet. Two plates are stacked under two bowls, one of which is chipped, the glaze cracking.

'To one of the safe centres, in a church near Milnerton.' He talks into his chest, still checking his phone.

'That's nice. Good, I mean.' Only one pint glass. 'Lindiwe was saying that no one had been to see the refugees yet.' I won't call her Lindi in front of him. Not here. 'She'll be happy you went.' Just two sets of cutlery in the drawer.

He looks up. 'It's my job, Jo.'

'What happened with Lindiwe last night?' I ask, filling the pint glass with water. It's my first chance to ask him. After Lindi left, he shut himself in the office and I went to bed with a crime novel I found in the living room and in which every chapter ended on a cliffhanger.

'I don't want to talk about it,' he says as I move the fern into the sink. I pour half of the water into the soil. 'What happened with the brigadier yesterday?' he asks.

I put the glass down. I'll water the fern again before we leave. 'I don't want to talk about it,' I say, leaning against the counter and folding my arms. The pain in my shoulder is deserved punishment for my childish tone.

'Christ.' Paul drops his arms to his sides. 'We have to stop doing this, Jo.'

The carpet is dark where he stands, the door still open behind him. I wonder if the backs of his legs are also wet. If he'll come inside.

'I know. I'm sorry.' I walk back to the couch. 'How was it, this morning?'

'Terrible.' He puts his phone in his pocket. 'I don't know how long we'll keep these safe houses open, or where they'll go after that.'

The picture frames on the sideboard are empty.

'I was talking to this woman from Somalia. Her name was Senga and she'd lost two of her children in the riots.' He lifts his chin and runs his hand over his stubble. It sounds like rain. Everything does. 'I mean, actually lost. As in, she didn't know where they were. And there's no way for her to find them, because she can't go back into Du Noon.' He loosens the knot on his grape-coloured tie. 'She started crying, hitting her legs. Saying, "Fuck off my black skin."'

I wait, tracing with my fingertip the outline of a shield on a couch cushion, wanting to touch him instead. He clears his throat. A set of World Book Encyclopaedias fills two shelves of the sideboard. The second volume for the letter C is missing. I turn away from Paul. There are two doors off the kitchen.

'So. Yesterday?' he asks.

'Not great.' The bathroom door is open. In the shower cubicle is a fishing rod, a bag of coal and a cricket bat. I open the medicine cabinet. 'He wasn't very helpful.' Cologne. Floss. A pill bottle with the prescription scratched off.

'What did you ask him?' Rather than coming any further into the flat he raises his voice.

'About Gideon's unit.' The mirror is flecked with toothpaste and shaving foam. I decide against telling Paul about the shotgun. 'What they did after they left the army.' I wet a square of toilet paper and wipe the smudged mascara out from under my eyes. The face that stares back at me doesn't feel like mine. It looks different, older, tireder, but it's more than that. It's less important now than it used to be, mine only incidentally. I remember that Paul is waiting for my report. 'I think Jaco Eloff was killed to stop him talking to the TRC, as a warning to anyone else who might be thinking about it.'

Paul remains silent, so I flush the toilet and step back into the living room.

'It made me feel a bit sorry for Danie,' I go on, realising immediately that it's probably the wrong thing to say. He doesn't react but I try to explain myself. 'Because I believe he's changed. He can't come clean about what happened and he knows he can never make up for what he did.' I remember having this conversation with my father outside Danie's house.

Paul's suit swells with wind. 'I think most of us are in that position,' he says. Almost the exact words my father used. Then, I had no idea how much my father might have been referring to, what he was capable of. I thought he was only acknowledging his absence in my life. Here, at least, I know what Paul is talking about, though trying to get to my father through me is not something he needs to make up for.

The front door shudders, straining against the chain keeping it open. 'What else?' Paul asks.

'A lot of the guys from Koevoet went into the security forces doing counter-terrorism stuff.' I hope he knows air quotes are implied. 'If Gideon was as good at his job as Nico said, he probably did too. The brigadier definitely knows about the work they did after the army. And he mentioned a Van Vuuren, but he wouldn't give me any more details about him.'

Paul holds a pair of latex gloves against his leg.

I feel the need to explain why I've not been a very good spy. 'I was alone with him in a garage full of knives and he could tell, or he knew somehow, about my shoulder, because he made a big show of not touching it.'

'And Danie?'

I sigh. 'We should probably talk to him. Just – I dunno – try to remember that he's different now. If that's worth anything.'

He shakes his head. 'I don't know that it is. If it is.' He turns away from me, thumbs on the keys of his phone, and steps out into the rain.

I push the bedroom door open. It still smells of my father's cologne. The room is too small for a double bed, and the mattress is folded in half on the floor. The flat must be cheap, I think. He'd been telling the truth when he said he hadn't been getting much work. There's only one thin pillow and no cover on the twisted, yellowing duvet. The window is small and bare. Police sirens throw their voices in blue and red across the ceiling. An ashtray stinks in the corner next to the mattress. It's balanced on top of a small pile of books. I twist the spines towards me. Wyndham. Gibson. Le Carré. I lift the pile and pull out the bottom book. *The French Lieutenant's Woman*. On the front page, under the title, someone had written: *Would it spoil the romanticism to make a joke about menstruation?* I leaf through the first few pages. In the margins, in pen: *Sounds like a catch!* I don't know if it's my father's handwriting. I throw the paperback onto the mattress and pick up the ashtray, closing the bedroom door behind me.

Paul is back and the door is closed behind him. He stands in the middle of the room. He's wearing gloves now too.

I leave the ashtray on the counter next to the sink. 'Cigarette butts, for DNA?'

'We already took some,' he says. His jacket is folded neatly over the armrest of the couch and his shirt sticks to his chest where it got wet. 'But thanks.'

He holds my gaze but I have to look away. I open the fridge, unscrew the top on a bottle of milk and sniff it. It's thick and sour.

'I'm sorry I asked you to see van der Westhuizen by yourself,' he says behind me. 'I needed to go to the lodge before we came here or spoke to Danie again.'

I turn back to him. 'It's OK. I want to help.'

'I know that,' he says. 'Listen, I've been wanting to ask, why didn't you call me after Alex? Before you went on the run with your dad, I mean.'

I have to stop myself from laughing at his choice of words.

'And why did you keep working on the riots story?'

Here it is, finally. 'I had to,' I say, slamming the fridge door shut. A magnet drops to the floor. 'Have you gone back to Alex since that night?'

'No. You?'

'No.' I lean against the kitchen counter and sip the water meant for the fern. 'A few other townships, though, as the riots spread.'

'I know. I read the articles. It seemed like you wanted to get hurt.'

'Maybe.' This is the first time I've admitted it, even to myself.

'Why?'

I put the glass down. 'You know why.'

'There was nothing you or I could've done to save him,' he says, undoing the top two buttons on his shirt. The collar, no longer stiff, lies flat. 'That's how necklacing works. Once the fire starts, there's nothing you can do.'

'I know.' My face is warm. 'There's just so much to feel guilty about. The woman in the shack. The woman whose husband was burning to death in front of her. We just left them there. We did nothing and then we just left them there.' I close my eyes. 'And it just keeps getting worse. Your dad. Nico.'

Paul was right when he said I was running away by going with my father. He was wrong too, but if I was up in Jo'burg right now, I know I'd go back to the townships again. I wouldn't be able to save anyone, but maybe telling the story of what is happening would help in some way. That's what I've been telling myself since the night in Alex. And I hope it's true even more now that I know what my father did, when not flinching away from the violence and poverty would make me less like him and his selective lens.

'I know,' Paul says in front of me. Water shines on the scar above his eyebrow. His eyes are bloodshot.

'What have you got to feel guilty about?' I ask.

'At least you tried to put out the flames. I just stood there.'

'I'm sorry,' I say. 'For everything.'

He steps forward and puts an arm around my shoulder, pulling me towards him. 'Me too,' he says, his voice in my hair. He's cold against me, shivering.

I pull back and his hand slides down to my waist. I reach up and wipe a drop of water from his temple with my thumb. The latex squeaks against his skin. He smiles at the sound. The fridge begins to hum as I pull his face down towards me, my fingers curled behind his ear. His lips are slightly parted, his breath hot. I close my eyes as he brings his other hand up to my cheek and into my hair. His stubble is rough against my skin.

It's structurally almost identical to the first time we kissed, but the content is different.

I lower my chin. 'I'm sorry,' I say into his neck.

'No.' His voice vibrates against my chest. 'I'm glad you did that. Before anything else happens and we can't.' He leans back and brushes my fringe behind my ear with his fingers. 'I wanted you to.'

'Good.'

His watch sounds the hour and he drops his hands to his side, stepping back. 'So, is there anything useful in this dump?' he asks.

'Not really,' I say. 'Apart from what looks like secondhand books, none of this stuff is his.' I would gesture but my hands are shaking.

'Shit.' He glances around the room.

'But I'll keep looking.' Now that I think about it, I'm surprised Nico hasn't kept any copies of his photos, either in albums or on the walls. Not even the one of the little white bird perched inside a basking crocodile's mouth, which he said was quite famous. Maybe he hadn't lived here long. But then where's the rest of his stuff, his music, the antique floor lamp he bought during my second visit to Cape Town?

I walk to the rubbish bin, the milk in one hand, ashtray in the other. The lid of the bin hits the wall behind it when I press down on the lever with my foot. Inside the bin is a baseball cap, the one with the springbok on it. It looks wet, still, and there are bloodstains on it. The police have been sloppy.

He's been here. But what did he come back for? Is this his way of letting me know he's OK? Or did Gideon save the hat when he got rid of my father's body so he could plant it here? Make us chase a ghost?

I let the lid drop and put the milk down on the counter.

I want just one more minute. Just one.

Paul's putting on his jacket, struggling to push his arms through the wet sleeves. I wait, watching him. 'Let's go,' he says.

I shake my head. 'No.'

'What is it?'

'He's been here,' I say, pointing at the bin. 'His cap, from the crash.'

'For fuck's sake.' He grabs his phone from the counter and sprints outside, leaving the door open. It slams against the security gate, but the wind has changed direction and keeps it pinned open.

I sit down next to my bag. Inside it is the pencil tin my father gave me in Nature's Valley. The sea-urchin shell broke in the crash but everything else is still intact. I pull out the case, running my thumbs over the faded corners. I don't want it any more. His treasures are not mine. I push it down into the couch for the next tenant to find.

I turn on the TV. There's no remote, so I kneel on the floor, scrolling through stations. I want my email, a computer. My phone. None of the channels is showing news. When I come across a station showing *Dr Phil* I crawl back to the couch and sit on the floor against it. Dr Phil is talking to serial cheaters, telling it like it is. Women cry.

Sitting still reminds me of being in the car with my father. I mute the TV, stand up, and turn to the sideboard. All I can hear is rain.

In the top drawer, under a faded Yellow Pages, is the profanisaurus I gave my father when he came to visit me in London. The spine is cracked, pages folded over to mark favourite swear words. I leave it where it is.

I move the bank statements and bills in the second drawer onto the top of the sideboard for Paul. My father owes a few hundred rand for electricity and there's a notice to say that the phone line has been disconnected. His credit card statement shows a few small grocery trips, each no more than five hundred rand, at the beginning of May, but nothing since then.

In the bottom drawer, among plasters, a crumpled packet of menthol cigarettes and a roll of black rubbish bags, is a key, small and silver. The letterbox.

One winter's evening three years ago, I met my father on High Holborn. As we walked through the stretch that smelled of sewage, I told him about the building works, pointed out my favourite falafel bar and the inn built in 1585. A man passed us and laughed loudly into his mobile phone; in Afrikaans, my father described the colonies of shit particles annexing the man's nose, his lungs. 'Just like the British did to us,' he said. I had to think for a second before I realised that I was included in that *us*.

We went to a busy pub on Chandos Street. It served bitter, and that was what he wanted to drink. 'I want to *know* that I'm in England, damn it,' he explained.

It was the second time we'd met during his trip. I'd seen him the day before, when I took him to the second-hand bookshops on Charing Cross Road. He'd bought me an expensive coffee-table book of photos taken through a microscope I didn't want.

'I don't have a coffee table,' I'd said.

'Well, now when you get one, you'll have a book for it. Actually, you can learn a lot from this book, so you should get a coffee table just to have somewhere to put it.'

'But it costs twenty-five pounds. That's almost four hundred rand.'

'I want to get it for you, so shut up.'

Later, at a coffee shop, he confessed his disappointment with the English. 'I thought they would all be so well read and educated. I went to a big bookshop – a Waterstones, I think – and looked around, hoping to see better books, or more people, or just a wider range of people. But I've come to the conclusion that dumb people here are the same as dumb people in South Africa, maybe even worse. They don't have any excuses here. This is the land of Milton and Shakespeare and fucking dickhead Keats, and some excellent atheists. Arthur C. Clarke for Chrissakes!' He was shouting.

'People are looking,' I said, downing my coffee.

'Fuck 'em!' He was expansive, forgetting his cup was in his hand as he gestured; black coffee slopped onto the floor.

At the pub the next day, he ordered fish and chips – he wanted it to be bad so he would *know* he was in England – and a round of drinks. As we waited for his food to come we smoked the British cigarettes I'd bought outside the tube station.

'So, I'm putting together a book,' he announced.

A couple sat down at the end of our table. The girl wore a top that gaped in the front, exposing a purple and black bra: the colour sex is supposed to be. My father stared at the lace.

'What about?' I asked.

The girl leant over the table to kiss her boyfriend, and a matching triangle of thong showed above her jeans.

'*Jissus*, man.' Nico looked away. 'Veld fires. Mainly the animals that get caught in them. I think the way animals die says something about the world. Especially tortoises and leopards.'

He was uneven, and it always worked to his advantage. I hated how he could swing between ogling the girl's bra in front of me and saying something that could pass as insightful, beautiful even. That he forced me to see him as a whole person rather than just my father; I wished I didn't know that he preferred brunettes and one-night stands. I hated that I knew my father as an adult, but my mom only as a child.

The couple kissed, tongues like flags. My father was eating. Empty condiment packets stretched out in front of him, banners of blue, green, brown, burgundy, yellow and red. 'I don't know what brown sauce or tartare is, but I'm going to eat them,' he said. 'These chips taste wrong, though.' He looked at me as if it was my fault.

'They're wedges.'

'Fuck wedges.' He ate them anyway, swirling the quarter-moons of potato in the six different sauces – now bleeding into a grey-brown puddle – then spearing them onto pieces of fish.

I was one drink ahead of him. The girl had moved over to sit next to the boy, and I thought that he probably had an erection.

My father finished his fish, leaving five or six wedges to turn to grey sponge, and pushed the plate away from him. 'Let's guess what that girl's name is,' he said. 'I think it's Sharon. Now you pick one, and then one of us needs to go ask her.'

'Staci, with an *i*.' I finished my pint.

'Good one. OK, I'm just going for a piss and then to the bar. You ask her and tell me what she says when I get back.' He got up.

I didn't ask the girl's name and when my father came back from the bar, foam on his cuffs, I told him it was Kate. He was disappointed.

Paul is still on the phone.

I duck my head and hurry to the letterboxes. Brown and metal, they remind me of school lockers. A mangled newspaper sticks out of the slot for number two, my father's flat. I unlock the box. A letter and a few flyers slip out onto the ground. I pull the newspaper through the slot from the inside of the door and bend to pick up the fallen envelope.

Back in the flat, I turn up the volume on the TV and spread the contents of the letterbox out on the floor. A guest on the *Dr Phil* show says: 'Like I would get pregnant on purpose!' No one laughs.

There are two pizza delivery menus and a handwritten note offering house-cleaning services.

Dr Phil says: 'Let me go over that again, because I'm just a country boy from Texas.'

I turn over the envelope. It's addressed to Glenda Thacker. My grandmother. I tear through the window with my nails. Inside is a bill for the annual rental of a storage container in Gauteng. It's dated 15 May but the postmark shows it was only delivered in the last two days.

The container is in her name so that anyone looking would think it belonged to the previous tenant, and no one – not the police, not Gideon – would know it had anything to do with my father. No one apart from me. The next clue. Maybe this one is a corner piece of the puzzle.

I stuff the bill into my bag. I don't want to show it to Paul yet; the police will check out the container before I've had a chance to look around.

Dr Phil says: 'Sometimes you make the right decision and sometimes you make the decision right.'

I realise how lucky it was that I gave my grandmother's death certificate to her lawyer for safekeeping. Otherwise, I would've no doubt woken up in the hospital to find it gone too.

After I've put the junk mail on the counter for recycling, I move my notepad so that it covers the bill in my bag, then turn off the TV and sit back against the couch, unfolding the newspaper. It's yesterday's and the top story is about the violence in Cape Town. Two policemen, shotguns just in frame, arrest a man outside a Somali-owned business. One kneels on his chest as the other cuffs him. I open the paper, turning past the xenophobia spread to national news.

There in the bottom right-hand corner of page seven is my UK passport photo. The caption reads: *Johanna Hartslief, 23, is in critical condition in George Hospital.*

'Jo?' The door slams shut behind him. 'Sorry that took so long.'

I pull a cigarette from the crumpled pack I found in the drawer and straighten it between my thumb and forefinger.

Paul sits down on the armrest behind me. 'Your dad's photo is going to be on the news tonight. And we'll be watching Danie's house to pick him up for a chat.'

'Good.' I turn up the flame on the lighter as high as it will go.

'Did you find anything in the post?'

I point to the flyers on the counter and light the cigarette. 'Just junk mail,' I say, exhaling. 'But his old credit card statements are in the sideboard.'

'Cheers.' He scans the top page. 'Yeah, that might be useful, Jo.' There's a smile in his voice.

'It's just a game to him, though.' I pull my knees close to my chest.

'What do you mean?'

'He'll play this with you until he gets bored.' My reflection in the TV is still, distorted by the curve in the screen. 'Leaving you clues, reeling you in. He'll probably give his credit card away to someone. I thought you should know that.'

'Thanks for the warning.' He puts his hand on my neck, his forefinger slipping under my collar.

Cigarette hanging from my lip, I pull the newspaper, quartered and fat, onto my knees. 'Is this what you meant when you said "before anything else happens"?' I point to my photo.

He takes his hand back. 'Yes.' He swings his leg around to the front of the couch and slides down next to me. 'I'm sorry, Jo.'

'Was it just to try and lure him out, or was it punishment for me too?' Our legs are touching.

'I thought he might try to see you.'

'And did he?'

He shakes his head.

'I get why you did it,' I say, looking at him. 'But this affects more than just me and my father.' I blink. 'My work, my friends.'

'At the time, I didn't care.' He puts his hand on my knee. 'But I am so, so sorry.'

I leave the cigarette to burn in the ashtray. 'Lindi? Last night?'

'*Ja*. She saw it in the paper.'

I nod. 'OK.' I put my hand over his, closing my eyes. 'At least that makes sense now.'

'Jo…' He doesn't finish.

'It's OK, really.' I can feel my chin puckering. 'But can I have my SIM card back, please? I know you've got it.' As soon as I saw the article, I realised he must have taken it to keep me unconnected, stuck in my fake coma.

He looks down.

'Please, Paul.' I don't cover my face as I cry. 'This is just what my father did.'

He straightens his legs. 'It's back at the house, in my bedside table.'

'OK.' I blink. 'Thank you.' There's mascara on my fingers. 'I think it'll be best if I go back to Jo'burg for a while and stay with a friend.' Naledi. Fuck. I hope she hasn't gone down to George. I hope she's OK. 'I'll go pack my stuff.'

He looks away. 'You're not safe, Jo.'

'My father got into the flat while your people were watching it. And we both know what Gideon is capable of. If either of them wants to get to me, it won't matter if I'm with you or back in Jo'burg.' I squeeze his hand. 'I'll be careful, though. And if I can think of anything else to help you find my father, I'll call you.'

He nods. 'Thank you.'

'Let me know when you want me to talk to Danie.'

'I will.'

I lean over and press my lips against his cheek. He's stiff, but as I stand, pushing up with both hands even though it hurts my shoulder, he turns back towards me. 'I'll put it out on the wire that you've made a miraculous recovery,' he says.

'Thank you.' I smile at him, step over his legs and walk out, leaving the door open behind me and the fern only half watered.

I sit in the car Paul lent me, watching the waves come up onto the bluffs at Three Anchor Bay.

I'm booked on the seven-thirty flight back to Jo'burg. A present from Paul. When I'd packed everything and dragged my bags to the garage, I searched the house for a phone. There was one on the floor in the study, hidden behind the desk. I felt sorry for him when I found it, for how we met, what he'd lost. I called the number on the storage bill and waited to speak to the manager. I'd need my grandmother's death certificate to gain access to the unit, he said, and the key. I'd told him I'd be there first thing on Monday morning and hung up. I wouldn't be able to get the certificate till then, which left a day to kill in Jo'burg.

Now my phone lies on the passenger seat, dark and quiet. I need to call Naledi to ask if I can stay with her for a few days – to let her know I'm out of my coma – but I can't quite face having to be cheerful and call what happened a mix-up yet.

This is where that poet killed herself. I haven't been to this bay since I was ten years old. Two years running, I came down to Cape Town for a week's holiday with my father. The second time, we jumped into the winter water. To make us feel alive, he said. To remind us it was right that all most people could remember about the poet was that she'd killed herself.

'Don't dive,' he said. 'There are sharp rocks and I'd rather you cut your feet than bumped your head.' Seagulls struggled in the wind coming off the water. Our towels waved at us from the railings as we climbed onto the rocks. My feet hurt already.

'We go together, on three.' Along the breakwater, the waves played thumb piano on a small pebble beach. We jumped in reckless arcs, his higher than mine, and my feet touched the black Atlantic first. The cold winded me as I sank into a kelp waltz. I opened my eyes underwater and saw my father, legs shining white, but then it was black as the veld, black as fear of the dark.

When I breathed again in the dusk, my father was holding on to a rock, fingers in fossils, waiting for me.

'Thank fuck.' He shivered, his lips white.

My feet were numb. Kelp curled around my calf.

'Did you see anything?' he asked.

'What do you mean?' I swam towards him, not wanting to be the furthest out to sea of the two of us.

He looked around. 'Her. The poet. I've heard she haunts the bay.'

I kicked as hard as I could and pulled myself out of the water.

Later, we put a blue plastic bottle filled with sand and a joke about the Afrikaans version of Paddy on the water and watched it sink. It was to buck up her spirits, my father had said.

When we studied Sylvia Plath in secondary school, I looked up Ingrid Jonker's poems. She was better than Plath, I thought. Not the kind of poetry you'd easily remember, but better, even in translation. Not so easily read through the lens of her suicide.

Finally, I reach over and switch on my phone, resting my chin on the steering wheel while it finds a signal.

My father told me the story every night during that second visit. In 1965, almost ten years after he was born, Ingrid Jonker had walked into the sea here, where only white people were allowed to swim. It was mid-July and the storms were thick on the water. A twilit horizontal rain kept tourists and runners from the seafront. She was alone on the shore, in a pale yellow dress and brown flats.

OK, OK, so I made that part up, he'd say when I'd ask how he could know. But it made sense. Sensible shoes. Colours that don't draw attention. She also chose the dress because it had two deep pockets. She was wearing hold-up stockings, which she stuffed with dark pebbles as though it was Christmas. She'd planned this, he said. The wind could not lift her dress or her thick wool cardigan, also with pockets. The cardigan, just so you know, he'd say, touching my nose, would never be found.

The pills started to take effect: she stumbled as a wave hit her calves. He'd hold his arms out in front of him like a zombie. The hem of her

259

dress skimmed the water then sank, defeated. Thighs and waist; it was cold between her legs. He'd cross his legs at this point in the story, chattering his teeth.

A wave stretched back, yawning, and pulled her over. My father would reach up, miming a yawn, and pull me over onto the bed, tickling me. She cut her hand on a rock but the blood ran away. Then the wave blessed her. He'd draw his thumb across my forehead in the shape of a cross. The water ran out again, this time to the Point, and the olive cardigan turned in the water as the current took her. At this, I would climb onto his back and he'd run around the room.

When Ingrid washed up later, back onto this beach, she was soft and swollen. Her dress was a paler yellow. There was water in her mouth and a starfish over her belly button. She wore a garland of kelp flowers and a bruise on her forehead where she took communion with the seals. She was thirty-one.

He'd kiss me on the forehead and turn off the light.

Hers was an open casket.

15

The Blue Plan

A shaggy blond man, bracelets like springs on his arms, brings our drinks. Lynda sits back in her chair as he lowers the tray onto the table, the menu closed in her lap.

'White wine?' he asks, peeling two serviettes from a small stack on the tray.

Lynda raises her hand. 'That's me.' She touches her short brown hair, laced with grey, as though to make sure it's still there.

When we sat down in the patio café, I hoped that Lynda would order first, but the waiter turned to me. I expected her to at least raise her eyebrows when I asked for a cider, if not override my order and ask for a pot of tea and two cups instead. When I'd called her yesterday from the bluff at Three Anchor Bay, she'd invited me to the morning service at her church, and she's still in her Dutch Reformed Sunday best. Actually, her navy-blue pantsuit seems kind of revolutionary for a church where the ministers preach hellfire and the hymns are in formal Afrikaans; judging from the dozen or so times I'd been to church when my grandmother was over from the UK, women in anything other than flower-printed dresses were fashion-forward. But that was almost fifteen years ago now. Another out-of-date assumption. Lynda winked at me when she called after the waiter to make sure her glass of wine was a large one.

'Hunter's Dry with lemon.' He puts the bottle down on the place mat in front of me.

I pull the bottle towards me. Hunter's Dry is what my mom used to drink. 'I don't need a glass,' I say.

He nods, watching me push the wedge of lemon deeper into the mouth of the bottle. I can't tell if he's older or younger than I am, but I think there's an invitation in his eyes. When Naledi came to visit me in London a year and a half ago, she was surprised by how shy people were on the tube, even the men, how they avoided your eye. On a crowded Central Line train to Tottenham Court Road she said loudly in Afrikaans: 'This journey feels a lot longer when there's no one to eye-fuck.' Our laughter crept in under earphones; passengers were pulled out of the corridors of Hogwarts, the grand gallery of the Louvre, and looked up to frown at us.

Other versions of me might think about kissing the waiter over a cigarette while Lynda waits at the table; or, even better, fucking him in the storeroom after the restaurant closes. It could be fun, or it could be pathological – I can't decide which. And the latter is too much of a cliché to risk it.

Displaced cider splashes over the mouth of the bottle and I reach for a napkin.

'Are you ready to order?' the waiter asks.

'Not yet, no,' Lynda says. Her nail polish matches her lipstick. Each coral nail is like the inside of a shell, or a perfect pink tongue. The waiter nods and picks up the tray. I wonder what his name is. Nick? Steve? I'm better at this game in London.

'Actually, can you leave her glass, please?' Lynda asks.

'*Ja*, sure.' He puts the tumbler, half-full of ice, down in front of her and turns away from the table, his eyes skimming over me.

Lynda sits forward to spoon an ice cube into her wine. The ice cracks but doesn't break apart. 'This whole complex used to be a park, you know.'

I shake my head. 'We didn't come to Pretoria much.'

'There was a merry-go-round and a witch's hat and a big jungle gym.' She looks past me, as if remembering the primary colours, the sound of swings. 'It's sad, really. But this is nice, isn't it?'

I nod. From the car park, the shopping complex looks like a stuccoed fortress. But in the centre of the building is a small lake, complete with a willow tree and a pair of peacocks. I can hear them calling to one another.

I look around but I can't see the man who's been following me. I haven't seen him since he pulled into a parking space a few cars from mine.

'Do you remember me?' Lynda asks.

I haven't been asked that question since my first month in the UK, when friends of my grandmother's, whom I'd last seen when I was six and an unaccompanied minor on my first overseas trip, would bend down and press caramel candies into my hands.

'Yes,' I say, rolling a sliver of lemon between my fingers until it bursts. What my biology teacher had labelled vesicles, my mom had called soldiers, performing battle skits with orange wedges even after I no longer needed encouragement to eat my five a day. 'I think so. Well, I remember your swimming pool.'

She smiles. 'Good. I remember you too, although you were a lot smaller then.'

'Yes.'

The last time I saw her was when I was about seven, before we'd been able to afford a flat in a complex with a pool, before she and her family had moved up to Louis Trichardt. While Lynda and my mom talked, I practised my dives and handstands in the pool. Lynda, who was always pregnant, would sit under the gazebo where her husband was barbecuing the meat. My mom would sit with her legs dangling in the water, talking to them over her shoulder, and I'd pretend to be a shark. Later, my fingers still wrinkled from the water, I'd fall asleep in front of a Disney movie; I'd always wake up hours later in my own bed.

'Thank you for coming.' I straighten the place mat so that its edge runs parallel with the table. 'I'm sorry I didn't call sooner.' It's a lie, but I hope she can't tell.

'That's OK.' She reaches for my hand over the table. Her engagement ring is twisted around and the diamond digs into my hand as she squeezes. 'I had to pray when I saw the newspaper article about your accident. I didn't understand why God would take you just like He took your mom.' She shakes her head; her hair, sprayed stiff, doesn't move. 'But when you called, awake and alive, I knew that God had a plan for you.'

This is very familiar territory, but I feel unprepared somehow. 'Thank you,' I say.

'Of course.' Lynda pats my hand and sits back.

'I don't believe in that stuff, but thank you for thinking of me,' I add.

She sips at her wine. 'I didn't think you would.'

'Why? Nico?'

She smiles. 'Not just him – although steam came out of his nose when your granny asked if they were going to baptise you.'

I'd never called her *granny*.

Her thumb drags the lipstick mark on her glass into points, a sun setting at the edge of a page. 'You don't hear good things about England – all the drinking, the sex.' I'm surprised she doesn't whisper that last word. 'Growing up there – not even your granny could keep you safe from everything,' she says.

The high school in Jo'burg I was supposed to go to the January after my mom died – the one Naledi went to – had daily prayers, a hymn book, Bible education classes. Naledi wrote to me about a book that was making the rounds, called *I Kissed Dating Goodbye*, which said you shouldn't kiss anyone till marriage. The girls who did were called sluts. The girls who didn't, prudes. Were they being kept safe?

'Mostly because I didn't believe when I was your age,' Lynda says.

I push the slice of lemon further into the neck of the bottle until it drops into the remaining inch of cider.

'But life gets harder – trust me – and knowing that God has a plan for you makes it a lot easier.' Lynda will be praying for me tonight.

'I bet,' I say. If God can forgive me, I must forgive myself or else I'm implying that I have higher moral standards than he does. I think that's how it goes. But God hasn't been to Alex lately.

'Do you want some nuts? Let's get some nuts.' She raises her hand to flag down the waiter. 'Or some bread.'

The grass in the shopping centre oasis is bright green, even though the willow tree is empty of leaves. A painting left half-finished.

One of Grant the waiter's shoes squeaks behind me. 'What can I get you?' He looks only at Lynda. There's a pencil behind his ear.

'Do you have any peanuts?'

'*Ja*, sure.' He stands with his hands slid into his back pockets. 'Anything else?' His t-shirt is too faded for me to see which band it's advertising.

'Jo?' Lynda motions at me.

'Um, yeah.' I look up at him. 'A Diet Coke, please?' I move the empty bottle towards him.

His fingers brush mine as he bends to pick it up. 'With lemon?' The hair on his arm is gold and fine as a heat haze.

'Please.' I push my fringe back behind my ear. Lynda is watching us. 'And some tap water.' I smile quickly and turn back to her.

'OK.' Robert leans forward and sweeps the pile of curled-up pieces of label into his hand, his arm almost touching my stomach. 'I'll be right back.'

Lynda watches him over my shoulder as she spoons the remaining lozenges of ice into her wine. Please don't acknowledge this, I think. Suddenly, I'm angry at Robert or Steve or whatever his name is for looking at me that way in front of Lynda. Angry at myself for noticing the way he looks at me.

'You don't really let me see a lot of you, you know.'

'Excuse me?'

'You're very guarded.'

'Well, I don't really know you,' I say, letting my fringe fall back into my face.

'You don't really remember me – that's different. You do know me. I loved your mom very much, even though we didn't see each other a lot in the years before she died.' She smooths the tablecloth. 'Isn't that enough?'

'It hasn't been.' I remember my father in the pub near Charing Cross, boasting about how he'd never been in love. I look up at her. 'But maybe it should be.'

She nods as though that's settled something.

The wind scurries in under the thatched awning, dragging its leafy feet. The serviette that was under my drink takes off and settles under the next table.

'Let me get that for you.' Nick – it must be Nick – slides his tray onto our table and crouches to grab the serviette; I can see the waistband of his boxers.

I pick up the bowl of peanuts and push it towards Lynda. Then I take my drink from the tray and, before he can turn, the two pint glasses of water.

'Doing my job for me?' He crumples the serviette and stuffs it into his pocket.

'Sorry.' I close my eyes and take a long drink of water, bumping my teeth against the glass.

'Thanks for that,' I hear Lynda say.

Perhaps she wouldn't look at him either, because when I open my eyes, Nick and his tray are gone. Grateful to her, I smile.

'So what can I do for you?' she asks.

I planned to ask her about my father, what he was doing while he lived in the commune, if she'd ever met a Danie or a Van Vuuren. I wanted to know if she'd ever seen any good in him or if it'd only been me and my mom. If we'd been the only ones he'd fooled.

'If you have something to ask about your mom, go ahead,' Lynda says, her elbows on the table for the first time since we sat down.

There are so many things I want to know about her. My mom watched *Aladdin* with me every Friday, but what was her favourite movie? Did she ever dye her hair a weird colour? What did her room look like in the commune? Did she start eating sugar on white toast because it was cheap or because she liked it? What did she want to be when she grew up? What was her favourite album? I want to know what her life would have been like if she'd never met my father or had me, what that trajectory was. All the different futures she could've had. A career, a house, enough money to pay the TV licence. Her thirty-fifth birthday.

'Do you think he – Nico, I mean – loved her?' I want to know that he was worth it, even just a little bit. And I hate that I want to know.

'*Ja*. I think he did.'

I wish we'd done this over the phone. 'But you think the best of everyone.'

267

'Not him – not later on. But before they moved out, it seemed pretty good. He'd kiss her neck when she was washing up – I used to be so jealous of that. I thought that's what love was. Now I know it's him offering to *do* the washing-up.' She laughs, but it sounds almost canned, as though the punchline was written by someone else.

I've spent the last two weeks hoping my mom never knew my father the way I do. 'She was younger when she met him than I am now,' I say. 'Only twenty.'

'I know, but she was so sure of what she wanted.' Lynda picks at a piece of nut lodged in her bottom teeth, trying to hide it with her other hand. 'When she told me she was pregnant – I remember, we were sitting in the garden in our cozzies – I was really worried. I hope you'll forgive me, but I offered to help her find the money to fly to London to get an abortion.'

'Of course. It's what I would've done.' I've never worried that she hadn't wanted me; rather, I felt guilty about what she'd given up to have me. If she were still alive, I know I'd try to earn enough money so that she could quit whatever job she had and go back to university to finish her degree. 'But I'm a heathen.'

Lynda smiles. 'Your dad didn't have a job. Well, he was trying to be a photographer. It wasn't about the money. When his parents died that first year in the commune, he had more than enough to live on.'

I lean forward. 'Sorry, what?'

'I just thought he should take responsibility and get a job to support his family.' She reaches for more nuts.

I stop her, my hand over hers. 'No, I mean about his parents.'

She frowns. 'They died in eighty-four, I think. I remember because he had to miss your mom's twenty-first birthday. The house they left him somewhere up near the border with Zim – Tzaneen, I think – needed some work and he wanted to do it by himself.'

Another house, this time up north. I'll need to ask Naledi to check the property records.

'We offered to go with, but I think it was his way of grieving.'

Nico told both me and my mom that his parents had died before he went into the army. Which version of events was correct? Maybe my grandparents are alive somewhere, with small dogs and a loud TV, wondering when they'll hear from their son. I'll have to ask Naledi to check for their death certificates. I'd google it, but I don't know their names. And there's no guarantee anything would come up even if I did – South Africa is a country still only partly online. The rest of its history, its records, is hidden – in the memories of men like Brigadier van der Westhuizen – or destroyed.

Lynda pulls her hand out from under mine. 'Did I say something to upset you?'

I could tell her – tell her everything – right now. Make it partly someone else's problem. She fiddles with the locket around her neck, opening and closing the heart. Inside are two school portraits of blond children.

'No,' I say, sitting back. 'No, sorry. Go on.'

'Shame, he had to go up there every month for a while. Some problems with selling it.'

Where was he disappearing to so regularly? I nod. '*Ja*, shame.'

If he told me the truth, if his parents had died years before he met my mom, what was he doing for money while he was at the commune, and where was he going every month? Why resurrect his parents if not to hide something? I'm so tired of his lies, of his twisted take on choose-your-own-adventure stories. Carrying the different versions of his stories to their logical conclusions – if not A, then B, where B stands for things like kidnapping and torture – is worse than just knowing, once and for all, what he did. I have to wait till tomorrow morning to see what's in the storage unit, but after so long, I'm too impatient. Danie's the only one left who can tell me about what happened at the lodge, what my father was capable of. I'll go back to his house this afternoon, I decide. I'll make him talk to me – threaten him with prison, tell him talking is the only way he can protect himself from his unit, cry over my missing father. Whatever it takes.

'Even when the money came through, I thought he should get a job.' She pushes the nuts towards me. 'Please, or I'll eat them all. He was always taking photos of her. Drinking coffee, walking through the quad, everything. He'd go with her to the demos to make sure she was safe. I told him he should try to sell his photos of all the protests, but he refused.' She shakes her head. '*Ja, nee.* It was sweet, but not how a man who was almost thirty should be spending the day.'

'No.' I poke at the ice cubes that have settled like tetris pieces in the bottom of my glass.

'What's he doing these days?'

'I don't know.' The truth, finally. I'm tired of controlling my body language, of watching my reactions, to protect him. 'Don't worry, it doesn't bother me,' I say before she can sympathise. I realise that this is almost the truth. Not quite yet, but soon.

'Did you know that Karen actually wanted to call you Hélène? Like the French way.' She looks at the bowl of nuts and back at me. 'But Nico wouldn't let her. He said he'd met a Hélène when he was in Belgium and that she had the kind of nose that you could see up her nostrils even when she was looking straight at you. And no daughter of his…' Her impression of my father is actually quite good: over-emphasised words and wild hand gestures.

My phone vibrates in my jacket pocket. I wonder if it's Paul, calling to say he's found something or explain why a man's been following me since I got back to Jo'burg. More likely, it's Naledi asking what I want for dinner.

'He was funny,' Lynda says. 'The thing with him is he could tell a good story, but it was almost like he was telling you what you expected to hear.'

'Like a trope?' I remember the nameless Dutch couple, taking a chance on a down-and-out man in an ice cream parlour meet-cute.

She hooks her arm over the back of her chair. 'More like…the thing that would make the most sense, or was the most convenient. And then just embellishing it with some funny or weird details to make you forget that.'

I'd underestimated her. She'd picked up that his stories were collages of other people's experiences, of things he'd read. I wonder if my mom had realised that, before they split up.

'But your mom loved him, so I didn't push it.'

It wouldn't be fair to tell her that maybe, if she had pushed, my mom would still be alive, so I nod instead.

'Even when they moved out just before you were born and I didn't hear from her for ages.' She shrugs. 'Not until Professor Webster's funeral, God bless him,' she says, touching the crucifix around her neck. 'But by then, Nico was long gone.'

'Who was he? Professor Webster?'

'He taught in your mom's department. He was an activist. Murdered by some government-sponsored shithead.'

Cursing doesn't suit her. I bite my bottom lip to keep from smiling.

'You must've been about four.' She looks up at me. 'Your mom brought you to the funeral. It wasn't a good idea with all the police and everything, but she couldn't find anyone to look after you.'

I shake my head. 'I don't remember it.' I want to say sorry for not remembering, but I wouldn't be apologising to her.

'I brought something for you.' She lifts her handbag onto the table. 'When your mom died, your granny took a few of Karen's things back to England but she asked me to give everything else to charity.' I swallow, gripping my knees under the table. 'I kept a couple of things for you.' She pulls out a small gift bag and puts it down in front of me.

'Thank you,' I say, keeping my hands under the table.

'Open it.'

'OK.' My hands are shaking as I push apart leaves of tissue paper. Inside them is the pottery jewellery box I'd made for my mom when I was eight. I lift the box out of its tissue nest. It's light blue, with zigzags etched into the sides. The lid doesn't quite fit. I don't have to look to know my name is scratched into the bottom of the box.

'When I saw it, I knew I couldn't give it away.' Lynda's voice seems to come to me as if through water.

I put the box down on the table, tracing the patterns with the fingers of one hand. Blood buzzes in my ears.

I didn't realise it before, but I've always wanted something that was hers. All that my grandmother brought back to the UK was photos, but I wanted something that she'd bought for herself or kept in her pocket. Something that told me about who she was as a person, not just a mother. Any normal mom would keep her child's art projects. If she was still alive, she would have given this back to me when I was in my twenties and she was moving house. I would've kept it for a few years before it got lost along the way. Now it's all I have of her.

All ten years of missing her shiver up my body. I close my eyes. My face is wet. I cover my mouth, my ugly, tight mouth, to silence the sobs.

'Oh *liefie*, I'm sorry.'

I feel Lynda move the jewellery box away before she grips my wrist. I curl my fingers and hold on to her arm. My breath catches in my chest.

'It's OK,' she says, stroking my hand.

I shake my head. I don't know how to stop.

'It'll be OK.'

I leave a message for Paul asking if he wants to meet me at Danie's house later today. I'll give him an hour, maybe two, to let me know. I can't wait any longer than that. As a distraction from the jewellery box, I read. I bought every book I could find about the Border War, which isn't many. After all my father's versions it seems strange to be able to leaf through a book and find the definitive, accepted account of an event, indexed neatly at the back. Naledi's laptop warms my thighs as I scroll through pages of search results for the term Koevoet, opening each one in a new tab.

What I have learnt so far:

At the Koevoet reunion in 1997, the men wore t-shirts that said: *Killing is our business. Business is good.* Some of them told journalists how misunderstood they were. Like the Vietnam War vets.

'We were brainwashed,' one soldier said. 'We were fighting against the black danger and the commies, but really we were fighting for nothing. And we've been forgotten. We're the forgotten soldiers.'

'We fought as soldiers for our country,' another said. 'We have a right to exist, even if the people out there think we don't.'

'We shot better than them and we shouldn't have to apologise for that,' said a third.

I try to imagine the reunion, which took place in a large conference room in a hotel in Camps Bay. On each table were ten bottles of red wine, called Koevoet, made specially for the occasion, one article said. The label listed the statistics: only three hundred soldiers in the unit, which had killed three thousand, eight hundred and sixty-one terrorists and lost only a hundred and fifty-three of its own men during the seventies and eighties. Koevoet was, the label said, the 'best anti-terrorist unit in the world'.

I can picture the clashing carpet and tablecloths, the chairs fold-up and cheap. At the head table, I can see Brigadier van der Westhuizen, fat as butter. He officially founded the union for former Koevoet members that night. He even led a prayer, one of the newspaper articles said.

I hate how easy it is for me to put words into his mouth.

'Father, we thank you for bringing us together tonight to help one another. We are outcasts. Some of our brothers have killed themselves. Some have gone off track and can never be gotten back. We ask for your forgiveness and your guidance in these difficult times.' The brigadier opens his eyes to survey his audience. 'Now, Father...' he says and pauses. Give a man a microphone and he thinks he's Elvis. 'I just want to open up the floor to any one of the heroes here who might want to talk to you. If anyone wants to talk to God, just put up your hand and we'll bring the mike over to you.'

I can see the clouds coming in, flags of an advancing legion. Men scanning the crowd for any sign of Jaco. The brigadier making a start on the potato salad while the others pray.

I read about how soldiers struggled when they came back from the border. Solitude was a luxury after so long sleeping in barracks and sweating in the back of Casspirs with a dozen other men. One soldier wrote about how he'd been called a hero, his parents throwing him a welcome-home party with champagne and a blue, white and orange banner. His auntie said how nice he looked with his hair so short. His father had made a speech about heroism and what makes a man. 'From life's military school: what doesn't kill me makes me stronger.' People had passed around cake on paper plates. The guests were clapping and singing the national anthem when he'd walked to the bottom of the garden, climbed on top of the bins and over the wall into the field behind the house, leaving a rosette of blue and white icing on the bricks.

Paul texts: *In a meeting, but will come asap. Blue camry outside house – get them to come in with you. Be safe x*

While making a flask of instant coffee for the drive, I read about the army's euphemisms. Playing radio. Making knots. The helicopter. Even if he's not used it in decades, I want to be able to speak to Danie in his own language.

16

In Other Words

No one answers when I buzz at the security gate, and there's no sign of the men in the Camry. Dusk filters yellow through the smog as I call Danie's number, but it just rings. I'm not going to let him hide behind a fence. So I drive up as close as I can get to the gate and climb over it from the roof of my car. The pain in my shoulder makes my eyes water as I lower myself on the other side. If my bodyguard is watching, he doesn't stop me.

The front door is unlocked. Only when I'm already inside do I remember stories I've heard from Naledi about home invasions and how the security guards summoned by the alarms would often be too scared to go into the houses for fear of being ambushed and gunned down.

'Danie?' The lights are on and water is running somewhere. A small TV next to the toaster shows *Days of Our Lives* on mute. A woman talks, facing the camera. Behind her, a man emotes. His hair is big and solid.

There's no answer.

'Mr Gerber?' I call. The scullery is empty. I close the tap. 'Patience?' The keys are missing from the coat hooks. All of them. The kitchen smells of rotting meat. A fridge left open? The pot of grey stew on the hob? I'm too late. He's gone, run from the next round of questions that the police had promised him.

'Danie?' The voice that comes back at me doesn't sound like mine.

In the dining room, nine high-backed chairs are pushed in under a large glass-topped table. The tenth has been tipped over. Serving spoons are fanned out on a sideboard, bookended by warming plates. Up close, I can see that the table is made out of an ox-wagon wheel, the rims sanded and smooth. There's a crack in the glass. A calabash gourd, shaped like a butternut squash, is balanced on the window sill behind the sideboard, a leather thong tied around its neck.

I stand with my back against the wall, listening, before venturing further. The study is quiet; when I push the door open with my foot, the curtains are still drawn and there are more cigarette butts in the ashtray.

I head back to the kitchen. The sliding glass door onto the porch is open.

'Mr Strydom?' I try, stepping onto the veranda. The smell that had been mild in the kitchen now rushes at me, and I gag.

The one-armed bandit is lit up, playing its creepy carousel music. Three cherries. Jackpot. The tray under the cherries is full of one-rand coins.

The bougainvillea shudders in the wind.

Patience is lying next to the table-tennis table, her green headscarf unravelling. She is on her side, her back to me. Blood grouts the bricks under her.

A dark car approaches the house and parks on the opposite side of the street. It must be Paul.

I called him first, then the police, before moving my car away from the gate. The police took twenty minutes to get to Danie's house; Paul has taken just over an hour. Even though he was still in his meeting, he answered this time. 'Danie's gone and his maid, Patience, is dead,' I said. He was quiet but for a hurried 'I'll be right there' before he hung up. The speed traps will have caught him on his way here.

There's blood on my shoes, but the trail stops on the driveway bricks. I sit in the car in my socks, smoking, my shoes on the pavement collecting ants and leaves.

Paul gets out of the driver's seat of the car. No chauffeur today; I wonder how much the party knows about what he's doing, looking into his father's death. He slams the door and walks towards me, his head ducked against the wind. I move my handbag from the passenger seat onto my lap.

He opens the passenger door and sits down next to me, pulling the door closed behind him. He's wearing a dark tweed suit, fine blue stripes running through the herringbone. Smoke hangs between us. 'Hi,' he says eventually, running his hand over his hair from the nape of his neck to his forehead and squeezing his brow bone between middle finger and thumb.

'Hi.' I take another drag of the cigarette and offer it to him, but he shakes his head. 'Thanks for coming.' Smoking reminds me too much of my father and I drop the butt onto the road, wishing for rain to carry it away.

'Are you OK?' he asks, turning towards me, knees pressed against the air-con.

Three weeks ago, I would've attempted a joke, a *what do you think?*, some sort of deflection. Now, I say: 'No.'

His fists white on his thighs, he closes his eyes and leans back against the headrest. 'I'm sorry I wasn't with you when you found her.' He sits forward and hits the dashboard with the flat of his hand. 'Fuck.' My phone slides down onto the floor.

'Wasn't someone s'posed to be watching him?'

Paul twists in his seat to scan the road behind us. '*Ja.*' He checks his watch. 'Shift change was two hours ago, but there was a big accident on the N12 from Jo'burg.'

278

Maybe Gideon's been watching the house, waiting for an opportunity. Or maybe he was already here when Paul and I were in Cape Town and since then the men have been watching an empty house. I rest my forehead against the steering wheel.

'Why did you come here?' Paul asks.

I sit back. 'To ask Danie exactly what my father did for Gideon. If he was still doing it when he met my mom. It doesn't really matter, but I wanted to know.'

'I get it,' he says, as a beige van passes the car and turns into the driveway. An acronym I can't decipher is stencilled on the back and sides in black. 'Listen, maybe this was just a break-in gone wrong or something.'

'There was a word painted above Patience's body.' I swallow. '*Impimpi*.' Traitor.

'Jesus.'

My father was a traitor too. What has Gideon done to him, to Danie? And why was I spared when Patience wasn't?

'Gideon came for Danie,' I say, shifting in my seat to look at him. 'And all she was worth was the blood he could write his message in.' The muscles in Paul's neck are raised. 'Danie wouldn't have done that to her. I know you find it hard to believe that he's changed, but I know he wouldn't have done that.'

'Either way, I'll get Danie's photo out on the wire,' Paul says. 'Maybe we'll get lucky and someone will have seen him. With or without Gideon.'

It'll have to do. 'Thank you,' I say. 'And thank you for having me followed.' I have a sudden impulse to laugh. 'I appreciate it.'

He nods. 'I should go let the cops know I'm here,' he says, opening the car door.

I put my hand on his shoulder as he turns. 'Paul?' He looks back at me, one foot in the dusk. 'Can you find out how long she's been dead?' I bend forward to pick up my phone. 'If that's possible?'

'Why's that important?' The dome light flickers.

'I want to know how late I was.' I've been moved around the board by everyone, especially Gideon and my father, but also Paul, and I'm tired of it. Maybe I'll find something at the storage unit tomorrow morning that'll help me catch up.

'OK.' Paul looks down. 'Why don't you go back to the house in Jo'burg.' He doesn't say *the one we were in together*. 'They can interview you there.'

'No.' I turn on the radio. 'I'll wait.'

17

This is how it happened, I think. Maybe it was like this.

Gideon drops his backpack and kneels on the rocks. The river is quick and cold, straight from the mountain. He bends down and laps at the black water. He cups his hands and washes the mud from his hair. There's blood under his fingernails.

When he lifted the girl from the car and put her down in the road, she was still breathing. Scree was coming down off the rocks in sheets. There was glass in her hair. He found a gun under the passenger seat and aimed it at her – it would have been so easy and much cleaner to kill her – but the woman in the yellow car was only a few turns behind them and he had to get his *bakkie* off the road. And he could always find her again if he changed his mind. He moved her into the recovery position. Maybe he was getting weak, he thought. For good measure, he kicked her in the hip. He would do no more for her.

The storm announces itself above him. He holds his water bottle in the stream; it fills up quickly and he slings it across his chest as he stands up.

The trail crosses the river up at the rapids. There's a chain strung up between two trees to help tourists over the slippery rocks. But he's not interested in the trail, nor in going any further inland. Not yet.

He turns away from the water. Sickle-shaped leaves, wet and heavy, spin down to the forest floor. It's dark, but he's worked in worse. Tall ferns leer out at him. He pulls a torch from his belt. Really, the rain is a blessing. It makes dragging the man behind him that much easier.

Roussouw tried to run. Why do they always do that? He should've known better, gone down like Eloff, willingly, quietly. Accepting of his fate. Loving it. Although Gideon has to admit that hunting him has been fun. And Strydom will be next.

A blue damselfly whirrs past Gideon's ear. He wonders what Roussouw told the girl, if she knows what part he played. No doubt, Roussouw played the victim. Blamed the whole thing on Gideon. No matter, he thinks. This country was built by people who weren't afraid to do dirty work, even if they were reviled for it later. History would absolve them.

Gideon ties his backpack to Roussouw's and slings both over his shoulder. He picks up the end of the rope tied around Roussouw's waist and ankles and turns, heading downstream. Roussouw, on his back, blind to the sky, follows.

Underground People

An empty plywood bookcase is wedged into the back of the storage unit next to an upright, faded box spring. But the couch is upholstered in black leather, rather than African print, and behind it is a yellow-wood dining-room set, the chairs upside down on the table. This is more like him. I've been worried that he might have got here first; maybe he has and he's taken all he needed. But I hope the roadblocks and army presence around Jo'burg will have put him off. That I mean little enough to him now that he no longer cares about what I find here and how it might change how I feel about him.

I walk quickly back to the end of the row of lockers to see if anyone is coming. The corridor to the lift is empty. No security guards patrolling the storage units. It's a good thing my father is both cocky and cheap.

I return to his storage unit and crouch down next to the empty box I brought with me, unzipping my backpack. I drop the padlock shim kit and the instructions I printed out at Naledi's back into the bag. Lock-picking: just another thing I thought I'd never have to do. On the way here I stopped at a hardware store and bought a boltcutter as well, in case my father had used a combination lock; I knew I wouldn't be able to crack the combination if he had. But the shim kit had done the job. Now, the padlock hooked over the waistband of my jeans, the metal cold against my skin, I pull the box into the unit and find the light switch. The fluorescent lamp fizzes above me as I slide the door closed. It rattles, so I'll have some warning if someone – a security guard, Gideon, my father – tries to open it.

It's musty inside, but at least the corrugated walls block out the music. I'd forgotten how much I hate post-grunge. Since I got here, the greatest hits of Creed – so well utilised to sell God and off-road vehicles to Americans and South Africans alike – have been piping into the self-storage facility over tinny speakers. The man behind the counter had hummed along as I showed him my passport, the bill I found at my father's flat in Cape Town and my grandmother's death certificate. 'I have her key,' I lied.

The storage unit is only half full, and there's a clear path to the bookcase between a two-deep row of boxes against the left wall and a sideboard pushed up against the dining-room set. I move my back-pack and the padlock onto the couch. If I have to, I'll cut open each cushion, pull the table and chairs out of the way to gut the box spring. But for now I'll start on the boxes, working left to right.

I lift a box from the top row and put it down on the sideboard. The flaps at the top are taped shut, and the initials *NR* are written on the side in thick black marker. I pull the Stanley knife from my pocket and slide the blade out a half-inch.

The night before the accident, my father and I got drunk. Me, to make the gun in my handbag lighter in my lap, the image of my mom's car catching fire in Gideon's rear-view mirror fade; my father, because he was thirsty.

I'd waited for him for twenty minutes while he watched Patience put the rubbish bins out on the street and made sure Danie was staying put. I'd go along with him, I'd decided. Sympathise; say how hard it must've been for him, how I didn't want him, my one remaining parent, to go to prison for a crime he didn't commit. He wouldn't expect that. And he wouldn't see it coming when I delivered him to the police. I wasn't sure of that part yet. A quick payphone call to Naledi, giving her our location, perhaps. Or maybe I'd have to use the gun.

He'd moved the coolbox onto the back seat before we left Danie's and handed me a beer when he got into the car. I'd finished three and a half cans by the time we passed through Kroonstad.

After that, my memory is patchy, less linear. In a way, I could've been anywhere, our itinerary an accumulation of words on road signs, slides out of sequence. Swallowing beer, I watched the landscape – what I could see of it in the dusk – speed past. Millions of other people had looked at the countryside from their cars. And millions more would do so in the future. I was alone and yet the same as everyone else.

'Why're you slowing down?' I asked as he switched on the brights.

'There are speed traps around here,' he said, opening another beer.

I wondered how many times before he'd travelled this way, and why.

'Once,' he said, feeling in his pockets for his cigarettes, 'I got stopped by a traffic cop and he asked me what it was worth to me for him not to write me a ticket.'

I pushed flat, warm beer through my teeth with my tongue.

'I told him ten rand.'

I laughed. 'Did he fine you?'

'No,' he said, offering me the half-empty pack. 'He just looked all depressed and said: "OK, well go then."'

'Oh.' I shifted in my seat. The burn on my thigh was itching.

'*Ja*, but I don't want to risk it tonight,' he said, opening his window an inch. 'Circumstances being, hey.'

The roaring of the road beneath us testified to our passage through space and time, but I felt as though we were sitting still, talking in the same way we always did. It was comforting at the time.

'Are you glad you came back?' He kept his eyes on the road.

I watched the flame on the lighter move in the dark. 'I dunno.' I felt dirty, inside and out, and dropped the lighter and the cigarettes into the ashtray.

'Furry muff,' he said, a smile in his voice. 'I know it's been hard, but you'll relive all the moments you've had here over and over in your memory, and you can never change what you've done, so you might as well not give yourself any shit for it.' He scratched his chin, the ember of his cigarette almost close enough to his beard to singe. 'Just embrace it, hey.'

I could believe that he was capable of that, even given everything he'd done. I wondered if I was. 'That sounds like something from a self-help book.'

'That's all religion and philosophy is, in my opinion.'

I turned towards him, pulling my knees onto the seat and the seat belt taut over my shoulder. His face was illuminated by the white-green numbers shining on the speedometer. 'Are you glad I came back?'

'*Ja*, of course.' He shook his can, listening for beer.

'Why?'

He passed me the empty and I dropped it behind my seat. 'Because you're my kid,' he said, rubbing the condensation from his hand onto his trouser leg.

This, like so much else, was familiar. I wondered which TV show he'd quote from next. *Because you're the only good thing I've ever done. Because you remind me of your mother. Because I want to get to know you.* Or he'd try to deflect with some unexpected follow-up. *Because I wanted to ride a tandem bike and needed one more person. Because I need a kidney.* Those were the options, I thought then, not realising that the truth was probably more along the lines of: *Because you're easy to play and useful, to an extent.*

'And I'm sorry for everything.'

There was already so much to apologise for; at the time it seemed impossible that there would be more.

He dropped his cigarette butt through the open window. The moment was over.

'Does Gideon actually exist?' I'd wanted to ask this for almost a week but I hadn't had the courage. I asked then because I was drunk, because I was tired of the way he ended a conversation whenever he wanted, just by putting out his cigarette. 'He's like a bogeyman with a buzz cut. You say his name and I do whatever you want. And you can just pin anything that happened on him, even if it wasn't him.' I was thirsty; I wanted water, not beer.

I expected him to shout and swear but he just shook his head. 'Shit, man, Jo. Of course he exists. I wouldn't just make up what happened to your mother.'

I didn't know whether to believe him, whether I wanted to believe him. 'Well, how can we find him, if you don't know his real name? There's no proof of him anywhere.'

'There is, and we'll find it,' he said.

'How?' Jaco's disappearance and Danie's reaction to my mention of Gideon and the lodge were hardly proof, but it was all we had so far. What else wasn't he telling me? 'We can't drive around forever.'

'I know. Just, I mean…just trust me, hey. We'll find it.'

I was angry that he'd asked me to trust him, after everything. And at the same time, I really wanted to be able to.

'Do you like what you do?' He reached past my seat, feeling for the coolbox.

I undid my seat belt. 'Have we only just met?' I leant towards him, my arm behind me, and found the lid. The cans were slippery in my fingers.

'We can play that game if you want,' he said.

I shifted a can into my left hand and nudged his shoulder with the wet metal.

'I'm Dylan Snodgrass,' he said, taking it. 'I'm a pilot and I like to make fertility gods out of bottle caps in my spare time. My sexual kinks include getting women to trample my balls and dressing up like a giraffe.'

I tapped twice on the top of my can. 'I don't want to play.'

'OK.' He held the beer between his thighs, opening it with one hand. 'Fuck,' he said as a fine mist of lager sprayed his trousers.

I laughed. 'Serves you right.'

He didn't rise to the bait. 'Writing is so passive. You're just reacting to what you see. You're just a witness.'

I pulled the tab on the can. The noise it made as it opened would be the sound I'd associate with my father in the future, I thought. 'What about photography?'

'I know, I know. But I can admit that all I am is a stupid, blinking eye. It's not about you – it never is.'

'I'm surprised you like it then.' I closed my eyes and leant back against the headrest.

'That's exactly why I like it.' He paused. 'And why you want to write.' He dug his fingers into my leg and squeezed. 'Don't forget: I know why you do it because I know why I do it.'

I pushed his hand away, tipping beer onto my skirt.

He laughed. 'Serves you right.'

I needed to pretend that I believed his story, that I was on his side, so he wouldn't see it coming. I finished the rest of the can, breathing through my nose as I drank.

'We should of both become builders or something,' he said. 'Instead of hiding all the time, done something honest and active with our bodies. And in the sun.' He looked at me, but I didn't want to talk about this any more.

'Let's play a game,' I said.

There's nothing useful in the boxes. Three of them contain cutlery, crockery and bulky electrical equipment in pastel shades, all wrapped in newspaper. I unwrap each plate and spread the newspaper out on the sideboard, looking for notes in the margins, for crosswords filled in in pencil or circled personal ads. Nothing. The final box on the top row holds videos of rugby and cricket matches taped off the TV, the teams, date and location of each fixture noted neatly on the labels. I stack them in the box I brought in case the labels are lying. Underneath them, still in its original packaging, is *Debbie Does Dallas*. On the cover, a blonde cheerleader in a cowboy hat leans forward, her cleavage the focus of the image. Above her, the strapline reads: *Everyone on the team scores when her pom-poms fly*. Sport and breasts: I suppose I shouldn't be surprised.

The bottom row of boxes contain only books. I open each one and check for receipts or notes pressed between the pages. Those with my mom's name written inside the front cover – the *K* and the *H* always a lot bigger than the other letters – I drop onto the couch to take with me.

I'm relieved that I haven't found anything of mine in the boxes – photos of me or cards I drew for him. He's never thought of himself as a father, and I'm grateful for that here.

Having moved the boxes back against the wall, I check the drawers of the sideboard. They're empty, apart from tobacco dust. I kneel in front of the sideboard cabinet. This is the last place to look before I begin pulling out cushion stuffing. I open the doors. Inside is a small collection of audio tapes – Wagner, Strauss. Elton John's greatest hits.

I haven't seen a stereo in the storage unit, but next to the tapes is a speaker. It's small, but I recognise the make.

I look up, listening for security guards, but the corridors are still quiet. I push the Stanley knife blade out as far as it will go and turn the speaker so that I can see the back and feel for a joint. The blade slips in easily between the backing and the speaker case. I lever it, hoping it won't snap, and the backing pops free.

Inside the speaker is a thick plastic envelope. And inside that, a roll of film. I sit back on my heels, the envelope on my lap.

I have to see what's on it before I show Paul, but the fact that the film was hidden here tells me enough for now: I can't risk going to a one-hour photo shop to have it developed. I hope Tumelo will have time to help me develop it. And that when he sees whatever's on it he'll be able to forgive me for bringing it to him.

I stand up. My mom's books half fill the box I brought with me. At the top of the pile, under the envelope, is a book my father gave her for her twenty-first birthday. It's a book of Afrikaans poetry by a writer whose first name is repeated in his surname. My father had written the date in the corner of the title page and, underneath the author's doubled name, signed just an uppercase N. I sit down on the cool leather couch and try to decide whether to take the book with me.

Ten minutes later, I stop at the front desk on my way out of the building, the box under one arm. The man behind the counter stands up, but before he can speak, I push the padlock towards him. 'I've got what I need,' I say. 'Do whatever you want with everything else.'

19

The Red Plan

Tumelo stoops under the half-open garage door, wearing a navy-blue apron and shielding his eyes. He smiles as the door rolls up behind him.

I pull the key out of the ignition, my car parked halfway up the sloped driveway, and take a deep breath. I don't know what I'll see today – Gideon's face, my father's, for the first time, as he really is – but I'm ready for it, I tell myself. I grab my handbag, the film inside it, open the door and step into the morning sunlight.

A black sausage dog runs past Tumelo and points itself at me, barking loudly.

'*Thula*, Butch,' Tumelo calls, patting his thigh. The dog pauses and catches its breath, but doesn't look back at him.

'Hello,' I say to the dog. 'Hello, Butchie.' I slam the car door and he flinches before rearing and beginning to bark again, this time more urgently. I take a step to the left to move around the dog, but Tumelo walks quickly towards us and scoops Butch up under one arm. Being airborne shocks the dog into silence.

'Sorry,' Tumelo says, tapping the dog's nose with one finger. 'He's Gugu's.' The dog growls as Tumelo moves closer to me.

'Where is she?' I ask. His daughter's a junior doctor. He'd smiled as he talked about her. He was proud of her; the boyfriend he wasn't sure of yet.

'At a conference in Bloemfontein.' The dog squirms against his chest, its claws slipping on the plastic apron.

I hold my hand up in front of Butch, my fingers curled downwards like a paw. I've seen this in a movie – a man trying to calm a Great Dane wearing roller skates – but I don't know whether it actually works. Butch frowns up at me and sniffs my fingers.

'Good little bugger,' Tumelo says, running his hand along the dog's flank.

'This is a nice place,' I say, as Tumelo bends to set Butch free. 'Very arty.'

His house is painted a light blue; the front and garage doors are white. It looks out of place in a Johannesburg suburb, more like a beach house. I look up at the porch, expecting wind chimes; a motion sensor stares back at me. His suburb, Melville, looks the way you might imagine Paris to be if you'd never been there: people drinking coffee and smoking at tables on the pavement, shops selling out-of-print books and records, and bars with x's and z's in their names. But the numbered roads are dotted with palm trees and empty jacarandas. And you don't find this kind of light in Europe.

Tumelo rubs his right palm against his thigh and holds it out. 'Do you remember?' he asks.

'I think so. Zulu or Sotho?'

'You choose.'

I clear my throat. '*Sawubona*,' I say, shaking his hand. *Hello* in Zulu. His fingernails are brown from the developer.

He nods. '*Unjani?*'

'*Ngikhona, ngiyabonga.*' I'm fine, thank you. Maybe if I know those words in enough languages, they'll be true. '*Wena unjani?*'

He smiles, pulling me into a hug. 'Very good, Thulisile,' he says into my hair. Thulisile is the name he gave me on our second trip together. I googled it that night: it meant *she who made things quiet*. I felt Thulani,

292

the masculine version of the name, was more applicable to him.

'Thanks,' I say, blinking. I'm surprised by how much I've missed him.

He pulls away. 'Back from the near-dead, then?'

'So I keep hearing.'

'Come in,' he says, clicking his fingers to call the dog. 'The dark room's around the back. I was just getting everything ready.'

I turn towards the street. If he's watching – if my father is watching, or Gideon – I want him to see me. The look on my face. But no one ducks into a bush or behind a tree. Apart from my guard, who's parked at the end of the block, the street is quiet. I turn and follow Tumelo up the driveway into the garage.

Tumelo's old blue Golf is just small enough to fit between two long shelves stacked with tools, ageing electronic equipment and lengths of wood. Its windows are grainy with dust. At the far end of the garage, a door is outlined in light.

'Butch,' Tumelo calls, waiting at the door, the remote in his hand.

I put my hand on the roof of the Golf. Every morning at dawn, my breath in empty speech bubbles around my head, my bag stuffed with fruit from the breakfast buffet, I waited outside my hotel for this car. This is where he taught me the Zulu and Sotho phrases for *hello* and *how are you?* Where he told me about his wife and children and showed me how to adjust the f-stop on his camera.

'Let's go through,' Tumelo says as the garage door starts to roll down. 'Butch'll come.'

We shuffle past the car, feeling our way over bumps in the thick, oil-stained carpet. I check that Tumelo isn't looking and stop to wipe the grit from the back window of the Golf. The first-aid kit is still there, under the front seat. But from this angle, I can't see if there's blood on the back seat. Butch skirts my ankles.

I started checking the back seat after our first trip to interview refugees who'd fled the riots, four days after they'd started in Alexandra. The violence had spread across the Transvaal, jumping highways and rivers and leaving the landscape smoking in its wake. Army helicopters circled the cities; Tumelo's police scanner buzzed on the dashboard.

We spent five hours sitting in a roadblock outside Roodepoort, sharing cigarettes and dried fruit. The last time he'd seen the townships burn like this, he said, was just after Madiba had been released, back in the early nineties. During the Hostel War, as he called it, in the run-up to the first democratic elections in 1994, ANC and Inkatha Freedom Party supporters tore up the townships, fighting for territory. Tumelo was on assignment for the *Mail & Guardian*; every day for nine months he drove into Thokoza or Soweto to document the fighting. One of his photos had been submitted to the Pulitzer Prize – a picture of an ANC supporter hacking at the body of a Zulu man.

Listening to him talk about the war, it seemed impossible to me that I was alive when it happened. Other than the day Mandela was released, which I remember only vaguely, and more from reading accounts of it than from actually seeing it, and the election day in 1994, my mom hadn't allowed me to watch the news until I was ten. Like everything else that had happened worldwide since then, the war was mediated. But unlike the natural disasters and terrorist attacks of the recent past, there was limited footage of it: no YouTube videos of the fighting to watch until it became real.

Some days, Tumelo said, the photographers wouldn't be in the townships long, instead rushing injured fighters to the nearest hospitals, making tourniquets out of t-shirts to stop them from bleeding out in the back seat. As the traffic began to move ahead of us, I wished that there had been someone in Alex to do the same.

'Are you coming?' Tumelo asks from the door.

'The dark room used to be the maid's quarters.' Tumelo pulls a key from his pocket. 'It's the reason we bought this house.' He unlocks the metal door and flicks a switch against the wall. The strip light on the ceiling begins to glow from right to left. He motions for me to go ahead.

The room is small, even by London bedsit standards, the concrete floor unfinished and uneven. This room, I realise now, is what Tumelo's clothes always smelled of. One wall is painted white; the rest are cement-grey. An extractor fan hums above the toilet, coppery at the base, and a sink, which huddles in the corner at the join of two long perpendicular counters. I'd expected photos hanging from a clothesline like black and white bunting, but the air is tidy and square. The back wall is covered in prints and a framed cover of *Drum Magazine*.

'Stay,' Tumelo says to Butch, before closing the door.

'Did you take that?' I ask, pointing to the cover. A pretty black woman in a sailor's hat poses against a blue backdrop.

'My first cover.' He laughs.

I turn away from the photographs. Against the far wall, four labelled trays – developer, stop, fixer and hypo – are sunk into the counter. Bottles of solvent and glass jars stuffed with cosmetic pads line the shelf underneath the trays. A rubber pipe is attached to the tap in the basin next to the toilet. The windows, which should look out over the garden next to the driveway, are blacked out. Blue plastic tongs, slightly discoloured at the ends, are balanced on the corner of the tray closest to the sink.

'What's this?' On the counter against the white wall, attached to a wooden board, is a cross between a traffic light and coin-operated binoculars – the kind you find on tall buildings. Beneath it is a small yellow easel.

Tumelo follows me to the counter. 'The enlarger.' He switches on the electricity at the socket and the red light blinks on the extension cord on the counter.

'And that?' I ask, looking at a small plastic container, its top red as a button you're not supposed to push.

'The developing tank.' He takes a pair of scissors down from the shelf. 'Are you here for a lesson in developing photos?'

'No, not really.' I wipe my hands against my jeans.

'Then sit,' he says, pointing at a stool against the back wall.

'OK.' I drop my bag on the stool and turn back to him, still standing, holding the roll of film against my chest. 'They might be very bad. The photos I mean.'

Leaving the scissors on the counter, he locks the door, before bending to push a towel into the crack of light where the concrete sinks away from the frame. 'I know,' he says, and waits.

'I want you to know that if they are, I'm going to do something about it.' I made this promise to myself driving back from the storage facility. 'Even if I get in trouble for stealing the film or my part in helping my father get away. I don't care.' I skipped between radio stations, all four windows open, music whipping away into the night. 'But I might need your help figuring out what to do.'

Tumelo nods. 'OK.'

'OK.' I put the film down on the counter near the enlarger. 'Thank you.' The stool wobbles as I sit down, my bag on my lap, my back against the cool wall.

He flicks the light switch and I can't tell whether my eyes are open or closed.

I hear him walk across the room, his steps practised and confident. Something clicks, and a red light bulb begins to glow above the trays. He pulls a cord hanging from a second bulb above the enlarger.

I watch the bulbs brighten until they're as warm as the noon sun on closed eyelids.

He washes his hands in the sink. The apron is tied in an even bow in the small of his back, the loops long and sagging like an old dog's ears.

I have to fill the silence. 'Do you believe what the government is saying about the apartheid security forces?' The ANC has blamed the security forces for starting the trouble in the townships to destabilise the government and jeopardise the World Cup preparations.

Tumelo snorts. 'No.' He pulls a bottle opener from his pocket, using it to pop open the film canister. 'They're just passing the buck.' He takes out the film, handling it at the edges. 'These problems aren't going to go away.'

I nod, hugging my bag to my stomach.

He cuts off the first part of the film and drops it onto the counter where it curls. He feeds the film into the developing tank, twisting the reel back and forth until he can cut it away from the spindle on the roll.

'How long will this take?' I ask.

'Another forty minutes,' he says, putting the reel into the developing tank and screwing the lid on.

I close my eyes. My father's secrets – the dark parts of him I've always known were there – will soon be exposed to light.

'And then another four hours for the negatives to dry.'

Respite.

We sit outside in the afternoon sun. I keep trying to read Tumelo's face, his watch, to see how long we have to wait. Butch digs at the base of the pecan-nut tree that shelters the garage and a small compost heap in the corner of the back garden.

I stayed sitting in the corner of the darkroom while the negatives dissolved out of the fixer, while Tumelo hung the strip of film up above the sinks to dry. He turned on the radio; he said it was what he usually did when cleaning up, but I wondered if he'd already seen something on the film that he didn't want to talk about.

Tumelo's wife, Lebohang, has brought us tea and rusks. An hour earlier, the three of us ate lunch together, before Tumelo and I went into his study, he to answer emails, me to listen to him type as I read a Dick Francis novel. The formula of it was comforting: a flawed-but-ultimately-good hero discovered a nefarious plot, got laid exactly once and beat the baddies at the end.

Now, I want Lebohang to sit down with us – for the talk to be small and surface again – but Tumelo asks her in Sotho not to.

'How long still?' I ask, cupping the enamel mug in both hands. I like drinking out of what my father would have called the gardener's crockery.

Tumelo looks at his watch, squinting in the bright light. 'Twenty minutes,' he says. He spoons the end of a rusk out of his tea and drops it onto the gravel. 'Butch,' he calls, but the dog has found some squirrel's cache of nuts and is splintering his way through them.

'I'm really sorry,' I say. 'I didn't want to take them to a photo lab, and you were the only person I could call.' It's an echo of my father's words on that hill in Empangeni thirteen days ago.

'You did the right thing.' His forehead creases under his hand. His wedding ring is cloudy with thirty years of wear. 'And until I saw those negatives, I would've said you'd done the right thing going to see your dad when he called.'

Next door, a child screams. I look up, but Tumelo smiles.

'Trampoline,' he says. He waves as a blonde head appears above the wall for a second.

I'm not sure the girl can see us, but I wave too at the top of her next arc. 'Why did you think it was the right thing?' I'm trying to ignore his reference to the negatives.

'I thought it was a good idea for you to get away from the townships. So did Lebo.' He pulls a crumpled pack of rolling tobacco from his trousers. 'Want one?'

I shake my head. 'Why did you stop covering the riots?' At Naledi's place I'd raided her recycling for the newspapers I'd missed while on the run with my father. I found two further notices of my accident and countless front-page photos of the riots, none credited to Tumelo.

'Working with you made it bearable.' He dabs tobacco into a silvery paper. 'But when you left, it was just what it was again,' he says, rolling the cigarette between his fingers. 'Sad. A step backwards.'

A faded basketball skids past the table, Butch close behind.

'I went into Alex a few times, though,' Tumelo says.

'Why?'

'Looking for her, for both of them.' His face flares behind the lighter.

Without asking, I know who he means. I'd told him everything about the night in Alex. We were in the car outside Kagiso, on our way back to Jo'burg after a day interviewing refugees. It was four days since it had happened and I needed to tell someone. The streetlights were out and he couldn't see my face. I told him how the woman had cried out as the men raped her, how long the man had burned before I thought to do something. How sure I was that the man with the machete came back to punish the wife for marrying a *kwerekwere*.

'I found her,' he says. 'She's alive.'

I look up at the pecan tree, my eyes full of tears. 'Who?'

'The wife of the man who burned to death.'

He coughs once into his fist. 'I said I was doing a photo story on survivors.' My father would have been proud of the ruse. But Tumelo isn't bragging; it's more of an apology.

'Why did you do that?' I push my mug towards the tray.

'I was worried about you, hey.'

'And now?'

'More so.'

'Was she OK?'

'She has a broken cheekbone, her husband's dead and she's squatting in someone else's shack with her kids and her brother because hers was burned down.'

I know what I should do: give my grandmother's money to Lindi to help the refugees. Help this woman. Is that what guilty white people do, unburden themselves of their money and their culpability at once? And is that better than nothing?

'But Jo – at least she's alive.' He drops his cigarette onto the flagstones and squashes the butt under his foot. 'I know you were worried about that.'

I sit back and lift my face to the sky. It's the watery blue of spring in England. Next door, a man calls out and the girl stops jumping.

'There was nothing else you could've done,' Tumelo says.

'I was such a coward.' My head is heavy in my hand. 'Instead of trying to put out the fire, I just stared at that machete.' I was too scared to do anything. Just like my father had been.

'*Eish*, Jo.'

'What about the other woman? The one in the shack?' I ask, but when I look up, I know the answer. The dog blurrily pushes the basketball around the garden as I cry.

'I tried,' he says, offering me his handkerchief. 'But I couldn't find her. That doesn't mean—'

I shake my head. He pulls a folded slip of paper from his pocket. 'Her name, the woman you saved.' He uses my empty mug to anchor the paper. 'In case you wanted to know.'

I lift the mug to look at her name. Lerato Tshuma. Below it, another, one Tumelo didn't warn me about: the burning man's name. Dakarai Tshuma. Below that, an address in Alex. 'Thank you.'

'What're you going to do?' he asks.

'I'm not sure.'

He turns his watch strap so that the face measures his pulse. 'The negatives are ready.'

I wait outside the door, Butch's slobbery basketball in my hands, while Tumelo cuts the strip of negatives. Seated at my ankles, Butch looks up at me, wagging his winter-dry tail.

'Come in,' Tumelo says, opening the door.

I step past him, handing him the ball. There are three piles of negatives on the counter next to the enlarger. Behind me, Tumelo throws the ball over Butch's head and closes the door. I sit down on my stool as he plugs the enlarger into the timer and the timer into the socket.

'I'll make you a contact sheet,' he says. 'So you don't have to carry them around.'

'Thanks.'

He bends over the enlarger. 'Come look.'

I take a deep breath and stand up, dropping my bag onto the floor. The negative is loaded into the enlarger, projecting the image onto the easel below it. Tumelo twists a knob on the side of the enlarger and lowers the head by about half a centimetre. The picture focuses. He whistles.

'What is it?' I ask. He steps away from the enlarger and gestures for me to take his place.

The photo is of page ten of a document, written in Afrikaans. The title, right-aligned at the top of the page, is *Operation White Lion: Feasibility Study (Region 6)*. There's no indication of who wrote it.

'What is it?' I ask again, looking up at Tumelo.

He leans forward and pulls a sheet of photographic paper from a black bag under the counter. 'Read on.'

Underneath the title is a short paragraph, which Tumelo helps me translate: *As mentioned above, subject undeniably presents a risk to national security, especially in the light of his manipulation of international sympathies. Decisive action is required. Subject's international links call for more than a good hiding.* Beneath that, a bolded sentence: *Loss of life is anticipated. Obtain approval from CoA.*

The last paragraph reads: *Operative has considered the following actions: contaminate the subject's prescription medication; parcel bomb; car bomb; ambush outside subject's home. Operative and handler recommend either of latter two actions. Recommend recruitment of third-party operative for ambush. Estimate production bonus: R10,000–R40,000. Recommendations for third-party operative:*

The page ends there.

'This is ordering a…hit on someone, isn't it?' I ask, not knowing what else to call it. Tumelo nods. 'Who?'

'Dunno. Could be a lot of people. Albie Sachs, maybe.'

'Who's that?' I can recite the kings and queens of England from the Tudors onwards, but no one ever bought me a wooden ruler listing the names of civil rights activists.

'*Eish*, you need some history lessons, my girl,' he says. He turns off the enlarger and the document disappears. 'He's a judge now. But in the eighties, he was in exile for helping black people fight security laws. The government went after him. He lost his arm and the sight in one eye in a car bomb.'

Why does my father have a photo of this document?

Tumelo replaces the negative with another from the same pile.

———

302

There are thirty-five photos, now in miniature on four contact sheets laid out on the counter.

The first contact sheet contains the shot of the feasibility report, close-ups of other documents and a picture of a man neither Tumelo nor I recognise. Assuming he had access to the whole thing, my father must have hidden photos of the rest of the document – the pages that could identify the target, the author – somewhere else, spreading the risk. There's no way to know where.

Tumelo waits, sitting on my stool, as I move along the counter to the second sheet and place the magnifier over the first photo.

'What are these?' I ask, looking up.

His eyes are closed. 'Keep going,' he says.

A young Danie Strydom smiles at me from the bottom photo, his top lip pulled high in a snarl and too many teeth on show. In the photo below it, Danie and my father pretend to throttle each other. My father's hair is shorter and lighter than I've seen it, and his ears stick out more than I've ever noticed before. He looks relaxed, hamming it up for the camera. He was at home there.

In the next photo, they're joined by another man, the three of them doing a Chaplin yawn, heads thrown back, mouths open, using their guns as stand-ins for canes. The third man must be Jaco: the features are just as my father described – the deep-set eyes, the mole – but here they combine to look wicked, not dumb.

In the photo at the top of the second row, my father and a fourth man – turning to look at someone out of shot, blurred – are giving a thumbs-up, a bloody ear hanging around each of their necks on a piece of wire.

'Jesus.' So much for just taking photos. I study the image, but I have no description of Gideon to go by, apart from that he had red hair. These photos were taken on black and white film.

Tumelo's eyes are still closed.

The first photo on the third sheet was taken through a small, concave window. In the foreground is a pool, lightning veined across the sky in the distance. I know this place. It's the lodge in Dundee.

In the next image, Danie and Jaco drink coffee on the sun loungers outside one of the rondavels. Jaco smiles into the camera. Danie wears oversized sunglasses with thin metal frames. His cup is a blur on its way to his mouth. If I didn't know better, it could be one of my father's tourist pictures.

In the third, Jaco is crouching between the sun loungers, his back to the camera as he strokes a dog. My father stands smiling over Danie. His hair is wet and he's not wearing a shirt. He's just got out of the pool. He looks so young. A finger has strayed into the shot.

He lied to me about everything, I realise now. He was their friend. He wasn't forced into letting them use the lodge. Maybe he even suggested it. And he didn't just stay in the main house while they worked. He swam and played with the dog and made them all coffee.

I step back and over to the final contact sheet, which has only two images.

In the first, a black man lies face down on the grass. His wrists are bound behind him. A stream of water arcs towards the hood over his head. His back is puckered with round scars.

The second photo is of a thinner, taller black man slumped in a chair, his arms tied behind him, the hood over his head soaked. The floor around him is wet, but I can't tell if it's blood or water. The wall behind him is straight, rather than curved. This wasn't taken in a rondavel at the lodge.

Could one of these two men be Paul's father?

Tumelo stands up. 'It looks like he chose these photos really carefully and then photographed the original prints so they'd all be on one roll. Maybe they were his insurance?'

Or trophies, I think.

'There's nothing to say he took the originals,' Tumelo says. I know he's trying to comfort me.

Butch scratches at the metal door, whining.

I trace the shorthand symbols for *trophy* on my thumbnail. It loops back on itself.

20

I try to imagine what happened. I don't want to but I have to. If I look away now, the photos will become nothing more than images, signifying nothing. The men who died at the lodge will be reduced to nothing more than part of my father's story. I try to imagine Vusi Silongo and his last days.

The man sitting on the imaginary chair against the wall is shaking. A slow landslide of sweat breaks over his swollen knees. He pushes his back harder into the wall to steady himself, hoping for an uneven brick to take some of his weight, but the walls are smooth. He has to keep his arms stretched out in front of him at shoulder height, or they'll beat the soles of his feet with *sjamboks*. In between cigarettes, the men balance open cans of Coke on his hands to weigh them down. When his arms sag, the tins fall and bounce, and the spray burns where his toenails used to be.

Outside, a pink lilo floats in the empty swimming pool. Gideon van Vuuren sits at the shallow end, his feet in the water.

The man in the thatched hut screams. The sound is wet and the wind cannot carry its warning far. Birds do not scatter and no one comes.

When I picture Gideon, it's the fourth man – the one with his arm around my father's shoulders, severed ears around both their necks

– that I see. I don't know what Vusi looks like and it's hard not to picture Paul instead. I remember my father saying he didn't recognise the photo of Vusi the police showed him because all black people looked the same to him.

They brought Vusi here from Mamelodi. It was Gideon alone who drove him through Johannesburg and across the Vaal; the others had gone ahead to set up. The air in the long black car came hot off the engine, so he drove with all the windows open, smoking and trying to recognise songs on the radio. Vusi was quiet. Gideon took the long way through the pass, the crook of his right arm moving to the window whenever the turns weren't too tight.

Vusi had been an easy target, on stage almost every night playing bass for jive singers in a township shebeen. On the nights Vusi wasn't performing in the shebeen, Gideon had listened to him playing in his shack, picking out tunes by ear as though catching flies in his fist. He was working on Stevie Wonder songs, fretting the strings forcefully and singing loudly so that neighbours and stray dogs could hear. The first time Gideon had heard Stevie Wonder was while he was tracking guerrillas up in Namibia; no one bothered to inspect the few tapes that were passed around for banned music. But he liked this man's versions better: the music was harder, a tin cry.

Gideon had watched Vusi for three weeks, longer than was necessary. It was sport – a doss – despite the handicap of his white skin. Tracking the man from his shack to the factory to the shebeen was the biggest *jol* Gideon had had since coming back from the Kavango. Granted, there wasn't much need for bushcraft here, but he could piss into Coke bottles and live off biltong while he stalked him, and that was good enough for now.

They'd gone in to get Vusi at 3 a.m. on a Thursday. Dressed in police uniforms, the men surrounded the shack. Vusi had come home two hours earlier, but he hadn't been alone.

'Fuck me,' Gideon had whistled. 'We'll have to wait for him and that *meid* to be finished.' They'd watched for the lights to go out and the air to still with sleep.

'Let's move.' Four torches lit up, splintering the night as the light bounced off the corrugated-iron walls. Gideon hammered at the door. 'Come out, *kaffir*! It's the police!'

Jaco was pressed against the recycled perspex windows, his torch cutting through the swaddle of blankets and falling on the frightened faces inside the shack. 'You can always find them by the whites of their eyes,' he laughed.

'Come out! We know you're in there!' Gideon could feel the neighbours stir, but their lights didn't go on. Better not to draw attention.

The door opened. Vusi was still trying to pull on a second shoe, but Gideon stepped inside and pushed him off-balance. He fell hard onto his coccyx. The woman screamed.

'Tell that slut to shut up, *kaffir*.' No 'or else' was necessary.

'*Thula*, Thembi,' Vusi said from the floor, still trying to get the shoe onto his foot. 'It'll be OK.'

'Get dressed.' The man's nipples were hard with cold and fear, Gideon noticed. He kicked the guitar that stood by the door; the sound of the strings snapping was dramatic, appropriate, he thought. The woman was quiet now, trying to put her panties on under the blanket.

'Hurry up, you son of a terrorist.'

Vusi flinched. He had nothing to do with the ANC. But he knew better than to object and finished dressing.

'*Kom, kom*, into the car with you.' Gideon pushed Vusi in the direction of his friends and their hard, metal edges.

The uniforms were already bloodstained, Vusi realised now. To intimidate him. 'Thembi, I'll be at the police station, OK? Come for me tomorrow,' he called over his shoulder in Zulu. The leader of the group closed the door behind them and Vusi suddenly missed his shaving mirror and his wife's red tablecloth. Outside, the policemen lost what little humanity they'd had, becoming silver and angular as the lightning.

'What've I done? Where are you taking me?' He used the formal version of *you*. Compulsory Afrikaans lessons had done their job.

Vusi looked at the boot the policemen were trying to fold him into. He thought of the van parked in front of the butcher's every morning, doors yawning to show three carcass tonsils. There was blood magic in this dark space, he knew it. He started struggling against the men, becoming heavy in their grip, hoping they'd give up.

There was the sound of feet slipping on stones. And Gideon liked playing with this man, with the man trying to become hammock, but there were better places to stretch him out, hang him up. He opened the front passenger door and picked up the crowbar.

I can imagine the panic, the fear. But I know too much about men like Gideon and not enough about Vusi.

The only furniture remaining in the rondavel is a chair in the centre of the room, a shower curtain underneath it. Gideon had the other men carry the zebra-print lamps and cane-framed bed into the courtyard. He needs room to work and the sockets free.

He leans against the wall, looking at the curtains and smoking. He holds the cigarette between his thumb and forefinger, the ember close to his palm. Each rondavel is named after an animal. Maybe it gives tourists a kick. The sign next to the door is orange and the name is shaped out of black rosettes. He thinks of asking Danie to take it down; it irritates him, making him work harder and faster. Right now, the others are outside, hosing the evidence of this irritation off the man, spraying him back to consciousness on the grass. He needs to pace himself.

'Come get the hose in here, Jaco,' he calls. 'There's piss and vomit all over the chair and we need to change the sheeting.' He sits on the table, in his playground, legs swinging.

'OK, *baas*.' Jaco's silhouette fills the door, the light behind him. He's a dark blue potato-print on white paper. He lifts the flaccid stream of water into the room and puts his thumb partway over the hosepipe's mouth. The water sits up straight in the chair. Marbled in red and yellow, it pools in the folds in the plastic.

On the bed outside, their instruments sleep. A *sjambok*, a tyre, bricks, a cricket bat. But they'll work their way up to these; first they're using the man's body against him. Plastic, rubber, wood: they'll come later.

Jaco comes back with a broom. He likes having people tell him what to do; he excels at it, able to translate words into bruises and blood so skilfully it hints at an undiscovered artistic side. But Gideon doubts that Jaco's secretly writing poems about his mother and his soul. Torture is the only poetry Jaco knows.

'Thanks, Jaco. The sheet's pretty clean now, so we don't have to change it. Will you bring him in?'

'Yes, *baas*.' Jaco turns towards the door. Gideon puts his cigarette out on the table. His ashtray is still outside, coughing and wet.

Danie and Jaco bring the man in between them like a couch, turning him sideways through the door.

'Set him up in the chair. Let him rest for a while.' Gideon watches the man take the shallow breaths of a cat with a cold. 'What's wrong with him?'

'He swallowed a lot of water just now.' Danie looks down, knowing he fucked up.

'Sort it out.' Water-balloon lungs will make the man too weak for what's coming.

Danie nods. '*Ja*, will do.'

Gideon stands up; water moves in folds across the sheeting. 'And when he wakes up properly, let him pick one tin from the pile outside.' There are peaches in syrup, pilchards and a few tins of dog food, all without their labels. It won't matter which one the man chooses: he'll be throwing it up soon enough.

'Yes, boss.'

'Give him just a bit of *tik* to keep him awake. It's boring when he's out for so long.' Gideon cracks his knuckles against the tabletop. 'But, while he's sleeping, go for a smoke.'

'OK, thanks.' Danie's relieved. He's more comfortable tracking the enemy through the bush, interpreting the marks in the ground. He's no good at interpreting the marks on the body.

From the door, Gideon watches Danie and Jaco tape the man's arms to the chair. He's too weak to run away and they've scrubbed his feet with a wire brush, but it'll help to keep him still when the current goes through him. The man is naked, the hair on his thighs singed.

Outside, Danie fills a glass bowl with water for the dog. Gideon gives Danie a cigarette. The dog snorts as it drinks and they laugh. It wags its tail and puffs of dust come off its back. It runs to lick the calves of the man getting out of the pool.

I can't imagine the pain, just the torturers' words, their actions and instruments. Is that how they could do it? I wonder. Because they couldn't imagine the pain they were inflicting either?

––––––

They've overslept. It's almost eleven and they're behind schedule. They left Vusi outside overnight, hanging from a tree by his arms and legs, which were bound behind him, his body a bow. At dusk, they beat his back with two-litre bottles of Crème Soda; standing on either side of him, they took turns, making his body spin. This was known as the helicopter. Then they sprayed the sticky green cool drink over him and walked back to the rondavels for beers and a *braai*. He'll be covered in ants by now, Gideon thinks, as he hangs his towel over the fence around the swimming pool. Time to get to work.

The men are on the grass playing gin rummy. Jaco has all the face cards. He's cheating. Gideon whistles, his pinkies in his mouth. The men look up.

'Go fetch him, will you?'

They nod, putting their cards face down in the grass.

'And take a sheet, in case you need to carry him.'

Gideon turns and walks over to the rondavel. It stinks. The plastic bag they submarined Vusi with, still full of dogshit, lies on the floor by the table. Gideon dribbles the bag between his feet out into the sunlight, remembering how the man struggled, his head in the bag, and then went limp as they took turns punching him in the stomach. It's time to ask him some questions.

When they stripped him yesterday, Gideon noticed a constellation of cigarette-burn scars on his back. Those between the shoulder blades were the newest, still pink and puckered, evidence of a recent stay at a police station. Gideon was disappointed. He likes virgin territory.

I am looking away. My father was there. I know that. He was there, taking photos, maybe doing more than that. The attitudes and thoughts I'm ascribing to Gideon are based on him. But it's not enough. I have to see him there. What he did.

———

Rain is in the air; it'll be here in less than half an hour. Danie moves the car battery and wires into the rondavel. The *sjambok*, bat and bricks can get wet: it'll probably make them hurt more that first strike. Jaco's in the pool. He likes to swim in the rain. The sky above the pool is empty but for two or three hamerkops whose webbed feet surf the wind.

Inside, Vusi is awake, a tyre filled with bricks around his neck. Gideon is with him. So far, he's been working without comment, the only sound in the hut that of the flash of a camera, the spooling of film. He wants to remember what pain looks like, to be able to show it to their next guest to help them know what was coming. The door is open, as it has been since they got here. Gideon wants the man taped to the chair to see the rain on the horizon, giving shape to the wind. To see the dog near the door, watching flies.

'Look at me,' Gideon says.

Vusi is slumped forward, bleeding into the tyre. They woke him by forcing a knife up his nose.

Gideon knows that the man's world is ending, his vision blurry, his hearing dulled. Flies circle the man's left ear, which lies on the table. The camera flashes. Vusi doesn't even blink.

Gideon knows that each time the man takes a breath, his world shrinks. That although he can't see his torturers' tools, he knows they're out there. It doesn't matter though, because this room and this failing body and the white men in front of him are all that's left. The shower curtain under him is his last and only map.

'Look at me.'

The man lifts his head.

Flash.

'How'd you like your stay in our guesthouse?' Gideon wants him to talk, but the man is quiet. Maybe because his voice is his only agency and he wants to keep it to himself for as long as he can. Well, Gideon knows how to deal with that. He steps forward and punches the man hard on the sternum.

'You're going to spill your guts for me.' He hits him there again. 'Tell me you did it. Cough it up.'

Flash.

'Did what?' Vusi rasps from behind bloody teeth. Everything is a weapon, even his own body. He's forgotten his children's names.

Finally, Gideon thinks. He steps back and folds his arms. 'Raped that girl.' It will do. He smiles.

'What girl?' The rasping gives way to the real voice, the person underneath the screams and groans. Gideon remembers the man singing in his shack.

'You know what girl I mean, moron,' Gideon says, circling him.

Flash.

'No.' Vusi shakes his head as best he can, but his neck is full of knots from having to throw his head back and swallow his own spit for an hour, and the tyre is heavy. 'I swear.'

He's relieved that there's a reason for this, Gideon thinks. He hopes that if he can just convince me that he never even saw the girl, this will all end. Excellent.

The dog lies down in the doorway of the rondavel.

'You saw her in Lynnwood near the Pick 'n Pay and you followed her to her car and you raped her. And now she's pregnant with your filthy child.' Gideon almost laughs at the details he comes up with.

The man tenses, the tape around his wrists shifting into the grooves cut into his skin by the rope. 'What? No, I don't know what you're talking about.' He can't get the words out fast enough.

Flash.

'She's pregnant and can't get rid of it and you carry on like you've done nothing wrong.' Gideon's enjoying this. He cracks his knuckles.

'No!' The man knows what's coming. He's seen the Bible on the table.

'Yes, and we will stay here until you admit it.' Gideon punches the man on the sternum again. 'We'll carry on until you confess.' He stands back, waiting until the man can breathe.

'No,' the man says. His voice is blood.

Flash.

'All you have to do is confess.' This is an ancient skill, from the days of ox wagons and skulls on spears. 'And this stops.' It's charting new territories.

Flash.

'Just say it.' It's making maps. It's This Big.

Gideon puts his foot between the man's legs, bending his penis over the edge of the chair. 'I'll let my foot slip and take it with me,' he warns. 'Tell me you did it.'

Flash.

The man is crying for the first time. Gideon presses his foot harder against the flesh.

'I did it,' the man shouts. He sags forward, the tyre almost touching Gideon's boot.

Gideon laughs. 'That was easy,' he says, lifting his foot and stepping back. He turns away and kneels in front of the car battery. There is no woman, no rape. The man, his noisy kidnapping and his disappearance, is simply a message to someone else running a resistance group out of the shebeen. 'You did well.' He flicks the switch. The battery begins to hum.

The rain is here. The dog sits up in the doorway. In the pool, Jaco does a handstand and feels the drops on his feet.

Flash.

Gideon untangles the electrical wires. He finds the ends and pulls one wire around the chair, attaching it to the man's fist. The man is still.

Gideon kneels next to him. 'Do you think this will hurt?' he asks, holding up the sharpened gold-tipped wire. The man raises his head. Gideon smiles.

'Please. Please don't.' The man knows then that he will die here. 'Please.'

Gideon is wordless, grunting as he pushes the clip into flesh. Vusi shakes, curling forward as much as the tape will allow. He's screaming. He has no more words.

Flash.

Outside, leaves and withered fruit are coming down. Gideon switches the battery off and bends to scratch the dog behind its ears. He lights a cigarette. The rain plays piano on the can of petrol standing outside the rondavel. It will pass soon; the sky is already clearing.

Twenty-four photos. The film rewinds. Nico Roussouw ducks past Gideon, the camera under his jersey, and runs out into the rain.

Later, when it's dry, they'll take the man up the hill near the farm. They'll lay him down in the scrub, wrapping him in the sheet they carried him up in. And then, when they've knocked their beer cans together, they'll light a match.

Maybe, some day, a summer storm will unearth his bones. More likely, there'll be nothing left of him to wash clean.

21

Johannesburg Streets

'Is this the adventure you remember it being?' Naledi's ball rolls along the green felt fairway, settling against a rock. 'Shit,' she says, tapping the tip of her shoe with her putter.

'I can't believe you're losing.' I drop my ball and stop it with my foot. 'I'm only using one arm.'

'I know.' She shakes her golf club at me like a fist. 'People in comas shouldn't be able to play so well. I'm sure you're cheating somehow.'

'Hey – don't tune me because you're playing like a complete chop.' My ball rolls down the slope and slows on the bridge across the stream.

Our adventure golf phase was just after our ice-skating and arcade games phases, and we came here – or somewhere like here – every week during my last winter in South Africa. Our moms would take turns ferrying us to and fro; at first they'd played as well, but we were too impatient to explain our invented rules to them and they mostly waited in the car. Maybe my mom would've waited for us outside nightclubs too, years later. Maybe she would even have come in with us. I wouldn't have minded, I think now. It could've been fun.

The water running under the bridge is too blue.

Naledi laughs. 'Nice. See – it only took a few weeks and you're speaking the language again.'

My minder's 4x4 is parked next to the golf-course fence under one of the palm trees. Even though it was dark when we arrived, finding shade is a habit.

'Fully, *bru*,' I say.

Naledi measures three putter heads from the rock and bends to move her ball. 'Maybe your accent will even come back.'

I roll my eyes. '*Ja*, fine, but only if that means people stop thinking I'm Australian.'

'I'll hold thumbs for you.' She swings and the ball runs down the slope and across the bridge. 'Being mistaken for an Australian is the worst. Luckily it'll never happen to me because I'm black.'

I laugh and she waits behind me as I putt, the club handle held high against my inner arm.

'Shot,' she says over my shoulder as the ball stops near the yellow flag. Insects halo the light above us. 'I'm sorry, but it's time for the dreaded question.'

'As in?' It's almost cold enough to see my breath. 'Am I seeing someone? Do I have a boyfriend yet? When am I gonna have a baby?'

'No, I fucking hate those questions. But luckily people never ask me because they don't want to think about the mechanics of fucking a woman.'

'Their loss,' I say. 'I'm always happy to talk about scissoring.'

She laughs. 'I meant as in what're you gonna do now, Hartslief?' She lines up her next shot, looking between her ball and the flag.

'Whip your arse at adventure golf?'

She shakes her head as she swings, and the ball bounces off a rock anchored in the felt and back towards her. It stops next to her feet. 'That's just what I was aiming for. Part of the strategy.' She steps back off the fairway. 'Your shot.'

My ball is only a few feet from the flag. 'Should I play with my eyes closed?' I ask, looking at her over my shoulder. The golf course is empty behind her.

'Fuck off,' she says.

Carousel music drifts across the car park from the shopping centre, gaudy as Blackpool. I turn and putt. The ball pauses at the edge of the hole before falling in.

'Bitch,' Naledi says behind me. 'I think you got a lucky ball.' She lifts the flag; the ball spins in the cup attached to the bottom of the flagpole.

'Only a bad player blames his balls,' I say. 'Or something like that.'

She picks up my ball, dropping the flag back into the hole. 'Whatever – it's mine now.' She pushes the ball into the back pocket of her jeans. 'And it's my turn. Come on, Hartslief – what now?' She swings her putter, trying to make the question casual, spontaneous. 'You can stay with me as long as you want, obviously.'

I nod. 'Thanks.'

'But?'

'But I'm not sure why I'd be staying.'

She swings again and the ball rolls past the hole. 'For fuck's sake,' she says, lifting the putter over her head. 'Actually, do you think they'd charge me extra if I broke the golf club?'

I pull the scorecard and short pencil out of my pocket. 'Probably. But I'd pay half just to see you do it.' I write down our scores, pressing against my thigh.

'Nah. This is already a rip-off. And lamer than I remember. How many strokes am I behind you?'

'Shitloads,' I say, handing her the scorecard.

She looks up, folding it in half. 'You never used to beat me this badly. Maybe I'm getting stupider.'

'One more hole to go.' I point across the log bridge over a deep pond, smiling. 'And then we can eat.'

'Or drink,' she says as we lean forward over the green wooden railings of the bridge. The reeds and ferns growing around the pond look plastic.

'Again?' Koi fish bask near the surface under the lights, bright as tattoos.

'Not if you don't want to.' She turns to face me. 'I don't know what to do to make this better for you.' Behind her, across the car park, animated steakhouse and fish-restaurant signs flash.

I smile. 'Playing so badly is helping.' An Indian headdress is sketched across the shopping centre wall in white and yellow light.

'Are you gonna stay in SA?' Her braids hang out over the water and I can't see her face.

'I dunno.' I really don't. I have a flat, friends to go back to. 'Maybe.'

Three days ago, I drove straight from Tumelo's house to Paul's and waited in the car until he got back from the office. I wasn't sure if I was doing the right thing, taking him the photos of the lodge and the two men, but I had no right to keep them from him.

He'd been expecting me, he said. My bodyguard had told him about the trip to the storage unit and he'd been wondering how long it would take.

We sat together as he tried to find his father in the photographs.

The documents were front-page news in *The Star* yesterday and in all the other papers today. Tumelo was quoted in every story, under headlines about hit squads and mercenaries. The word *skeleton* was used both literally and figuratively. One of the papers used the TRC statement about the Civil Cooperation Bureau as a pull-quote: *The CCB was an integral part of South Africa's counter-insurgency system which, in the course of its operations, perpetrated gross violations of human rights, including killings, against both South African and non-South African citizens. The activities of the CCB constituted a systematic pattern of abuse which entailed deliberate planning.*

I'd asked Tumelo not to publish the photos of my father and Danie yet – not while Paul was still trying to find them – but I'd left it up to him whether to use my name, or my father's. We'd argued when he pushed me to go for a byline on the article. But when the story ran, there was no mention of either Jo Hartslief or Nico Roussouw.

The car park is almost empty. The golf course is closing soon.

'I keep wondering why he called me in the first place,' I say. 'Maybe he was bored.'

'Or maybe he wanted to see you,' Naledi says.

'Family bonding over a racist murder.' I drag a yellow lily pad across the surface of the pond with my club. 'Lovely.'

She pushes her braids behind her ear and looks at me.

'Actually, it was probably to help him find Danie and check what Jaco's girlfriend knew. I think the old boys' network isn't what it used to be. Or maybe he just needed enough money to get to his stash of coins.' I won't ever know for sure why he called but I can't keep searching for reasons. 'It would be easier for me to believe that he crashed the car because someone was following us. And when I blacked out, Gideon took him. I've been lying awake at night picturing Gideon dragging Nico away from the car. Probably to kill him somewhere in the forest.' I pull the club up over the railings and dry the head against my jeans. 'How fucked up is it that that's the better option?'

'Pretty fucked up,' she says.

'But I know it's not true.' There's too much evidence against this version of my father, the would-be reformed character, trying to do the right thing. Naledi had confirmed that at least one of the stories my father told me – about when his parents died – was true, although they'd never owned any property in Dundee or Tzaneen. Which meant he lied to my mom and Lynda about where his money was coming from, where he was disappearing to once a month. My bet's on the lodge, or some version of it. And he lied to me about why he was in Dundee in the first place, how Gideon found him, the blackmail. Everything. 'Whether or not Gideon ever even existed doesn't matter any more.'

She closes her eyes. 'I've been meaning to ask – and I hope this is OK – but why did you go with him? Or stay with him, if you get what I mean?'

He asked me this same question, but I can't lie to Naledi the way I lied to him, or to myself.

'At first I thought I could help him. He'd never needed me before or anything.' I look over her shoulder so that I can't see her feeling sorry for me. 'Why I stayed is harder. I think at some points, it was because I hated him and wanted to take him to the police myself. Sometimes it was to stop him from doing anything crazy.' I can hear my voice cracking but I have to say it. 'But I guess mostly because he was my dad, you know?'

She rests her chin on my shoulder. 'Well, since I've ruined the mood, I hope it's OK for me to say that you deserve a better one.'

I nod, wiping my face with my sleeves.

'Just let me know if there's anything else I can do,' she says.

'OK.'

The waterfall on the fifth hole has been turned off. In the silence, the road feels closer.

'Do we have to play the last hole?' I ask.

She opens her fist and tips her golf ball into the water. 'Whoops.' The fish scatter. 'Now we can't finish the game,' she says, smiling. 'What a pity.'

A horn sounds. I turn, searching the car park for my mom's car. To see her leaning against the bonnet, waving. But it's not her and never will be.

I look back at Naledi. 'Home?'

22

We Who Are Homeless

The grave is small, differentiated from the rocky scrub around it by a two-foot-long oval of grey bricks and a baby bottle as a headstone. A pink stuffed elephant lies on its side, dusty, one eye missing. A sign near the entrance of Alexandra Cemetery said *Full house*. This part of the cemetery is relatively new, but already it can take no more dead.

When Lindiwe called this morning, I was still asleep, feet hanging over the edge of the too-short bed in Naledi's guest room. Lindiwe left a message, asking me to meet her at the cemetery at eleven. Paul thought I might like to come, she said.

Coming up the N3 to Sandton, I'd passed the building site that would be the Gautrain station. It was still a mine dump, but a banner stretched between two poles promised a June 2010 opening. I crossed the Jukskei River again, this time heading in the opposite direction, and parked at the Marlboro Gardens entrance on Pansy Crescent. There were three cemeteries in Alex, this one the furthest away from where we'd watched the man burning. I hoped Paul had chosen it for that reason.

The graves are close together, starting about five feet in from the fence and stretching up the hill into the smog. In the winter morning, the grass is sparse and yellow, without trees for shade. The drought is a tea stain. Between the graveyard boundary and the river, a space that's no doubt empty on maps, thousands of shacks glint in the sun.

Beneath the cemetery, Alex smokes. The army came in last week and the evening news is no longer full of people dancing in the dust, their machetes raised. Instead, politicians accuse each other of sabotage ahead of next year's elections. The leader of the AbM, Lindiwe standing to his right, used the word *pogrom* in last night's broadcast. I wonder if Paul saw it.

This part of the cemetery is empty of mourners. The graves have no headstones, just numbered plaques planted in the hard soil. Long numbers to remember the dead by. The earth isn't even raised where they lie. Lot 3475 is marked with a two-litre Coke bottle.

Lindiwe, in a bright blue dress, waves and walks towards me. 'Hey,' she calls. Paul turns, his sunglasses blinking.

I smile, clamping my handbag to my side as I jog. 'Hi,' I say, slightly out of breath. There's a white flower behind her ear. It brushes against my cheek as she hugs me.

'That wasn't too hard, was it?' she asks, stepping back.

'No.' I shake my head. 'It doesn't really hurt any more.'

'You look much better, actually.' She hooks her arm through mine and we walk together towards Paul. 'Thank you for coming,' she says. A hadeda lands nearby, but it might as well be a vulture.

'No problem. It's good to see you.'

'You too.'

Paul, in black jeans and a dark green jersey, stands next to an unnumbered grave.

'What're you guys doing?' I ask, turning towards her so that the wind won't carry my voice.

'Remembering our father.' She looks at me. 'The way we want to and not like he could've been in those photos.'

We stop on either side of Paul. Lindiwe smooths her dress, waiting for one of us to speak.

'Hi, Jo.' He takes off his sunglasses and hooks them over the neck of his jersey.

'Hi.' I turn towards him, the light behind me.

He steps forward and hugs me with one arm. His neck smells of soap. 'I thought you should be here,' he says.

Broken glass, blue and green, shines in the scrub, a map.

'How's it going?' I ask.

'If you mean finding your dad, not well.' He looks up. 'But if you mean me, better.'

'Excellent distinction, big brother.' Lindiwe's silver bracelets slide down her forearm almost to her elbow as she waits in vain for him to return her high five. 'Face forward.'

He smiles. 'She says that all the time now. I blame you, Jo.'

Lindiwe sticks out her tongue. She circles the grave and sits down opposite us, crossing her legs and putting her bag in her lap.

'No surprise that Danie hasn't turned up.' Paul rolls a stone under his foot. 'Patience was dead at least forty-eight hours, but they couldn't be more specific than that.' A bird, black and flat, glides over the graves near the fence. 'We interviewed the brigadier, but he couldn't identify the fourth man in the photos. Or wouldn't. And all the Koevoet records were destroyed long ago now. All we found at the lodge was another stash of Krugerrands hidden in the wall of one of the rondavels. Worth about ten thousand dollars.'

That's why he took me to the lodge.

'There were a couple of holes in the same wall,' Paul continues. 'Memory's not what it used to be, obviously.'

A month ago, I might have found the thought of my father being confused by interior design and scrabbling at walls trying to remember where he'd long ago buried treasure strange or funny. Now it's just repulsive; desperate.

'A dead end, hey,' Lindiwe says, squinting.

'I'm sorry,' I say. 'Do you need me to do anything else?'

Paul holds up his hand. There are calluses on his fingertips. I wonder if he's learning the guitar. 'No,' he says. 'That's it.'

'Oh.'

He smiles. 'But thanks for the offer.' He lifts his face to the sky, his eyes closed. 'I used to think there had to be a reason for it happening,' he says. 'That they must've planned it, picked him on purpose.'

'Why?' I clear my throat. 'Why must they have?'

'Because otherwise everything can just go to hell at any second. Every single decision, like going to the shop for toothpaste, can mean life or death. Everything is just random.' He shakes his head. 'It was too much.'

I remember the man on his hands and knees in the dust, the fire underneath him.

'But that's Africa,' Paul says.

'That's everywhere.' Lindiwe sits up straight, her hands curled around her knees. 'That's life.'

'*Ja*, no. I know.' He looks down. High on the hill, women sing, a slow call and response. A funeral song.

'Anyway,' Lindiwe says, looking at Paul.

'Anyway,' he says. 'We wanted to pick a place to remember our father together.'

I swallow. 'Why Alex?'

'It seemed right,' Paul says. His hand touches mine, and I know he has chosen this place so that we can remember Dakarai Tshuma too.

'So we thought we'd borrow this person.' Lindiwe pats the soil. 'No one else looks after him, anyway.' She opens her bag and pulls out a shallow red tumbler and a trowel.

'Will you help?' Paul crouches and looks up at me. I nod. 'Thank you,' he says, straightening the few bricks still surrounding the grave.

I drop my handbag and bend forward to pick up jagged pieces of broken concrete. I pull my top out in front of me, placing the stones in it. The wind is warm against my skin. Lindiwe hums as she scratches at the soil, making a heap at the head of the grave. I turn back to them, my t-shirt heavy and sagging with stones. Paul looks up, his eyes pausing on the pale half-moon of stomach above my belt.

'To fill in the gaps,' I say, kneeling next to him. I lean forward, tipping the stones onto the ground.

Together, we build a solid line of stone around the grave. Lindiwe, on her hands and knees, twists the base of the tumbler into the heaped soil. Small glass flowers on green wire stems bend over the rim of the glass. She sits back on her heels, singing softly in Zulu, and drops the trowel into her bag.

'OK,' Paul says. His hands are grey with dust.

'Yes.' Lindiwe holds out her hand and he helps her to her feet. She takes the flower from behind her ear and bows her head to smell it. 'For Vusi Peter Silongo,' she says, giving the flower to Paul.

'Do you want me to go?' I ask, standing up.

'No,' Paul says. 'Stay.' He bends forward and plants the flower in the glass.

'For Vusi. In his last resting place,' he says.

A monument to their dead.

Lindi and Paul stay at the grave while I hurry back to my car, the police report on my mom's accident in my handbag. I couldn't read Paul's face when he gave it to me. He must have looked at it, but he gave no indication as to whether my father had been telling the truth. I count the steps back to the car park, down from one hundred and back up again. Ten steps to the grave with the Coke-bottle headstone.

Forty to the toy elephant. The air is thin and for the first time since the night in Alex, I can feel the high altitude burning in my lungs. Five steps to the gate.

I unlock the car with the immobiliser. Eleven steps to go. I open the passenger door and sit down, my bag on my lap, locking the door behind me.

The report is thin, only a few sheets of paper in the brown cardboard folder.

I drop my bag onto the driver's seat and check the clock on the dashboard. Green quarter-inch lines tell the time: 12.08. I wait for the eight to flip into a nine, and then for the zero to become a one. Just after 12.10, I open the file.

The first page has a seven-digit number running across the top left corner. Underneath it are six tick-boxes. There's an off-centre cross in the box marked *Fatal*. I blink. The report lists the date, day of the week and time of the accident. The accident occurred off the roadway, another cross through the box marked *Overturned*. She was headed south. Headed home. Her name, driver's licence number and date of birth, our address: I hate seeing all this in some stranger's handwriting. A table follows, with only the first line filled in. The police noted that she was thirty-three, that she was sitting in the right front seat. That she was wearing her seat belt. In the column marked *Injury* are two two-digit codes. I skim over the car's make and VIN, the insurer's information, looking for the key to the code. In the right-hand corner of the page, I find it. The first digits mean her visible injuries were on her head; the second set, *Killed – chest*.

Mascara stings my eyes as I turn over the page. On the back is a diagram of the accident. I read the instructions to the officer: use solid lines to show route before accident, dotted lines for after. I trace the solid line, my mom's final moments. Just after the Louisa Road

●

turn-off, where the road starts to curve, the car began to drift onto the dirt track separating the northern and southern traffic. She swerved back into her lane, the line dotted now, but went too far and the car sped off-road. Underneath the diagram is a short description of the accident. The car went down onto the hard shoulder, hit a three-foot wall and overturned.

Why did she let it drift? Was she tired? Had I woken her the night before, to tell her about nightmare? Or was I up too early, too noisy with my recorder? I want to find the people she worked with, ask if there was anything different about her that day. But no one will remember it or her in enough detail. Even I can't. I slide the police report onto the dashboard.

The medical examiner's report is next. On the front page are two sexless outline drawings of the human body, one from the front, the other from the back, where the coroner fills in marks and wounds. I cover the drawings with my hand. They're anonymous; they have nothing to do with her. Below them is another table.

I close my eyes. Her death wasn't so organised; tick-boxes and columns can't make a straight line of what happened to her that night, of what happened after.

Under the heading *Probable Cause of Death*, the medical examiner had typed: *Multiple blunt thoracic and abdominal injuries with aortic transection*. The words move on the page, blurred and meaningless. I blink, wetting the tick-box marked *Cremation approval*, the cross in the box soaked grey. Overleaf is a detailed account of her injuries, *haemorrhage* the only word I understand. But at the bottom of the page is a list of the blood results. Ethanol in post-mortem blood was 0.02 per cent.

She'd been drinking.

I can hear my father's voice, himself drunk on bitter as we left the pub on the Strand. 'Your mother's perfect because she's dead,' he said.

'No, she's perfect because she stayed,' I shouted at him before leaving him to find his own way to the tube station.

Now, I think of all the beers my father has drunk in his life and wish it could've been him. My knuckles are white as I crumple the autopsy report and throw it onto the driver's seat. I cry loudly, doubled over, blood noisy in my ears, my chest shuddering.

Tears drip onto the pages in my lap and I sit up to wipe the paper where it's bubbling. I blink quickly, trying to focus on the top page. It's a witness statement, a short, typed-up paragraph, signed by someone named Gareth Bruyn. My hands are shaking as I hold the file up against the steering wheel.

At approximately 18:45, I was heading north on the M45 [Great North Road] towards Kempton Park. A blue Toyota was coming towards me very quickly. It was the only car in the oncoming lane. When it was approximately fifty metres away, the Toyota began to drift towards me into the area between the lanes. I honked and it swerved back onto the road, before going too far and mounting the hard shoulder. The car hit a small wall and overturned. I pulled off the road, called an ambulance [call logged 18:48] and ran to check on the driver. She wasn't breathing. I flagged down the first car coming south [see witness statement 4673398b by Jodie Booth] and we lifted her out of the wreck. We continued performing CPR until the ambulance arrived.

His signature is neat, the foot of the *y* looped.

I look for the second witness's statement, but it's not in the folder. Jodie Booth, Gareth Bruyn. No Gideon van Vuuren.

My father has lied to me, again. I don't know whether to be disappointed or relieved.

I take the long way back to Naledi's, past Edenvale on the R25 towards Oliver Tambo International Airport and onto the Great North Road towards Benoni. This is the road she died on.

Paul and Lindi are a few cars behind me. Naledi is meeting us there.

Traffic is slow. They're doing roadwork to widen the road ahead of the World Cup, so they've closed off one of the lanes. Men in bright orange bibs move between trucks parked in the scrub that separates the north and south lanes. The new tar is dark and smooth. Nothing has melted into it yet, trapped in the blacktop and never reaching its destination. A sign flashes the waiting time to the N12. Twenty minutes.

On the seat next to me are photos of my mom that Lynda sent to me with a note that said: *Love is doing the washing-up.* I haven't yet been able to look at them but I want to see her face and remember her as she was, rather than as a series of check-boxes and medical terms. In the first photo, my mom stands in a quad at Wits University, holding up a placard that's turned away from the camera. In another, taken during a sit-in at the same quad and again from a distance, she passes a cigarette to a male student.

She smiles at the camera, lifting her shirt to show a cricket-ball-sized welt on her stomach, to the left of her belly button. It bleeds at the edges. I remember tracing that scar, the skin smooth and light purple where the rubber bullet hit her.

She lies on a low bed, pregnant and asleep. There are candles and an open tin of fruit cocktail on the bedside table. In the mirror above the bed, I can see my father's shoulders. His face is hidden behind the flash.

The cars ahead of me begin to move. I put the photos on the dashboard, covering the police report, and change gears, ducking to look up at the sign straddling the highway. Louisa Road is fifty yards away.

I check the rear-view mirror and pull the car onto the hard shoulder, leaving the hazard lights on. Pushing my back against the seat, I lift one leg over the gearbox and grab onto the headrest, pulling myself into the passenger seat. Handbag slung over my shoulder, I open the door and step out into the sun.

The tar breaks up into dust as the road slopes down into a long black field. She was just ten minutes from home. I had to sleep over at Naledi's that night. Looking out at the burnt field, I remember that whenever she was late coming to pick me up, I'd imagine her car overturned among some trees, one wheel still spinning and blood and petrol making dark mud. Her body lying surrounded by flattened frogs and snakes. Then one morning, Naledi's mom, crying, had told me it was true.

Paul coughs behind me to let me know they're there.

I crouch on the slope. There's no landmark or monument. Just the veld fire's trails, dark as a lithograph or a potato print. It's enough.

I pick up some earth and hold it in my hand.

Acknowledgements

Thank you to my mother, Lise Roode, for her faith in me, for reading every draft and for giving so generously of herself over the past twenty-eight years. I couldn't have done this without her.

Thank you to Jamie Knight for his kindness, for believing in me and for distracting me with his complete otherness, his soldering iron and his dinosaur t-shirts. To Renée Hložek, for her insights, her random messages of love and encouragement, her inventive use of Afrikaans. No matter where we are, she is a piece of home. Less than three to you both.

To Claire Urwin, a thoughtful and inspiring reader and writer, whose love of and belief in the novel saw me through even the most difficult of times. I'd pretend that Johnny Cash's cover of 'Hurt' is better than NIN's original for her.

To Sarah Chandler, Hannah Dedman, David Hiles, Clare Hodder, Medi Jones, Mila Roode and Jessica McNeill for their support and friendship. To F. A.

To everyone at Manchester University's Centre for New Writing, especially M.J. Hyland and Geoff Ryman, for the time and space to write. And for their deadlines.

Enormous thanks to Elinor Cooper for her help and guidance with revisions. Working with her has been a pleasure, even if she dashed my secret hopes that the first draft would be good enough. And to everyone at AP Watt for their support.

And finally, huge thanks to my infinitely encouraging editor Margaret Stead, James Roxburgh, Louise Cullen and everyone at Atlantic for their support and advice, and to Clara Finlay for her insight and mastery of track changes.

A Note on the Author

Marli Roode was born in South Africa in 1984 and moved to the UK when she was seventeen. After earning an MA in Philosophy and Literature, she worked as a freelance journalist in London before studying at Manchester University's Centre for New Writing. Marli won the 'Is There A Novelist In The House?' competition at the Manchester Literature Festival in 2009 with an extract from *Call It Dog*. She lives in London.